# ACCLAIM FOR NATIONAL BESTSELLING AUTHOR SUZANNE STREMPEK SHEA

## *AROUND AGAIN*

"Satisfying, porch-swing summer entertainment as pleasing as a summer breeze. . . . Once again steeped in lush local color and regional flavor, Shea's fourth novel is . . . filled with the ordinary yet vibrant western Massachusetts characters that fans have come to expect. . . . Upstanding, wholesome, unadorned prose is Suzanne Strempek Shea's trademark, and we're thankful for that."

—*The MetroWest Daily News* (MA)

"Shea brings uncommon depth and richness to her narrative, which powerfully conveys both the adolescent push for independence and the adult need for connection."

—*Booklist*

"A heartwarming story."

—*Library Journal*

"*AROUND AGAIN* captures how summertimes sometimes change our lives as no other season can. . . . The book provides the sweet flavor of a place and time idealized, left behind, but never really lost."

—*The Capital Times* (Madison, WI)

# LILY OF THE VALLEY

"[A] satisfying tale of dreams realized in peculiar ways. . . . Shea lovingly renders Lily's family and friends . . . with the same affectionate brush strokes she employs to describe her protagonist's beloved art. . . . Readers may well count themselves lucky to have gained vicarious admission to her colorful circle."

*—Publishers Weekly*

"A refreshingly heartwarming novel, upbeat and unsentimental . . . very funny. . . . Every paragraph is a delight."

*— The Plain Dealer* (Cleveland)

"Told with a freshness and real grace."

*—Kirkus Reviews*

# HOOPI SHOOPI DONNA

"Deeply satisfying . . . a bittersweet tale of dreams deferred but not discarded."

*— The Philadelphia Inquirer*

"[A] sometimes rollicking, sometimes heartbreaking, effectively quirky read."

*—Kirkus Reviews*

"A wry, beautifully rendered novel that is touching but never sentimental."

*—New York Newsday*

"Shea's voice, channeled through Donna, is simply a delight . . . sarcastically funny and poetically moving."

*—Pittsburgh Post-Gazette*

# SELLING THE LITE OF HEAVEN

"Wonderful. . . . *Selling the Lite of Heaven* is a charmer."

—*The Washington Post Book World*

"Shea's wry yet warm rendering of a community where strong mothers rule and meek daughters find creative ways to rebel is satisfying on many levels."

—*Glamour*

"Shea's comic odyssey . . . overflow[s] with charm . . . irresistible."

—*The Patriot-News* (Harrisburg, PA)

"IT IS A GIFT TO TAKE THE ORDINARY AND MAKE IT EXTRAORDINARY, to reveal the lives we see unfolding every day, and add a charm and warmth to them that those of us who move around them sometimes forget to notice. But this is what Suzanne Strempek Shea does for her readers."

—Ann Hood, author of *Ruby*

"SUZANNE STREMPEK SHEA HAS A DISTINCTIVE VOICE—comic, bittersweet, a bit old-fashioned—and a distinctive sense of place. . . . In her novels Shea has quietly created a quirky American version of English village fiction, wry and closely observed. Though her heroines' horizons may be narrow, their sorrows and triumphs are no less affecting for being confined to the most prosaic of hopes and the most prosaic of places."

—*Boston Sunday Globe*

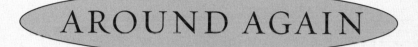

# AROUND AGAIN

## SUZANNE STREMPEK SHEA

**WSP**

**WASHINGTON SQUARE PRESS**

New York   London   Toronto   Sydney   Singapore

Copyright © 2001 by Suzanne Strempek Shea

Originally published in hardcover in 2001 by Pocket Books

All rights reserved, including the right to reproduce
this book or portions thereof in any form whatsoever.
For information address Pocket Books, 1230 Avenue
of the Americas, New York, NY 10020

ISBN: 0-7434-0376-2

First Washington Square Press trade paperback printing July 2002

10  9  8  7  6  5  4  3  2  1

WASHINGTON SQUARE PRESS and colophon are registered trademarks of Simon & Schuster, Inc.

For information regarding special discounts for bulk purchases, please contact Simon & Schuster Special Sales at 1-800-456-6798 or business@simonandschuster.com

Cover design by Jeanne M. Lee; cover illustration © Darrell Gulin/Stone

Printed in the U.S.A.

*For Cindy Hamel, friend in all seasons*

# ACKNOWLEDGMENTS

Once again, I celebrate the kindness, generosity, and expertise of Tommy Shea, John Talbot, Greer Kessel Hendricks, and Elinor Lipman.

During my final time around with this story, Holly Angelo, Tanya Barrientos, David Bergengren, David Hamel, Sue O'Hare, Susan Tilton Pecora, Judi Kauffman, Katherine Kelly, Leo Moran, Mary Ellen O'Shea, and Padraig Stevens provided unforgettable help and support.

# · 1 ·

He was the brother they called Peabrain.

I never knew his real name.

Only Peabrain.

So that's all I ever called him, too.

Though I never once stopped to think what I was saying about him by doing that. Or how it might make him feel. I only knew that's what he answered to. So that's the name that I, like everybody else, used.

Peabrain had a sister. She was . . . who? Some name, solid, that was like a stone dropping when you pronounced it. She regularly chewed paint off pencils. Neatly, leaving them the color of their wood.

Every Sunday night, their mother would drink a single beer. She sprinkled salt into it after filling her glass. I'd never seen that before. Not the salt. But a woman, with a beer.

The brand name on the label, the shape of the glass, the hand she held it in, everything would come to me in time. All I had to do was think hard. And that's what I was doing right then, with great intent. Thinking, thinking, rooting around the long sealed-up cartons in my brain, bringing into light harmless memories from the old days here, thoughts I'd stored from that time. Something, anything, other than why I really was back and what that meant. Something other than what this place once was for me—the setting of almost an entire childhood of summers so pleasant and cheerful they could have doubled as coloring book illustrations. Something other than what the farm was for me the final season I lived here, a lesson as black and white as the dictionary page you consult because you need the definition of a puzzling word.

What I had been trying to define in that summer of 1976 was the adult universe, where I, then about to turn 18, swiftly was headed, baggage packed for me, ticket purchased, brochures offered but merely glanced at because the destination seemed too unbelievable to be my own. The grown-up land might as well have been India, with its jarring class levels and mysterious religions and exotic garb. Countless subtle languages, strange foods, extreme climates, customs you wouldn't finally learn until after you'd broken every one of the rules. I inched forward without a map. Then came the summer of Lucy Dragon. Though my very age, she already had visited places light years ahead, landing at the farm for a breather, only to become my erstwhile guide into reality. Most people can call up merely the most general, fuzzy memories of leaving their innocence and getting the first real idea of what it would mean to have eyes open to the way things really are in life. This place, this farm—mostly this worn circle of earth where she and I spent so many hours—I actually could put my finger on and point to and say right here is where I caught on to the idea of the bigger world. Right here also is where I was broadsided by it for the first time, a slam I am embarrassed to confide I can feel keenly even more than two decades later, courtesy of the boy I believed to be the love of my life, and the girl I was hoping would be the friend of my dreams. Good and bad, it happened right here on the ground on which I once again stand. All this because Lucy Dragon came to stay in the nice clean room we had for rent.

The ponies were the ones who witnessed it all. Watching then just as they were watching me on my first day back. Without a look at them, I couldn't help but know this. Their stares pressed into me, their eyes the color of rich earth and as big as the oval you make when you join your thumb and first finger together to signal that everything is okay. In a wasted effort, I tried to pretend they really weren't only a couple feet away as I started the walk from the barn down to the big sign at the roadside, carrying in my left hand the plain piece of cedar shingle onto which I had written the single word.

With every step, each time I swung that arm forward, a cold wave of general sadness broke over me. Then followed a pail full of guilt, right in the face. I knew well that my uncle would have spent all morning in his shop, firing up his fussed-over collection of power tools to perfect the look of the word I was delivering. He would have taken a router or some other kind of loud machine to carve the letters. He would have added a fancy little scalloped border. There would have been a coat of milky white primer. Then, after the proper amount of drying time, a small sharp-angled brush would have been dipped into a can of bright orangey red paint so that anybody, no matter their level of eyesight, could easily and without squinting read this from well down the road. I never have had any of my uncle's creativity, and right then it was tough to drum up anything coming close to resembling his enthusiasm for such work.

So all I'd done was take a laundry marker to the piece of wood I'd found in a box of scrap beneath the workbench, and I'd started and finished the job in the short few minutes it took for the hose to top off the water trough.

My uncle never would have stood for displaying these few inches of unadorned wood anywhere on his property—let alone out in the front yard for both passing strangers and lifelong friends to view. But, suddenly, my uncle wasn't standing at all. And because he wasn't, just as suddenly, there I was, three thousand miles from my home, to begin the end. To put his place to rest. To clean out, wash up, sort out, pack up, give back, give away, sell off, ship off, move out, and move along everything and everyone for which and for whom these rolling 152 acres were home. The little white farmhouse with the neat horseshoe shapes cut into the many pairs of green shutters. The hunkering barn, color of fresh blood. The thirty-eight Rhode Island Reds worrying beneath their slanted roof. The couple of rabbits that followed on your heels if you allowed them loose from the pen. The four quick goats named for the Evangelists. And the six ponies who for so long had made this address some degree of what you actually might consider a place of interest.

After this summer, so much of what was right in front of me on this day of my return would be gone. Relocated somewhere new and, as of right now, unknown. And the first step in all this was for me to head down to the sign and nail my square of wood over the number forty-four. Right in the middle of the line that tells everybody exactly how many consecutive summers the Happy Trails Pony Ring has been in operation. How many seasons in a row, it has without fail been offering any kid with enough coins five slow and dream-filled trips around the perfect circle etched beneath the sugar maples.

I stuck my hand in my jacket pocket and a fingertip found for me the point of the wide-headed silver nail I'd taken from a coffee can on the workbench. I pounded it in the proper place and then stood back to take in how three whacks of the hammer were all that was needed to announce the great chore I'd been asked to perform. To turn last year's message—"Our 44th Season"—into "Our FINAL Season." With my version of handiwork, a thick, wavering black line under the length of the middle word.

That's when I finally turned and brought myself to really look at the ponies for the first time since being delivered up the driveway an hour earlier. For the first time since I was last here, twenty-two years ago. And they were staring, as usual, like no time at all had passed, all six heads over the fence, lined up side by side in the same order they'd always been: Star. Pan. Tony. Princess. Zoey. Chester. I'd always thought they were the smartest animals ever born. But as far as I knew, they were unable to read. And, enviably more often than not, their awareness and concern was limited to the very moment happening right now.

Which is an end, but also must be given some credit for being a start. Of simple-sounding things like a summer, and a request to be fulfilled. Of a real breeze, too, one that began waving up across the back field while I was down at the sign, and that now ruffles the new leaves overhead, an entrancing sound you could tape and sell to be played on the stereo at day spas. It moves around to push the tail of the copper rooster posing on the barn cupola, and to sway the triangle that hangs from the fence and calls the ponies in from the farthest edge of the field at night. The air is circling, a piece of hay scuttles past on the ground, followed by the purply feather of a jay. It's moving my hair, now free from behind my ears and sliding across my eyes. All I can do is listen. To the whoosh of the breeze and the souvenirs it carries past me—my uncle's whistling, and my aunt's laughing, and the ponies saying the only word ponies are able to. I enjoy all of this fully, as you do the last bits of a dream when it gets to the point where you are waking and you realize what's happening is not real life, yet it's still very nice and good so why not get every moment out of it that you can. One more thing I haven't heard for a lifetime: Frankie's voice saying he loves me loves me loves me. I'm standing in the barnyard blinded by the sweetness in all this and that's when the wind kicks up and—bam!—the door of the nice clean room for rent flies open and there is Lucy, who took what she did and ran away from us all, but who never really left me.

I shove the hair from my eyes and I shake the last thought out like sea water sloshing in the middle of my head. "What was that?" But the wind is gone and there's nobody left to ask. Except the six of them there at the fence.

Executrix, I was to be.

Originally, I was to have been called owner.

"The farm will go to you," Pal repeated throughout my childhood, like mortality was something a kid would want to dwell on. But he'd made the right choice. I knew the place as well as they did. From my eighth year through my eighteenth, I spent every summer there. I don't say that I simply stayed there, because I did a lot more than just sleep in the little spare room that was straight ahead as you cleared the top step onto the second floor of the farmhouse. I lived there as much as did Victory, in the room to the right of mine, and Pal, in the one to the left, joining them in the cycle of the place, the working before light that is more than a butter-commercial cliché. I was far from a guest who needed to be entertained or who scuffed around bored, having to be given a constant handful of suggestions for ways to spend all her free time. I was there to help out. To work. To feed and groom and tack the ponies, then to head back to the barn to rake and shovel, sweep and pour and fill, and to interrupt any of that only when a car pulled up the drive and its doors flew open and a stream of kids ran to the ring, climbing onto the fence rails and pointing and yelling and attempting a pat. To take their money and settle them on and give them their five times around, then to head back to my chores until somebody else happened by. That was my day, always ending with a ride into the fields, a two-helping supper, a warm bath in the short deep tub, and up to bed usually even without a lengthy look at TV. Those three months of the year, I grew taller, tanned, and got from the sun the kind of streaky golden highlights in my hair that my mother's girlfriends paid good money to have professionally applied. It was as if the farm were one big vitamin pill. That's what Pal, flexing a bicep, liked to tell me.

But that was before the summer of Lucy Dragon. After that, I remained away, my choice of school and job taking me far from Massachusetts, and my career in education earning me nowhere near the income required for the upkeep and taxes on a place that size. The farm was a sentimental luxury I wouldn't be able to afford until I hit the big-bucks state lottery, which there was little chance of because, not liking to waste a dollar, I never bothered to play. The same way I never bothered to visit. Not once after that last summer, after the disappointing post-dentist-visit taste left in my heart regarding the place I'd long considered my true home. After that summer, I made up—or conveniently actually had—one excuse after another as to why I couldn't come out for a stay: Heartbreak. School. Heartbreak. Love. Heartbreak. Motherhood. On and on. And all the many obligations that each one stacked on my head. The string of reasons I never could fly east eventually got so long that my aunt and uncle stopped raising the topic, which was a relief.

My uncle's whole, complete name—Pawel—was what they gave when they phoned me from Mary Lane, the hospital to which he'd been brought.

"I'm calling on behalf of Pawel Panek," said a nurse who didn't identify herself personally, just rushed on to say that I was the family contact listed on Mr. Panek's wallet identification card, even though I was out of state, and, hey, where is the 206 area code anyway?

Seattle, I said as slowly as if the word had forty-five syllables, and she informed me, "There's been an emergency."

When I arrived there the next day, red-eyed from my first red-eye flight, my uncle was left to bits of whisperings. A monster had been growing in his brain for who knew how long, and the morning before it had flattened him to the kitchen floor linoleum, where he was discovered by farmhand Jerzy there for chores. Once located, the thing had been determined too tricky to remove, especially from the head of someone elderly. When my uncle's words came, they were little and soft, and I had to stay close to make them out. My ear was almost on his lips when I made out the message: "It's time. Close the farm." I almost asked him to repeat this, but what he'd said sunk in. Of course I replied, "Nonsense, you'll be back there soon." But however I tried to puff up the words, they came out steamrollered. Both of us knew better. "Nonsense, you," my uncle said back. "Close.

End. Get rid—everything." There was a space here, and I studied the weave in the flimsy ecru blanket. He jarred me, with this: "But run the ring. One more season." Machines on either side of the bed purred and clicked. "Please?" Pal asked. The man in the next bed, about ninety years old, screamed for his mother. My uncle finished. "Nice round number before you take the sign down."

Twenty-two years after last doing so, I am taking in the sound of it all. The snap of the crossties. The creak of the leather as you secure the saddle, bringing the strap up into the metal ring, through and down to the right, around to the left, back through the ring and down behind the crossover of leather you've already made. Pulling it tight. Sort of like how you tie a man's tie, as my uncle instructed back when he, rather than I, was the one closing the gate now that the six are tacked and waiting in the ring.

All that is why I now sit there, hand curled around the whip, mind wrapping around the past. I look to the left, to the right. There are no cars. No sounds. Nobody. Nothing. I look down at the sign. I look over at the ponies. I am back here. They are here, as they always have been. We are open for business. All of us, ready for the first of the final trips around the world. Wherever they might take us along the way.

# · 2 ·

I have returned to the first place I ever traveled to in my life.

My debut at the farm, forty years ago, was much more ceremonious, made via a tenderly driven Chevrolet Belair the second Sunday of July, 1958, ten days after I was born. Springing my mother and me from our sterile hospital confines, my father took us on a roundabout way home, three extra miles over to Route 9, just so he could stop at the farm and show off his first-ever child.

My Uncle Pal and my Aunt Victory—my father's little brother and his big sister—lived at and worked the farm that my grandparents had started, and on which my uncle and aunt and my father had been raised quite comfortably. The place long was known for its fine beef cattle, and its lush pastures were dotted with dozens of massive ink-colored animals the size of the two-hundred-gallon tank of heating oil hidden under our back stairs. The meat that grew on their bones was literally prize-winning, and if you wanted proof of this you could walk inside the barn and over to the pretty oak-edged glass-front case my uncle built just for displaying the many ribbons Panek Farm beef cattle had won at agricultural fairs and expositions held over the years throughout New England. Many of the animals were auctioned off to exclusive restaurants and your more notable butcher shops right after they received some of these prizes, and in this way my uncle and aunt made a decent enough living. As they did selling the asparagus in the spring, the tomatoes and cucumbers in the summer, the sugar pumpkins and winter-keeping squash in the fall, and the reliable brown eggs all year 'round.

He widowed, she never-married, both of them pretty much keeping to themselves, they didn't live too loudly. Yet nobody could say the two of them ever wanted for much. Even so, Pal always was thinking they could do better than they were. Old age had been a big concern of his, long before he even got to the halfway point. He and Victory had personally escorted their parents through the final years of their lives, and that naturally got them thinking, especially considering how there'd be no offspring to do that for them. Saving to insure Victory and himself a comfortable existence right to the very end became the goal, and over the years a lot of my uncle's spare time went to growing or putting together or coming up with something extra to make money on, everything advertised out in front of the house on the neat rectangular signs my uncle cut out, painted, and then hung from cup hooks, one below the previous, like those that on the day of my first visit made up a swinging block-lettered chain of hopefully irresistible offers:

Clover Honey
Brown Eggs
Miracle Herbs
Rope Swings
Manure
Firewood

Onion Sets
Birdhouses
Perfectly Round Rocks
Lucky Horseshoes (Used)
Your Name in Cement


Over the years, Pal opened up and sooner or later reluctantly closed down a series of generally ignored ventures including an iced-down boulder-strewn toboggan run, guided walks over to a tree knot roughly the shape of a pair of praying hands, and a small sideshow of poultry cursed with a range of deformities. Five winters before the July that I came into the world, he worked many nights constructing a big wagon wheel that Victory at first could only guess the prospective use of because he wouldn't reveal it until the very end of the project. Then, the Friday night after that Easter, my uncle went off to an auction and came back with the first of the ponies—Star—standing in the footwell of the backseat of his Chevrolet. A month later, on Memorial Day, after he and Victory had made their early drive over to leave a bark-covered log planter of salmon geraniums at the family headstone, my uncle poured the final wheelbarrow full of concrete around the two square legs of a big rectangular sign on which he'd printed elegantly and in black:


"Happy Trails Pony Ring"
Our First Season
Five Cents for Five Trips Around the World


The "Happy Trails" part had been Uncle Pal's idea. He was an admirer of Roy Rogers and once read how Roy had the habit of signing all his publicity photos with that wish. "The World" part had been Victory's suggestion. My uncle had wanted the line to end at "around," but my aunt pointed out that everybody then probably would ask, "around what?" So she suggested he add "the world," despite this technically being false advertising. Unless you had one good and big imagination, as most kids did, and do.

At noon that Memorial Day of 1953, the first rider arrived. Victory always told how she knew the exact time of day because she was just about to fill up Pal's ginger ale glass for lunch, and as she uncapped the soda, the loud fizz roaring up from the neck of the bottle made the appropriate sound of applause. Like something big was just starting. She looked out the side window and this was what she saw: all finished with marching in the morning's big parade downtown, a dark-haired floppy-eared boy wearing a too-large Cub Scout uniform and still holding a tiny American flag and hopping out of a long gray car then standing still before the now-complete circle of animals Pal had assembled over the previous month. And a man in a good dark suit stepping from the driver's side and pushing back the brim of his fedora and holding out a nickel.

My uncle lifted the U-shaped piece of metal that secured the gate closed, and slowly swung it aside. Star stood there in the opening, as he would always, because, as Pal was told at the auction, and went on to relate to everyone who might ask over the years, ponies live forever.

Sunday drives were still a huge deal in those days, happily uprooting family members from their daily routines and getting them out into the country for a free day of fresh air and a glimpse of the contentment being enjoyed by farm families who, regardless of how busy they were in actuality, looked to be living the coveted simple life. Panek Farm, so well cared for and inviting, was located perfectly for the convenient viewing of this life, up and off a main and paved road that was smooth and edged with forest. This also was the same route you had to take to get to the new reservoir, so that meant steady tourist traffic on the weekends, people intent on getting a good first-hand look at the nearly forty-square-mile expanse of dammed-up river that was being billed as the largest water supply ever created by the impressive and often surprising hand of man.

Over twenty years of construction in the 1930s and '40s, the Commonwealth of Massachusetts obliterated four entire towns in the making of the enormous Quabbin Reservoir. It was not created for the needs of most locals, but to charge down a long gravity-fed pipe and into the kitchen sinks, drinking glasses, clawfoot bathtubs, and swimming pools of people who lived in the Boston area a hundred miles east. Uncle Pal and Aunt Victory's property abutted what once had been the town of Dana, a place that now, according to the black-on-orange signs nailed to tall trees at the boundary, is known as nothing more than State Property. If they wanted to walk far enough into the woods, as they used to once in a while for recreation, or if they wanted to ride one of the adult-strength ponies, like they once did often enough that the animals knew their way in and out without having to be given any kind of commands, my aunt and uncle eventually would come upon places that had ceased to exist.

In preparation for the flooding of the valley, houses and barns and shops and municipal buildings were moved or were demolished. Trees and fences were felled. A rail line was dismantled. Residents scattered to find new places to call home. If you can believe or at least imagine this, even the dead were disturbed, what was found to be left of them—sometimes only the hardware from their coffins—dug up and moved to a new main cemetery on the other side of the state road, a parklike setting offering higher ground and even quaint street signs that would allow you to that much easier locate the latest eternal resting places of your disrupted loved ones.

Stone walls that once delineated the properties of the towns now ran down to a long and quiet shoreline, and continued straight on in to disappear beneath cold eggplant-hued depths. While the water level was still inching up during its seven-year-climb, some people said you could spot building foundations intact and still poking up from the rising surface. And, truth be told, the chance of catching memorable and unsettling sights like that, rather than just the stark beauty of the massive lake, was what was drawing many of the visitors years after the maximum capacity of gallons had been reached. But "How long can you look at water?" was how Uncle Pal saw it. Folks soon surely would want something else to do after a few minutes or hours of staring at scenery, they'd certainly crave somewhere else of interest to go. So, he hoped, they'd drive down the road in search of some new diversion, and—hey—wait—look—stop—ponies!

By the end of that first summer of business, from no formal advertising but my uncle's sign and the powerful means of word-of-mouth, families were seeking out the pony ring. Groups on their weekend outings were making the farm a regular stop. Little vans and big buses labeled with the names of churches and camps and youth organizations from crowded cities as far away as Bridgeport and Providence would fling open their doors and children of all sizes would charge to the ring. Nickels imprinting their palms, the most impatient kids would count aloud the number of times the bell rang to mark the number of times the ponies circled. The wheel spoke to which Star was tethered was a few inches longer than the other five, and reached a brass bell that hung from the gatepost. Each time he came up to it, the bell sounded. Five rings meant that particular ride was completed. Some of the riders wailed when that happened and when Uncle Pal moved forward to advance each animal to the gate, to free the littler ones strapped to the saddle horn by an old trouser belt and to assist each to the ground. Sometimes the kids on the ponies cried when the ride started and the animals stepped off and the stationary world began to revolve past. Or they screeched the entire time they were on, as if being put through some horrific form of torture. I am told that my parents and I got cuts in line the day that I showed up as a brand-new infant child, and that our being ushered to the front for my very first pony ride caused one little girl to have to wait that much longer and she broke into tears and, even though she was dressed in Sunday church clothes complete with straw hat, went and had a rolling fit right there on the dusty ground.

My family visited the farm every summer Sunday until I turned seven. In the first pictures of me from many of those times, I am still so small and young that I need assistance to keep from falling off whatever pony I've been placed on. Skip a few album pages and I am sitting proudly without anyone's aid. Arms reaching farther, legs longer, feet finally making it to the first stop, the high hidden little loops just below the saddle that are like a beginner's set of stirrups. My face grows more at ease in each photograph as I ride Chester, Tony, Princess, but mostly Star. Until I turned seven and my father's telephone company, without much notice that I ever was aware of, transferred him to Chicago. And, of course, what could be done? My mother and my brother and my sister and I had no choice but to go along.

The littler kids did not care about relocating. For them, the farm held nowhere near the great degree of fascination that I knew. During visits, they chose to stay on the porch with their G.I. Joes and fake versions of animals and around two in the afternoon would begin screaming for home. I'd beg to be left behind. By age four, I was working at the farm every summer weekend, pitching in with a seriousness that had visiting adults elbowing one another as I passed them by in my blue felt cowboy hat and fringed shirts, boy's dungarees, and black-and-gold boots, hefting a pitchfork or some other implement a couple times my size. Once we moved, I whined and pleaded and stopped eating to achieve the only thing I wanted in life—permission, with airfare, to spend the whole of every summer at the farm. So, starting with my eighth summer and ending with my eighteenth, for most of each June, all of every July, and the whole of all the Augusts, I had right heaven on the good earth I knew so well.

And then came Lucy.

All because Pal had gotten the big idea to add to the usual lineup of signs—

Miracle Herbs
Mulch Hay
Peony Roots
Laying Hens
Pickled Tree Mushrooms
Sharpening of Various Implements

—an additional one:

Nice Clean Room for Rent

It sounded great at first—when Victory wrote me over the winter about my uncle's latest moneymaking idea and the plan to let out the extra room, a small sunporch that hung off the back of the kitchen, I loved the idea. This meant anybody from anywhere could be living with us. Somebody from Africa or Taiwan or the South Pole or Idaho. Somebody famous. Rich. In hiding. Somebody with a past that needed sheltering, here, far away from most everything. Where they wouldn't be found. And where, if anybody did come looking, my aunt and uncle and I would be so loyal we would show blank faces and shrug in response to every question, and we would never, ever reveal there was anybody else here with us on the farm. Anybody human, that is, except for her, and him, and me.

But such exotic tenants never appeared. Those who did rent were just regular people passing through on their way to somewhere else due to nothing more than the most boring of reasons. They needed a place while awaiting an apartment vacancy nearby. They were hunting for work, or exploring a largely ignored part of the state. One sturdy young couple who daily wore matching his-and-hers khaki shorts claimed the porch for their two weeks of vacation, and bravely set out toward the dead village each morning on map-guided hikes lengthy enough to keep them gone until way past suppertime.

Only one boarder—a young man who stayed the June and July the summer I was sixteen—was remotely intriguing. While slowly drinking the can of Schlitz that Pal offered him as a welcome gift his first night with us, he told the three of us that he was on a leave of absence (though he never detailed the job he was missing from) and that he wanted solitude so he could write the play he'd long dreamed of creating. No, he'd never written anything other than letters. And he'd never been an actor, he told Victory when she asked him that question as well. Truth be told, he'd never even attended an actual play. Nor seen one on film or on his TV. But he'd heard about plays and he said he did have to his benefit the fact that he always was a good listener.

"Just as I'm listening to you now," he told her, even though right then, if you wanted to get technical, he was actually speaking rather than listening. "Everything people say sounds to me like words on a page. I just thought it's time I wrote it all down."

Nobody on the farm was going to stop him. We all had our own business to tend to, and he stayed well out of our way, in the porch room all the time, writing longhand on unlined paper. I knew that much because I'd see him through the many windows as he hunched at the little table on which Victory the rest of the year displayed her Christmas cactus. He stared down at his work with the type of laser-beam concentration that I employed only on things like the Iowa test. None of us ever knew the topic or content of his play because he never revealed that. Or anything else. He took his meals in his room, on a tray, like you do when you're sick. He didn't bother us with chatting or company. The minute he left on the exact last day of July, just as he told Victory he would when he first arrived, it was like he'd never been there. I am lucky to even be able to recall his name. But, then, it consisted of only three let-ters: Ron.

I could have sat on that porch in my solitude for a dozen Junes and Julys and still never could have written the plot for what would happen after the sign got hung the following year. About that next boarder, I remember a whole lot more than the four letters of her name. She doesn't so much stick in my mind as she occupies a territory of it. Still living, rent-free, these many years since the last time I saw her.

I'd been hearing about her the entire spring, in all my regular and greatly anticipated cards and letters from the farm.

"Guess what?" my aunt asked me in her usual typewriting, done on her old Royal that couldn't decide between red or black ink so democratically split each letter in half and printed both. "Guess who'll be renting the room! A granddaughter of my friend! Coming north from the south! Loves animals! Is in need of fresh air!"

And the best news, Victory pointed out with another exclamation point—the girl was just my age! Maybe a tad older by a few weeks or a month, but still replying the same number of years when somebody asked her age. Which, this summer, would be seventeen!

"Do you know this girl?"

I first asked this question back in Illinois, during the spring leading into that summer, one late afternoon while my mother peeled side-dish carrots down the drain, into the brand-new garbage disposal that had been her big present from my father for their last wedding anniversary. I couldn't imagine ever wanting such a regular boring thing for a gift, especially if you were an adult and therefore could ask for or afford anything in the world. But these were the kinds of things my parents traditionally exchanged. An electric knife for a garage-door opener. A machine that scrubbed your rugs for another gizmo that shot a fierce stream of water at the dirty aluminum siding on your house. A tube with a plastic claw on the end that extended so you could reach up and easily change a lightbulb on a ceiling fixture. Snow tires. Overshoes. Storm windows. A pressure cooker.

A rolling trash can. Matching Water Pics. As Ma worked on her carrots, the floor of the stainless steel sink disappeared under big orange curls that piled like chopped-off locks beneath a beautician's chair. She didn't look up from her chore as she asked, "What girl do you mean?"

"Do you know the girl, the one who's coming to the farm this summer? Some granddaughter of one of Aunt Victory's friends?"

"I don't know many of her friends anymore," Ma told me. "Some I knew—one used to make a decent crumble but would never write down the correct recipe for me—one of those people who on purpose leaves out a crucial ingredient just to throw you off track. But I don't remember anyone well enough to know who their grandchildren are. I'm sure Victory wouldn't offer to take in a girl who wasn't good and nice and respectful and helpful. Don't you worry."

"I'm not worried," I said. "I think it'll be fun."

I did. What I actually thought was that it would be like camp. My summers always had been taken up by going back home to the farm. And despite how much I loved doing that, and that I always knew I had a better time there than anybody in the world, I once in a while found myself a bit jealous when catching up with my friends each September. They all made it sound that in groups they'd been having a kind of great time I was somehow missing all by myself at the dark end of the day with nobody around but my aunt and my uncle and the crickets, never the company of a real girlfriend like you might otherwise hang around with for the summer months.

Except for Judith and Joan, sisters who were sent off to a special camp in New York state where everybody talked Hebrew, and Gay and Darlene, two other sisters from a separate family that every summer without fail shipped them off to a place in Pennsylvania that was supposed to teach them how to eat better and exercise and bring themselves down to a healthy weight that they might maintain until the next year, Girl Scout camp was where most of my friends spent their summers. Some woodsy place up over the Wisconsin border that bore the same multisyllabic Indian name as did the freezing island-dotted lake on which it was perched. There, for a month at a stretch, wearing forest-green shorts and matching T-shirts and kneesocks and beanies that varied in style with the wearer's level in the organization, these girls made their homes in tents, washed without hot water, used latrines, lit actual fires, sang songs, presented skits, and told terrifying stories late into the night, doing so even after the third warning from the counselor, and the threatened penalty of busing the dining hall.

They envied me in turn, but only for my access to boys, which they were offered maybe one Friday a month at disastrous mixers with the Scout camp on the other shore. Daily I saw boys, many of them my age, passing by on bicycles, slumped into the backseats of family cars that stopped at the ring, behind the counter at the feed store. And so extra lucky was I that the only one I ever wanted to have in front of me—Frankie—literally was delivered to my door.

Our Day 'n Night Dairy order arrived every afternoon around four-fifteen; two quarts of whole milk each visit, half a pound of butter every second one. The delivery truck was a rusting boxy thing colored the same shade as coffee is if you put too much cream in it. Which, I guess, the dairy would have liked you to do so they could come to your house maybe twice a day. Its slow, clattering arrival up the driveway always coincided with my aunt's starting supper. That was one thing I liked about seeing it. There also was the clean formality of the old milkman, known to us as Fred. His dirty work done for the day, he was now outfitted in his blue-and-white-checkered over-alls and white button-down shirt and work shoes painted the color of his bestseller. The fact that he also delivered chocolate milk already mixed and tasting better than anything you could concoct in your own kitchen no matter how much Bosco you added, that was good, too. But nothing beat what the truck delivered in its passenger seat. And that was the old milkman's young son, Frankie.

He started with the deliveries when he was nine. It was star-tling the first time I saw the truck stopped at the front of the house and watched from the ring, ready to wave to Fred, and out hops Fred's outfit—only a tiny version, with this smallish white-haired boy in it. Rushing, bent forward as he ran up the steps. You could hear the soles of his boots catch on the rough cement, the muffled clinks of the full bottles as they knocked against the metal basket he lugged, Fred's voice sternly remind-ing him to slow down. The boy swapped the full bottles for the empties left rinsed shiny in the box, collected the next day's order form, and ran back down the stairs to the truck. Fred honked a little tune at me as he backed down the driveway. I waved. From the usually vacant seat next to Fred, the smallish boy pretended he had something on the floor important enough to look at, and he kept his eyes focused down there until he was out of sight.

The summer we were twelve, he told me he liked me. I'd felt that way about him for three years, had been waiting two long years to hear it from him, and answered as much. When I returned to the farm at thirteen, he said he wanted to go steady.

At fourteen he said it was love. He'd say it in multiples. Love love love, like once wasn't sufficient, unlike you'd expect a boy to go on. But he did go on, and how could you not believe it: Love love love. I'd say it back to him the same way, to the only ear of his that worked, which was easy to remember the placement of because it was on the same side of his body as his enthusiastic heart. The summer we were fifteen, Frankie on purpose dropped his brand-new high school class ring into our delivery box, just so he could come back on his bike the next day off and say he was on a search for it. That his parents would murder him if he couldn't find it. They'd sprung for real gold rather than just the plated stuff that most of his friends had ordered, and now look what had happened. Gone and he'd only just gotten it. Victory said she hadn't a clue where it was. But I had a lot more than that. The thing was upstairs in my trunk, hidden deep in a nest of seamless bras. I'd kept it there since finding it the day before he came looking, when I removed the quarts from the box and spotted the gold shining down from the corner. It fit on my finger quite perfectly, and I played with it after bedtime, making up some kind of eternal vows and pretending that my right hand was Frankie's slipping this onto the ring finger of my own left one. He was saying my name as he did, three times, and with a peculiar Boston accent he used on no other of his words, without fail pronouncing it kind of like how I imagine the Kennedys would if any of them had ever met me. I never heard him do that to anybody else's name, to give it that twist, and that took a big electric mixer to the blood around my heart.

"Oh Robyn, I love you love you love you."

In the bath, I'd turn my hand to admire the green stone that represented the school color of Ware High School down the hill in the valley, home of the Indians, one of which was profiled in detailed relief on the left side of the band. On the opposite side was a small crest bearing the word "WARE" and then "FIDELITY" in an arc over that. To people who thought they were funny, that they were the first to ask, "Where's that? Where'd you say you're from? Where?" the town name was a joke. But if you lived here, you really didn't think twice about the name of your home, it being what you'd known all your life. As for the word *fidelity,* I knew that meant you stayed true to something. I held the word in my vocabulary, and practiced it like some people work at good posture or an Olympic sport, constantly and with great future purpose. The same summer I snapped up Frankie's ring from the milk box this kid Kevin Powers back in Illinois was after me to be his girlfriend. He wanted to know how I could have any kind of a relationship with a boy half a country away. But even if I could have put my feelings for Frankie into some kind of comprehensible words, he wouldn't have understood them. Kevin Powers lived back in Illinois, which from the first year there I always had seen as a separate life from my real one, on the farm. It was like my blood ran down different veins when I got back to Massachusetts. One minute there and the air in me went down different tubes and passageways. Parts of my brain that I never otherwise used kicked into gear. Sounds went in the same ears, but were replayed to my brain on what was like a far better set of speakers, the type you'd pay lots for on a trip out to some specialty store in the city. There, my eyes switched, gained new abilities, like when the optometrist sets your face into the little mask of lenses and clicks a selection past you—which ones are the best, he wants to know, which ones allow you to see the way you really should? One or two? One or two? And at first, the lenses are all like how I view my existence in Illinois–you can see fine, but everything has a vague fuzz to it, a muddiness around the edges, everything is off. Then clearer, clearer, that's it. That's the one. I am back home. I know who I am.

And this summer, this last summer before college, I would have a genuine girlfriend along for the ride. I just knew we'd have adventures, and they'd be the best kinds, ones you couldn't list or predict ahead of time because they would just happen on what had started out to be the most boring of days and then you would reminisce for hours, years later even, on the fun or the fright. We'd cook over an open fire all the meals that my aunt would allow us to. Even cake, which I heard from the Girl Scouts that you can make over coals if you use some kind of tin-foil contraption. We'd invent ourselves a code in which we'd write letters every month all the way until next summer, unlike my friends' new friends, whose correspondence bulletted with hollow-dotted *i*'s and smiley faces at the closing usually petered out after the pages detailing the sender's choice of Halloween costume. We'd swap clothes, invent hairdos. I'd leave for college in the fall wearing the beaded jewelry made in our own version of craft class, displaying my enviable matching necklace and bracelet and pinkie ring while showing off photos of this girl and me, of us riding, riding on real ponies, not just sitting on one of the couple of trailweary nags the Girl Scout camp each July trucked in for the many who'd registered to take part in Equestrian Day. It all was going to be just perfect.

At least that's what I thought until my first day back at the farm that final summer. When all of it really started–when Victory had her talk with Mrs. Chichon, her closest friend in the whole world.

.       .       .

As usual, my steamer trunk had been deposited by my uncle in the far corner of my room, and I had the lid open as I knelt to admire all the things that I had thrown in haphazardly the week before, and that my mother had immediately come along to fold and neaten and mark off on a detailed checklist because that's the kind of organized person she is. We had a couple of packings to tend to that May—both this old beat-up black trunk, and a new white golden-hardwared one bought just for college. I maybe should have felt sadder about all this, the fact that once I left Illinois for Massachusetts the day after high school graduation I really would not be going back but for that week in which I hoped to catch up with, and brag to, the other girls on the block. When the new year had turned and my plans got so real you could see them printed on the current calendar, my mother often would get weepy, not really crying in front of any of us, but heading behind the sliding door of the bathroom to address her sadness in front of the double sinks. Maybe some daughters would have joined in, would have banged on the door until the mother unlocked and over the threshold they'd fall into each other's arms, sobbing out their feelings. But I couldn't work up to that. I was so excited about the prospect of going back to the farm, and, of course, to Frankie. Then off to college in Washington, at the far other end of the country, a school that not only wanted me but was willing to pay my way. And then looking forward to returning to the farm, of course, like always, at the end of the school year. All these huge and wonderful things happening to me one after the other that even in the dark I couldn't help but smile every time I thought about the life that awaited. My future was like a pizza that had just been delivered to the front door, made to order, all so right out of the oven and baked just for me that the steam making its way through the cracks in the corners of the box is writing my name in the air.

The farm was the first course. My favorite place in the entire big world, and now I was back there. Back home. Back in time.

It was old both physically and in the ways that were practiced there. Fish on Friday, cleaning from top to bottom on Saturday, Mass on Sunday, every night sit in the same rocking chair my grandfather once rested in, awake to the same scene he saw when he opened his eyes in the bedroom that was now mine. A man I never met, but felt like I had thanks to the many palpable links to him. My uncle was always telling me stories about his father, the original Pawel, a music lover who dragged the phonograph out to the barn and cranked up classical records for the benefit of the animals decades before anybody else in the world ever thought anything similar. He loved to walk to the edge of the field and pick a handful of plants, some for medicine, some for supper, some just to rub between his fingers and hold beneath his nose and inhale for the healing powers they surely were emitting. Always, in a custom that my uncle continued, rattling off the old-country sayings that were the answer for any situation. Proverbs for everything—even one about exactly that—*"Na wszystko jest przysłowie,"* which translated to "There is a proverb for everything."

The sayings became the sum and total of my knowledge of the language the older Pal, and Sobota, his betrothed, had used when they turned to one another and decided this was the parcel of rocky land on which they would plant their please-God comfortable future. I loved the language, the soft waves of the sounds that it called for, how those collided up against the harder pilings of the consonants, all of it stitched together in the secret code to God with which we began each day, *"W imię ojca i syna i ducha swiętego,"* as we dipped fingers into the holy water font at the door of the kitchen and blessed ourselves in thanksgiving for what we had, and in preparation for whatever the day might bring us.

Pal would never rise from the breakfast table before announcing, *"Bez pracy nie ma kolaczy"*–"Without work there is no bread." If the work ahead was not going to be greeted with enthusiasm, *"Lipiej nie zaczynać niż, zaczynać i nie skończyć"*–"It is better not to begin than, having begun, to leave unfinished." If I beat him to that one, he'd concede, *"Mądzejsze jajo od kury"*– "Wiser the egg than the hen."

There was a pile of sayings suitable for the end of the day. A million times I heard *"Starosc nie radosc,"* that it is not good to get old. And *"Zycie jest jak księżyc, teraz ciemne, teraz pełne"*–"Life is like the moon–now dark, now full." The later hours were when Victory and Pal would reminisce, and she would agree with him, who'd been there all those years gone past, and with me, who'd seen a fraction of them, *"Wszystkie stare czasy są dobre"*– "All old times are good."

And they were. I would think this even as they were still young and still taking place.

On my first day of my last childhood summer there, most of the windows were open. It was already so nice out you couldn't help but do that, even if you hadn't had time yet to install your screens for the season and prevent the earliest of the bugs from buzzing in. That was what I was supposed to be doing this late morning. I was supposed to be out in the barn, getting the window screens from beneath the tarps up in the loft, then scrubbing them with Clorox and water to get them all fresh before putting them into their respective tracks in each window, following the room names Victory long ago had penciled onto the aluminum frames: Victory Room Front, Parlor Side, Robyn Room Back. Robyn Room—even seeing my name written on an aluminum screen was a level of thrill. I was home. Back on my farm. With my own screen. And with Frankie due at seven, my first sight of him since last September. I was all caught up in the contents of my trunk, debating my outfit for the big reunion, when I heard the voices outside. When I heard Victory say the word. She spoke it quietly. But I have two very good ears, so I picked it up right away:

"Suicide."

My aunt always read a lot of books. There were constant stacks of them, titles borrowed from friends, bought from stores and tag sales, checked out of the bookmobile when it made its weekly stop each Tuesday afternoon at the Meetinghouse. They were piled on her nightstand. Next to her TV chair. On the radiator next to her place at the kitchen table. In a basket in the bathroom. She often read two or three in the same span of time, something I always found confusing when I attempted it. But she switched without problem from the final chapter of the one on the porch to the big charging middle scene awaiting her upstairs. The books were mostly what she called "women's stories," ones that probably would appeal only to females. Not the out-and-out romancey things many ladies enjoy, Victory's selections were more like those about pioneer ladies and female detectives. Courageous nurses. Spy girls. Women politicians, saints and social changers. Some were simply female relatives of famous men telling the behind-the-scenes stories of how their brothers or fathers came to be so well-known. She was constantly recommending stories to Mrs. Chichon, though I don't know if the woman ever actually went and picked up the ones Victory told her were so fabulous.

"Some said it was merely a cry for help," Victory was informing Mrs. Chichon in a low voice as they stood beneath the clothesline, Mrs. Chichon just standing there, never once offering assistance, her arms folded while Victory worked to stretch a fitted sheet along a vacant line. "But others said she really meant to do it. Imagine! Being so desperate . . ."

Here I peeked higher above the windowsill, and I saw Mrs. Chichon shake her head. Her eyes were big and sad, and she looked a lot more impressed by this book than by any of the others I'd ever heard Victory review for her. "Then what?" she asked, and she leaned in as if she anticipated that the answer was going to be a real good one.

"Then, then there was a period of time spent in one of those mental institutions, the poor thing." Victory said this, softly, which I have to say added to the building drama.

"No!"

"Yes."

"No!"

"What'd I just say?"

*Tsk. Tsk. Tsk.*

That last thing was the sound coming from Mrs. Chichon.

In front of me, on top of the nearest corner pile of clothes in the trunk was my new summer sweatshirt. My mother bought me one every spring, and between my own steady growth and life on the farm, depending on its looks come September, the thing either became a hand-me-down or a rag. This year's was royal blue, with the word *Chicago* spelled out in blocky white iron-on letters of fluffy looped felt. I hadn't actually gotten the shirt in Chicago—it was kind of far from our town, even though it was the answer we gave when someone asked us where we lived, close enough and big enough to give people the general location. Ma had bought this new sweatshirt in our town, at a shop that sold athletic wear at reduced prices because maybe the team name was misspelled or the wrong mascot was sewn on or there was a pull or the zipper at the neck was stuck. Like the Chicago one—the *o* at the end of the word was half coming off, but a few stitches at home surely would do the trick. If you didn't mind those sort of defects, you could pick up some real deals there, and my mother loved a bargain. She came home that day with a second shirt, all goldeny yellow with the name of our state scrolled in black over the left breast. The incorrect spelling—*Illinios*—made it seventy-five percent off. It was to be for the summer girl. Ma said giving her this present would be the least I could do to welcome her. To make her feel that we liked her right off. Not knowing the girl's size, Ma had bought a medium, which seemed like the safest bet, nothing that could really insult somebody who truly was small or large.

I unfolded my sweatshirt, then folded it back up the way Ma had taught us kids long ago because, what was she, our maid? Anybody could fold a shirt—and certainly should know how. Lay it front side down, she instructed, bring one arm straight across to meet the other shoulder, do the same with the other arm. Fold the bottom up to meet the top. You're done. I flipped mine over and the "Chicago" was centered and displayed as perfectly as if I were working in the seconds store, which, actually, the previous October had been a dream of mine, only they hired a boy instead. The position turned out to be nothing as fun as working the cash register—they kept him in the back room, stacking one heavy box on top of the next. You can pick up one shirt or a pair of socks and think it weighs nothing. Try lifting a couple dozen at a time. That's what the boy, a skinny little defenseman hopelessly stuck for three whole seasons on our j.v. hockey team, told me when I had asked him how he liked working there, which he didn't, and he soon went on to quit and take a job washing glasses and trays down at The Finish Line.

I picked up the second sweatshirt, the one that was to be the summer girl's. I shook it loose to admire it, then flipped it over to fold, pulling the manufacturer's tag from inside so it could cascade over the front collar, underlining that this indeed was a brand-new item. I wondered if I should get some paper and wrap it up, making it look like that much more of a gift.

"Can you picture it, being in a mental institution?" Mrs. Chichon was asking this. Victory was silent for a few beats, and then offered, "Well, not only that, but just think of being in there at that age."

I peeked over the sill now. My aunt had progressed from hanging up the biggest pieces to pinning up smaller items—her aprons, blouses, various undergarments, a solid purple Sunday dress she'd washed separately and by hand in a plastic basin kept under the sink for such purposes. Pal's green work pants, a pair of new denim overalls, his sleeveless T-shirts, thick white socks and balooney briefs took up the next line. As I'd been at the farm not even twenty-four hours, none of my things had yet made their way into the wringer washer. But even this I anticipated. There was a comfort about seeing my tops and bottoms slowly working their way onto the line, populating among Victory's and Pal's things, all of us and them waving

together in the wind, the simple little poke-on clothespins linking my shorts to her clamdiggers, which went on to pin up a
chain of his plaid hankies.

More *tsks*. About what Victory had said: "Institution."

I placed the girl's right sleeve over to meet the beginning of
her left shoulder.

"Well? Tell me! Whatever happened to her?"

Mrs. Chichon obviously was not interested in going
through the trouble and time of reading this particular book,
probably one of those people who, if they did pick up a copy,
would flip to the last line and read that before anything else.

I placed the left arm over to the right.

"She got better." Victory said this with a genuine sound of
relief. It was the kind of perfect happy ending that I knew she
preferred, even though she always stressed to me, usually right
after finishing another book, that neat and clean and tidy
unfortunately is not how life usually works out. I folded the
bottom of the sweatshirt up to the back of the neck, and flipped
it to admire that professional fresh-from-the-store-shelf look I'd
created.

"And then what?" Mrs. Chichon couldn't get enough.

I put the summer girl's sweatshirt in the trunk, then mine
on top of it. I could see us sitting on this very floor once she
arrived in another two days, and I could imagine the hidden-
camera film of myself bringing the sweatshirt out from the
trunk, the one I'd so kindly brought for her. Years later, I predicted, she would tell me how that was her first clear memory
of me. How her pulling up to the house and shaking my hand
and saying my name for the first time—how all that was nice,
but faded. What she would replay clearly over the years would
be how I had gone and brought something for her—a total

stranger who I couldn't possibly predict would click with me. And she would say how that moment was the one in which she realized that we would be friends for life.

"Well," Victory said to Mrs. Chichon. "Well, then her family decided a change of scenery would do her some good. So that's why she'll be arriving here on Monday."

# · 3 ·

Back in Illinois, we had our own institution. Hidden away at the edge of our town, like they so often are, all brick and looking from very far away like an exclusive college that you would have to be a millionaire to afford.

It technically was called the state school, but nobody I knew referred to it as that. It was not the kind of school my friends and I attended, the type with classrooms and lessons and books and papers and crayons and paste and tests and recess, and, most importantly, moving up through the grades and finally getting out once you'd done all the required work. The state school was a place where insane people were kept. For good, and forever.

Many people in town called it the crazy house. Some of them used the term *nuthouse*. "The loony bin." Or just "the bin." If you acted weird, that was where your parents said you were headed. If you liked to cross your eyes a lot, if you made weird sounds just for the fun of it, if you had the habit of being unable to stop laughing at something long after everyone else in the room had, if you got very curious and, only because you genuinely wanted to know, you asked questions about deep

topics like death and hell—keep it up, they'd warn, you're
going to end up in the bin.

It was an enormous place, so a lot of our adult friends and
neighbors easily found work there. Like Buddy Davis's quiet
father, in some capacity that all of us—including Buddy—could
only guess at. Mr. Davis wasn't the kind of father who would
ever say anything to you outside asking what you wanted on
the hamburger he was burning on the hibachi, so he was no
help in our finding out any details. But we got more than an
earful from Linda Darnley's greasy oldest brother, Gordon,
who was of the age when he should have been off studying in
college like everybody else's oldest brother, but who instead
stayed in his room playing his records at top volume when he
wasn't off mopping floors on the night shift of eleven P.M. to
seven in the morning.

All of what he told us was stark and shiver-inducing. According to Gordon Darnley, most of the people at the state school
were kept in cages. When you walked down the hall they
reached out at you through the bars, pleading, weeping, moan-
ing. Wearing hardly anything, or, if clothed, bound up in straight-
jackets. To demonstrate what these were the first time he used
the term, Gordon crossed his arms and bugged out his eyes and
slurred, "Pretend you were tied up like this and couldn't move.
At all. All day." We'd put our arms over our own selves, in that
same manner, but not for long, as we couldn't stand even the
few seconds of simply imagining. "I'm working on sneaking one
out to wear for Halloween," he added, excited.

The state school wasn't just one structure. There was a whole
bunch of buildings over there. A "complex," Gordon said they
called it. Most of the buildings held men, and two of them were
reserved for the most dangerous, including the kind of criminals

who are determined by the courts to have done something awful, but because they are insane rather than normal they get to come and live in our town, rather than be shipped off to real prison. Inside these particular buildings were actual genuine murderers. Not fake ones like on TV, actors you might one night see on "The FBI" shooting somebody in the back of the head, then the following week serving floats to the Brady Bunch. Those caged up here were seriously dangerous. It wasn't Gordon's usual area, but he once was sent to work in one of their buildings, and he got a look at a man who, long before any of us were born, had gone and killed his entire family and an unlucky overnight guest, then progressed to do away with the neighbors on both sides of his house before somebody across the street heard some kind of commotion and summoned the police. Of course one of us had to ask what did the man look like.

"Oh, you wouldn't want to see," was Gordon's answer. "He kept crooking his finger at me through the little window on the steel door they keep these kinds of guys behind, inviting me over, whispering, 'You don't know . . . You don't know . . .'" Here Gordon mimicked the voice, rough and scratchy, that of somebody who hadn't swallowed in, like, ten years. No, no, he didn't go over to the man. What did we think he was? Crazy?

Gordon also said there also was a whole building full of women and nobody else. He said these were all older than a certain age, which he estimated to be around that of Mrs. Kelvey over on the corner, who wasn't yet grandmotherly, but old enough to have a daughter moved out of state to take some kind of bigshot job to which she had to wear an expensive business suit every day.

"It's like women hit this number and they go off their rockers," Gordon said. "Their families bring them out and just leave them there. They tell them it's just for a week or so, until they feel better. But it's usually forever. Once they realize that nobody's coming back for them, that's what really pushes them off the deep end."

He went on to elaborate. These ladies wore housecoats and slippers all day long. They shuffled around, hairdos a mess, makeup off-target, big hollow eyes staring out the windows at the fence they couldn't climb even with the tallest ladder, never mind what they would do when they got to the top and met up with all that flesh-shredding wire. Nothing made them happy. But why should they be, I figured, if one day you're fine and smiling and scooping everybody their second helpings of the favorite macaroni and cheese that you went out special, maybe in a storm, and bought for them because you are one big happy family with strong love binding you all, and the next day these same people you have pampered and spoiled are giving you their big thanks by loading you and your nightgown into the car and dumping you off to be locked up until the day you die.

"From what I dig, it's a very common problem for the ladies," Gordon said quick and matter-of-fact. "No doubt it'll happen to you guys one day."

If it didn't occur that far in the future, it could hit us as soon as tomorrow: Gordon had proof that kids also went crazy. The state school included another couple buildings packed to the gills with them. With real, regular kids. Ones our ages, even. Sure, there were the deformed, whose appearance was a lot less than what most of society would consider pretty or cute, but a fair number of them looked shockingly normal, and that just had you wondering day in and day out what was the thing that had landed them there?

"The kids, they look just like you," he would say, then point, usually at me. "And they're going to be there for the rest of their lives."

Whatever the age of the patients, Gordon told us, their most terrible behavior came on the nights of full moons. Tides, gravity, whatever was connected to that, it all did something awful to the mind, and for the duration they were at their worst. Shrieking so constantly that Gordon hardly could hear his Blackhawks or Cubbies coming in at top volume through the earphone of his pocket transistor. There was constant commotion brewing on these nights once a month—twice a month in the rare and dreaded occurrence of a blue moon. The patients shoved their food trays back through the slots in their cell doors. Tried to choke the nurses who had to get close enough to administer medications. Actually howled, and Gordon was not making that up. He also said these were the times you had to worry most about them getting free. Because on the nights of the full moons crazy people gathered such superhuman strength that even bending the bars at their windows, and making it over the fence outside, were not beyond their powers. On full-moon nights those first few years we were in Illinois, I'd check at least twice to make sure my windows were locked and I'd slide my blanket chest against my door and I'd take to bed an uncapped can of my mother's Super-Hold Final Net, having overheard one of her friends from ceramics class tell how a lady down in the city blinded her attacker with a good long blast of something aerosol.

Once in a while after listening to Gordon, I'd have an awful dream. There I'd be, in one of the kids' buildings, insane, locked up, nobody but the likes of him passing by, poking his wooden mop handle through the bars, taunting me, laughing.

I'd flip around in bed so many times that I'd bind myself in my sheets and I'd wake in hysterics, sobbing. My mother, who'd managed to shove her way into my fortress, would be hugging me and warning me never to go over to the Darnleys' again, how many times did she have to tell me that?

"I'm crazy! I'm crazy!" is what I'd throw at her in big sobs, believing I was still back there, locked up for good in my damp, dark cage.

"You're not crazy," my mother would comfort, hugging me to the fabric-softened lapels of her avocado terrycloth robe. "Nobody here is crazy! We're normal people. Nice and normal. Nobody's crazy here."

As a way to get me to meet new friends the first year we lived in Illinois, my mother enrolled me in the ballet lessons she'd seen advertised on a poster at the fabric store. The only friend I even half-made through this plan was Deborah, a very quiet girl who constantly pulled her chewing gum out of her mouth in a long rubbery strand and who lived on a street just beyond the state school.

Driving Deborah home, we'd actually have to take the same exact driveway that you would if you'd been declared nuts. "Northern Illinois Regional State School," read the big blue sign at the start of the drive. "All Vehicles Must Stop at Gatehouse."

The first time she instructed my mother to turn in at the sign, Ma slowed the car, looked in the rearview, and asked, "Are you sure?" as if Deborah didn't know where her own home was.

"Yeah," Deborah answered in the kind of sigh that told you everybody who ever gave her a lift home asked the same question.

"I'm only wondering because it looks like we're going to the . . . the . . . institution." My mother tried to sound proper and unflustered as we drove up the long straight driveway right toward the hulking main building. I could tell she was nervous, which, of course, got me feeling the same way.

"The town made our road before the state built that," Deborah said all in the same low tone, almost mumbling, pointing to the school. "Take a right just before you get to the gate."

Ma said, "Oh," and I saw her reach up with her left elbow and lock her door in that quick manner she also used whenever she came upon an apparently black section of a town.

We rolled almost to the gate, where a big van with no windows was stopped, a uniformed guy with a clipboard writing down its license plate. He waved the vehicle in, and pulled a heavy sliding gate shut behind it. Even from inside a moving car, I could feel the heavy closing of the latch. I swallowed hard and, in plain sight, reached to lock my own door. Ma took the right and we traveled along the side of the complex, a series of plain two-story brick buildings linked by straight sidewalks that cut through a neat lawn. Picnic tables had been placed here and there in the yard, and you could make out figures at them, not really picnicking, just sitting stooped or exaggeratedly erect. On the otherwise deserted sidewalk that ran on this side of the fence, a normal-looking man was walking toward us, holding the hand of a short apey guy in a chunky hockey helmet, all bearded and sloped of shoulder, arms hanging past his knees. His eyes met mine and that's when it happened. In a half-second, he jerked free and into the road he leapt, his keeper in pursuit, both of them waving frantically at the car as Ma screamed and swerved to the right and Deborah and I scrambled to the far end of the backseat. Ma blew past the ape guy just as the man caught hold of him by the back of his shirt, and when I peeked over the top of the seat, I saw him calm once again, like nothing had just happened, being led by the arm in the direction of the gate. I got one of those big shudders that takes over your entire body. Deborah slid down in her seat, her aqua tutu crinkling. I nervously played with the net on mine. I hated wearing the thing in public, but Madame Tayna had only the one dressing room and by the time our class was over it was jammed with lipsticked high school girls who locked the door on us younger kids while they changed into the cool black leotards in which they practiced their modern jazz.

"Just a little farther," Deborah told my mother as we passed a sign that read "Leaving State Property" and big trees began to spring up and more and more of the kind of familiar houses that sane people lived in could be seen on either side of the road.

Whenever a bulletin was broadcast over the radio or crawled along the bottom of our TV screen warning that somebody from the state school was on the loose, my mother would run to lock our doors and slam down any open windows even though the announcer never failed to note that "The client is not dangerous." Gordon Darnley told us this was a bunch of bull. He asked us what did we expect? That they'd say what was more the truth—that there was a homicidal mental case hiding somewhere nearby, probably in your bedroom closet? I once mentioned something about this to Deborah—I asked her wasn't she petrified living over where she did?

"They're just people, like you or me," she answered, chomping on her Juicy Fruit. "How do you know what kind of people even live next door to you?"

I thought about that and tried to imagine Mr. and Mrs.

Scercer doing anything other than what I knew them to do, which was, thanks to the perfect view of their TV room that I had from my bedroom window not twenty feet away, a lot of boring stuff. They talked often on the phone equipped with a really long cord that allowed them to do things like dust and search through drawers while having a conversation. They rolled up their spare change on the coffee table. They paid bills at a corner desk. She sewed things at a machine that folded into a little cabinet on which she kept a small bowl of wax fruit. He sat in a corner chair and read a lot of books with pictures of war planes on their covers. Some nights they shut off the lights and I got to see slide shows of their vacations. Usually at a pond, she posing on the dock in a bathing cap, bashful in a swimsuit that had the attached skirt to shield the upper thighs, he fishing but never holding up any results like you so often see men proudly depicted. Despite that, it still looked like they had a nice time. Everything normal.

On the other side, it was harder to tell the situation, as there were no windows on that end of our house. The four Balfrys, whom we would have been spying on had there been some openings, appeared in public to be no different from the Scercers. Or from us. Regular people living regular lives, except that both those couples attended Protestant church. Before Deborah's comment, nobody ever had me considering how the people at the state school were like the Balfrys, or the Scercers, or us. Because, except for Deborah, nobody I knew ever had that thought cross their mind.

"Do you know this girl?"

The clothes were all hung. Mrs. Chichon had left. Victory was upstairs now and setting flowers on the little desk in my room, where I'd been stuck to the bed by the weight of what I'd just learned. The vase she brought in was small and made of rubyish Depression glass and filled with the kind of bleeding hearts that bloom all summer, not only in the spring. Without fail, thanks to Victory, there was a new arrangement in my room every few days. Just like in a fancy hotel, she'd point out, like either one of us would know this for a fact.

"What girl?" she asked as she picked a spindly green bug off a blossom and squished it between her fingers in the casual manner that I never managed to acquire.

"The one who's coming."

"I don't," she said. She searched the serrated leaves for any other freeloaders and then turned to go.

"You don't know anything?"

Victory looked at me. "Oh, no, I don't. Just that she's coming here, that my friend—her grandmother who used to live up here, now lives with the son, she says the girl's nice. Like I told you in the letters."

She knew more than that. I knew this. I couldn't believe she was lying to me, because I don't think she ever had before.

"What else?"

"Let me think . . ."

I couldn't stand it. I remember shooting to my feet without really meaning to.

"I heard you," I said to her louder than I'd ever spoken to any adult. "Out the window. Talking to Mrs. Chichon. Saying those things."

Victory looked at the window. At my uninstalled screen leaning below it. Then at me. "What things?"

The walls blurred like spin art as I punched out the words, "You're making me stay with a crazy person!"

"Robyn." My aunt said that calmly, but at the same time she looked kind of shocked. "Why do you talk like that? There is nobody crazy here."

"I heard you tell Mrs. Chichon. This was somebody who got locked up. Who had a, a suicide."

Victory sat on the bed and put her hands on her knees. She had on a new pair of apricot polyester bellbottoms she had sewn over the winter from a raised weave patterned like that of a honeycomb. Before she spoke, she placed each of her fingers into one of the little compartments in the fabric that covered her knees. I couldn't tell if that was on purpose. She said to me slowly: "Now, the girl didn't have a suicide, or—think about it—she wouldn't be alive to be coming here. She didn't actually . . . I don't know . . . sometimes people just do things. Really—a little trip off the tracks doesn't make her that strange. We all have them now and again."

I thought about this and was ready to say, no, I know that at least I never did. Not me. But just as Victory had never lied to me before this, I'd never lied to her at all. So I had to admit, if only in my head, that I always got very sad when it was time to put away the Christmas decorations. My mother always took everything down on January the sixth, the afternoon of the Feast of the Three Kings, sticking to old-country traditions even once we moved to a diverse, modern neighborhood with all kinds of people living in it, hailing from the most different backgrounds, even the kind that had one family who all day long wore towels on their heads like you just stepped out of the shower. Just as excited as I got when the boxes of ornaments and festoons were brought down from the attic the Saturday after Thanksgiving, I got equally as low and blue when we had to pack everything back up. The rooms that had been so colorful and softly lit for those many weeks suddenly seemed bare and dull. Even the top of the toilet tank, where during Christmas season my mother stored a spare roll of paper beneath the crocheted hoop skirt worn by a Mrs. Santa doll that was really an old Barbie in disguise. The sight of the fake tree trunk being unscrewed from its color-coded branches and folded back into its huge coffin-like crate was enough to make me curl up on the couch and hide my head under an afghan. Okay, from this, I knew what it was like to feel less than good and happy. But, for me, that always had disappeared by suppertime.

"They put her away!"

"People sometimes need help," Victory offered. "And they can get better. They go to a doctor. And get help. Like how you go to a doctor for anything—bad cold, broken arm . . ."

I cut her off: "What'd she do?"

Victory looked into her honeycombs. "Pharmaceuticals," she said without protest. "Lots and lots of them."

I thought of Paula Whitman's big sister, who once got into huge trouble for having a tinfoil packet of colored pills in her hobo bag when her mother went looking for the car keys one night, and after that I was forbidden to go over there or even to call Paula's name from down the street. *Go Ask Alice* had been on my summer reading list, "Drug Downfall" was the corny filmstrip shown to every health class. So I knew. I knew some of what all this was about. But the girl who was coming to stay with us must have been absent the day they assigned the book or showed the beep-cued stills of the good girl overdosing. Maybe that was the same day she starred in her own version of these stories, and already had been hauled off to her nearest hospital to have the pills removed from her system by some method that Victory told me I didn't need to know the details of. Maybe by that particular health class, the girl had already been admitted to a place that sounded not unlike the institution I had in my town. The girl's grandmother had told Victory just that it was no vacation spot, no place for a child. That there were people in there with real, genuine problems, and you would fear for your life if you weren't in the state of mind that had you pretty much not caring about it anyway. She went on to tell Victory stories that would have chilled Gordon Darnley, and that would have shot me right back to the practice of dragging furniture against my door. So Victory didn't share those with me, only gave the important facts that after five months in this place, the girl was determined to be well enough to go home, just in time for the annual hopeful season of Easter. She never returned to high school, never formally finished up, never knew a single day of her senior year. She had missed out on all the things that I was fresh from enjoying, the very best being the loping Pomp-and-Circumstance walk up to the podium to collect the little pebbled vinyl folder that contained my hard-won diploma. The day she should have gotten hers, the girl probably had been home, maybe lazing on the couch watching a black-and-white Sunday afternoon movie and pretending none of this bothered her. But it did, and her parents could tell, and so they thought it would be nice for her to air out, far away from the scene of all her woes, and so they had the grandmother call her old friend Victory up on the peaceful New England farm and make the arrangements to send the girl here.

I still felt sick. I shook my head. This is not who I'd been expecting.

Victory shook hers back at me. "Look." She said this, and I did what she asked. I looked into the face that, for three quarters of the year, I could conjure up in front of me whenever I had the need to be back at the farm. Mine, only decades of life later: Round as a slice of bologna, wrinkles concentric like ripples from a stone that's been tossed, mouth shaped like a watermelon slice, nose that turned to the left because her mother always set her facedown and in that direction when she was a sleeping infant, eyes that bordered on the lands of gray and green but that never claimed residency in either.

"I would not have agreed to this if I didn't have faith in you—that you wouldn't be as nice to her as you would to anyone else. I didn't think you had to know everything, because it's a lot for somebody young to understand. All you needed to know was what I'd been telling you: That she's in need of a nice summer, and that you're going to have a good new friend. There is no need to let her know what you know. Think of how hard she's had it already. To have somebody else looking at her odd, it won't help, not at all. If she wants to tell you, she'll tell you. Which she might. Just be nice to her. Don't get her mad, if you can help it. Don't get her mad. Show her a nice time. Treat her like she's anybody else, would you? As a favor to me? And to her? All this will make sense when you have some more years on you. Trust me for now, okay?"

There was nobody I trusted more than Victory. I sat down next to her on the bed and, as it gave a big tired creak from holding the two of us, I told her yes. That I would do what she wanted. She had to be right. This was just a girl. Just a girl. Like me.

Mr. Maytaz, whom you could without any guilt ask to do such things because he had taken early retirement from the shoe shop and was a still-youngish older man looking for something to fill his many suddenly free hours, brought the girl from the airport to the house late that next Monday afternoon. He did the same for me every spring, picking me up when my plane landed down near Hartford and for the hour and a half it took us to get back to the farm he let me work the various buttons that moved his fancy car's seats forward or back, the windows and aerial up and down, made the interior lights dimmer or brighter, shot the true miracle of air conditioning straight into your flushed face. That Monday, he was chauffeuring some-body else. I sensed rather than heard the smooth arrival of his mirror-polished Delta 88 and looked out the upstairs hall win-dow to watch it slow at the front steps.

"She's here!"

Victory yelled this from downstairs, hepped up like this was some good news, and I heard her scurry from the kitchen down the little hall to the porch. Fast steps. The screen door squealed open and then came my aunt's cheery odd "Hallooo!" that always got me pretending I was someone in a foreign country.

I'd been hiding. Doing that as much as I could in the two days since I'd overheard the conversation with Mrs. Chichon, and had my own personal one with Victory. And when I was not hiding, I was cleaning—Pal's idea so I wouldn't have time to think.

"*Czem chata bogata, tem rada,*" he said. "The humblest cottage joyfully shares what it has."

"Uh-uh."

"*Gość widzi więcej w godzinę niż gospodarz w roku*"—"A guest sees more in an hour than the host in a year," he reminded me while he held the stepstool steady so I could safely dust along the tops of the doorsills.

"Yeah, okay."

In between each of the bright time-consuming ideas—turning mattresses, like the girl was going to try each and every one of them out, joining pairs from a box of mismatched stationery and envelopes in case our guest wanted to write home in a formal manner, trimming the goats' beards to make them more presentable—there was the old-country wisdom.

When not being made to listen to it, or do the work assigned, I sat at the ring for only as long as I was supposed to. I hurried off to my room when no customers were there, and I returned for only as long as it took to send a couple of kids five times around the world. Or to see Frankie, of course. No dallying in the yard, no extra riding around just for the fun of it. What if the girl arrived early and Victory and Pal were gone or busy and I was alone out there? What would I say to her? What would I do? What would she do? I hadn't the smallest idea.

I was functioning on very little sleep, getting hardly any rest in the two previous nights as my head swelled from the frosting I was applying to the startling facts I'd been given, reviewing all the ways I knew of that people did themselves in. Movies and TV and books and newspaper stories were full of suggestions. There was jumping off bridges and other high places. You could run out in front of a car. In these days, so many people— many of them the children of celebrities—were accomplishing what this girl had unsuccessfully tried. I guessed there were many more ways than I knew of to end your life, but those were far more than enough for me to list. Each I could counter with a reason I'd never try it—being afraid of heights, not liking to feel pain, hating the sight of blood, and most of all, simply not wanting to die. My life was fantastic. I'd have to be crazy to want to end it.

Every time I did manage to grab a piece of sleep, my dreams would be taken over by an ape girl, short, all bearded and sloped of shoulder, one arm hanging past her knees. She leapt at me, waving frantically at the car in which I was riding. I screamed and pitched myself across the seat—into the side of another ape girl I didn't realize was next to me. She bared her teeth and laughed back when I shrieked and jumped to the front seat, where another ape girl at the wheel was driving us right past the gatehouse without stopping to show an ID, delivering me right into the land of the insane.

"Robyn—come downstairs, please."

Victory was calling from the front yard. I rolled my head back and rubbed my eyes. When they were closed, the ape girls were there, behind my lids.

I opened and closed the front screen slowly and quietly, to buy myself that many more seconds alone, also to not cause a sudden noise that might frighten the girl. Who knows what this kind of person might do if spooked? Don't get her mad, I remembered.

Victory and Pal were at the car door, leaning in and talking loudly to Mr. Maytaz, happily thanking him for his help in driving once again, and ordering "Take them take them" to Mr. Maytaz's "No no no" as my uncle pushed into his hand some dollar bills that eventually were accepted.

"Come on out, dear." Victory was now over at the passenger side. The door unclicked, my aunt stepped aside, and there was the girl. Regular height, maybe a little taller, regular weight, maybe a little less, long black hair that made her look like Buffy St. Marie, white skin that had been inside a lot. Yellow-and-black-striped top, bellbottom jeans, jute platforms. I went

over all this once again, how she looked and what I knew of
her and I couldn't help but say in my head, wow, if you put her
in a crowd you'd never be able to tell. Then I remembered:
That was what Gordon Darnley had said about a lot of these
kinds of people. Those very words.

Mr. Maytaz popped the trunk by using my favorite button, the
toggle one hidden inside the glove compartment. Lucy walked
around back and pulled out a small suitcase, blue and red
plaid, brown vinyl sides, a zipper closing the whole thing. She
hung a denim purse from her right shoulder, and the orange
suede fringe at the bottom of it fell into place neatly once she
stood still.

"I want you to meet my niece," Victory said, and she guided
the girl over to me, putting an arm gently around her shoulder.
"Lucy Dragon, this is Robyn." Lucy looked at me and Victory
looked at me, both of them in a way that told me I was now
expected to contribute something to the greeting.

"I'm glad you're here," I said just a little higher than what
you'd call flatly. I don't know where this came from, because it
was the opposite of the truth. I saw Victory nodding in appreciation of my few little words.

"Thanks," Lucy said, and her smile unveiled teeth that
looked like those on a family I know back in Illinois whose
father is a dentist. All shaped the same, loose-leaf-white, shiny
as shower tile on a Saturday morning.

Since it was that correct time of day, it was handy for Victory to say what she did next, which was, "Let's go in and eat."

First we gave Lucy a tour of the house, which was not really
necessary, as even if it was your first time there you could move

through the place yourself and figure out from the furniture or appliances just what kind of activities each space was used for. Victory was anxious to narrate, so she walked in front, the girl in the middle of our procession, me in the back, Pal still outside, discussing car batteries with Mr. Maytaz, where I wouldn't have minded being. Instead, I was behind Lucy, and I began studying every inch that I could without getting caught doing it. The worn backs of her sandals, the gray line of dirt on the bottom of the pink heel flesh, the little square of a purple patch on the right back pocket of her jeans. The beads, green and red, wound around her left wrist in an order that made me wonder if it held meaning. Her shiny hair rocked slow like a solemn bell when she moved along. You could see the clothing label sticking out the back of her jersey top—the product of a line titled "Way Out Fashions"—upside down because she hadn't tucked it in when she'd dressed. Had I known her well, I would have had no problem reaching up to slip it back into hiding, where it belonged, like any friend would. But we weren't anywhere near friends at that point. I kept my hands at my sides.

The tag told me that the girl was a size medium. As usual, Ma had been right. Thinking of the sweatshirt, in the proper size for her, I began to realize the girl indeed would need clothes. I was carrying her suitcase, which felt like it was empty except for the times when we'd round a doorway into another room and a few soft items would shift. Maybe she'd destroyed all her wardrobe at the same time she tried to do what she had tried to do to herself. A fire would do that. Maybe she had set her house on fire and took a bunch of pills and tried to do herself in that way. If so, she'd failed, her clothing the only victims. Maybe all she had left was what she wore. And, somehow, this empty suitcase as well. I watched the girl when we went past the kitchen stove and approached the fireplace, to see if the prospect of heat and flame had any effect on her. But she showed no reaction I could detect.

"This is the parlor, complete with fireplace and, more interesting to you, I'm sure, the television," Victory said when we got in there. "It's a color set, of course, you know. And, here, this is the kitchen, complete with table. We do not have a dining room. The other room down here is a little office, for me, for the farm. That door there, that goes out to the porch, which also is a spare bedroom, where Pal will be staying for the summer. He likes that—don't worry that you are an inconvenience because that is not the case. That door there, that goes to the cellar. Nothing much for you to be interested in down there, root cellar, winter clothes that you won't be in need of—though we might ask you once in a while to go and get some eggs from the extra refrigerator, or something canned because we eat a lot of homegrown things here—I hope you won't mind that, it is very good for you, your health. There are plenty of lights down there, and everything's labeled so you should have no problem. It's not scary at all, if you're concerned about that sort of thing as I know some girls are (here she shot me a wink I didn't appreciate). That door, that's the one to your bathroom. See? Very clean, I will say, but not too modern. And it's the only one we have. We all must share, the four of us, I hope you won't mind."

"It's okay," Lucy said, an answer from which I could take no interesting details.

Victory then announced, "Upstairs, now," and the both of us followed.

As we climbed, my aunt pointed to the right. The white chenille spread covering the foot of her bed was visible from the hall, as was the round wood-edged mirrored dresser reflecting all her grooming implements clean and shiny and lined up for their next use, and a small photograph of her parents, like the one my father kept on his dresser, two formal and separate sepia-toned full-length shots glued together as if in all those years that they were alive, my grandparents had been too busy to ever pose together even once. Next to them, a little bottle of Victory's special-day cologne stood in a glass ashtray to prevent it from damaging the wood surface should it leak. "My room," Victory explained proudly to the girl, who nodded.

Across from the top of the stairs, Victory opened the door. You could see the chair that I'd only throw my clothes on, and the little table I never spent any time at, only piled mail and books and magazines on, the double bed I normally looked forward to, the nightstand with its little lamp and the gray folder displaying the senior-year portrait of my Frankie wearing his father's oversized navy suit and tie, and the chest beneath the window I never rested at because there was too much to do in every day to have much time for sitting and staring—except for the minutes I'd hidden there after I peeked out and got knocked into the wave of the conversation between Victory and Mrs. Chichon, something I regretted because there are some things you are better off going through your life never knowing.

Now Victory was saying, "Robyn's room," loud enough to make me jump a little, drawing me back into real life. And then she was pointing left, telling Lucy, "Your room," and waving the girl past her, and inside. Normally, as it had been since time began for him, this was Uncle Pal's room—actually once shared with my father in their childhood. But for this summer, my uncle had decided to stay out on the back porch, feeling it would be better to give the females their own complete floor. "Like a dormitory," he had said when he told us of his plan and started hauling his blankets and clothing down the stairs. He told me I'd better get used to that, living on one floor that was home to a bunch of females. "Being headed to college and all like you are," he added, "can you believe it?" and Victory had answered for me, as enthusiastically as I would have said it if I'd beat her to it: "Imagine."

Lucy walked through the doorway in the cautious manner of somebody who expected the next floorboard to be rotted away. I lost patience and went around her to place the case down on the bed that I'd been ordered to fit with new floral sheets the previous day, after Victory brought them home from the sidewalk sale at Durand Sisters.

"This is very nice," the girl said. I noticed how she made her first bit of a smile when she looked at Victory then and said, "Thanks."

"You're welcome," Victory answered, kind of dramatic on the first syllable like she was on stage in a play, maybe one that had been written by Ron, had he been around to tune his great listening ear into what was happening to us all right there. Next, Victory looked at me and I knew I had to contribute at least some of the dialog.

"I'm just next door," is what I said, though, from the tour, the girl already knew that. "Knock if you need anything."

"Thanks." Now she was playing with her beaded bracelet, the kind all my Girl Scout friends always came back from summer camp with and showed off once Labor Day weekend ended and we girls all met in the middle of our street and caught up on the previous months. Lucy looked like she'd already been to camp and back. Wait—this was supposed to be camp. This was supposed to be a bonus of a summer. But now everything was going to be different. We were standing in Uncle Pal's room with somebody who was crazy. The summer was ruined, and officially, if you go by the dates on the calendar, it was just the beginning of June and the season hadn't really even started.

# · 4 ·

The reporter visited the farm on my fourth day back.

Phoning the newspaper had been Jerzy's girlfriend's idea. Not mine. She came over and told me she knew about such things as publicity and would take care of everything. By this she meant telling the world, or at least the towns in this corner of it, how this would be the last season for the pony ring.

As for Jerzy, he knew about such things as running a farm. He'd been helping Pal out for the dozen long years since Victory's death, and indeed had been doing the very good job that Pal always reported to me—at a bargain price I never had been told. But the detailed ledger informed me that my uncle had been paying him a flat twenty dollars a day. It said this under each Friday:

"Jerzy Weekly Wages: $140.00."

"I've always done my best for him," Jerzy said when I phoned him after that first hospital visit. Just from his voice I could tell he was being truthful. I didn't know this guy other than all the many positive things said about him by my uncle, who always used the Polish pronunciation "Yehz-she" for his name, rather than the sporting "Jersey" the spelling would have

you concluding. I knew that he lived in an apartment somewhere down past the public pool, that for his more lucrative day
job he repaired cars, specializing in tricky foreign transmissions
at a place halfway down the road leading to the university, and
that he came to the farm before or after that obligation. Often
he stayed late, much later than my uncle thought was necessary,
or good for a younger man who certainly had to have other
things to do with his time. I didn't know the exact projects or
chores he was up to on any given day, but I was pretty confident that I knew what he was doing there in general—walking
around the place like I used to, enthusiastically performing the
endless chores, imagining that nobody else could have done
them so well, at the end of the day standing with hands on hips
pretending the place was all his. I know that at the farm I always
had done a lot of pretending. It was like some kind of spell came
over me at that place. Everything grew fast and lush there.
Including the world that had existed inside my young head.

Jerzy had given me fair warning about Jeannie. Back that
first time we'd spoken, he'd mentioned a girlfriend who often
came out to the farm to help him and enjoyed it more than you
would expect. I was surprised to feel envious. Maybe it was as
simple as Jerzy having somebody who wanted to be there.

"Get one of the kids to come along," my mother had suggested when I called to tell them my plans for the summer. By
kids she meant my grown siblings. But they didn't care any
more for the farm now than they had as children. I had my
own kid, no longer a child, and indeed had asked her along,
said I'd pay her way, that she'd probably enjoy it.

I think I was tempting her at first. Tina had never been east.
We hadn't made the trip a dozen years before, because Victory's passing was marked without formal ceremony—just the

way she'd wanted it. She had arranged to donate herself to science, and after one of those diseases that women don't like to talk about finally claimed her, the next thing to take her was a hearse that safely drove the speed limit as it transported her willed remains all the way to Tufts School of Medicine over near Boston. "Just go outside. Wherever you are when you get the news, go outside." That's what she had said to me over the phone right before she got very bad, and you knew time was short but still you didn't want to hear someone talking of the end. "Go outside and think of me," she said. "Riding away. Healthy. Happy. On Pan."

I was then what I am now, a community college physical education teacher with her own office, which was where I was when I got the call from Pal. I drifted down the stairs to the gym and pushed open the back door to the track. It thudded right into Russell Morgan, a troublemaking sophomore sneaking a joint in one of the most popular places to do so. He stammered some excuse as he shoved the roach, still burning, into his pants pocket. "Just go away" is what I barked, and he did, quickly, and then I was there alone, like I wanted to be, looking across the snowy athletic field to the little tree-covered hill beyond that. And I imagined Pan there, as she'd been in her prime, carrying Victory as she'd been in hers, moving beyond the bleachers, up past the concession stand, in back of the press box, and back into sight. Then, up again, through the few bare trees, slowly and with the awkward climbing motion a pony must use on an incline. They made progress, creating their own path as they moved farther away, and I watched them until I was totally sure I could see them no more.

Tina is still in college and, when you stop to think, only a bit older than I'd been when I last saw the farm. She was more than half interested in coming out to join me. But at a backyard picnic on Memorial Day weekend, she'd gotten what she had been waiting for since junior year of high school: a proposal from her boyfriend Manny, who'd frozen a small diamond ring in an ice tray and then asked her if she wouldn't mind going into the kitchen and tossing a few more cubes into his glass. There was no way she would spend the first couple months of her engagement on the opposite coast, far from Manny and his bottomless stash of unpredictable romantic acts. Though also a student, he worked overtime delivering bottled water so he could afford to surprise Tina with hot air balloon rides and picnics on blankets of rose petals, the kind of stuff typically boasted about by contestants on television dating programs. Tina was in love and she said "I hope you understand," regarding her staying back there, and I told her I did, because it was true. I knew all about love—both the world-without-end variety and the pointy cactus-edged kind that had kept me from ever returning to the farm. Until now, until I had no choice.

There could be worse last requests—to promise to marry a sad-sack jerk just so he'll have a body around to clean up after him and make his bed in the daily manner of the old mother who's begging you make this commitment. Or to take in and raise a friend's kids, whom you secretly loathe. Plus, if you wanted to think more positively, even though what my uncle had asked me to do was sad, it also was comparatively easy. It had been years since the pony ring was so busy that somebody had to be sitting out there all the time, so I most likely wouldn't have to be in two places at once. Sunday afternoons were still the best for customers, though they were nothing like the ones way back before the abolition of the Blue Laws that prevented stores across the Commonwealth from opening on the Sabbath. Come Sunday afternoons, I'd probably welcome a break from the week's work of clearing out the place, and I might enjoy sitting on the porch, reading the big fat paper, and awaiting the few riders.

And, really, if he had to pick a time of year to give me this task, Pal couldn't have selected a better one. I just hope it doesn't sound too crass to say that. But the school year was just wrapping up and I was facing the three months of free time that long ago had been my main incentive for becoming a teacher. I'd certainly have the time to sift through years of accumulation, emptying closets, drawers, chests, attic, cellar, desks. The bathroom drawer in which Victory kept the heating pad and the neck brace and the envelopes of powder for soaking her feet. The rusting gray file cabinet in the barn office that held the lincage of every animal that had ever set hoof or claw or paw on the farm. The glove compartment of the old truck, where Uncle Pal always kept pink Canada Mints long after they lost their snap, the way he preferred them. The seat of Victory's sewing machine with the tan vinyl cover you could remove to access the rows of thread organized as neatly as if they were still on sale at the shop. The little table near her bed that held the Bible from which she read a passage each night before sleep, sticking to the New Testament because, unlike the original one, it didn't have too many of the kinds of stories that give nightmares.

It didn't strike me right then in Pal's hospital room, but I soon after realized how this was the same time of year I long ago would have been all wrapped up with packing for my summer at the farm. Counting the days to the beginning of summer vacation. Buying the few new essentials to fold and set aside and pack and not wear until I got there, when, finally,

after nine months of dreams, Frankie would be real and in
front of me me me. Sure, it would be just like the old days.
Except it would not be at all.

Everybody leaves piles of stuff behind. It would be hard not to.
Though I personally know of one exception—on my mother's
side, up in Buffalo, my great aunt who was a nun. Once her
health began to fail, Sister Beatitude sent to my mother packets
of her meager belongings: two sepia-toned photographs of her
on the day of her final vows; a full-color one taken at the small
tea-and-cake reception that marked her golden anniversary; a
starched and folded doily; unworn flesh-tone Supp-Hose; one
time a half-used bar of soap and a pocket package of Kleenex
with only several sheets remaining. The final mailings were thin
envelopes containing a five- or a ten-dollar bill folded inside a
piece of paper marked with the name and address of a priest
back in Poland to whom the money should be sent, when the
time came, to say Masses for her intention.

When Sister Beatitude did expire, she was shipped down
from the Mother House to our town undertaker, packed in a
long white coffin that contained her body and all she owned at
the point when her perfect soul had floated up from it. The
white floor-length habit, on her. The rosaries, in her hands.
The silver bride-of-Christ ring, on her finger. That was that.
Neat and clean and tidy. What was left went right into the
ground. Good-bye. Good luck. See you later.

"Cleaning out the farm's not going to be anything like picking up after Sister, I can tell you that." Ma said this, though she
offered no help.

Not that I expected her to. She and Dad still lived back in
Illinois, happily wrapped up in lives of community service. My

mother was the backbone of a large ecumenical women's club that ran an annual fall pie festival complicated enough to somehow kept her active and running year-round. She had been co-chairwoman for at least eighteen years now, coming to wield such power that she alone could determine the flavor of pie filling and the exact type of crust that contestants had to create for each year's competition.

My father was big into the Lions Club, retirement giving him more time than ever to tend to his duties as King Lion. He was always busy selling scholarship raffle tickets and specially sized Tootsie Rolls from a card table set up outside the grocery store. He worked the phone finding homes for exchange students who'd be arriving here any minute and can you believe that their host families all of a sudden changed their minds? Always, he collected out-of-style or old-prescriptioned eyeglasses for people too poor or living too far from an optometrist to obtain pairs in the usual manner.

My parents absolutely and totally loved retirement, and their adopted home out there. Except for the couple of times when Lions conventions were scheduled in the northeast, they never ventured out. When they did, they drove their rental car to the farm for a quick afternoon, turning down offers to stay the night, or longer if they wished. After all, Pal and Victory would point out, isn't that what retirement is for—to relax? And my father would say there was no time for that. He was busier now than he'd ever been with the phone company, so let's say our good-byes and we'll be on our way. He'd tell them this while walking toward the front door, a moving target being harder to lasso. I expected that the next time my parents would visit the farm would be when Pal died.

.        .        .

In the meantime, I'd get a bit of company from Jerzy, and from Jeannie, but she might stop only once in a while. Jerzy warned me she was a very busy woman, had a great interest in the world of public relations, which was what she hoped to go on to one day but for right now she was busy running the office at the turkey farm out near the Warren line.

She'd created her favorite task there—getting as much good publicity as possible. People can buy their turkeys any old day from the deep freeze at the Grand Z. They need to be reminded that also very nearby there is a farm that sells healthfully raised and freshly killed turkeys of all sizes. So Jeannie worked to develop a nose for news. She used that exact phrase. Near her phone she kept the numbers of the *Pennysaver* and of the radio station in Ware and of the television station in Springfield and of the bureau the city paper maintained in town. Anything close to interesting—a newborn chick that had taken to the family dog as if it were its mother, the local daycare center coming by to collect feathers for a craft project, a new recipe for gizzards—she started dialing.

"P.R.—you know, that's public relations," Jeannie educated me on my fourth day back, giving the definition in case I was some kind of an idiot that might think she was talking about Puerto Rico. "I know news people. I'd be happy to tell them you're selling the place. A local landmark. I bet it would make a great story."

"If you want."

Maybe she didn't like me shrugging right there as I did, but I also knew about P.R.—the kind the farm once had gotten plenty of. None of it sought, none of it positive. I hadn't been at fault, but I'd been mentioned. And I hadn't enjoyed it. I'd be mentioned again this time, too—what might that kick up in a town with a good memory for the bad? Plus, I didn't have great confidence that the sale of my uncle's place was any kind of a real story. Farms all over the country—most of them much bigger than this one, most of them struggling for years—were going under with great and sad regularity. I'd seen the stories in the papers, on TV, always headlined something like "The Last Harvest." Coverage of the depressing auctions at which an entire family history disappeared when the highest-bidding stranger lifted his hand. Couples sorting through family photos that showed great-great grandfather, with mule and plow, and themselves, present day, driving a combine equipped with computer. No, none of the dying farms that I'd read about had a pony ring in their front yard. Well, maybe it would make a nice photo feature. Story short, or nonexistent.

It became much, much more than that. However many numbers Jeannie dialed the next day, only one person ended up being interested in doing an interview. But one was all that was needed. The reporter who did respond, a too-warmly dressed middle-aged woman thick in the midst of a terrible bout with allergies, stayed for only about twenty minutes and in that time asked a child-sized handful of questions. Most likely due to her fresh entry into the world of journalism, she hadn't done her homework and ventured nowhere near the subject of my last summer here. But, despite her lack of experience, she ended up writing a touching article that got picked up by a wire service and was transmitted, photos and all, to newspapers nationwide.

When the story ran in our paper the next day, I clipped it carefully and went to visit my uncle. He hadn't improved any in the five days since I'd come back. But neither had he worsened. He would open his eyes at unexpected times, but mostly he'd lie there as if sleeping soundly after a long, hard day's work. Even though I couldn't be sure he was able to hear me, I did read him almost every word, exactly as it was printed in our paper, the first positive publicity connected to the farm in twenty-two years. Starting with the first lines, the simple roll call of pony names, each of them awarded their own line complete with a period at the end of it. Typed out, I was pleased to notice, in the correct order, starting with Star, corresponding to the animals' places in the ring. Which was the point the writer was trying to make. That this is where they always have been, and still are.

Then came the meat of the story. How the ponies had thrilled generations of local kids. How their caretaker and life-long friend—"That's you, Uncle," I noted for him—no longer was able to be there. How someone else—that's me—had come out for the last summer. The reporter told her readers what I'd be doing at my uncle's request—selling everything. "A painful commitment rooted in love," was how she put it, which I thought was nicely put, and true, but also very sad, so I didn't read that line aloud and risk making Pal feel worse. She wrote how this summer would be the final chance to enjoy a ride, to experience a slice of life that soon would evaporate. She used that word, like the farm was a rain puddle that sooner or later would be dried up come the August dog days. Regarding the end of the season, I had been asked for my thoughts—what might happen? The reporter said that I began to give a reply, then hesitated—something I don't remember doing but I have no reason to believe she made that up. She wrote that I looked to the ring, an action I do recall, because I was hoping one of the six over there might send me a fitting quote. But all she has me saying is, "I don't know." Which is correct. That both being what I said at the time, and exactly the case.

Before my reading hung in the air for too long, I quickly went on to describe for Uncle Pal the pictures that ran next to the words. I laid some decoration onto the one that had me in it. "The big photo is of me and Star," I said. "And I look gorgeous. Like from the movies." I glanced to see if he was smiling at just the idea of that. I half expected him to wake any second, though I was told I should know better than to hold such an idea. The outlook remained bleak and the doctors were using the line I only thought they said on TV dramas—that it was just a matter of time. But, really, when you think about it, bad or good, in this life what isn't?

The next day was a Saturday. And locally and nationally, when they opened whatever were their newspapers, people were seeing the picture of me looking not at all movie-starish, a bandanna around my head, one of Pal's workshirts hanging down to the knees of my jeans, then his ancient lace-up leather boots that fit me despite his feet being those of a man. I am dressed down as you are when you have dirty work to take care of, which I had that morning, in the chore of getting the ponies out to the ring, and everything else.

It was not the kind of picture they warn you is about to be taken. I was shown giving the last yank to a girth. Pulling down mightily. My face is strained because even though this is a pony, there's still effort involved in the process of tacking up. Later on someone will tell me that even though no real muscles are showing I look strong in the photograph. Very strong. Another will say that I look like Victory did at my age, a nice compliment. So I guess it could have been worse. In the other picture that ran, I am thankfully less the center. The fuzzy-haired photographer, who drove his own car over shortly after the reporter arrived, shot his other picture from up in the hayloft he somehow found the ladder to, catching me unaware and standing at the gate after everyone had been put in their places. I look at Star and vice-versa. The lens was the type that at the same time condenses everything, but spreads it out as well. The farmhouse appears to be miles away. The trees arc around the pony ring in a protective curve. Beneath their fragile new leaves, we are there, the seven of us. Looking very small. Very small, and alone.

But that state does not last. The day after the story runs, there is a car in the driveway even as I stumble outside to feed the horses their breakfast.

No occupants are visible to me as I head down the stairs. Just the vehicle. Midnight blue and angled, bullet-shaped in the way Ma recently told me in a letter she thinks the new cars all resemble. Bullets. And I wonder, what does she know about bullets? Closer, through the tinted windows, I see many heads inside, most of them small and restless. At the driver's side I wave. The glass rolls down electronically. A young man—he has to be the father—smiles at me.

"I know it's early, but we read the story in the paper," he apologizes, and he has a copy with him, folded so that the piece and the photo of me and Star is on the front even though it had run on the second page of the Local section. He waves it for emphasis, in case I don't know what he is talking about. "We live in town—not far, just down by the redemption center—and we had no idea the farm was going to be sold. We had no idea at all. We wanted to bring our kids one last time. So they could have a ride. Both of us came here when we were their age." Here he nods toward the woman in the front seat—she had to be the mother—who nods at me that he was telling the truth. And then the husband asks, "We're a little early?"

"There's really no set time for opening," I tell him, "just when I get the ponies out here. Which I haven't done yet. I'm sort of out of practice. Do you want to go have breakfast and come back?"

From somewhere inside the car, a kid whines, "Awww." The wife grimaces at either the sound, or my suggestion.

So I had an audience for my work. An enthusiastic one that took still more photographs plus operated a video camera. All the four kids wanted a try at brushing and feeding, at holding a bridle or a saddle just before it went on, at fastening a buckle, at pulling the stirrups back down into place when all the adjusting was over.

They were nice kids. The kind I had tried hard to raise when Tina was still small enough to impress with the importance of please and excuse me, which was what these children said, often, throwing in other endearing acts like letting the littlest one go first at everything, without their parents even having to tell them to. I didn't mind them being there. There were four children in all, very near or just into grade school, and I let each lead a pony to the ring. I let them have their pick of the ones they wanted to ride. I let each go around an extra five times, for the same price as just one set of trips. I answered all their many questions, and those of their parents as well. When they all left, it was just me and the ponies again.

I no sooner had gone over to feed the goats when I heard another car. Then another. And more after that. Whoever was driving, all echoed the first set of parents—how they'd visited here once or twice or more or very often as a child, so often, in fact, they were surprised I didn't recall them, and that the memory of the place is so dear that they just had to make sure they got here before we closed.

"Kids I knew were getting radios and watches for their presents that day. I just wanted a pony ride." This from a woman in a pink track suit who held out a black-and-white photo of her dressed much more formally, on the day of her first communion about twenty years before. In a white lace dress and Jiffy Pop veil she stood at the gate to the ring, Zoey's head just to the left of hers. Farther left, attempting to stand out of the picture but caught in it nonetheless, there was my uncle. Back when he still resembled the irresistible Little Joe Cartwright. Back when he was still young and healthy and upright.

"My parents brought me here every other Sunday. I'd mark the weeks off on the calendar and remind them, in case they forgot." This from a small, nervous red-haired guy with eyes that didn't leave yours for a second as he told you how he'd count the days until he could return and that you, you were here in the summers. From early June to the very end of August. You were here every time. He was jealous of you. He wanted a pony so bad. And you, you had six! His father wanted to get him one—actually, one of these right here.

"The black one," he says, and he points over to the ring even though he's still staring right at me. "Right over there! That one!" He means Star. "I remember the farmer who lived here brought that very same pony out to the field and you got on him and rode and put him through his paces, so my father could get an idea of whether or not he was worth the money that was being asked. Which, in the end, my father complained was too high."

Pal back then never for one moment would have considered selling Star. Or any of the ponies. I just said, "Uh-huh," and asked him for the $1 cost of the ride for the hip-high little girl who stood silently at his side, staring, too, like an extra from a horror movie in which evil children take over an entire town.

"That one," her father said to her, his eyes finally leaving my face. "That pony there was almost mine. That one."

I didn't want to argue with him. I had too much else to do. It wasn't every minute, but maybe every five or ten or fifteen that somebody would appear, car doors would open, and another wave of kids would crash onto the dirt drive.

The lying father wanted a photograph of himself with Star, of his kid with Star, of him and his kid with Star, of Star alone, of the kid alone. Everybody else wanted some version of themselves. Then and now. The grown-up kid posing with the present-day child, next to the horse that each of them had ridden at the very same age, many years apart. Hand tentatively on a pony nose or pony ear, or arm around a pony neck, they posed again and again. I handled all sorts of cameras that day. The video kind that shows you the image on a little screen like real life is being broadcast the exact moment it happens. Polaroids that eject little split-second all-American family scenes of the type that sell milk and cotton clothing, nonskid tires and life insurance. An aunt remembered exactly which pony had been her favorite, and introduced her niece to Princess. "Well, hello, Princess," said the girl, around five, sticking her hand between the fence boards to offer a shake, like that was what ponies did at first meeting.

Then came the visitors who bore other kinds of memories.

"I was, well, I was one of those who helped search."

The woman in the Buffalo Sabres jersey was looking at me expectantly, like I was supposed to go and thank her after all these years. In case I needed a reminder of the details, she pointed. "Through those woods right back there. I was twelve. It was like a game. Exciting. Even if I didn't know exactly what was missing. Mainly because the adults wouldn't really tell us kids. It was exciting, like a big adventure. Because not too much ever happens around here. You know?"

"This was the place where that girl lived—I always think of that when I drive by. It's automatic. I'm driving up the point when I'm passing this place and I'm thinking, 'That's where the girl lived.'" The historian looked familiar. Arms skinny and long and almost mechanical, moving slow like arcade cranes poking from his body. I remembered those arms belonging to a young boy who'd stop at the ring, and their being the same length and appearance even back then. "I told the kids all about it," he went on, "but, no, you weren't the girl, were you? You were the other one, right? The one who wasn't crazy, right? See, kids? I told you, kids—I told you the crazy one is long gone. Gone. There is nothing to worry about anymore."

"Worry? I used to lose sleep over her," a woman about ten years younger than me said a lot louder that I would have liked. "We lived up on Cherry Street, on the other side of the town, but that crazy girl got my mother paranoid. Even when it was a hundred degrees out we couldn't sleep with open windows. We had no fans, no air conditioning, of course—who did then? That crazy girl was all locked up somewhere safe, but my mother was torturing us in case she broke loose and came looking for some other kids. Every night we'd check under our beds . . ."

"Hey, yeah, hey," piped up the man whose T-shirt read "Male Mega Models." "The crazy one—whatever happened to her?"

Somebody's kid acted up in line and another boy shoved him and I was grateful for the interruption. There were little fists pounding a crew-cutted head as a woman came up and asked, "Where'll they all go now?" and she nodded at the ponies as she said this.

I told her what I had told the reporter, what I was telling everybody. That I didn't know. I skipped adding what I'd also skipped telling the reporter—that the ponies would figure that out. And that, with nothing more than their one word, they would tell me.

At least that's what I was hoping.

Lots of people wanted to take the ponies home. Maybe if I had no connection to them, or to this place, maybe I would have said that any price would be fine, that I'd even deliver. All six, and their tack, could fit with room to spare in the long, rusting, red trailer in which Pal once delivered and received cattle before the last head of the dwindling herd was sold five years back. But I was me, standing in the barnyard of a fading-but-still-alive man, and at this early stage I couldn't imagine handing any of the ponies over to anybody, stranger or friend—even though it eventually would have to be done. Furniture, clothing, bric-a-brac, all that would be much easier to unload. And I was going to start with that, beginning with the contents of the parlor and maybe a few things from the kitchen cabinet closest to the parlor door. That had been my plan for this weekend. To put a few things on the lawn, to sell them for whatever fair price I might ask or people might offer to pay. All I'd brought out so far were small things, items easy to carry by myself, ones that contained little to no sentimental value—a plastic hassock, a wobbly magazine rack, a cheap set of laminated TV tables, the Superstation portable radio I'd sent the previous Christmas, still with instruction tag for receiving faraway baseball games hanging from a thread looped around the antenna.

Pine end table, blown glass statue of a duck, braided throw rug. Toothpick holder, lint picker, crocheted antimacassar. Painting—really a print on bowed cardboard—of three dogs sleeping in front of a fireplace. Empty cookie tin with worn-off brand name. A carton of yellowed business-size envelopes. A basket of buttons. One meat pulverizer. Two shoehorns. Three flashlights. An unopened tube of VO5.

Will you take a quarter for that? This is what they asked me. Is that the best you can do? How about two for one? This is broken, you know. Broken. Did you know that? Did you? Ha? Did you?

All the bargainers who came to my tag sale, both that first day and most of the rest, wanted something for nothing. I didn't give them that, but in the interest of making progress I gave them much better than they deserved. Items moved off the front yard in a slow procession, fitted into trunks, onto roofs, on back window ledges, around passengers, beneath legs, onto laps. Pieces of Victory's and Pal's lives being dispersed, like the farm was softly exploding and things were being shot to the globe's four corners. Packed into cardboard cartons, grocery sacks, trash bags, carried in the back of that truck headed toward the reservoir, that compact going the other way, lugged by hand or pulled in a wagon across the field and through the woods and even somewhere up Fisherdick Road.

The most interested people knocked on the door of the farmhouse. May I come in? May I take a look at what else you have here? I love antiques. I collect antiques. I sell antiques. I bet this place is full of them. Just let me have a look. How about that barn? Those sheds? Oh, animals? Well what else you got? Not living, I mean. Things. You know. You never know. And you won't know until you have a professional take a look. You could be the owner of something you think is worthless, and it might be something that could fund your old age. Most people who are sitting on a goldmine never know it.

I took names. Phone numbers. Business cards that contained both those pieces of information, plus mobile numbers, fax numbers, and e-mail addresses, should I have such urgent needs. I promised I'd get in touch when it was time to move to the next room, floor, building, pile of junk. Until I'd get the chance to look up the word, I was answering no, I had no ephemera. And no, I didn't realize what some of this stuff was worth. But today wasn't the best day to find out. There was too much going on. Jeannie came by with the excuse of bringing her smallest nephew for a ride I let him have for nothing, considering her help, but obviously also to stand and be all so proud of her part in the successful confusion.

"See?" she asked and she poked her finger in the direction of another two cars pulling in and depositing a total of seven more riders, all while Victory's three-legged footstool and Pal's never-correct banjo-sized barometer were sadly disappearing behind the sliding door of a worn family van. "P.R. rules!"

I told her she was right indeed, and I went back to work to get away from her. I'm sure she was nice under regular circumstances, say if I'd met her at a party of Jerzy's if he ever threw such things, but that was far from what was going on right then. It's one thing to say, yes, Uncle, I'll do this work for you, and it's another altogether to actually start it, and watch bizarre reality take on a life of its own. I walked away from seeing her to her car, returned to the ring, hat on the head, hand on the whip, money in the box, line all neat and reaching to the short row of cars, pick who you want, latch the gate, parents on the outside, please, bell ringing on the fifth pass, children jumping, crying, laughing, crying, say cheese, camera flash, crying, bye, silence. The kind of silence that is so sudden that to your ears it is like a sound itself. Quick as a gunshot, and still, so anything that falls right after gets magnified. Which is how I came to hear the car long before I ever saw it. The tires crawling slowly up the drive on the other side of the house. The dark hood—plum or at least some dark shade of that—coming into view over the rise. The shine of it all, the kind priests' cars used to wear. More of this sedan came into view. It parked itself in front of the house and stood idling.

As I approached, the engine was shut down, the driver's side opened. Somebody got out and stood up straight, arching shoulders back like it had been one long ride. Here was a woman, one with black hair shorter than that of most men. She pulled on a blazer all formal and stayed behind the door like it was a shield she needed. When I got to the hood of the car, she put up a hand and stuck it in the air for a single wave. I heard the words, timid at first, coming across the air, from her and from a time long gone past us both:

"Do you know who I am?"

She used to ask me this, only back then it was from across the ring, from her place on Pan, the pony she favored. She'd make a game with her talent for mimicry. She'd be there asking if I knew who she was, then she'd turn into somebody—head bowed, shoulders hunched, one somehow suddenly placed higher than the other, both shifting right and left and right and farther right. Knuckles knocking loudly on an invisible back door.

Lucy was so good I'd know the answer well before she croaked out the final clue, which was, "Ehhh, yer uncle home?"

"Marbles Midura."

"Right again!"

We'd have a good laugh. Circle the ponies some more, go around again. Move on to other important topics. How it'd been a week since we'd last gotten a supply of those little wax soda bottles with the syrup inside and wouldn't that be a perfect excuse to get the truck and head downtown. Then maybe get a pu-pu platter takeout from Debbie Wong. Sneak it into whatever's playing at the Casino. You never ate Chinese food from a bag on your lap in the dark? We'll do that tonight. Then from nowhere she'd begin again.

"D'ya know who I am?"

She held her hand up to her ear, like she was on the phone, and she spoke like she was a frequent caller who always asked for Victory by surname.

"Paahneek?"

Lucy was fantastic. Right on. Could have had her own comedy program if anybody but a handful of people knew the locals she was imitating so perfectly, even after only one or two encounters with them. Beneath me, Star jerked when I yelled out: "Magda!"

Having no mercy, Lucy went on to recount the back-and-forth of the last time she'd answered the phone and found Magda Zielinski on the other end.

"Don't panic?" Lucy would answer. "Don't panic about what?"

Me, I could never get away with such things. But Lucy was a guest. And, if you knew the facts that some of us did, she also was nobody you'd want to go near upsetting. I'd catch even Victory—Magda's good friend—getting a kick out of Lucy's imitations, and she'd playfully swat her away from the phone when she caught her provoking a caller.

Once we'd get into it, we'd slay the whole town, or as much of it as both Lucy and I knew. It made no sense to imitate somebody she hadn't yet met. We stuck to the ones she'd come across. Diamond, Ace, Noxie, Scuffy, Guts. Bosco, Basia, Tootsie, Purdy. Dingo, Cal, Chicken Bigda, and one guy who, depending on the day, was either T-Bone, T.J., Tommy Joe, or just Tee. Peabrain. His sister. His mother. People we knew by only their first names, which were sometimes nothing more than noises—Pudge and Dimp and Hub. The way they rolled their $r$'s, nodded while you spoke, said "sure" after everything you said even if they were in disagreement, played with a belt buckle the entire time they were talking to you and what did that mean? Lucy didn't even spare the priest, who must have taken extra seminary classes in hand motions. She wouldn't so much imitate his National Public Radio voice, as the actions he made as he went to fold his hands or extend his arms in a blessing. Elaborate almost cheerleaderly moves that cracked us up even days after Sunday was over and done with. Lucy'd sit there on Chester and announce, "Let us pray," and then launch into five minutes of gyrations.

All this was fun back when we were teenagers. Now, it didn't seem like a game when she asked me if I knew who she was. I could only answer: "You're here."

I said this slowly, words unadorned, the truth, the only ones I could locate.

During the school year, I always tape my favorite soap operas to watch in my spare hours. And more often than is plausible, the shows have people returning either from the dead or surfacing after so many years that all hope about their ever being seen again long ago dried up and blew away. I've always been disappointed in the reactions of those who are coming face to face with the returned. Despite all the ragged edges of unfinished business still dangling there, the words are always something plain set against dramatic music, a starch-stiff "You're here," which I now know must be not so much due to bad writing as to honest reacting at such a time. The kind of reacting I did when Lucy Dragon, on whom I had not set eyes or heard a word from since just before she was loaded into the backseat of a police car twenty-two years before, whom I had given up for as good as dead even though in spirit she'd lived a few inches behind my back all that time, suddenly was standing in front of me in the here and now.

There was a hug that I didn't see coming because why would I expect such a thing? Plus I was still in some freeze of a shock when she walked over and put her long arms awkwardly around me. My shorter ones stayed in their places at my sides, and we stood there, everything back to quiet, once the words about her being sorry over Victory and then Pal and then all my new obligations faded and the space in which any other words would have been said was taken up by early crickets and an angry crow. Over Lucy's shoulder I got a view of the inside of her car. It was a BMW, the letters on the key fob still in the ignition informed me. The black rug and mats obviously freshly vacuumed. A big bottle of fancy imported drinking water was jammed behind the gearshift, half empty. Nothing rested on the leather seats except for a pair of costly looking sunglasses and a road atlas, closed, its cover a photograph of a station wagon overbrimming with family traveling on a desert road toward one of those big dramatic rocks that tend to jut from the flatness of such places. I don't know how long Lucy and I stood there in our odd embrace because all this was like a dream that you wake from not knowing if you've been sleeping for ten hours or ten minutes. I suddenly began to float, following Lucy as she finally moved and walked up the porch stairs and into the house, where she began to name each room, even though both she and I knew firsthand their functions.

Since returning, I had moved a few things around, and had already sold several others she amazingly began to scan for—stuff you'd never imagine anybody would remember so strongly that they're the first things that would be sought. Where, she wanted to know, is the red-white-and-blue umbrella can? And the birdcage that never had held any birds? The pillow that was a souvenir from Atlantic City? The small wicker plant stand and its family of Wandering Jews? How about the framed rose-edged poem that had hung since time began in between the two windows over the kitchen sink. She closed her eyes, placed a hand over her heart, and recited:

> I've got a sweetheart,
> And I would have no other.
> She's more than all the world to me,
> Because her name is Mother.

"Gone." I'd carefully chosen my third, fourth, and fifth words to her. "All gone."

But even with these things missing, the house still looked much the same as it had the first time Lucy and I made this tour, room by room, she in front, me carrying nothing this time but a load of questions on top of the dizzying reality that she was back. Here. Right here. Not in an old photo, or in a memory, but real, moving, and moving away from me if I slowed down as she made her way past me into the next room, here, real, alive.

Again, I recorded every bit of information I could. The shape of Lucy, which was pretty much the same as I'd remembered, and I wondered how much work it took her to keep it that way at this point in life, or was the maintenance all due to her metabolism, done without thought or effort? Her hair, still very black, was snipped short to a shape that flattered the wide face she used to complain about the size of, all the strands sitting just so without the help of any spray or gel that I could detect, lessening in length the nearer the stylist got to her collar, where, if she had any growing, stray neck hairs had been clipped neatly. I detected a perfume, the smell of something nearing citrus, the kind suggested for warm weather as it would be pleasant and not nauseating in the season's extreme heat. I scanned the back of the tan suit—expensive, I guessed, from the looks of the neat and wearless weave, wrinkled a bit only at the knee backs. There was a white blouse beneath, its collar flipped up over that of the jacket, and a decorative line of tan stitching crawling along a quarter inch or so from the edge of the collar. With each step, sheer hosiery blinked between the pant cuff and the brown flats. The thick gold chain on the left wrist was interrupted by a quarter-sized watch face. A string of pearls circled just above that. Fingernails weren't polished, but definitely had to be buffed somehow to attain the degree of sheen they displayed. Her right hand wore no rings, nor did her left.

Suddenly, okay, there we are—we've rounded the stairwell and are back at the front door, where we'd started.

"Upstairs, then," Lucy announced, and I trailed her with an obedient immediacy I found startling.

Near the top, she stopped and pointed to the right. My uncle had kept Victory's things the way they'd always been, and the chenille still covered the foot of the bed. The dresser, with all the grooming implements that remained clean and shiny but would have no next use. A viscous quarter-inch of special-day cologne aged scentlessly in the bottle on the ashtray.

"I always loved that room," Lucy told me in a tone I believed, and since I agreed with her, we stood there on the stairs together, wordless, paying some kind of respect, it seemed, until she decided to continue on.

At the top of the stairs, she proceeded into my room. There in front of us was the high-backed chair I never sat in, the little table I never spent any time at, the window I never looked out. There always had been too much to do, especially now, with only me here to do it. The big chest was in the corner as usual, stuffed awkwardly as is the only way I know how. The only object that brought the scene up to the present was the framed photo I'd set on the nightstand once I found it wrapped in pink paper and hidden in my stuff, of Tina holding a computer-print-out reading "I Miss You," which, considering even one-hour film processing, had to have been written way before that emotion was felt. I didn't see Lucy take any notice of the frame, or its contents. She simply narrated, "Your room," and walked out of it.

In the hall, swinging her arm to the right, she announced a little louder, "My room."

Uncle Pal had moved back from the porch to his regular quarters after the summer Lucy had been here, so between that and being carted off to Mary Lane he'd a couple of decades' time to settle back in pretty completely. The double bed and the dresser and the little upholstered chair were in their same places as when Lucy had lived here, but unmistak-able man things long had taken them over. I hadn't moved anything of his in my short time back. I knew that job awaited, but I didn't want to rush it. Big shoes and bigger pants hung near and on the chair, suspenders and his two good ties were slung over the footboard, a hairy brush and flat old wallet and tube of Mennen Speed Stick reflected in front of the slanted mirror.

"How is he—Pal?"

Now at the dresser, Lucy arranged my uncle's spare change in a neat stack as she asked this. Pennies first, working her way up to quarters. Her air was nonchalant, she was talking easily.

Like she'd lived next door for a hundred years, and had just seen him maybe last night or the morning before. Like even being within a hundred miles of the farm hadn't gotten her considering a big fast run in the opposite direction.

"Uh, no better," I said. "No worse, but no better. Though they don't have a lot of hope for him."

"A nice man. What a nice man." Now she was looking at the only two photographs I ever knew my uncle to display: the faded half-dollar-sized squinting headshot of his late wife, my Aunt Tut, who I always wished had survived her car wreck just so I could make aloud, whenever I wanted to, the sound that was her name. And then there was the photo of me and Pal and Victory taken on some regular August afternoon my first summer back after moving to Illinois. We stand in the opening of the barn, side by side, he to the left in his overalls and big hat, she in the middle in her jeans and workshirt, I at the end, in a checkered sundress and cowboy boots, holding Chester on a lead. The darkened doorway behind us makes us look like we are at a photographer's backdrop. I don't know why my uncle chose that one to put in a frame and stand in a place where he'd be face to face with it every day. But maybe he liked it for the same reason I did. That this here was all of us. On a day that wasn't special for any reason you could see listed on a calendar. Yet, simply because of that, it was just as remarkable as any one of your most major of holidays.

Pal was the one who had encouraged me to write to Lucy. After it happened, after that last summer, "She'd love to hear from you," he said to me when we'd speak. I didn't agree. But after his bringing this up each time in about a dozen phone calls, I mailed Lucy one half-hearted letter. Not because I wanted to, but because I'd been asked to. By him. The guy who loved kids. Even ones that were very messed up.

I hated getting out the sheet of paper. I hated uncapping the pen. I hated making the few words as much as I hated the envelope I could hardly work up enough spit to seal. I hated mailing it off to Victory, who forwarded it on to Lucy's grandmother, because that's the route I was told it had to go due to the way things were with the girl—you never really knew where she was. All Lucy's grandmother had to do was fill in the address of the most recent place where her son and daughter-in-law had put their daughter, for a while, for this one more time, for her own good.

I put next to nothing inside. Marked the date and greeted her "Dear Lucy," which she wasn't to me in the least. I was reluctant to go on to the next thing you usually cover in letters— the recipient's health—so there was no "How are you?" because I knew good and well that if she were anything in the area of fine, she would not be where she was. I did not go on to say "I am well" because that would only rub in the glaring fact that I was so free and fortunate as to be out here living a regular life, and she was locked up in there, enduring only God and some equal of Gordon Darnley knew what. Weather was a safe topic, so I gave her mine. That from end to end of my campus here in Washington State, it had been pretty clear for three days in a row and it was killing everybody—no, change that—I put how it was very difficult to attend classes and not skip and enjoy the sun. Skipping, I'd point out to her because she could not have known this, was something so much easier to do in college than it ever had been in high school. In college, nobody cared if you showed up or not, even for the biggest exam. If you did stay out, next time back in the classroom nobody pestered you for a note from your mother explaining your recent absence. The teachers—in college they all were called professors like they were from some laboratory—only told you what work you'd missed, and gave you the dates by which they wanted you to make it up. If you cared to do so, I pointed out. Although I didn't get into this, I found the new freedom both heady and scary at the same time. There I was, doing okay considering the summer I'd just been through, on the road toward some form of a real new life. And Lucy, she was back in the crazy house.

There they must not have given her access to such things as pens or pencils, because she never wrote me back. The letter I sent was not returned to me, so I felt sure she'd received it. She either couldn't respond, or didn't want to. Whatever the reason, I really didn't care.

"You can understand her position, can't you?" Ma asked this in one of her own letters to me.

My mother wrote me often. Telephone calls were expensive, and even if your father worked for the company there was no special discount to make the most of. I spoke to my parents on only the first Sunday of each month, at seven P.M., the very minute that long-distance rates plummeted, and I stood in the dorm hall guarding the pay phone, awaiting the ring. And even then, the conversations were limited to two rotations of the stovetop egg timer at the other end of the line.

"Lucy's obviously still not well," Ma wrote. "She needs to get better. And once she's better, she's going to be embarrassed about what she did. Wouldn't you be? Think about that now. Think."

Halfway across the continent, my mother was giving me an order on paper. But I did as I was told. I stopped and thought about that. I thought. I even imagined, as Victory might have suggested. To do this, I put down my mother's letter as I lay on the upper level of the bunk bed set I shared with a girl named Katie, who had enrolled here only because her high school boyfriend had chosen to do so. They had been named class couple back in some high school down in Arizona, and the photo of them that had been taken for the yearbook's page of such honors was displayed on her side of our shared desk. An expensive-looking silver frame shone like a halo around the image of Katie seated on Erik's lap, his head resting right on top of hers like they had grown that way in the womb. Frankie and I could have grown like that, could have lived like that, I could have been mooning over his photograph right then. Except Lucy had gotten in the way.

Katie and Erik stared up at me like they wanted to know more. I ignored them and studied the correspondence from Ma, who always used old greeting cards for her stationery. After they'd had a suitable period of display on top of the stereo cabinet, she took down even those presented her by my father, scissored the spine, and separated the message page from the front one that held the image and greeting. On the back of the illustrations she would write her letters, whether or not the topic or the time of year had anything to do with the flip side, which could be a strutting Thanksgiving bird, Band-Aid shapes spelling out get well messages, angels announcing the Messiah, or, after the death of Victory, oceans or meadows rolling all peaceful beneath scrolling words that were meant to soothe your grieving soul. "Wouldn't you be embarrassed?" Ma was asking me in this particular letter on the back of a birthday greeting, a bland bouquet of nondescript flowers that had embossing as part of their effort at decoration. Her words flowed neatly as usual until they dropped down into the gutter of the daisy-shaped indentations, then crawled back out onto a flat stretch to finish her empathetic message: "Just imagine how Lucy feels now."

Imagine.

I didn't need that particular command. Not then, nor in the Grand Canyon-sized span between that summer in Washington and this last one back in Massachusetts. Over the years, I often stopped and tried to imagine how Lucy felt. Though, as with all imagining, it was only my own thinking, what was known inside my own head. And my own head, as weird as it could get, did not contain the information as to how to feel like Lucy had that night on Fisherdick Road. Still, I have to say I once made as valid an attempt as anyone could have.

Now Lucy was in my driveway, opening her car trunk with her keychain remote, and now she was around back and reaching in to take the handle of her black rolling case, the kind with sturdy wheels and SWAT team fabric and all sorts of Velcro loops capable of attaching securely to any other carryons. This suitcase looked heavy—though I couldn't right then say for sure because she, rather than I, was carrying it this time. But I was still in the back, walking behind her yet again, up the stairs, where she took a few steps to the left, then stopped, and asked me, "Can I have Victory's room?"

"What happened that night? And all the next week? Why did you do it? What happened in all the years after that? Where have you been?" I wanted to ask everything. But no words came from me. It was like I'd never even learned any. Like nobody ever tipped me off that breath, tongue, palate, lips, all could combine and cooperate to make the sounds I so badly wanted to right then, that would have asked Lucy even a question as short as the name of Ron: Why?

Unable to do anything, I stood next to Victory's bed as Lucy moved right in. I might as well have been in a theater watching her on the screen as she drew the suitcase, twirled a tiny combination lock to a number I couldn't make out, and pulled a zipper that made a throaty, expensive sound. I stole a quick inventory of the contents, the neat pile of tops and pants and a fleece pullover, balled-up pairs of socks, and dazzlingly white underwear that looked right off the neat color-coordinated piles on the store tables. I saw one Victoria's Secret tag, which informed me Lucy was a five-six.

"This is okay, right?"

What was okay? Her being here, or being here like she was, putting her stuff in Victory's dresser, like she was, without an answer from me, going ahead and opening drawers now, and motioning to the emptiness that ran all the way down to the purple liner I remembered buying with Victory down at Grant's back when there was a Grant's. The sheets of paper were printed with faded lilies of the valley, which had been my aunt's favorite flower. The matching but overpowering smell long since had evaporated.

She didn't await my reply and her back turned quickly as she became the first person in a decade to put anything in that dresser.

"I don't like to live out of a suitcase," Lucy told me. "Unsettling."

Anyone else would have told her to make herself at home. Which she already swiftly was doing, removing a few stretchy dresses from the bottom of her load and hanging them in the tiny closet that had been constructed back in the days when people had very few pieces of clothing to their names.

That done, Lucy kicked off her loafers and then slipped her feet into a pair of black velvet travel slippers resembling the kind of dance shoes Deborah and I once wore back at Madame Tayna's. Finally, she sat down next to me solidly and patted the bed.

"This is going to be easy," she said and gave a big happy face and began, rummaging through a toilet kit, using the fast jerky movements you'd need if you were going in search of one specific thing you knew was in there but was just not visible though right in front of you. The tote, a square zippered thing covered with satiny purple paisley, had little spare room. I recognized a jammed collection of the same shapes and colors of bottles and jars from the lines that Tina prefers—the exclusive and expensive ones that you must ask a clerk to fetch for you from behind locked glass at the department store counter, rather than the regular hit-or-miss bargain brands you—or at least I—grab off the shelf at the hanging hooks at the drugstore.

I couldn't help but look for what I ended up not seeing—the plastic amber-colored bottles that hold pharmaceuticals.

"What's going to be easy?"

She didn't hear me. "Here it is," she announced happily, oblivious, pulling a fat tube of something from her kit. I read the big label: "Sunblock." Factor 50. Being applied now by someone who once sunbathed on long sheets of tin foil and basted herself with baby oil.

"You can never be too careful," she told me, and by this I saw she meant regarding sun exposure, because she had squeezed herself a length of cream and now was holding out the tube. I took it only because I didn't know what else to do. It was after five o'clock by now, and I was covered with the dust and sweat and surprise of the day. It was the wrong point at which to apply sunscreen, but I did anyhow, out of politeness, I guess. There was no scent to it, which was probably one of its touted selling points, and a little greasy blob of it went on for miles. I only meant to do the tip of my nose, which I have tended to try to remember to protect ever since a friend's father several years back was diagnosed with a melanoma and had the end of his sliced off as clean as the last of an olive loaf at your neighborhood deli. I coated my entire nose, and still had enough to take care of both arms and the front of my legs as well.

"Now we can go out and say hi to the ponies," Lucy told me, standing up.

But not before she reached over to her case and took out a camera. A small but fancy model, compact and black with lots of buttons, the kind that wouldn't require you to think very much except to decide what to look at. She confessed this last part to me—I didn't guess it, as I don't know a lot about photography.

"It's the company's," she said as we were headed to the stairs. "We used to pay a photographer to go out and shoot the houses we were going to feature in our ads, but now we just save a lot of money by doing it ourselves. Because, really, what skill does it take? It's nothing you have to go to school for."

"Won't they miss it?" This question, having nothing at all to do with anything, had no trouble finding its way out of me.

"They who?"

"Uh, your boss. Won't he—she—won't they miss the camera while you're gone?"

"I am the boss," said Lucy, and, beaming, she pointed the camera at my slicked face. "Smile!"

The flash went off. Then, with a quick flip of a button that probably shut the whole thing off, she stepped past me, out into the hallway, and ran her hand over the wood of the banister. Sharp-edged blue zeppelin shapes floated wherever I looked. I blinked as I heard her say something.

"What?"

"I said this'll be easy—we'll have no problem." She called this out, more than yelled it. Still, she was loud considering we were only a couple feet apart.

"Really?" I had no idea what she was talking about.

"No problem at all," she said. I left the room and watched her nod to herself. "This is quality. Oak. Plaster. Dovetails. Tongue and groove. No laminates. No sheetrock. All of this is by hand. Probably without the aid of any power tools at all. Look at the detail! The work that went into this place . . . this is something you just don't see nowadays."

"What will there be no problem with?"

"Selling it," she said, and she handed me a bright yellow business card.

Lucy Dragon
Leading Multi-Million-Dollar Realtor
1997, Eastern Pennsylvania District III
"Buying? Selling? I'll help you home!"

"That's what I'm here for," she said brightly. "That's why I've come back. To be of some help for the family. Really—seriously—it's the least I can do."

# · 6 ·

We took Lucy to the reservoir the first free day we had.

Tuesdays were usually good slower days for the farm. The rush of the weekend was over, as well as the big scramble that the world makes of the first working day of the week. My aunt packed a lunch for us all and we took the truck over to the Quabbin so we could properly show Lucy most every detail of this famous place abutting our very own property.

Anticipating questions, and hoping for great interest, my uncle brought along his prized file folder of newspaper clippings that told why and how the reservoir had been conceived and created. He didn't like to even leave the house with it, say, if some parent at the ring happened to ask a question—how old was the reservoir, or can you really get arrested for swimming in there when there's all that water waiting, or, the frequent and best one, how did the state ever get away with killing four towns? So I thought it was sweet how he put the folder in a grocery bag for that much more safekeeping, and sat that on the front seat next to him where he could keep an eye on it. Victory stayed in the back, in the truck bed, with us two girls, narrating information, statistics about legislation, funding, workmen, lengths of pipe, gallons. Numbers and names that filled the time as we rolled from the pretty brick administration building, over the thick dam, above the silent spillway, around the curve near the boat launch, up the steep hill, and around the rotary to the turnoff for the lookout. After a stop there to study the before-and-after map of the valley, my uncle drove us back up to the circle, and took the second right that led us up to the big stone tower overlooking practically the whole entire world. First we climbed the many stairs and took in the view while catching our breath, my uncle pointing out for Lucy where we'd come from and where we might go later, all of it just a mass of dense green but even so the girl nodded like it all made sense to her. At the base of the tower we unfolded two old bedspreads and unpacked numerous containers of food. Then we dished out, chewed, and swallowed, staring northeast to Mount Monadnock all the way up in New Hampshire while Victory gave my favorite of her stories. How, at the age of nineteen she had been present just outside the gala that marked the end of existence for the four towns now drowned in the valley below.

Victory hadn't been a resident of any of those lost towns and villages, but she and her family had lived close enough to know plenty of people there, and she was among those Pal's clippings referred to as the "curious onlookers" drawn to the event held at the Enfield Town Hall on April 27, 1938.

"I didn't feel I would be out of place," Victory noted in case we were to get the wrong impression. "A boy from Prescott invited me, and he being a resident, I thought it would be appropriate to accompany him. Not just to go and be nosy, but to be with someone who belonged there."

With the usual drama she employed while retelling this, Victory described for us the mix of vehicles that lined the town's streets that night—farm trucks of residents alternating with the fancy sedans of project engineers and family cars of gawkers from out of town. The Town Hall accommodated a thousand people, who made sad souvenirs of the black-bordered admission tickets and programs. Twice as many others milled about outside, some trying to look in the windows of the hall, others telling stories, cultivating rumors, or moving to the swing music and square dance numbers that McEnelly's Orchestra played inside.

"You could hear the music as clearly as if you'd paid to go inside and my date wanted to dance, but I thought it was neither the time nor the place," Victory told us. "I was only nineteen years old, and had never before found myself in such a situation, but I knew that much—that you don't dance at a time like that."

The stroke of midnight was the towns' death knell. At that point, according to what Pal read from one of his stories, "A hush fell over the Town Hall, jammed far beyond ordinary capacity, as the first note of the clock sounded; a nervous tension . . . had been felt by both present and former residents, and casual onlookers . . . muffled sounds of sobbing were heard, hardened men were not ashamed to take out their handkerchiefs, and even children, attending the ball with their parents, broke into tears."

The orchestra did the "Auld Lang Syne." Victory acknowledged that she was one of those weeping down there in the pit of the valley now being closed off by a rising dam and dike, and soon to be covered with the cold waters of the trapped and slowly rising Swift.

"The town," Pal read as clearly as you'd ever hear him, "was now a nameless waste."

He put down the folder and we were all quiet. Until Victory spoke:

"Imagine."

I did. I looked down toward Mount Ram and the old grave-yard's terraces still visible and I tried to envision the roads and the dots of houses, barns, shops, the hard lines of train tracks, the softer ones made by puffs from chimneys. Maybe with the miracle of an eagle's eye I could have zoomed closer to see men walking to work, women hanging clothes, old people chatting on porches, children in some running game outside school, vaca-tioners moving their belongings into cabins set at the edge of the many small lakes. Even closer up, a good-sized farm like ours— the wagging tails of dogs, the sturdy hooves of cattle, the golden beaks of chickens, the tufted ears of ponies. You could try to pic-ture all this, but it was difficult to succeed. You'd have to be some sort of talented artist or psychic, because now down there was just the wide, winking blue water and the hills that had become islands, and that, really, was all my eyes were taking in.

I turned to see Lucy looking down toward the piney island that marked where Enfield used to be, in the direction Victory had gestured as she began her story about the final night. Lucy's head then turned to the left, out toward Holyoke, to the abrupt mountain scarred by the trails of a ski hill. At the base of it was Mountain Park, where Victory and Pal took me and Frankie once a summer and we rode the amusements while they stood in the shade and smiled each time our boat or train car whizzed past. Would Lucy enjoy an amusement ride? What would such a person like at all? I of course couldn't yet know, nor could I tell what she was thinking as she looked down into the valley. There had been no questions from her all along, so I began to supply them. Asking my aunt and uncle things I already knew the answers to, in an effort to make all this more interesting for the girl. Where had the best sliding hills been located? Where were the pool halls? Where were the factories? Where exactly were the lakes before the flooding made everything into one hand-shaped sea?

That's when Lucy finally spoke.

"Where," she asked, "are the dead?"

We rolled through the gate of the stone walls that mark the entrance to the Quabbin Park Cemetery. Uncle Pal was driving slowly now, at the pace we would have been using for an actual funeral. We were standing, leaning against the back of the cab like Victory had suggested so we could get the full effect she thought was intended by the designer, who placed the monument of the Gettysburg soldier just so that it is the first thing you see when you've come through the wooded entrance and up over the rise. The statue came into view and Victory asked, "Isn't that magnificent?" but neither of us answered her. I was instead noticing for the first time in all my visits here the two big cannons on either side of the monument, trained right at our truck.

As these kinds of places went, the cemetery was a lovely one. There were pleasantly named street signs where the paved lanes intersected. Contours to the land, not just a typical flat football-field of a space. Trees and shrubs interrupted the stones and created little neighborhoods, whether or not that was the intention.

Uncle Pal parked at the end of Sunset Road and we all got out and stood in the silence the place deserved and was lucky enough to have. Victory then said to Lucy, "You won't see many places like this, dear. Very old stones, very unusual stones. Look closely at the detail. Some people make rubbings of them. To frame and display on the walls of their homes. They come out quite nicely, however it sounds. We can come back and do that sometime if you want."

I couldn't believe her. Suggesting a return.

And, yes, "I'd like to try that," Lucy was answering, and she looked brighter and happier than she had in the whole day since she'd arrived.

"Wander around. Go," my uncle told her. "You won't get lost here. Just remember we're on Sunset."

I slouched against the truck and watched Lucy stroll along a row of stones. She'd stop at one, crouch to read, maybe trace a word with her hand, then continue on until another caught her attention in some way.

"Go on with her," Victory said, quietly and encouragingly, using her hand as kind of a broom to sweep me past. "Go."

"No way."

"But it's fascinating! Show her around! Show her. Look at this one." Right in front of us was the stone so badly timeworn that it was difficult to make out name or age or date, only a few words from the poem carved into the very bottom. I could make out the line "your cold dead."

"Imagine!"

Victory was right. And, on any other day, I would have agreed with her, how this indeed was something to get you thinking. Any other day it would have been fun to do what we did every once in a while each summer, to walk around and try to find the oddest names, the ones that weren't at all peculiar two hundred or so years ago. Girls named Chlorenda, Philura, Flora, Armandine. Boys who for eternity would be known as Stilman and Elect. The dignified name Elkanah, gender unclear to me. Then there was Zelotus Cooley and his wife, Verlina. And Fannie Horr, always spotted by visitors. But this wasn't just any stop on a holiday. It was our first free day with a crazy girl, and this is where we were having to waste it.

"I think that's a morbid poem," I said, "and, most of all, I can't believe you brought her here."

"You know it's a popular place, Robyn. And Lucy is curious, she asked the question. She wanted to come here. All kinds of tourists come here, you can't blame them—it's something to see firsthand."

I wasn't happy. "Yeah, well, all of them are probably not crazy. You want to bring her to a cemetery? Her? You know what she tried to do—she'd be in a cemetery right now if somebody hadn't saved her. Don't you think this'll give her, I don't know—ideas?"

Victory *shhhsshed* me, and frowned. "Look at her," she said. I lifted my eyes from the cold dead stone and saw Lucy now resting, lying on her back, hands behind her head, as peaceful against the green grass as a lady in a deodorant commercial. "Does she look upset to you?" Victory asked. "She's come up here to relax, and she's relaxing. Go. Go and make friends. I'll pour us all some lemonade."

I sighed loud and scuffed down the row, passing stones marked with fountains, urns, angels, a sun face, then a moon, a boat, and a leaping fish. I knew that all these things held some sort of meaning regarding the person whose name they adorned, but wasn't sure exactly what. Never mind symbolic carvings, the writing itself was hard enough to make out— swirly, the old-fashioned kind that makes an *f* out of an *s*. So the "Famuel Fawyer" planted beneath that stone there was really "Samuel Sawyer." This I planned to point out to Lucy once I reached her, it being the only thing I could think of to say right then, other than "Let's get out of here."

"Hi."

Lucy squinted up at me and said, "Hi—isn't this great?" She looked content. At ease. A lot happier than most people are on a cemetery visit.

"You know, you know that their *s*'s look like *f*'s . . . that's how they used to write the alphabet. People back then, in the olden days. That's how they wrote. Weird, huh?" That said, quickly, I was now completely out of conversation. I looked back at the truck. Victory was offering Pal a Dixie cup of refreshment. I heard a flat tapping and looked down. At my feet, Lucy was patting the thriving grass. Slowly, I sat where she was inviting me to.

"That's perfect, then," she whispered, excited, and leaned toward me. "About how they write, I mean. Because, look . . ." And she pointed to the skinny timeworn stone leaning between us at a sunken angle, the marker of Kittie Evans, cherished daughter of Zilpha and David, 1815–1832. Lucy ran a long finger beneath the name. "Look—she was only 'feventeen.'" And then she added just slowly enough, "Just like we are!"

I slapped my leg and pretended something had bitten me. I stood up on the earth that covered Kittie. I rubbed at the fake bite and said, "I have to get some ice." I tried not to move as fast as a run, but I was back at the truck in almost a second, reaching into the cooler, my aunt fussing and wanting to examine me though I wouldn't let her as there was nothing there to look at. What she should have been examining was the head of the person over there with cherished Kittie Evans, sunning herself over bones, content as could be. The same girl appearing suddenly, at our side, all cheery and bright and winking at me as she told Victory: "Thank you! This place is fantastic! Can we come back here again someday soon?"

Had it been up to me, the answer would have been no. But I was not in charge. And Pal, one of the two who were, told Lucy, "Yes, whatever you'd like." And, "Certainly," he'd said, "no problem." Then added, "Why not?"

I could have given some reasons why we probably shouldn't be carting this girl back to a place like a cemetery, but who was listening to me?

Frankie did, but he had no pull. At the shore of Lake Wyola the night of my first day back, just hours after finding out about Lucy, he sat attentive and didn't interrupt as I went through as much of the story as I'd learned at that point. "I don't know a lot about these kinds of people," he told me, "but if she's okay with your aunt and your uncle, well, they wouldn't bring a weird person here."

"That's what she told me."

"Then believe her."

"If this girl freaks out, you'll save me, right?"

"She tried to kill herself, not somebody else. Right?"

I nodded.

"Then I wouldn't worry," he said, and he reached over suddenly and pulled me close like there was something big and scary approaching right that second. "I'll always save you," Frankie said. He laughed, he made it a joke.

But I wasn't kidding.

Victory wasn't worried, either. She displayed utmost confidence that our guest and I were the perfect fit she'd predicted. There she was, doing all she could to make Lucy happy and at home, and also doing all she could to get the two of us to bond before we had the slightest chance of heading in opposite directions.

This far from thrilled me. In the twenty-four hours since Lucy had arrived, I walked around like there was a wall built on either side of my head. I looked only at what was in front of me, which I limited to my food plate, the work that needed to be done, and Victory's suddenly fascinating books. I hid away with Anne Morrow Lindbergh as carefully as if I'd been told to look for a secret message written by her just for me. I was deep into anything that involved concentration, all just to avoid looking directly at Lucy, or having to say more than a greeting when she came into a room. My uncle quickly caught on and took a sledgehammer to what I'd been constructing around myself. He asked that Lucy accompany me when I went to the basement to get a couple jars of string beans, when I chained the goats in higher grass, when I went out to the ring.

It never had occurred to me when Ron or any of the other boarders, including the bearded guy who held two-sided conversations in his sleep, were living out on the back porch, that they might get up in the middle of the night and do me some harm. Certainly, all had been strangers, some of them big strong men who undoubtedly possessed the power to just go and kill Victory and Pal and me in an instant if the idea ever struck them. But as far as I knew, they all had been normal. And though I looped the little hook through the eye my uncle screwed into my doorjamb the first summer the "Nice Clean Room for Rent" sign was swaying there out front, I never lost any sleep over a single one of them.

That first night Lucy stayed was a different story. With only a wall and a door and a hook between me and the girl, I was on guard. As I stared into the black, every normal little shift and pop of the house got my heart racing more than I'd like to admit. Some point after two-thirty, I'd heard a door open, and then, to my relief, Victory's soft familiar steps on the less-creaky side of the stairs as she made her way down to the toilet. A cheerfully sunny morning lasered through my eyelids an instant later, my aunt rising again, earlier than anyone, and getting the aroma of Canadian bacon and rye toast floating up the stairs to wake us.

I cracked my door and peered into the hall before heading to the kitchen. I was happy to find Victory there alone, standing at the stove, nudging a cloud of scrambled eggs onto a white serving platter. I went over and stood next to her and she put an arm around me. Then she pointed her spatula in the direction of the pantry door, through which Lucy was passing with a stack of juice glasses, and she told me to say good morning to our new friend.

"After breakfast, why don't you show her all of the farm?" Victory asked, making it into a question, like I was going to have the opportunity to give an answer. "You can get yourself better acquainted."

By doing this, I was allowed to skip the breakfast dishes, the most likely highlight of the day. "Let's go," I said to Lucy, and I motioned a little to indicate the direction. Through Pal's room, through the back porch, down the steps, she was behind me before I could put much space between the two of us. We were in the middle of it right then, so I pointed out Victory's kitchen garden. All kinds of plants that you could add to your cooking grew there, lush and close and handy. Knitting-needley chives, shiny basil that came even in the color purple, firecracker explosions of dill, the tiny-leafed thyme all in their places, everything in neat clusters. Tender plants like rosemary and basil grew in pots that Victory lugged inside at the first hint of frost. Mint, oregano, anything else tough and invasive, was kept corralled by cement blocks sunk into the soil. Victory had designed the garden in the shape of a boomerang, running it along the stepping stones that curved left in the direction of the barnyard, and pushing the back center of it out to a rounded point at which she'd placed a knee-high cement statue of Jesus holding a hand up, one finger of that extended hand pointing in a way that looked like he was trying to make a point in a crowd that was not including him in its conversation.

Maybe he was saying "Wait!" because Lucy was moving past and I was behind her again, as she swung her arms and headed toward the barn. She was wearing a halter top made of blue bandannas stitched together, and her hair was twisted up and secured to the back of her head by a trendy piece of leather with a wooden stick poked through it. Her spine was straight but the bones that made it up were bumpy, like there was a necklace of beads lying beneath her skin. She had long legs that covered lots more ground than mine did even if we were taking the same number of strides. I ran a little to catch up with her and I said, "Uh, my aunt told me that you like animals."

Big space here.

Then, "Yeah."

Another space.

"Have any?"

Silence.

"No."

Nothing.

"Ever have any?"

More of nothing. Then, "No. You?"

Enthusiastically I bubbled, "Well, these . . ." Here I pointed to the ring, where the six ponies were tacked and snoozing in the still, warm morning air. Uncle Pal, probably thinking he was doing me a favor, had completed all my morning work, leaving me that much more time to get to know Lucy.

"They're all yours?"

"Well . . . they're my uncle's."

"Oh."

Her little word just drifted there pitifully. So I added, "But I can do whatever I want here," not so much to be haughty but because it was the real truth.

Lucy stopped, turned to me, and said, "Cool." Then she smiled, small at first, then larger, then as much as I think her face would allow, like somebody was turning a dial and had gotten up to one of the higher numbers.

I smiled back. But I'd say that if my controls could go up to ten, it was probably a three and a half.

"Wait—" she pointed at the ring, "these are them? The horses?"

Her words were slow and drippy, thick with disappointment. I felt bad, but only for the ponies, as if some of her disapproval was a physical thing that was going to fall on them, and hurt when it landed.

"These are the ponies," I said cheerfully.

"Where are the horses?"

"Well, we don't have any. No horses. Just ponies."

Lucy's eyes got daggerish. "My grandmother, she said you had horses here."

"I don't know about that," I said. "Maybe she was thinking of somebody else."

"She was talking about here. She told me I could ride horses here. Here. She said you had lots of them."

"You can ride these around, really," I assured her, yet Lucy didn't look happy. She linked her hands behind her back like a prisoner and made surprisingly loud cracking movements with her bare toes. My heart started knocking in all directions. I didn't want her to get upset. Especially when there was no one else around.

"Uh, want me to get my aunt?"

Just like that, Lucy's face changed and she knocked me on the shoulder and said, "Don't panic, Panek . . . Panek—get it?" happily, as if all of a sudden there was no cause for any concern.

I didn't know the response. I took a few steps backward, toward the house, out of the reach of her long arms, in case they started flying out at me. "Uh, she knows somebody with a horse. A guy down the road. It's the kind for pulling a huge hay wagon, but he still rides it anyway. With a saddle even. He's a big guy, but he gets on the big horse and he looks small. It's really something to see. Somebody the size of you, well you'd look really, really small on it and . . ."

I realized I was sweating now, as much as I would have if sent up to the attic for something on a hot afternoon. The sudden rivers pouring down my back felt like a million bugs crawling. So I looked to the six ponies for help and I brought her over to the ring. By that I don't mean I led her, or touched her arm or anything, as I didn't quite have the courage. I just walked over and she followed. Star was standing just inside the gate, as usual. I opened it and I introduced her to him, and then sent him forward, announcing each of the others as they slowly paraded past.

"They're cute," Lucy said, sounding surprised. "They're like Volkswagens. You can ride these? Really?" She looked at me. I had the sun behind me and that made her squint.

"Most of them," I said. "That one"—I pointed to Star, of course—"and that one"—Zoey—"and those two"—Chester and Pan. "The others are way too small for people our size."

"What do they do all day?"

"Well, they stand there, and then when somebody comes along, a child, a kid, you know, they go in circles."

"That's it?" She wrinkled her nose.

"Well, then they go to the pasture at the end of the day, and they get to relax."

"Relax from what?"

I motioned to them standing there, sleeping, swishing tails occasionally, but basically looking like big furry decorations. I shrugged. "From this, I guess. But, you see, it does get busy. Sometimes we might have hundreds of kids come here. It just all depends on the day, and as we get into the summer, you'll see. It'll be very busy. You'll be surprised."

"Right." She seemed unconvinced as she leaned over the fence and put her hand onto the neck of Chester. You wouldn't have called it a pat, she simply placed her hand there and left it for a few seconds. Like a mother testing a forehead. After a little bit, she turned to me and laughed like somebody younger than her would sound. The effect, from her, who I knew to have had events in her life way beyond those your ordinary teenage girl might know, well, it was like dandelion fuzz crossing your face. So I couldn't do anything but laugh, too.

That sound went on to turn into words. My mind did that— had me going on from a laugh to a story, a bunch of them that fell easily from me. What I knew about what was right in front of us. A topic so easy I didn't even have to think: who the ponies were, and how they'd come to live here.

Only four kids showed up that day, so there was plenty of time for talking if you wanted to. Three of them—two shy brothers and a visiting boy cousin who loudly pointed out for the rest of us how the other two were afraid of everything and everybody—arrived at the same time, just before noon. The fourth— a sunburned toddler with one small forearm trapped in a hot-looking plaster cast—was driven over in mid-afternoon, around the time that Victory traditionally took a break for *The Guiding Light*. Soap operas lasted only half an hour in those days, and she took in just the first fifteen minutes. She'd come in and sit fully down in her armchair only after first opening a magazine and covering the seat to protect good upholstery from the reality of workclothes. That day, by the time the sturdy lighthouse was swinging its big warning beam through the title of the program and Bert had set yet another troubled son straight with her great wisdom, Lucy and I had progressed to conversation at least a couple levels above asking for the salt shaker.

I followed the same order in which my uncle had acquired the ponies, starting with Star and the groundbreaking presence he made when he'd arrived at the farm in the back of my uncle's car. I moved aside his forelock to show the true glory of the entire white blaze doing its fireworks show across his face. I've always thought of it as a work of art and was disappointed when Lucy just nodded to acknowledge she'd seen enough. "Thanks," she said, so I pointed to Princess, noted how she was tiny even for a pony, though, I have to note now, not as small as those little miniature horses people currently keep as pets walking around kitchens and TV rooms like they're regular dogs or cats. I patted her coat, soft tan like the lighter of the individually wrapped Kraft caramels we would melt in a double boiler each Halloween to coat apples, back in the days when you could hand out homemade stuff without anybody having reason to worry. Her mane and tail were as white as the bleached hair worn by Mrs. Bowler, the first neighbor person ever to come to our front door after we moved to Illinois. She brought with her a six-pack of Pepsi and a tuna casserole topped with an exotic crust of smashed-up potato chips, plus a bag of paper cups and plates and plastic utensils so that we, in all the commotion of unpacking, would not have to concern ourselves with locating, then washing, china. She said that, "china," like it might be what we ate off daily. I told Lucy this story, and she replied, "Oh," in an unimpressed way that made me regret opening up. Then I introduced Zoey, the small, spoiled red-blond animal who always had to be the first to be hitched to the wheel or later there would be a great deal of protest and noise and legs rooted to the ground. Her name meant "full of life" in Greek, though the Greeks would not have used the $y$ that my uncle threw in when he was carving the nameplate for the stall. I knew that, and other things that I told Lucy as thoroughly as if she'd paid for a ticket to learn something. How the many different kinds of ponies have in common the admirable attributes of being strong, compact, hardy, and blessed with good endurance. That a map of the world would help you trace the breeds' beginnings—areas of harsh environments, both hot and cold, each type of pony found there equipped with the proper types of coats, thick ones covering those from the frigid regions, lighter ones on those from warmer areas, powerful legs carrying the ponies who spent their days climbing rocky slopes. That wherever they had originally come from, all ponies are easy to train and can be useful in many ways. As pack animals, for one example. For such agricultural work as toting, for light harness, if you like to exhibit them in shows or if you live in an area where cars are scarce and you need to get yourself and your belongings from one place to the next. And for riding. The book said ponies are always good for riding.

"By anybody," I told Lucy, "even people my aunt's age—she goes around on Pan, you'll see her." Lucy narrowed her eyes, I could see her trying to imagine my aunt on a pony, but it wasn't something I was making up—Pan was Victory's favorite, Victory had even named her. Not after something from the kitchen, like you might suppose. It was from mythology—Pan was the goddess of the fields.

Originally, the pony carried no name at all. At least that no one could voice for her. Pal had found her at a tag sale on a front lawn on the road to Belchertown, just before the severe underpass where you must honk before entering to let other drivers know you are headed their way on the same thin lane. Somebody had Pan secured on a chain the strength of which could tow a barge, a dozen or so feet of that, the end of it hooked up to a cinderblock. That afternoon, hauling an empty livestock trailer just as if this was all the way it was supposed to work out, Pal scanned the long picnic table of unidentifiable machine parts, then saw the beautiful white pony grazing over near the little forest of dusty floor lamps. The man was asking $10, which Uncle Pal happily had on him.

Close up, she was a soft dust color, really, with little brown flecks all over her coat. The correct term for this is "flea-bitten gray," but I didn't think that was very flattering so I never used it in my narratives to those who admired her as they leaned at the fence. Instead, I'd point out the most lovely feathering on the back of her legs that, whether standing still or moving, always made her appear like she was rushing into that much more wind.

I moved on to Tony, brought to auction over in East Brookfield by a man who genuinely was sad that his children were no longer interested in riding. Budding pony collector, and high bidder, my uncle ended up calling the animal Tony the Pony, though he usually just stuck with the first part, correctly believing that the rest of the name was self-evident.

As for Chester, he really should have been Chester the Rocky Mountain Pony. Somebody's mother in the line once told me that was so, she'd had one as a child, she knew one when she saw one. Long neck, flaxen tail and mane, strong and slender legs. Pal gained Chester in an unbelievable swap advertised in an area radio program that broadcast just such matches waiting to be made, in exchange for only a young goat and a cord of unseasoned firewood. He said he had no papers to prove the pony's point of origin. But that didn't matter to me. As much as I thought it was fascinating how the others seemed to have been connected to some far-off places, I wanted this pony to be a Rocky Mountain Pony because a Rocky Mountain Pony was from here. Or, as the book put it, "Origin: U.S." An American pony. The only one listed. Not from the Russian Federation or the Middle East or Iceland or France. But America. Land of the free and the home of the brave people like me, Robyn Panek, who'd been standing and talking to Lucy Dragon for probably fifteen or twenty minutes straight now.

I turned the wheel until Pan came up to the gate, and I showed Lucy how to gather the reins in the left hand, to put that hand on the saddle horn, the other on the cantle, left foot in the stirrup, right leg swung over. The ponies were, of course, quite low to the ground, and she had the long legs my aunt had been making a fuss over since they'd stepped from Mr. Maytaz's car. So it wasn't that hard for her to get into the saddle. "You okay?" She was concentrating on her legs down there and her hands up here and so all she said was, "Un-hah," which I took to mean yes, so I sent them forward. Lucy rocked at first as Pan took the first few steps, and then she laughed. I let her go around a couple of times and then I stopped Star, directly across from them in the ring, hopped on, and gave a nudge. Now all of us were moving there under the sugar maples. Forward but around, ending up in the same place we'd started. Then heading off again, then coming back. Just the sound of the hoofs and maybe a snort, or tack rattled in the shake of a head, and, if you were lucky, and listening well, the neigh that held all you ever needed to know there, that day, on which Lucy and I, tenuously, bravely, began to move forward.

In the instant it takes me to decide to begin, the process of grooming floods back with the smooth ease of grain pouring from a scoop.

You start at the bottom. You face the pony so it's to your left, and in your closer hand you take and hold the part of the leg that on you or me would be called the ankle. Next you ask the animal for its hoof. If you are lucky and the pony is compliant, it will turn this up and back so you can hold it, and with your other hand you use a metal hook to clean out all the crevices that you as a human can be happy you do not have patterning the bottom of your own smooth and flat feet. In this V-shaped valley there sometimes are stones imbedded. Anything else the animal might have walked through. It is not the most pleasant or easy job, but if the roles were reversed you certainly would want somebody doing this for you.

Once done with the feet, you work on the rest of the body from front to back. Hard rubber curry comb in the right hand, soft brush in the left to pass over the spot where the other one has loosened dirt and dust and hair. One, then the other. One, then the other. You work from the top down, always progressing toward the rear of the animal. You pass over muscles and bone and cartilage, you cover the entire shape like you are carving it out of the surrounding air. If you do it long enough, and correctly, your arms tire and your back might complain and you don't like to think how there are five more ponies waiting for the same treatment. But you wouldn't want to skip any—it's good for them, plus they are eager with anticipation. Each has an unexpected spot that sends them right to heaven. For Zoey, it is the area a third of the way down her neck. Run the rubber comb over that and she turns her head and the left side of her lip curls up in bliss. I get to that place, now, today, and this happens. The last time I witnessed that, I was too young to vote.

That last summer, Lucy would come out each morning to help me groom. The first couple of days, she just stood at the mouth of the barn and watched wordlessly. Then she walked in and asked if she could try.

As I showed her how to run a wide comb through Princess's Miss America mane, she said, "It's sort of like being in a school of beauty, which I think might be fun to attend if you had to go off and learn something."

I wondered where she'd be headed after this summer had there been no crack-up to derail her high school career. What place was she dreaming of these days, in the way I was dreaming of Seattle? Replaying every minute of the weekend I'd spent there the spring before, me and my father and mother, the three of us touring the campus along with a dozen other parent-and-child combinations and an enthusiastic guide, a junior who was nametagged Irene but wanted us to call her Sophie. I knew where I was going come the second of September—straight into the dorm by the swan pond. I had no idea where Lucy was headed, just as I had no idea about the rest of her. I knew nothing of what she thought about after we chose three ponies apiece and got to work. We wouldn't speak while doing this, the only noises would be the stomp of a hoof, a comb running through mane, the soft things we whispered to the animals to get them to move where we wanted them to so we wouldn't get stepped on. Then we'd tack up and unsnap them from the crossties at the mouth of the barn and hook a second finger through the halters to lead them to the ring. Open the gate to spin the wheel to the next position in line. Ease the hindquarters into place and snap the halter to the clip on the spoke. The ponies in the ring have never worn bridles. It would be just too tempting for most kids to spend their entire rides yanking on a pair of reins. And how'd you like your head being pulled back all day, over and again, by some-body who either doesn't know better, or who is just plain mean, as some kids, believe it or not, are? There are reins for the riders to hold, but they are just a loop of leather fastened to the spoke. That way, the riders can pull all they want. That way, nobody gets hurt. So the last thing is to throw the reins over the necks, loop them around the saddle horn, and then close the gate and wait for the customers.

This was our job, Lucy's and mine, to run the ring. And when there wasn't anything to be running, well, we just stayed put. Sitting on the fence, or, more often, on ponies located opposite one another. We leaned on their necks, or sat sideways on the saddle, coaxing them forward every now and again, going around the same track on which, to my amazement, we eventually dumped over the surprisingly packed bushelbasket of things we held in common.

.          .          .

I first had asked the general questions you do when you want
to get to know somebody. I still wasn't sure if that was a desire
of mine, but here, with the ponies as sort of a buffer and distraction, it seemed less scary than if we were sitting across a
table from one another, alone. Lucy told me she was from
down near Washington, D.C.—just north of that in the suburbs,
if you wanted to be exact. I said I knew all about those, as a
suburb was where I existed when I wasn't living here. She said
she had never been to Chicago, but if it was as big a city as she
thought, she could pretty much guess what the surrounding
area looked like, and she made a face at the same time as she
was conjuring this image.

"I can't stand the suburbs," Lucy said.

"Neither can I."

She had a complete set of parents. A father who sold expensive women's shoes and a mother who went out in her own
sportscar a couple nights a week to demonstrate a line of
organic facial masks and cruelty-free cosmetics at ladies' parties
held only in private homes. For no charge, Lucy could get any
shoe or facial preparation, but she more often took advantage
of the footwear, which was something at least essential.

"I hate makeup," Lucy said.

"So do I."

She also said she had a brother and a sister. Whatever the
order in which they had arrived, there was only one thing that
was important as far as Lucy was concerned: just who had gotten there before they did.

"I'm the oldest," she said and I said, "Me too."

One day Lucy told me she had friends she would miss
while at the farm, and she might expect to get a few letters over
the next few months—maybe even a telephone call. But she

added that none of her girlfriends had really ever understood her that well, so it wouldn't be too hard to be apart from them. It sounded odd when she pointed this next thing out, but once I thought about it I realized she was quite right—she said sometimes it is lonelier to be standing right next to somebody than to be by yourself.

"I like being by myself," Lucy said. I said, "I know what you mean." And I gave this answer because, like everything else I told her right there in front of the ponies at the ring, it actually was true.

Another day, Lucy even brought up the subject of high school. She asked me about mine and I gave the basics, trying not to sound too excited about all the fun I'd had in the senior year she'd never experienced. For her part, and she couldn't have known that I knew better, she said high school had gone okay, but she was glad to get it over and done with and move on. She went on to say she felt that all the fuss over the country's bicentennial—weren't you sick of it already?—was a big waste of money that should have been spent instead on improving the lot of the nation's many poor people. One very warm afternoon she informed me her hair could stand a conditioner only once a week during the summer—more than that and it separated into ropy clumps as greasy as if she hadn't washed it in the first place. And she added that she got sick if she had to be in air-conditioning for more than ten minutes. She regretted not keeping up a scrapbook of Patty Hearst, whom she'd found fascinating. Green was Lucy's color. Orange, the soda she preferred. Soup was her favorite food year-round even if it was a hundred degrees out.

I told her how my family back in Illinois without fail ate some flavor of Rice-A-Roni four out of every seven nights, how we strung only garish orange lights on our front bushes at Christmas because that was the color on sale one year and they'd yet to burn out, how we recently redid the basement only to have some strange puffy fungus quickly come along and push up the edges of all the self-stick linoleum tiles we'd set down so securely. How the man who dreamed up cotton-crotch pantyhose had graduated from the very same high school I attended.

*The Six Million Dollar Man. Rocky. A Star Is Born.*

We agreed they stunk.

She hated Led Zeppelin, no matter the popular opinion, didn't care if I loved "Stairway to Heaven" like everybody else. On the other hand, she loved Aerosmith very much and even owned two of their eight-tracks and did you know that they come from Boston, which is in this very state? Was she interested in Peter Frampton? Was I kidding? We were of the same mind on this: Yes to Al Stewart, no to Rod Stewart. And yes yes yes, as Frankie would say, to Jackson Browne.

The give-and-take sprinkled over the first couple weeks of her being with us was enough to almost light some genuine interest in me. And, coming back at me in about the third week, I saw Lucy focusing the whole of her attention on me for the first time since she'd arrived at the farm. I know that was not a long piece of time in which that might come around, but most people I've met have given me that much right at first meeting. Lucy was sometimes late with true eye contact, but when it arrived I took it—even though that was a little startling, she looking right at me, she, the crazy one, looking at me with nobody around to deflect should she start getting weird for some reason. But we always were out in the open when this happened, in broad daylight, at the ring, with the scream of

Pal's table saw slicing through pine in the barn to one side of us, and Victory spray-starching shirts on the ironing board in the house at the other side, so I felt pretty safe whenever one of my fears about Lucy paddled its way to the front of the widening stream of the regular nice time the two of us were sharing. All in all, her attention was oddly and suddenly appreciated, reminding me of the way you feel when somebody comes in and turns on a light in a room when you'd been in there for ages and had not even realized it was getting dark out.

Which it wasn't really, but it was nearly time for supper, and for getting the ponies out of the ring, and fed, and for my favorite part of the day, Fred's old milk truck knocking up the hill, as it did right then, like it had been idling down by the road for hours just waiting for me to check the low placement of the sun and have the realization that it was time.

Lucy heard the truck engine and looked up from my showing her how to undo the triangle of a knot that held every pony's saddle in place—in this case, the one that straddled Pan's big flat back. She'd ended up liking Pan the best of all the ponies. As for humans, there was no way around the fact that Frankie was her favorite.

The only question Lucy wormed her way around was whether or not she had left a boyfriend behind. She's the one who started on the topic, wanting to know if I had a social life, as she put it rather genteely.

Pal would have whispered the lengthy *"Trzy rzeczy które są trudno ukrywać—ogień, katar, miłość"*—"There are three things that are difficult to keep hidden: a fire, a cold, and love." He would have been right. Even so, I did not right off tell Lucy about the extent of what was burning here between Frankie and me— nothing in detail, certainly nothing at all about how I'd known

him for eight years, how for the past four summers we had
been absolutely it for each other. The class ring. That this coming August 14 would be the second anniversary of his whispering we would marry. I would tell her, but maybe only once I
trusted her.

I never was much for formal competition. But the late
winter I was sixteen, my parents encouraged me to try out
for the town's colleen contest. The prize was a ride on a float
in the Chicago St. Patrick's Day parade, a big handknit
sweater with matching gloves and scarf, and a five hundred
dollar scholarship, an enormous amount in those days and
one that certainly would have come in handy no matter what
course of study you chose. We weren't anywhere near Irish,
but that didn't matter to the people who were running the
contest. All you had to be was a girl, which I was, and to be
active in the kind of things that might make you stand out
from the others. Volunteering for some tear-jerking cause, for
example, or able to beat everybody and set records in a
sport, or getting fantastic grades in courses most people
couldn't even pronounce. I was nothing better than an okay
student. I would have done a sport but my public high school
offered no equestrian team. And I really didn't do any kind
of work for which I was not paid. But my parents thought
that my summers on the farm might make me fall into the
category of at least interesting, so one Saturday they brought
home the application from a stack of them that had been
lying on the top of the cigarette machine in the grocery store
entryway.

Early that March, the town paper ran a special pullout section on the local contestants, printing all our various submitted
photographs, and the information we'd provided. Under the

green-inked shamrock-encircled headline "Colleen Hopefuls!" the editors had taken some liberties in condensing the many lines we'd all filled out on the applications. And in my category of hobbies, they'd reduced my five down to one. Not the impressive horseback riding or strenuous-sounding farming, or even the regular but admirable wifely skills of sewing or cooking, which I had to be forced to do but practiced enough to make the inclusion not really a lie. They left me with one hobby I'd practically made up just to fill in space. I long had kept a can of change on my desk. Nothing foreign or antique, but they were coins. From my pocket. They had been right in front of me the night I'd filled out the form, and inspired me to add "coin collector" under the hobby heading, which I didn't think was anything but true. And that following month, there in the special section, beneath my muddy junior class photo, the newspaper had gone and labeled me "Robyn Panek: Can collector."

I was mortified, feeling everyone would think I spent my days walking around picking up garbage. For the next few weeks, some kids got a great laugh out of driving by at night and tossing empty cans on our front lawn—food ones, plus some even from beer, which sent my parents right up through the roof shingles. They weren't happy about how the experience was turning out, but because they'd always stressed the importance of following through on things, they insisted I attend the pageant, that I put on my best dress and nylons and high heels and everything and go down to the Legion Hall and walk down a shaky runway made out of a line of banquet tables linked with duct tape. I didn't like it, but I did all that for them, and, no surprise, I came nowhere close to winning. I didn't even make it from the original twenty-three down to the final twenty, which the following weekend got reduced down to the final ten, which in the same night got shrunk down to the final five, which got reduced down to the all-important one: cute, freckled, rust-curled Mary Finucane from two streets away, who would get to ride on the float, wear the sweater and gloves and scarf, and hold a cardboard painted to resemble the scholarship check. And who, in her spare time, according to information that had been printed beneath her photograph, collected coins.

A couple years later, in the subtle pageant for Frankie's undivided attention, I was a much more enthusiastic competitor.

"Can you get me yogurt?" I heard Lucy politely asking my aunt one morning not long after that.

"Health food kick?"

"Well, I think I read it is supposed to be good for you," Lucy answered. "I read that. You can even apply it to your skin if you want to. It's a dairy product, you know. Like from the cows. Do you think the milkman has it?"

"He has everything." I heard Victory say this, and then I heard Lucy give a little short laugh. "Ha!" she went, just like you'd write it.

"I'll mark it on the order form," Victory told her, "and we'll make a special request. Just for you, my dear."

"Oh, thank you so much, Miss Panek," Lucy said. "Thank you."

And Victory, for the fortieth time, reminded Lucy to call her what everyone else did.

"Okay, oh, then thank you so much, Victory," Lucy said, correcting herself, but sounding just as genuine as she had the previous time. "Thank you, Victory."

.     .     .

Two visits later, Frankie brought Lucy's yogurt over. It was vanilla in flavor. Came in a very small carton, not even the size of what something like sour cream is sold in.

"We also have plain yogurt," he said to me when I met him out front, "but I've tried it and, really, it's nothing you'd want to eat if you didn't have to. This at least has some flavor to it. I hope it's a natural flavor. . . ."

He twirled the container in search of a list of ingredients, but this was way before such things were required on the label. He told me he couldn't find the information, and that he hoped it didn't matter to me. To me. Frankie was telling this to me, even though I wasn't the one who'd ordered it. I didn't stop him. "Go on," I tried to get my eyes to say. "Tell me more about yogurt. Everything you know about it." Any reason to look into the face of Frankie Mathews and know that he was speaking to me. Thinking of only me, and of yogurt, at that moment. There, right there, I would be crazy to say how this wasn't anything I'd ordered, and therefore direct him to somebody else.

My aunt took care of this for me.

"Oh!" She whooped this, all happy, from the other side of the front door screen. "Lucy's yogurt is here! We can try it out for dessert."

Her big hand came out through the crack in the door and she reached for the container and yanked it inside the house, where it, and she, disappeared.

I heard some excited voices from the back of the house, then footsteps that were lighter than Victory's, then the door scraped open and there Lucy was, for the very first time, between me and Frankie.

"Hi," she said to both of us, then laughed a little, turning girl-silly all of a sudden. I saw color flood her face and she

pushed back her hair slowly over her shoulder, for no other
reason than because all of its glory was there to move. It was
somewhat like watching one of those films in biology class. A
community of chimps, their social interactions interpreted in
the tired drone of the narrator. The preening, the baring of
teeth, the cautious approach, the offer of food, the picking of
bugs from another's hide. Everything you were watching right
there meant way more than just what it looked like. There had
been no mention in the films as to what a delivery of a carton
of vanilla yogurt might translate to, but I could just about
guess. I, the original chimp-ess in this film, and relationship,
stepped forward into the assaulted territory. Best defense being
an offense, I slipped an arm around Frankie, who kindly
repeated to Lucy everything he'd told me about the flavor differences. He even went into some vague information about
cultures of bacteria that lived in yogurt and went from the container into your intestines, where they did great things for
your well-being, thus all the interest in this time of great
health-consciousness. The dairy hadn't made this particular
item, he'd had to get it from a distributor. But if there was
enough call for it, maybe Fred—his father, he pointed out to
her, that's what everybody calls him, even his own kid—maybe
Fred would consider getting the machines necessary to make
yogurt. Whatever those were, as he had no idea, and noted
that fact.

Lucy listened as intently as if in a class, and brushed back
the hair again. Slowly. She touched her chin and tilted her head
like what he was saying about the workings of guts was just so
fascinating. Her eyes got big. Mine just rolled.

"Thanks," Lucy told him sincerely, then she looked past
Frankie to the truck, which was without Fred today.

"That's the truck." He didn't need to say this. Nor did he need to say what he did next—"Wanna go for a ride?" He was talking to Lucy, but he looked back at me and said genuinely: "I mean the two of you, of course."

One of us had to stay at the ring, of course. And guess who it was. I didn't care all that much, as I'd been in the truck a hundred times. Even so, I felt something other than hardworking bacteria in my stomach as I watched the thing back away, Frankie's arm flung for balance across the back of the seat in which Lucy sat, enthusiastically waving good-bye as the two of them disappeared down the slope and out of sight.

# · 8 ·

Whoever she was in love with secretly, I should add that Lucy also had a very public thing for Bruce Jenner.

Couldn't get enough of the sight of him there in his little short shorts, anatomy-book physique, Lord Fauntleroy hair, all that strength and skill. California boy, at twenty-six actually an older man. That last summer we were on the farm, Bruce Jenner was there on our TV, on the track and field, winning Olympic medals what seemed like every night. And in real life he was just right up in Montreal, that's like only up and over the border—can't we go?

This is why I ended up having to phone my uncle to say the red Ford had broken down on the way to a Monday morning trip to the post office, only before that it somehow had traveled two hours north. And—though I wasn't going to tell him this— it would have ended up a couple hours farther away, in an actual foreign country, had the engine not seized up like it did and stopped us dead just outside Bellows Falls.

Lucy's idea, that trip to just possibly catch a glimpse of some or all of Bruce Jenner, maybe buy a poster and get him to autograph it, and then turn around and come right home.

Directions? Tickets? Crowds? Canada? We'll worry about all that later, she smirked when I asked her these things, and she made me pull over, took over the driving, rolled down the window all the way, and speeded us up Route 91, staying in the fast lane the whole time.

"Didn't you realize you'd gone out of state?" my uncle asked when he arrived with Mr. Maytaz very late that day and got to work beneath the hood. I knew we'd caused a great inconvenience and had done what amounted to stealing the truck. But Lucy, whose idea it was, just shrugged and said, "These places all look the same to me," and my uncle hesitated then laughed at that, "Ha!" and then Lucy asked him, "Can we get back home in time to watch the Olympics?" and he said, "Let's go."

She got off easy, again, when caught swimming in Quabbin.

"It's easy to miss the signs," the state policeman acknowledged to Victory when he brought us home in his family car, rather than the cruiser that would have made it look like somebody at the farm had done something wrong. "And, really," he added, "nobody ever put one up to say that if you do swim, even though that's illegal, you gotta be wearing something."

I had warned her it was a crime but she'd waved me away, said I was a chicken shit, something she called me often, and each time she did she actually was correct. I stood there on a piece of driftwood as she stepped out of her shoes and shorts and left them in a nest like she'd been vaporized. She tossed her shirt to me and picked her way across the stones into deeper and deeper water. And, just like that, she and her skin were out bobbing there in the middle of what the governor himself one day might be drinking a glass of.

No, she told Victory the day Victory asked, she really, honestly, truly did not know the type of seeds she'd planted in the corner of the kitchen garden. Lucy said she'd found them somewhere, that she couldn't remember where, even though I clearly remembered her getting them from a stoned boy behind Friendly's. She just thought it would be fun to have a plant of her own to tend. Being on a farm and all. "Yes, it's thriving, yes, the leaves are lovely," my aunt said to her. "Kind of like hibiscus in how they point like a hand. Well, you just keep taking good care of it." And Lucy assured her that she would, but, then again, she thought maybe she'd just pull it out of the ground and hang it to dry because leaves like that would be nice in an arrangement, don't you think?

Everybody else in the car had been smoking on the way back from the mall, that's why she smelled like this. She'd only had a Shirley Temple at the disco dance, somebody must have slipped something into it. She'd fallen asleep at the movies and got locked in the theater, that's why she didn't come home until two. Fine, okay, that's great. Whatever she got into, she got out of without question. With a laugh. A hug. A wink. A jab. A joke. An attitude that wasn't questioned. I watched this with a fascination and awe. She was the person everybody, man, woman, child, fell in love with no matter what she did. And, next to her, amazingly to me, I fell under the spell as well.

She and I, it started to feel, well, normal. As nice as anything I knew back in Illinois with Gay and Darlene, who with nagging parents and nasty boyfriends and tough college prep courses certainly had enough problems of their own to go on about. Sure, with Lucy there was the big reality of what had landed her at the farm, and in my life. She never mentioned it, not once, but it remained on the front burner of my mind. Simmering there, always cooking to some degree, the fact that Lucy'd once done something bad enough to have her considered crazy. But try to put that aside in your mind, and in time you could, quite successfully. Shove it off into the corner with a good strong kick. And then it was very possible to have the best of times with her.

I was there as things changed. I was there every day of the five weeks over which Lucy's true personality surfaced like a bright bubble making its way up from the scary depths of a weedy canal. Strip away her story and you had just a girl, one made up of all the confusing flip-sided emotions that comprised a girl at that age. So shy she'd barely greet a guest, and then in a minute be babbling unstoppable even by her own brain, you could see her watching herself in horror, helpless as she gave away almost all of her most secret secrets. Marking off with a fat *X* the days on her calendar until she'd be leaving, but also wanting every one of them to last to the end of time and you knew this because she'd tell you so. Hair a mix of all the colors of the spectrum, a face that would never again be so perfect and flawless, a body molded by God's own hand on his best day, she could stare at herself adoringly, mesmerized for hours, but if she got caught in the wrong light she'd be running to her room feeling uglier than something from Pal's old poultry freak show. Petrified about truly growing up, but then she'd sneak the truck off to the drugstore to hunt for the equipment that might knock her out of the ballpark of childhood: Lee Press-On Nails. Sun-In. Jolene Cream Bleach. Nair. Barielle. Charlie. *Cosmo.* QT. FDS. Virginia Slims with free tennis-themed collectible holder.

I knew this because it was everything I was going through at the time. The flight and exposition, the self-love and automatic hate, loathing the minutes and waltzing happily with the slow day, searching fruitlessly for the one container of life-changing cream or goop or packet, all this shone back at me. A big gilt-edged mirror held up higher and straighter with each week that passed. So there was no way I could miss or ignore the truth. That looking at this crazy girl, clearly I was also seeing myself.

On a late afternoon, Lucy and I took one of our rides into the woods. She was on Pan, whose idea this was. I know this because Lucy told me it was: "Pan says we need to ride to the dead village." They did this a lot. Conversations, between girl and animal, only half of which I could hear. We'd be on the ponies, waiting for customers, I'd be reading a book or writing home and often enough she'd be seated on Pan, leaning forward and whispering in the pony's ear, waiting, then laughing at the space of silence that had to contain the reply.

Lucy believed she had a connection to Pan. Like Victory did. Only Lucy's and Pan's was different than Victory's and Pan's, which usually amounted to how it was going to rain despite there not being a wisp of a cloud to be seen, or wouldn't it be fun to just take off and go swimming right now? In Pan's conversations with Lucy, there was less frivolity. And due to what I knew about Lucy's past, the messages sometimes would give me a good shiver.

"What's that? Oh. Okay. Fine. Hey, Robyn, Pan here says you don't know."

"Don't know what?"

"You don't know, that's all. She says you don't know."

Lucy wasn't taunting me as it might sound—she simply was giving me the information. Like you'd relay a phone message that Wesley Elmer was going to start haying. Only this was the same thing I remember the murderer had said to Gordon Darnley.

"Fine. Okay."

"But you don't know."

"That's fine."

I'd continue with my reading or whatever, hoping to look normal, unfazed, wishing for a car to come by, or any distraction that would change the subject. Usually that wouldn't happen. But, just like that, their conversation would end and she'd start me guessing what Victory might come up with for supper and, if it wasn't what we were hoping, how could we talk her into that main course instead.

This day, Pan supposedly had suggested to Lucy that we ride into the woods, and that we travel farther than we'd ever been. It was her idea to head toward the dead village, but we never reached it. We did make it in very far, so far that we were in the middle of where they should have been around us, waving from behind trees, the visible souls of the disinterred and the disturbed. But on this day, for some reason, they were not. I know this because I do look for them, and I usually see them. Lucy stopped and asked me, "You see them anywhere? I want you to check." I stopped, and I stared into the trees that were filling the wide field of vision. Far away, a woodpecker was beating his face into a tree with the sound of a power tool. There was nothing else to note. I had to answer Lucy, "No, I don't. I don't." For the first time that I knew of in history, in all the years since the girl in line at the ring told me about them, they were absent. Somewhere else. Maybe vacationing.

"No," Lucy said after I nervously joked about that. "They weren't there in the first place. Don't believe every story you hear." Then, just like that, she clucked and nudged Pan, and, beneath me, Star naturally followed. And we all headed farther into the darkness, deeper into the woods that were on this day, just maybe as they always were, nothing but a plain old quiet beautiful sanctuary. I watched the back of Lucy as she led me into and through what long had scared me. End of the ride. We came back out again, nobody harmed, everybody fine, maybe even better than we were before we went in.

That night, just before bed, as Lucy and I were going up the stairs, I turned fast and hugged her. I wanted to do that in the very moment that I realized I had come to really like her. It was as basic as that. Something good and real and solid enough to put your touch on. And your arms around. I knew who she was—a real girlfriend. Which is just what I held that night on the stairs so late in June as moose-sized beetles threw themselves against the front screen, wanting the light that came from the front hall ceiling fixture, and from the two of us there on the stairs, a good surprise.

The previous summer, my annual trip to Mountain Park had switched from an afternoon with Frankie supervised by my aunt and uncle to a nighttime date without chaperones. This summer of Lucy, it became a double one—Frankie and me, and Lucy and Gumby. I was happy to see Lucy getting some attention from a boy, but at the same time I was aware he knew nothing about what he was getting into. Frankie'd been sworn to secrecy about the problems that had led Lucy to come live at the farm, and I wasn't going to be talking. The only source for information about Lucy would have to be Lucy. And all I ever heard her talk to Gumby about, over and over, was *Jaws,* which she'd seen with him when he picked her up in his father's Fury III and brought her to the Metro. She thought

Richard Dreyfuss was a dream, even with that beard, and she said so often. A classmate of Frankie's, Gumby worked at the dairy bar near Forest Lake and they followed up the movie with free sundaes that he made himself even though he had the night off.

"Gumby's just the kind of guy you could like," Lucy told me one day at the ring, "if he didn't have that huge head." And so I asked, "What kind of a guy do you want?" and she fired back, "Richard Dreyfuss." And then she said no, "Bruce Jenner." Then she said, "No, really," in a way that made me keep asking. She said, "Frankie." Then "Ha!" But I was well aware she wasn't kidding. I could like Lucy enough, but I didn't always like what she did.

I'd seen her stay busy at the front porch enough days right around quarter after four. Weeds hadn't a chance as she preened the gardens on either side of the steps, without being asked, and with her back to the driveway so she could easily be caught bending over in her microscopic hole-ridden cut-offs right when the milk truck came up. Just as she gave Frankie another view when we'd go to Snow's Pond and she'd jump from the rope swing and somehow a different half of her bikini would loosen and float away each time. I'd seen her follow Frankie up to the bar when we went to hear music at the Glass Crutch, the volume giving her a good excuse to have to lean in and put her whole mouth right in his middle ear just so he could hear her say, "Yeah, on second thought, order me one." I'd seen her at Mountain Park that night doing her best to fit next to him on the Scrambler, the Tilt-a-Whirl, in the stupid Futurama theater that showed a scratchy film predicting that we'd all be riding monorails to work and using microwaves and other modern conveniences we already were bored with. When we reached the Shipwreck, Lucy maneuvered to the point in line that would get her into Frankie's lifeboat, rather than that of Gumby. I watched them disappear into the dark, rocking and laughing. Next to me, in our lifeboat, Gumby was seeing this as a good thing, a welcome chance to grill me with, "So what does Lucy say about me when I'm not around?"

She and Frankie were one vessel ahead as lightning flashed and our boats narrowly avoided the floating debris, jagged rocks, and shark fin. While I told Gumby that Lucy thought he was very nice, that he was the kind of guy you could like, I watched Lucy jump with fake fright and land herself on Frankie when they veered around the dead man on the raft and Gumby saw, too, but he pointed and yelled to me, "You gotta love her!"

But I loved Frankie. And he was plainly in love with me. Sure, he was nice to her, maybe they even had their own kind of jousting, but he was mine, and I was his and we would be that long after this summer. Forever forever forever. I was the one to whom Frankie brought little bunches of yellow roses once they began blooming on the trellis in the garden at the side of his house. I was the recipient of the song requests he'd make each Tuesday night on WARE, sending anything from Bread's greatest hits from his telephone, to the station, to the clock radio next to my pillow. I was the one he whispered his dream plans to that night while we stood in line for both the little kids' and the giant rollercoasters, and for the Ferris wheel on which we rose to the top just as the sun was a big flaming Sunkist navel dipping down into the Connecticut River Valley. I was the one he took on the little train, where we claimed the last car and groped wildly for the duration of the slow dark tunnel that dripped water on you as you emerged, in need of the cooling down.

The four of us smashed bumper cars recklessly into total strangers, and each other. We all drank our quarters of a bottle of something pink and foul that Gumby bought off a man way in the darkest part of the picnic shelter. We all went off to hunt for more adventure when, hepped up and intent on getting his money's worth, Gumby grabbed Lucy and pulled her into the next building.

Before I could say a word, they'd disappeared inside the big open mouth of an enormous screaming head that wore as a hat an arched sign announcing "The Looney Bin." All around the head, all over the surface of the building, dark figures chased one another, eyes wild, arms outstretched. A loudspeaker asked, "Are you crazy enough to go inside? Remember—once admitted, you may never be released!" Then the voice launched into wild laughter that ran over a recording of wails and moans.

Imagine. I tried to be Lucy at that moment, being dragged through a place much too familiar and probably not her idea of fun. What would it do to me to be in there, reminded of all I'd gone through just so I could come up to New England and rest on a farm and as recreation come to an amusement park and be forced to enter a crazy house one more time. Frankie and I glanced edgily at each other. I grabbed the back of his shirt as we entered, calling out for the two of them but mostly going *owww owww owww* as we banged around the Labyrinth of Mirrors. Then Frankie was gone. Separated from me. I heard him, saw him, but when I reached out, I hit only my reflection.

"Over here!" He was yelling this but it was no help to me. His voice got farther away as I stumbled from the mirrors into a room lit only by the same color as our orange Christmas lightbulbs. A pair of boards moved one of my legs backward while the other was pushed forward. I hung onto a picky rope railing and made my way forward into a hall with a bowed floor that had me crashing into the walls. Overhead, speakers blasted pleas of the type that Gordon Darnley once mimicked: "Let me out! It's all a mistake! Don't leave me here to die!" I imagined the ape people approaching, and that got me rushing ahead, coming to a fork, and quickly picking the hallway to the left because it was illuminated in blacklight, which I was fond of at the time. I ran now, glowing in the dark, petrified, blinded by plastic fringes hanging from the ceiling, jolted by blasts of air being shot from the walls. "Let me out! I'm not crazy!" The voices were sounding real now. And real close. I called for Frankie. For Gumby. For Lucy. Unable to see a thing, I pushed my arms out. I felt my way along as the floor lowered and rose mechanically, and as the arms grabbed me from behind.

"Goddammit this place is fun!"

She loved it.

Absolutely loved it.

I knew who Lucy was. It's just that sometimes, I didn't. But when I did, the times it was clear that she was my friend, we could have been photographed for an ad that maybe my father's phone company would run—Lucy and me at age seventeen, at the ring, at our day of half-work half-goofing, she's asking me who she is and I'm telling her. Not so much giving her the name of the neighbor she's imitating, but telling her that I know she's somebody I'll always have as a friend. And then maybe thirty years later, we're on the line to one another, adults and mothers and businesswomen of some form, catching up, reflecting on our old times, maybe there is a slow-motion film of us riding over the fields, the announcer telling everybody that ponies live forever, and so can your friendship with your original real girlfriend. Just pick up the telephone.

People all over the country would be weeping helplessly, and then dialing information. Giving the operator names not spoken for decades, hopefully still living in the last place listed in an old address book. Please let them still be there. Please.

Me, I'd always know exactly where Lucy was. Through the years I would—this is what I thought back then. Because I thought we'd get and remain close. Frankie and I would have a bunch of kids, Lucy would be the eccentric aunt they would hate to see leave after she made one of her unannounced visits, wearing a big straw hat and flea-market shawl and jewelry box worth of beads, telling stories of her latest adventure as beautician on a movie set or some other glamorous profession. The kids would adore Lucy. So electrified and untethered and miles from predictable, she would be their favorite—that much would be clear, and that all would be fine. Because I'd know just how they felt.

In late July, after a trip of half a billion miles and eleven months, the Viking robot set down on Mars and sent back photographs of a rocky plain. It was the first successful landing on that planet. Signs of life were sought. There was a big exploration. I was on my own mission in a place just as mysterious and uncharted. The hidden world of Lucy.

I have to say that I really never did mean to start anything by following her. It's just that the temptation grew stronger every night I spotted her heading off into the dark.

I'd sit at the window and watch her form disappear, but I'd hang back. No, I couldn't, I shouldn't, it's none of my business. And, really, what she's doing is what a lot of people do—they go for walks. Although most of these people stick to the sidewalk. During daylight. While Lucy, she opted for the fields, and then the woods. Way, way past the time when she should have been asleep.

Once I became aware of this habit, a couple weeks into her being at the farm, watching her leave all those nights and not going after her was very much like standing on the beach and hemming and hawing about whether or not you're going to jump into the ocean. You've driven two hours and fought for a space in the parking lot, carried all your many necessities across scorching sand, pulled your clothing off in front of dozens of complete strangers, walked to the water, and there it is, right in front of you, but you're not certain if you'll even stick a toe in. The waves are freezing, sure, turning your feet blue, but sooner or later you realize you're going to throw yourself right into it.

Long into the hour I normally would have been deep in a dream, watching Frankie extend his hand lovingly toward me from gondola or hot air balloon or featherbed, I lay fidgeting and awake, clothed and shod, waiting for the eerie sound of the only crack in the dead quiet in which the farm was suspended each night. There it was, followed by a jolt that started in my heart and flew up to grab my throat: Lucy's door opening, then closing behind her. The soft fall of her feet on every other stair. One, three, five, seven, nine, eleven, floor. Then the tidy snap of the screen that all summer served as the front door.

I peeked from my back window as she started across the lawn and made an easy, careful arc around from the kitchen garden and, more to the point, well away from the back porch where Pal slept in his odd fashion, back of his head flat on his cot, pillow full over his face.

Finally, it was my turn to leave. My bedroom door came open and went closed without a sound, thanks to the drops of WD-40 that, in admirable preparation, I'd liberally applied a couple days earlier. I began the stairs, timing each double step to the loudest parts of Victory's big breathings, the last audible one allowing me onto the porch and Lucy's trail. I was frightened but confident. In my favor was my great knowledge of the property. Exactly where the outbuildings stood, where paths led, the location of most of the rocks and rises, junk heaps and fences. Fall to spring back in Illinois, I traced them in my mind when unable to sleep. There was a comfort found in their permanent locations, their solid footholds, the life they housed or restrained. Nineteen steps from wellhouse to coop, forty-seven from barn to ring, sixty-three from ring to house and the porch Frankie visited every afternoon. Thirteen steps up to my room. Three and a half strides to my doorsill, remember to set right foot first into the room for good luck. One more to the small, cool twin bed I'd just left. I always thought that I could find my way around the farm blindfolded. If nothing else, this night would be my biggest test.

Lucy had started off at her usual time, just as the most serious level of dark was arriving and the sudden depth of it was a new degree of black that made it hard to believe you could be moving along safely, without tripping or falling into a hole or crack that suddenly had opened into the earth. Even the air was a dark gray. Yes, you can give a color to something that is invisible. I know this because I saw it there in front of me. Walking through it was like working your way through smoke, or if you have the kind of eyes Victory used to tell me her crowd was starting to get, which Vaselined the center of an older person's vision and left clear only the edges, as if you unfortunately could only make out the frame of a painting, and not the work of art itself. The shapes of the trees and the path were visible only if you were looking just to the right or left of them.

Up and off to the side I could see the form that was Lucy, way ahead. Her white T-shirt was my guide. I'd been smart enough to wear spy-black, a tip taken from movies, which would make me much harder to spot. I also stayed behind as she progressed along the edge of the field, to the right-hand-side along the stone wall where dangerous snakes are known to sun. She continued to the corner where she would have gone right on, straight into the scary woods, had she not cut to the right sharply. I knew there was a path there, as it was the one I used whenever I thought I might be brave enough to pay a visit to the dead village. The path Lucy took strung along a little wet rut that fed into a small swampy area, where a few dead trees jabbed up from a green muck that grew thicker and more emerald the warmer the season got. Frogs congregated there, some of them loud bulls you could hear all the way over at the house.

I waited until she disappeared past them and then I ran through the field and caught up—but not quite up. I had to concentrate to follow her, watching the feet that were sometimes hard to see. I sneaked along on my trail, my heart making more noise than any other moving part of me. But not once did Lucy investigate. Wherever she was going, she was intent on her destination. Concentrating. There already, it seemed, before she came close to actually arriving.

The path ran out at the dead end of Fisherdick Road. Mary Ellen Watson lived out there, as did her sister, Margaret, and their parents. I was right in the middle of the girls' two ages, and, depending on my mood, I preferred the company of one or the other. Over the summers, once a week or so, they'd ride their banana bikes through the woods and over the field, and would keep me company at the ring. Their parents successfully had taught them to be afraid of all animals, so they had no designs on my job or any ache to lead a pony back to their own yard. They just liked to come and see me as there was really little else to do. Once there, they'd lean against a maple, well out of harm's way. Mary Ellen, the older sister, took piano lessons on Monday afternoons, including all summer, and she practiced for a full hour every day, without even being ordered to, which told you right there that she was serious about it. And a lot of the time when she wasn't talking to you she'd be playing away on whatever surface was in front of her—a board on the fence, a table, her leg, even the air. Not knowing much about music, I can't say if she was anywhere near truly talented. But I was impressed by this thing that seemed to be second nature, and that held her fascination on a level I could compare only to my interest in the ponies. Margaret, the younger one, liked to talk. Loudly and with great expression, endless stories of people she and Mary Ellen went to school with, so descriptive that I ended up believing that I, too, had been there in her fifth-grade classroom the day a frantically misguided stray cat fell through the decaying ceiling tiles right onto the head of the girl who sat in front of her.

Behind Margaret, as always, Mary Ellen played her fingers on her leg, as if accompanying her sister's retelling of such incidents, or her general orations, like the one she'd given Lucy and me the week before, all about her displeasure with the family's choice of summer vacation destination—Misquamicut rather than Old Orchard. The ocean up at Old Orchard is so cold, yeah, but, according to Margaret, there are too many weeds down at Misquamicut, deadly ones the length and strength of which can wrap around your legs and pull you under. What kind of parents would take their kids to a dangerous place like that? She had no intention of going. None at all.

Wherever they ended up, the Watsons wouldn't be leaving until the last week of August. They were home now, including Mary Ellen safely back from her first year off studying music education all the way up at the University of Vermont at Burlington. Mary Ellen right now most likely was in her canopy bed in the butter-yellow room she shared with Margaret at the back of the house, her parents in the one adjoining with its fancy headboard that was actually a very cool series of shelves onto which they placed books and magazines and family photos and a digital clock. This was the house Lucy was now coming up to, the stucco cottage to the right once you came out of the woods and stepped onto the ratty edges where the tar ended in cracks that disappeared into sand that sprouted with weeds then was covered with unkempt grasses then enthusiastic vines and prickly bushes and finally the many big stately trees that made up the woods beyond.

Lucy being headed this way, I was thinking maybe she somehow knew the sisters better than I imagined she did just from their few visits to the ring since her arrival. Maybe there was a secret late-starting sleepover that nobody told me about. Maybe Lucy'd been invited. Lucy only. I watched from behind a clump of birches. There she went, but fast and right past the Watson's place, no party, taking a right onto the lawn just after the neighboring house, a neat white ranch owned by the old man who every Saturday mopped his driveway from a pail of kitchen floor cleaner. He used Lestoil. We knew this because we'd seen the bottle, but we called him Mr. Clean just because he used any soap at all where you regularly drove a car. I traced Lucy's steps, crouching low as I passed the Watsons' big front window and I spotted Mr. Watson sleeping peacefully in his big television chair, wearing those weird short-legged summer pajamas some fathers are known to put on, all of him illuminated by the glow of the test pattern. Across the street, the Bertrands' overweight spaniel barked weakly from its shed under an apple tree—*"iff iff iff iff!"*—like it couldn't be bothered and did not waste the energy to even come out and see what or who I was. Even so, I flew fast across Mr. Clean's flawless front lawn, and veered in just before that of the Coburns, who hated kids except for on Halloween, when I unfortunately already was back in Illinois and when, in a good-will effort to prevent damage to their home, they set at their curb a card table heaping with full-size brand-name candy bars. I was told that they'd make up a big sign instructing "Help Yourself Please!"

At the neat row of square-cut yews marking the line between their and Mr. Clean's property, I stopped dead. Mr. Coburn, out very late, was just finishing up burning his trash in a big barrel next to the garage. I watched him poke at the contents with an old ski pole. Little scraps of embers flew skyward with every stab. Smoke puffed defeatedly from the opening as I waited for him to go back inside, which he did only after flicking his cigarette into the ashes and looking up to inspect the sky for what seemed like two years. I waited until I heard his back door shut and I tiptoed toward the woods. A trail back to the farm looped through there. Having lost sight of Lucy, I'd follow it home.

I was passing the Coburns' vegetable garden when I spotted her. It was only a fluke that I'd even turned. I just couldn't help

but admire the design of their plantings. This wasn't your typical big rectangle, like most people plow and plant in their back-
yards. This was a circle. With things growing in wedges, kind
of a big pizza. Triangles containing things you could eat—pep-
pers, beans, radishes—alternating with full sections of those I
didn't think you could—begonias, petunias, bachelor's buttons.
A circle of corn in the middle shot to the heavens like a foun-
tain. I looked down the section containing the hairy greenery of
carrots, and there in the distance: Lucy. Way in the next yard
over. Up in a tree—some kind of a small thing, like a pear or a
plum, a type that would be easy to get up into without the use
of a ladder or the flat of someone's back. There she was. Five
or six feet off the ground. Sitting and staring. At the house.

I didn't know whose it was. Sometime between last September and now, it had sprouted from the empty lot on the other
side of the Coburns', taking up much of the space in which
wild blueberries could be picked each summer if you wanted to
take the time and tie a bucket to your belt and stand in the sun
for how long it took to fill it. Spared were the couple of fruit
trees farther back, and that's where I headed, crossing the yard
and moving far behind Lucy. Behind another tree. To quietly
climb up a branch or two and crane my neck to see what she
was seeing. Which was only this: a small window—two actually—a pair of them set close together and framed with lacy
white curtains tied back all billowy at each side like this was a
stage and they'd been parted to allow the audience to view a
play. Beyond the curtains wasn't much—a little room with just a
single light burning, a tiny lamp on a high table set at the end
of a delicate crib over which a man and a woman stood doing
their own staring. Downward. Happily. Into whatever was resting before them. And if you took a few more steps up, which I

did as slowly and quietly as I could so as to not get noticed by either them or Lucy, you were able to see what it was. And that was a baby.

Just a baby. Regular in size, as babies go, and wearing what pretty much all of them seem to, a little one-piece outfit, this one sherbet green with the openings for its arms and legs cut short. I could see a small yellow blanket being pulled up to its middle and tucked in neatly around the margins of the little bean-shaped body. I could hear the parents cooing something that started out like words but got strung into a little song so nice you'd like to know it.

As odd as it was to have made the night trek all the way over here at this hour, and to be hiding at all, there was something pleasant about standing in the cool dark listening to these two people singing without accompaniment, without embarrassment. If I were that baby, I knew I would have been very pleased and happy and, even though I only had maybe a month or two of experience in being alive, I would somehow know that probably no baby, or person of any age in the world, had it better or nicer. At that point in my life, what would I know other than what was right in front of me—these two familiar people and their voices heard long before I'd ever laid eyes on them. The bars of my crib made up the world right then. I would not yet know anything of the space beyond that—not the pink-carpeted one between the spindly legs of the crib and the daisy-papered wall of the nursery, not the stretch between the wall's new set of weathertight windows and the trunk of the nearest tree, certainly not the curious world between the bottom of that trunk and the big branch above, on which a stranger-girl sat, staring in at me, a baby who, really, could have nothing to do with anything.

Lucy kept going back there.

And I kept following her.

Just about every other night or two or three she took her walk to the baby's window. And the next morning she'd come down to breakfast, or beat me to the kitchen, all fine, rested, refreshed, ready to go and do whatever it was that my uncle or aunt suggested. We'd go about our day, she in her own content orbit, me trying to act like I didn't know yet another secret about her. She'd pour herself an elaborate pancake in the shape of eyeglasses, then put that on her face and await our reaction when we finally looked up from our own plates. And, if you weren't expecting such a thing, it was funny enough.

"High spirits this morning," Victory would say, and Pal would look at her and agree with his, "You betcha."

*"Młodzież odwiedziny sa nazbyt krotkie"*–"Youth's visit is too short," he would lament, his all gone. I wondered if any of life got easier to understand during the longer visit of old age. I'd ask that of him another time.

"So let's go enjoy it," Lucy would say, and she'd yank me from my chair and over to the sink and she'd shoot way too much Joy into the sink and everything we washed would get very, very clean.

## · 9 ·

A rainy night was the one on which this happened. Soft rain like a steady breath. It made a nice and constant lulling sound, which was why I must have kept sleeping all through Lucy's sneaking down the stairs, across the field, along the path in the woods, out to Fisherdick Road, through the space between Mr. Clean's and the Coburns', over to the tree, and past that, to the window, which was open a bit to the lovely moist air, and also to any arms that might come through, as they did that night, to take little Amy Sutton away.

I remember waking to the scratchy sounds that come from a two-way radio, thinking the noise was birds squawking, or maybe one of the chickens had gotten loose and was out there rooting around down beneath my window. But it was numbers that were being pronounced clearly. Two-fifteen and six-eleven, ten and four and over and out. Often enough I'd watched the handsome and American-Indian-blooded, fantastically named Randolph Mantooth on *Adam-12*. And, thanks to him, I knew the sound of police talk even when I was half asleep.

I tripped from bed and down the stairs. On the porch, Victory and Pal were standing with a uniformed officer who was poised to jot something on a skinny pad of paper like he was a waitress down at Friendly's marking down their requests for medium-rare Big Beefs and a couple of strawberry Fribbles.

"No," Victory was telling him. "We've seen no one odd. Though we have lots and lots of people stop here, so I really can't say that is true about every single one of them—that I would know how they're odd from just looking at them . . ."

"You take in boarders," the policeman said, and he aimed his jaw down at the chain of signs, to which my uncle just yesterday had added "Old License Plates" because he'd looked around the barn last week and realized he had a bunch of them and somebody out there certainly had to be a collector, you'd think. Despite Lucy being with us two months already, "Nice Clean Room for Rent" remained there, between "Brown Eggs" and "Black Angus," basically because Pal felt if somebody did come along, the additional money would of course be nice for old age. He could always give the porch to the boarder and move himself off to the little musty cot he kept in the barn for when an animal was sick and he wanted to be nearby.

"Yes, normally we have boarders in the summer," Victory was telling the policeman, "but we've only a friend here this summer—a young girl, and another, who's my granddaughter, who stays with us each year. We've had adults, but not since last summer. And even then, nobody you'd stop and think twice about." She stopped and looked like she was doing exactly that. Then she concluded, "No, nobody like you're looking for."

"Uh-huh," the policeman said, and that's when he noticed me in the hall. I hid behind the door just because I had very little clothing on and he was a strange man, here on my porch.

"Anything you can add, please call me," he said to Victory and Uncle Pal.

"Okay, Officer Melley," my uncle answered, to show that he'd been paying attention to the degree that he remembered the guy's name without having to look down at his badge.

"Okay, Mr. Panek," said Officer Melley, and he nodded, but at me.

This made Victory spin toward the door and these had to be something like the words that flew from her—"Oh, Robyn, a baby's been taken! From right over there on Fisherdick Road!"—but I'm afraid I can't give them to you exactly because all that was coming across in the space between her lips and my ear was a full-color picture. Of Lucy. In a tree in a yard on Fisherdick Road. Looking into the house. At an infant.

I was still in the front hall, but the rest of me was suddenly bounding up the staircase. Somehow it had tripled in length since I'd come down, and it took me ages to reach the top and make the giant step over to Lucy's door. Just before I put my hand on the knob, I stopped. Nah, it couldn't be. She just likes walks. And peeking around. And maybe spying. That's all. Nothing I hadn't done to the Scercers next to us back in Illinois—nothing wrong with that. I tapped on the center of the door. Again. Louder. Again. She was just gone out for a walk. Louder. She was in the barn. Again. She was in the woods. Louder. I turned the knob a fraction and it was like starting the ignition of the engine powering something bad and unstoppable. Inside the room there were no sneakers at the edge of the braided rug. No Illinios sweatshirt folded and draped over the footboard. No jeans awaiting her on the chair. Lucy always kept everything neat, probably something they demanded of you in the crazy house. Order all around you, even if there is none inside you. My eyes jumped around the room that, except for the unmade bed, was as tidy and as empty as one in a decorating magazine. There was no Lucy anywhere.

"She's in the tub." I said this out loud, to only myself, and I flew down the stairs like I've done for years when in a hurry, grabbing both railings, swinging myself down to the fourth, then the eighth, then the short hop onto the climbing roses covering the half-circle hooked rug for which Victory once had won an impressive red second-place ribbon at the Big E but still came home and put the thing on the floor because that's where a rug belongs after all. I made the corner fast and flew into the kitchen, where the hall phone cord was stretched tight, Victory simultaneously whisking eggs over at the table and relaying the startling news to Mrs. Chichon, gasping, "Imagine!" as she walked past the open door of the empty bath and then covered the receiver so she could whisper to me, "Robyn! Go back upstairs, would you, and tell Lucy to rise and shine."

The search wasn't of the proportions of what you see nowadays, no thousands of participants, nothing televised instantly and almost from the exact point at which you realize there is the biggest of problems happening right there in your own home. That the girl who is staying with you, the one you were wary of who then won you over, who got you to drop your guard and fall into a good time, well, you were right in the first place—she was crazy all along, because look what she's gone and done now.

Then came the small-town manhunt—or a combination girl-hunt and baby-hunt in this case. Everything started quickly after I stared into that empty bathroom so long, right through to the mismatched hand towels Victory had made look a bit more related with the addition of bright blue crocheted edges, untouched yet by any boarder girl. I was looking at that sight with such fear that Victory put the phone to her shoulder a second and asked me what was wrong. "Is it the baby, dear? Don't worry, I'm sure everything will be cleared up soon, it's probably just the husband taking her for a walk without telling his wife." And I said, no, it wasn't that at all, and I can't remember much in the space between that and the cluster of cruisers appearing at our front door, two more joining Officer Melley's this time, four officers in all, I didn't know the town had that many, they were surrounding me as I sat in my usual back-to-the-porch-window seat at the kitchen table and stared down into the glass of water Pal had brought me. And I was thinking, thinking about anything else—a rich classmate with the gorgeous heated pool attached to her house and how I'd gone over there to swim in February, if you could believe it, and how that whole family pronounced *chlorine* like it rhymed with *fine*—chlor-ine—I was focusing on anything other than what I had to do right then, getting all caught up in how the water, and the glass that contained it, magnified the many golden flecks in the white Formica below. And then, because one of the officers spoke up and asked, and another said, yes, please start anywhere, and because the last voice on top of that was from Victory right next to me, I told them all what I'd told no one at all, not even Frankie—the story of Lucy's walks at night, and how I followed, and where she ended up, and what she looked at and what I'd seen, and, considering her history and the occurrence that had brought her to us, what I thought had to have happened here.

And that's when Victory added a whole part I knew nothing about, one that underlined how it made perfect sense for Lucy to have Amy Sutton.

Because someone once had taken her own baby.

"That's why she came here—she came here because she was disturbed. She was disturbed because there'd been a baby. She'd had a baby. And then she gave it up. That's what made her disturbed."

Victory walked us awkwardly backward along the major stepping stones of Lucy's rough travels over the past year. I scrambled to keep up, but slipped into the shockingly icy water between each rock. The policemen leaned in. Officer Melley and one other one scribbled on their pads. Pal, standing in back of me, settled his hands on my shoulders. The fact pin-balled around the insides of my head: There'd been a baby.

A baby.

This I had heard of. Not just people having them, of course, but about this happening to girls my age. In those days you knew about it instantly, practically before the couple had climbed back to the front seat or emerged from the coveted parent bedroom at an unauthorized house party. This was in the years before school systems installed condom vending machines next to hand towel dispensers, offered daycare programs for their students' offspring, won awards for the high quality of the fathering class being offered as prerequisite to college. A few of the wilder girls got in trouble, and I'd known who these girls were in my school because my neighbor Leslie worked at the town pharmacy and regularly handed out neat little pink plastic purses of birth control pills. If they said anything other than thanks to Leslie when she gave them their change and receipt and stapled-shut paper bag, it was the unrequested explanation of how these had been prescribed to battle acne, conveniently another use. One of them, who got excused from phys ed just because she was a majorette, would wink at Leslie, brazenly, like, "See what I'm up to and you're not?" That's how Leslie read it, at least. I'd walk past the majorette, past the rest of these girls in the hall, and I'd scan them quickly, wondering if, had I not known, just in passing would I be able to tell they were already actually doing it.

Of course I couldn't. They looked like, well, pretty much, the next girl. Or like Gay or Deborah or me. Or, probably, like the infamous girl in the next town, who Leslie swears she never saw picking up a single prescription at her counter. This girl had been her class valedictorian, no less—and had gone out and gotten pregnant and missed out on the last half of the senior year. No prom for her. No skip day. No rehearsals. No graduation ceremony. No walking to the podium and delivering a well-practiced speech aimed at sending her classmates hopefully and fearlessly into their scary, unknown futures.

I didn't know the girl's name, but she was brought up so frequently she might as well have been family. Before each and every date or general outing in the two high school years that followed the news from the next town, my mother would appear at my bedroom door to wish me a good time and tell me I looked lovely and then switch gears and solemnly warn me to behave myself, "Or you'll end up like that girl over in Buford. A valedictorian, no less. How her parents must feel. . . ."

My belief, as I stood at my dresser and clamped the curling iron to shape yet another face-flattering Farrah-like tendril, was that would never happen to me. I knew better. I had taken the required sex education course, and aced the tests that asked you to label the anatomy of not only the familiar females but the mysterious males as well. I even scored better than Bethany Fowler, whose mother is the school nurse, yet when she spotted the chart of man parts among Bethany's homework papers, she smiled and told her daughter, "Oh, I remember back when we were studying the ear . . ."

The biggest reason I knew it would never happen: I was a thousand miles from my boyfriend for all but three months a year. I had only a quarter of the year to be concerned about making the mistakes most girls my age were making every Friday and Saturday night. Maybe I wasn't as smart as the valedictorian, but I did know that I easily could end up being just like her in at least one way.

"Was she a valedictorian?"

The police turned to me when I asked this. Victory did, too. "You don't have to be a valedictorian to have a baby. Lucy was a regular girl—she is a regular girl. She got in trouble with a boy. That happened, she had to give the baby up. For adoption. Somebody else will do the raising, be the parents. She doesn't have the baby anymore."

I thought how that decision should have made Lucy happy. I mean, everything would be over and done with and you could go back to your regular life and plans. I'd heard how the valedictorian had hung on to her baby. As I understood it, she sat around with it all day, then handed it off to her mother at night, so she could start a few courses at the community college. While you might think this was admirable, it was also kind of sad. Because she'd been headed off to pre-law at Yale, and now she was spending her evenings sitting next to all the kids from her high school class who had been too dumb to get into any other school.

Victory looked at me and shrugged. "Her grandmother says she did seem fine at first. But, in time, I think if you don't address your feelings, events can affect you."

"This grandmother—we need the name," one cop said. Pal gave it: Anzia Dragon, and the phone number on the list tacked inside the utility closet door. In the next half of a breath he said to me, "You never asked her? You never said 'Lucy, what are you doing, taking these walks? Why are you staring into that window?'" His voice was just the carrier of these words, not a bat to beat me. He was almost businesslike, asking more questions than the policemen were, they with their caps off and their serious looks and their shining nameplates that jumped me to our game, one of them being a Borucki, as in Delka Borucki, who maybe was his mother but definitely was one of the people Lucy was very adept at imitating, in this case no big feat, just the way she said "stomp" instead of "stamp" when you paid a visit to her little barred window down at the p.o.

"You never asked her?" Officer Melley echoed my uncle.

"I, I was afraid to." Victory put her hand on my shoulder, on top of Pal's, and the next thing I knew I was hearing her make a picture of Lucy from a pile of adjectives. "Seventeen. Skinny. Tall. Like him"—here she pointed to the youngest-looking officer over by the refrigerator. "Black hair, long. Straight, though she has been known to wear it up. Skinny, did I say that? Dresses mod, you know, like kids today do. Beads, accessories like that."

I'd never heard the word *mod* come out of Victory. But things were going to get a whole lot weirder than that on this day. Slobbering police dogs sticking their big faces into a T-shirt of Lucy's that Victory had pulled from the hamper, as requested, because it is only dirty clothes, rather than the clean ones she would have preferred to offer, that hold a missing person's scent. Uniformed men, and a couple of women even, walking methodically around the farmyard, scaring the animals when they weren't stopping to investigate all the sheds and barn hideouts that Pal and Victory and I had already gone into a couple of times before my uncle went over to the telephone and dialed zero and solemnly asked for the police. Amy's young father in the kitchen garden like an apparition, not behind window glass, or singing, or smiling, as I was used to seeing him, his big shoes crushing down one then two borage plants as he advanced, as white-hot angry as you could imagine anybody in his situation being, shouting awful things and waving his arms wildly at Pal. His wife—Amy's mother—off to the side, her elbows supported by two women who in appearance looked like sisters of this caving-in woman watching all the sad commotion with a big hanky pressed to her mouth. Victory on the phone dialing Lucy's grandmother. Pal and I on Star and Chester, moving slowly along the girl's favorite path, the one that headed toward the dead village, yelling LUCY LUCY LUCY and hearing only the same thing back from the gloomy black hollow that was the rest of the wilderness. People from Fisherdick Road walking through the field and into the brush, linking hands to form a chain when they could, calling AMY AMY AMY, like a three-month-old baby was going to pipe up from some hiding place behind a rock and yell, "I'm over here!" In and around all this, cars coming up the drive. Safe, problem-free kids greedy for a ride, their parents so curious to know why the ring was empty, aren't you open today, what's the matter, I never heard of you being closed, ever. One TV news van that Victory chased away by helpfully directing it over to Fisherdick Road. And then, finally, just before the supper none of us were the least bit hungry for—the milk truck bearing Frankie.

I threw myself into the white salvation that was his uniform. My tears threatened the multi-colored stitching that spelled out "Day 'n Night Dairy" and then, below that, the name of the boy whose arms came around me slowly, embarrassed, you'd have to forgive him, to have this great display going on in public. I parted from him and he came into focus through the wet blur. He looked sad and beat. I had called him first thing, but there'd been no answer. I wanted to tell him everything, including whatever was my part. Obviously by now he'd heard about the little baby. And Lucy's whole story.

"Can you believe it?" I asked this, and Frankie shook his head. He couldn't, he told me slowly and just above a whisper. He truly couldn't believe it. I knew he delivered over to the Sutton house. Probably some of the Day 'n Night Farms dairy products had been fed to the same baby. Something like that has to connect you deeper to a tragedy like this one. And I acknowledged this in my head.

"Lucy was walking over there," I said. "To the baby's house. At night. A lot." He looked at me blankly. I'd never told him any of this. Maybe I should have. But all those nights of following Lucy in the dark, I'd felt hypnotized, or numb on something from Paula Whitman's big sister's pocketbook. It was like all this really wasn't happening, even as it was. Telling somebody, saying it out loud, that would have made her walks more real than they already were. And I wanted it to be a dream. I wanted to believe Lucy was fine. Normal, like a real girlfriend would be. Not somebody who sat in trees and stared into stranger's homes. "I'd follow her. I saw her staring in at that baby a dozen times. I never said anything. I should have. But I wanted it to be just a walk. . . ."

I said all this in bits, but fast. Frankie cut me off with a *shhhh,* but he didn't drag it out as long as I would have liked the consolation to go on for, so I pressed myself to the place just in front of his left ear, where I knew he liked to put his Hai Karate even though he wasn't supposed to wear a scent on a workday because who wants their butter smelling like Saturday night? Frankie wasn't doing much to help me. But I understood all that. The year before, I had attended the wake of Kevin Powers's old grandmother, which was indeed a death and certainly something that was a big deal. Yet the way he acted in the receiving line, it was like nothing at all had happened. As I hugged him with true sympathy or empathy or whatever word it is—I'd never known a grandparent, alive or dead, but felt it had to be a big loss—he asked did I want to sneak out and go to Burger King because he was gonna starve pretty soon. And then did I want to go on over to his friend Brad's house and see his new used bass guitar that was supposed to once have been owned by the brother of Robert Plant.

"Boys are like that. They are not as sensitive as we girls."

My mother, a girl too, explained this to me when I got back from the wake and I told her what Kevin had wanted me to do, proposing all this carefree activity just about three feet from his freshly dead grandmother, who certainly deserved some grief, or, at the least, the effort of faking a sad expression. "Don't expect them to get all weepy over every little thing." She'd added, "Or even big things." So I guess I understood and didn't feel that bad when Frankie let go of me and crossed his arms and said, "Uh, Robyn, I have to get going, Fred and Midgie are up at Hampton Beach this week. I'm up to my neck in work."

"Sure," I said. I remembered him telling us a couple weeks back about their vacation. Suggesting that maybe Lucy and I and he and Gumby could go up to the beach for a quick and free-of-charge overnight. Fred and Midgie were staying right on K Street, in a nice spacious place with a spare room and no other visitors coming. Lucy had said, "Wow!" to Frankie and told him she had a new bikini all ready. Frankie had looked helpless and said, "That's good, Gumby will be happy," and Lucy had rolled her eyes. When I want to remember things second by second, I am pretty good at it. I remember all that. Yes, he'd asked us. But now he was too busy, which happens in the kind of work he did.

If I were ever to become a farmer's wife, I had to get used to things like this. You couldn't drop everything just because there was a tragedy. Cows needed to be fed, milked, have whatever else was necessary done to them. We had cattle, ponies, goats, chickens, rabbits, to some degree it was the same story with them. I understood. I said, "Go," and that's what Frankie did, giving me a sad half smile and leaving me there on the drive-way just as a big long helicopter with "STATE POLICE" written across its belly flew low and loudly up over the rise and over my head. Over the farm, in the direction of the reservoir.

I had to stay and do what I could to assist in fixing the whole mess. I helped Pal tack up the four biggest ponies for any vol-unteer searchers who wanted to take them into other parts of the woods just before dark, and we watched three somber neighborhood ladies and one man head off, their feet almost scraping the ground. Late into the night I helped Victory make meals and snacks for the rest of those who were pitching in. They were using the Watsons' house as their headquarters. The Suttons' place down the street was off-limits to everyone but close family and law enforcement, that was what Margaret told me when her father drove her over to pick up the trays of deviled eggs and tubs of egg salad that Victory had phoned them to offer.

"Oh my God, to think that I actually knew her," Margaret whispered as we carried the food down the front steps. Her eyes were cartoony big. She was getting a kick out of this, even though she was trying to appear scared. "I'm trying to remember everything she ever said to me, and you know, I do remember her saying she liked kids. I asked her if she liked kids, and she said to me, yeah, I like kids. See? I should have known that something like this would happen. To think I knew somebody who would do this thing, go and steal a little baby! Ooooh!"– here she shivered from it all–"It really kind of gives you the creeps."

I didn't say anything. Not a word of what I was thinking– how Margaret hadn't known Lucy at all, at least not in the way you'd properly define the word. She and Mary Ellen had met her. Had gone to the Eastfield Mall with us once, and we'd picked them up in the truck a couple times when we went to Snow's for fries and then on to Howard's for clam plates and to Jeannine's for soft serve on the way home. Lucy had been there at the ring when the sisters came over and made their weekly visits to me. But she and they had talked about movies, television, music, calories, the layered look, a whole raft of stuff that doesn't really mean anything when you look back at it. They'd swapped issues of *Seventeen* and *Ingenue* and one of *Glamour* that showed Christie Brinkley photographed in a bubble bath with her French boyfriend. They'd talked and laughed about such things. But who Lucy was—and I mean the reality of how she kept going despite not too long ago wanting to stop for good—never even got approached. Margaret didn't know an original true thing about my friend. But she thought she did.

"Well, doesn't it?" Margaret was bugging me to answer her as she slid the trays of eggs onto the vinyl seats of her father's company car. "Doesn't it all make you feel weird?"

Victory said to me after I came back into the kitchen, "Go to bed."

Pal sat at the table with Wesley Elmer, who had a loud-speaker on the roof of his station wagon and regularly was hired out by businesses having sales and politicians seeking votes. He'd drive around town and recite propaganda into his microphone, not a bad job as long as you didn't care about what you were being paid to say. That day he'd been covering every back road he knew, sending AMY AMY AMY LUCY LUCY LUCY COME BACK COME BACK HOME RIGHT NOW PLEASE into his microphone, loudly, and often, out to the wild. Victory had made him hot lemongrass tea for his throat because even if you are using a microphone, if you talk long and hard enough, you're going to feel it. At least that's what Wesley had told her right before he asked for something stronger if she had it. Both he and Pal were tired from the day, nothing left in them but the ability to stare with exaggerated fascination as Victory sponged clean the table top that had been spotless before she began.

"I'm sorry," I blurted, and Victory knew where it was coming from even though it was out of nowhere. She said back as automatically: "You don't have to be." She pointed out that I wasn't even supposed to have known that Lucy had problems. And that once I found out, through no fault of my own, I was encouraged to treat her like I would had I never heard Victory and Mrs. Chichon that day. I had been told not to regard any little odd act or word as a sign she was anything less than a regular, normal girl. "Even if she walked in the dark," Pal threw in his two cents, "well, really, some people do that. How were you to know where it would lead? You didn't know about the baby, so the one she was looking at meant nothing to you in all this. If there's any fault, it falls on our shoulders. We opened our home to her, at the same time knowing her background. But, you know, we really did want to give her the benefit of the doubt."

He looked down at the floor after he said this, and Victory and Wesley Elmer did the same. So that's what I did, too, and as we hung our heads the room fell silent except for the soft animal-toe clicking of the second hand on the stove's clock, and the faraway voices streaming way out in the woods and along the field edges, still calling the name I hadn't known before this day, but would not forget after it.

I phoned the dairy again. No answer again. I pictured Frankie still in the barn, lights on, radio loud, lost in fixing some pump or line or other one of the many things that regularly seems to break over there. Pal always said beef was the way to go. No daily tending, he'd point out, just look at Fred's day, and his own day. Compare. Whose would you prefer? I'd answer, "Fred's," because Fred got to live in the same house as Frankie, and Pal would know what I meant and he'd snarl good-naturedly and throw something at me and never come close to hitting. Tonight he was nowhere near a light mood. He sat there with Wesley Elmer, didn't even look up when I said a quiet good night. As I cleared the top stair, something pulled me left. I entered the bedroom that once had been Pal's and now was Lucy's and I stood there wondering where in the world she could have gone off to—and with a real live baby? What had been going on in her mind all those times we were making up dance steps, fooling with blush, singing Top 40, or imagining stories about the people—usually just the man and wife—in the car that had just left? Had she been laughing with me and telling jokes while inside she was plotting all this trouble? And, think, what had it done to her all those times she had to hoist a genuine tiny little baby infant, probably the same size as the one that was hers out there somewhere, into the saddle and hold it safely on there for the five times around just because its parent was too nicely dressed to go near a real animal? I didn't know—and that fact bumped me up against a wall that surprisingly felt like a betrayal—I hadn't known every little thing Lucy was thinking. I had come to care enough about her that something like this would hurt to a degree.

The Nice Clean Room for Rent wasn't going to give up any clues. Though it wasn't my place to do this, or my right, I opened the drawers of Uncle Pal's dresser, now holding the few pieces of clothing Lucy'd brought, all arranged nicely. None of the corners or backs of the spaces yielded a diary or anything that could have answered the questions I would have asked. In the top drawer, underwear and socks took up opposing sides, neatly folded or tied, depending upon what the item required. There was none of the little keepsakes that for a girl usually make their home here. In Lucy's top drawer there were no notes, no dried-up flowers, no pieces of thread kept simply because it was something you courteously removed from the sleeve of a boy you deep-down admired. No poems, no matchbooks. No correspondence, that being no surprise as her parents never even called, never mind wrote. The only thing in there, other than something you'd wear, was a plastic shoehorn from Pee-Dee Shoes in Palmer, had to have been left behind by Pal, tortoiseshell in pattern but made of plastic, the advertising words stamped on in gold paint.

There were no photos displayed on the dresser top, which held only a couple pots of organicky creams from the line her mother represented, founded in England but produced out of a factory in Ohio. Lucy kept out an avocado/almond oil mixture that was meant for under your eyes, and a pure chamomile cream with a label that pronounced it suitable for all-day wear as well as nighttime moisturizing so you were getting double your money's worth, which her mother probably pointed out to customers was an offer no woman would turn aside. Next to that was a fat tube of lip gloss, a startling wintergreen flavor worn way down to a rounded nub that I uncapped and ran around my mouth, three times, and quickly, as if I was nervous Lucy was going to suddenly come in here and catch me playing with her stuff.

Even though it was an hour before midnight, I made the bed she hadn't neatened before she'd sneaked out into the light rain. I pulled up the yellow-flowered sheets Victory had bought at Durand Sisters' sidewalk sale in the interest of offering our boarder a cheerier room. Over those I drew the white flannel blanket that is more than all you need here in the summertime, and on top of that I arranged the white-quilted spread that is just for show. Then I turned a corner of the covers back, and I stood over at the door to see if this indeed did make the bed look more welcoming, whether or not you might come in from your wild day running through the trees with a baby in your arms and see the floral sheets smiling up at you and think how nothing would be better than to get yourself beneath the layers that were being shown off like that. I have to say that it did look inviting, so I went and sat down there, leaning back to look out the window, at Lucy's view of the barnyard, the empty ring, the sleeping truck, beyond that the barn full of its safe and secured animals. This is what I would see if I were she, here. Out past that, just the blackness that was the field and then the woods, and the world beyond. Lucy was out there somewhere, she and Amy the substitute baby, Lucy wearing the Illinios sweatshirt my mother had bought for a girl she didn't even know, and Amy wearing what the mimeographed flyers were describing as one-piece lilac-printed flame-retardant pajamas, brand-name Carter's size zero-to-six-months, sent to her by a great-aunt up in New Hampshire who'd bought them at a factory outlet and who'd yet to see her for the first time. And who, if you wanted to give in and think the worst, as was easy to do since the start of this, might never get that chance.

For the tenth time since I'd first stepped into Lucy's room, I said a prayer, in the language my uncle and aunt had taught me, an especially tongue-twisting one to the guardian angel, the unseen *aniot* Boze who floats behind each of us, all day, all night, during whatever we are doing, good or bad, remaining there to protect and guide. I instructed mine to please go and find Lucy and Amy and join up with the ones hovering at their backs and assist the pack of them in returning to the people who were so desperate to see them again. Who were missing them. As I found myself missing Lucy.

At the same exact time, I finally attempted to arrange the new information in my mind—that this girl my age was somebody's mother. A term I was used to giving to someone at least twenty ancient years older than me. The things this girl just my age already knew boggled me. From the brightly lit delivery room backing up to the probably dimly lit event that landed her there. Lucy was continents ahead of me in reality. Knowing first-hand in real life the things that had made famous the valedictorian, that dramatic characters like Erica Kane were going through on daytime television. A baby. She'd gone and had a baby. I rolled onto Lucy's pillow, the one that was normally accustomed to cradling a very mixed-up head of the girl who wanted me to know her. The case smelled of nothing but line drying, and the whole thing was good and soft and a relief, and it kept me there until Victory came in the next morning, to wake me and say it was time to help her make more food for the people who are so good as to still be searching but still without any luck at all.

The hours crawled in the same dull procession of kitchen work and farm work and worrying and waiting. Animals don't care what kind of crisis or drama you're smack in the middle of. They want and need to eat and drink, to be let out, to move around, to do the work for which they were made, to be put back where they came from, to have that done all over again for them the next day. So Pal and I took care of that, even reopened the ring because no matter how frivolous giving rides might have seemed at that time, more important was the ponies' routine. They'd been out there every single summer day of every single summer, so they automatically lined up at the crossties, waiting their turns to be groomed and tacked up, only to be led to the pasture. Confused, they'd ignore the salad bar of greenery that stretched out for acres, normally offered to them at the end of the day. They lined up at the fence next to the ring, staring as usual, waiting for an explanation, and to be moved to their usual stations, all six heads over the fence, lined up side by side in the same order: Star. Pan. Tony. Princess. Zoey. Chester.

"Neigh," they all said, not really all at once but in enough of a succession to make it one long word.

On the third day Lucy and Amy were gone, Pal turned to me and interpreted: "They're saying that life goes on." Which it does, and there is nothing wrong in addressing that fact. And in the same world where, just a block away, a set of young parents can be in hysterics over the loss of their infant, and just over in that house there, a pair of older ones can be so angry over the actions of their crazy teenage daughter, in that same square mile, a family having no ties to any of this, no knowledge that comes anywhere near, can drive up to the ring and launch toward me a tangle of cheering, yelling, fighting, shoving, pointing, begging children with not a single concern other than who's going to get to ride the black pony maybe twice in a row. Can we, ha? Come on! Please?

Lucy's parents and her grandmother arrived the day after she left us. They took a plane up to Bradley, and Victory accompanied Mr. Maytaz when he went to retrieve them, so that when the plane arrived the Dragons would have at their disposal someone to ask all the many answerless questions in their minds. My parents wanted to come out, too—but to take me home. They were not happy with my being in the middle of all this, and I in turn was not happy they knew what had occurred—before and during this summer. There was no way my family would have found out about the disappearance and kidnapping had Victory not phoned to inform them. "I'm responsible for you," was her explanation when I complained about that, and you really could not argue.

"If you don't want us to come out, we'll just send a ticket for you," my mother told me.

"No."

"We know best," my father told me from the extension.

"You don't." I was bolder than they were used to me being. Things happen and they change you. Even in just a couple of days. This was serious and I told them so. "I need to stay here."

I heard both of them make fed-up noises at me, way out here and out of their reach, living in what was nearly a crime scene. But, really, it was Victory they were upset with. Yes, she'd told them she was taking in a girl. It's just that Victory, feeling everybody deserved a fair chance, and Pal, more than agreeing with her, had skipped mentioning that the girl was crazy.

So, there, Mr. Maytaz's Delta 88 was rolling to the exact spot it had the day it delivered Lucy to us, only this time the door was opening to allow three more Dragons into our lives. Richard and Coreen, the parents, tall and dark haired, fancy Sunday clothes, walking slumped forward with no good reason right now to stand up straight. Anzia, the grandmother, the bulk of her hefty body shooting a couple feet out front from her spine, an icebreaker clearing a path through the dismal air that surrounded the car and its cargo. I watched from the ring as Victory rounded everybody up after they were let loose from the shining doors, and she ushered them into the house, where I left them to their deep discussion that really would have no effect on the search but hopefully would bring the participants some peace. I figured they'd come looking for me when they wanted me, which didn't happen for another couple hours, by which time I'd directed two more reporters in search of Fisherdick Road, and sent four more troublefree kids on their five times around the world.

"Are you the one that stoled that baby?"

This came from the last boy, roughly ten and grinning and trying too hard to act like he didn't know better.

When he came around to the gate, I stopped Pan, on which he was seated. I leaned over, leered at him, hissed, "Yes!" He launched himself from the saddle, fell onto the dirt, and sprinted shrieking back to the car.

I turned to latch the gate and the woman who had to be Mrs. Dragon was right there, standing in front of it like she'd instantly materialized from a spaceship. I wondered if she'd heard the boy, and what I'd said to him.

"I was just . . . ," I started to explain how I'd had enough wisecracks, but she pushed forward a shaky, "I'm Lucy's mother," then fell forward as a big wave of weeping knocked her right into me.

It was strange to have to console a grown adult. Especially one I didn't know. It was like a little waltz how I turned her around while she was still hanging on to me, and I got her to walk backward into the chair at the gate, where she set herself slowly and leaned forward, head in hands, careful, like it was a melon she was carrying.

"Lucy, Lucy, Lucy," she moaned, echoing the word I'd spent two days yelling as loudly as possible. "Oh my Lucy, my child . . ."

I didn't think I could be feeling any worse than I had been, but suddenly I was. Sorry for Mrs. Dragon, for myself, for everybody, I put my hand on her dark brown hair, which she wore long and unrestrained, unpinned and unsprayed, not something you saw a lot of mothers doing at the time. I gave the hair a bit of what I hoped would be a soothing stroke and noticed it had an admirable bounce and finish that my own had been acquiring since I'd started stealing bits of the beachy-smelling coconut butter cream rinse Lucy stored on the shelf my aunt had cleared for her use, noting to me before the girl's arrival that having your own space—even for something as friv-olous as beauty products—is an important thing.

"Now, now," I said to Mrs. Dragon. I wasn't sure what the expression meant, but I knew it got dragged out at times like this. I squatted to be level with what was the top of her head. "Now, now, now." And that's when she picked her face up from her lap and I saw Lucy's eyes for the first time in two days. But they were attached deep inside somebody else's face, and they looked a little older and a lot more sad as the mouth way down beneath them slowly asked me, "Where do you think she could be?"

As requested by the police, Lucy's parents and the grandmother had brought along a photograph. It ended up in the paper—and on local television even—the junior year portrait of Lucy that her father pulled from a paper bag when Mrs. Dragon brought me into the kitchen to formally meet the rest of them: the stern, word-stingy Mr. Dragon, who had to have contributed his height to his daughter, but nothing else that I could see. The sweating grandmother, who latched on to me and told me I was Victory's pride, that no one knows the worth of a good child until she goes bad. "Bad," she repeated, and Victory came and stood next to her and shook her head at me, without words telling me not to be bothered by this confusing sort of talk.

Down on the table, standing with the help of a little decorative easel, there were the head and shoulders of Lucy, all neat in a five-by-seven wooden frame, as she'd been way before anything had gone off in her life, smiling into the camera lens, hair pushed over one shoulder, brown vest, white big-lapelled blouse, huge square green beads for a necklace. Officer Melley drove out, removed the frame from the easel and Lucy from the frame and handed that back to her mother, carefully, for safekeeping. He was nice enough to say that after the Police Department had done what it had to with the picture, he'd of course return it—soon, he hoped—and she could have it back to display in her home once again.

Pal nodded, and then I nodded, but I noticed that all three of the Dragons did not.

"Do you think they've just run out of hope for her?"

I asked Frankie this when he came by that afternoon and delivered us one quart of two percent and a quart of buttermilk, rather than the gallon of whole Victory had checked off on the form.

He waited a couple beats and then said, "Nobody should ever give up hope, especially parents for their kids," but that basically was rattled off while he checked his order pad, and because of that sounded more like something from a bumper sticker than a pearl of advice you'd carry around forever. He'd miscalculated his inventory and delivery and that seemed to bother him. Frankie never made mistakes, but, hey, it was a nerve-wracking time for all.

"Are you free later?" I asked. "I had this idea—Lucy likes Amherst. Maybe we can drive out there and ask around town, maybe the campuses. See if any of the kids will talk to us. Things they wouldn't say to the police. You know, we could be like on the *Mod Squad*."

"Fred's still away." He said this and breathed out and I nodded my understanding.

"I'll drive over and help you."

"The vet's coming by last thing," he said, with a bit of exasperation that made it clear I'd only be in the way. Vets did things that even I, an animal lover, didn't always want to see. And Frankie knew that.

"Okay," I said. "Next week. Well—maybe by next week we won't have to look for her."

"Hope not," he said, distracted, and that trailed off into, "just a minute," and then he went off and hopped into the truck, came back and swapped the gallon for the two quarts, and then he told me he had to leave, sorry, but it's just a bad week. And I understood, right?

I needed Frankie. But he couldn't be there right then and I tried to understand. I found some measure of consolation in my own work, busying myself in the regular chores, sending another couple of kids on their five trips, and welcoming the additional obligations—making the refreshments and accompanying Pal as we drove them over to the new search headquarters, the big brick building at the Quabbin where the state police keep their offices. Five days into the search, officials felt the change of the center of the search mission was sensible considering both Lucy's interest in things related to the reservoir, and the dogs' having followed a track that led in that direction, which then just ended as if she and the baby had flown sky-ward from that point. Interest in our immediate area plummeted from where it had been so strong that even treehouses had undergone searches. Margaret came over and told me that they'd gone into hers. She had not been up there for years, a treehouse being a place for kids, after all, but having grown policemen climbing up there made her want to visit again. Now she sits up there in the night, she tells me, and peers down into whoever's windows she is able to see into. Unfortunately, her one and only choice is those of Mr. Clean's home, and it's not much—a view of only his clean kitchen countertop lit by a light overhead. A bunch of plastic flowers in a white vase on the sill. Violet, or lilac maybe—and isn't that spooky because that's the same color as the suit the baby's got on in all the reports? Lilac? One time she saw Mr. Clean come by and get a drink from the tap, then get out the liquid dish soap and sponge and wash the glass and dry it and put it away, all in a row, immediately. But there was activity only the one time. The rest of the time, there's nothing, she says.

"It's boring staring into a house," she says. "No wonder Lucy went crazy," she says. "Looking at nothing forever, that would be enough to push you over the brink."

Pal is sleeping on his cot in the barn now because Victory is in his bed because the two Dragons are in her bed. I'm in Lucy's room because the grandmother is in mine, which is next to the Dragons' room, rather than across, the reason given being in case they all need to get up in the middle of the night and have a big meeting about something, they would be closer. Our home is all populated by strangers who show no indication of or interest in becoming anything more than that. If not given a task, the women will mope about silently, stand at the

window or on the porch staring into the far distances. The
mother makes hushed collect calls, the grandmother sits in Victory's chair silently making her way through all the mysteries
on the brilliant crystal rosary that unintentionally throws hopeful little rainbows onto the far wall. The father spends the day
at the Quabbin, where he asks my uncle to deposit him each
morning and collect him at dusk. He comes back tired and with
his clothing sweaty and dirty, and never with anything new to
report, nothing much to say at all.

I drive over there in mid-morning to bring more trays full of
food, to pick up the ones from yesterday that the ladies from
church have washed and put aside under a piece of paper reading "PANEK" so nobody will take ours home by mistake. Victory has had us move on from churning out gallons of nothing
but egg salad to fortify the people who are out doing the hardest work of trekking around in the woods. Now we slice truck-
loads of carrot sticks. Mountains of pickles. Fleets of celery
boats packed with peanut butter or cream cheese. Buckets of
macaroni elbows tossed with chunks of the tomatoes that are
exploding from the garden. Nothing too imaginative, making
up in bulk for what they lack in creativity. But requiring
enough chopping and slicing and filling to keep us busy and
feeling like we are doing something, rather than nothing, as the
days drag. Daily, I count the hours until four, when Frankie
comes up the driveway, and once he's put our order into the
box—an extra quart now with all these people, plus a container
of half and half because that's what Mr. Dragon prefers in his
coffee over regular milk—I make some excuse, would he help
me bring something into the barn, and once we're in there I
grab hold of him, frantic for real comfort. "I hate this," I tell
him. "Why's this happening?" I ask. "Where could she be?"

Frankie just says *shhhh* and pulls me even closer as I collapse and then, the tears, for who knows how long, but way too soon Frankie says he has to get back to the dairy. And I ask him can he return later, and he tells me, maybe, can he call, he never imagined running a farm would be so much work and next time why don't they get his uncle to help out during vacation like usual and why wouldn't Fred and Midgie hurry up and come back from the beach to come and save him. He uses that very word. "Save."

The seventh night Lucy and Amy are gone, I tell my uncle and aunt that I'm going to drive over to the Quabbin with the food the ladies of our house have made for the next day. I'm restless. I hate being around all these silent people. You can hear all their breathing, and that's it. My aunt says okay, fine, go. It's a Friday night. Take your time. Mrs. Dragon takes hold of my hand as I pass to get the keys from the nail beside the door. She's looking crackly, like if you gave her even a slight knock she'd fall into a billion pieces right in front of you. I remember my mother telling me more than a few times how being a parent is the hardest job in the world. I'm thinking how they should make a poster of Mrs. Dragon as she appears right now and display it in high schools to scare fast girls and just regular teenage girls and they would never ever want to go near a boy even if it was just to shake his hand. If the lady depicted is a state you could be headed for one day just due to becoming a mother, you wouldn't want to have sex ever in your life. But this mother, Mrs. Dragon, is in front of me, not in a picture, in three dimensions, and I ask her if I can get her anything. She just looks through me for an eternity. Then finally she tells me, "No, Lucy, you're a dear," and I say thank you, without correcting her mistake.

I load the trays in the back of the red Ford. My aunt is getting a little more adventurous. She's used a whole box of toothpicks in spearing thin slices of the harvest, creating an assembly line that had Mrs. Dragon standing most of the morning, stabbing pieces of radishes, peapods, chives, then maybe a cube of cheese and an olive for an accent because, Victory noted, even in the worst of times there is a need for some aesthetics. There is a fresh sheet cake, too, with a rhyme made up by my aunt as she is the only adult in the kitchen with enough sanity right now even to come up with something as bad as

WE TRULY DO
APPRECIATE YOU

The lines are written in green frosting on a white field dotted with jimmies, sweet words for those who the paper tells us are getting scratched by briars and latched on to by deer ticks as they comb the reservoir land for Lucy and Amy. The night is cool. I wonder where you hide out with an infant, with no extra food or clothing, when it gets like this. Or anytime at all. That makes me shiver again, and I close the window when I get in the truck and turn the key and head down the hill to the road. On the radio, there is the jumpy *beep-beep-beep-beep-beep* music that signals the end of the news update, which is okay with me. I've read enough and heard enough, and it is the same thing over and over because there really is nothing new to tell. A girl and a baby have been missing for seven days now, they are probably together, but nobody knows where. The girl is seventeen, and tall and thin and dark-haired and can be extremely charming. She dresses in a mod fashion and has a history of mental problems that in the past have resulted in hospitalization. The baby, also referred to as "the innocent victim," as if there might be mistaking that she has played a part in this, is three months old and her hair is dark too. She is wearing lilac pajamas. The police implore anyone who knows the whereabouts of the girl and the baby to contact them by telephone. The news reports always point out that the police can be reached by dialing zero, like we are all stupid out here and wouldn't know to do that.

But, really, nobody's thinking straight. Down at the post office, the feed store, the steps of church, the parking lot of the Two Cows, rumors grow as fast as cherry tomatoes: Mrs. Sutton is supposed to be already on three or four different kinds of medication because she just cannot sleep. She stands near the window at all hours, and if you drive by slowly enough you plainly can spot her there. Mr. Sutton supposedly has consulted a lawyer about suing the Commonwealth of Virginia for letting Lucy free from the institution earlier in the year, and he's also thinking about taking Victory and Pal to court for inviting Lucy here and exposing the entire town, including its children, to the dangers of such a sick and dangerous person. He wants also to sue Pal, alone, for giving her a job at the ring where she had actual contact with who knows how many kids she considered swiping as well? The gossips ask these things: Did you know the Dragons had to be forced to come up here? They'd wanted to hide because they knew what kind of deeds their daughter might be up to. The grandmother, before she moved away a couple years back, didn't she admire a baby in the Grand Z once and tell the mother, "Oh, I could just go and steal him away from you?" Didn't she? Don't you remember people saying that? There was even a rumor about me, brought over courtesy of Wesley Elmer. That I'd shown Lucy the way to Fisherdick Road, and over to where the baby lived. It was all my fault. Without me, how would she ever have found Amy Sutton's bedroom? Don't I feel awful now? That's what people around here want to know.

There were rumors about Lucy, too. And in them she moved around quite a bit. She'd been spotted hitchhiking in Monson, at the edge of the river next to the toilet seat factory, holding the baby in one arm, sticking out the thumb of the other hand. Lucy and Amy were seen at the bus station in Springfield, boarding a Peter Pan headed for Utica. They were living at the commune out toward Palmer, eating yogurt, being sheltered by the hippies there who ask no questions of anyone because they don't want you asking any about them. Lucy and Amy had been taken in by the hermit who lives just past the Quabbin. You could never find just exactly where he lived, and, now, you'll never find her, either. And, of course, they said Lucy and the baby were still around here, but living in a cellar hole out the dead village, which, people who told these stories would point out, is where a crazy person like her wouldn't be bothered in the least.

They were right about just that last point. Lucy loved that place—rather, I should say, she loved the idea of it, as we never really made it all the way there. Once we started really getting along we'd head often in that direction, spurred on by Victory's descriptions of the spooky triangular common, the delicate patterns someone took the time to make in their foundation with stones dug from the ground, the old safe people go searching for, the reedy sound of the wind, and, hey, did you hear that, too?

According to Lucy, the woods held vibes that got sadder the farther in we went.

"Just our being here, acknowledging the loss of those people, that helps them, you know." She'd turn her head and yell this back at me as Pan carried her forward. I'd nod. I liked the idea of helping heal wounds. For years, ever since I'd first been told about the destruction of the towns, I'd try to imagine how I might feel if somebody came knocking at the door of the farmhouse and told us they'd decided to drown our entire section of the state. And that we had to get out.

"Imagine," Victory would say. And, really, that is all you can do. Because there is no way to actually predict the many things, both the shocking and the dull and the wondrous, that will end up happening to you in your own individual life.

I had to get rid of the food donation first. To take care of that detail, I made the right through the gates of the Quabbin, which was usually closed to visitors after sunset, but these days was busy with people at all times, coming and going, offering to help, offering food, offering paranormal information as to where the two might be found.

"A cake!" The officer who opened the door for me, wearing gray jodhpurs and tall black boots even though all he rode all day was a desk chair, faked like he was thrilled. "We haven't had a cake since this morning!" His laugh made the place seem like a fair, as if this was a bake sale at the parish picnic. And we were all out for the day, hoping to win the big 50/50 raffle, having fun at the dart throw and the water balloon drop and the money wheel, going for a polka, forgetting our cares, however enormous and hulking they might be. Yet I couldn't forget about Lucy, no matter how many jokes he made. I managed to smile at the cop, but it was half-hearted and he could tell and so he suggested I cheer up. That things would get better. That kids did things sometimes. He'd been a kid, so he knew that. I was a kid now, so I'd know it too, maybe even better than he did. "Come on, smile, come on now," he told me, but I just couldn't, even when ordered to by the law.

He went outside to the truck and I followed him and handed over the few other trays, the chewy date strips, the pecan sticks, the chocolate pinwheels, the spice drops. The cop peered through the layers of Saran and asked me, "What did you do—rob a bakery?" I told him I hadn't, no, it was just that Mrs. Dragon and her mother-in-law had been put to work the day before and were wearing out the pages of Victory's one cookbook. They'd decided that no recipe would be made more than once, as a way to keep the work interesting and their minds always turning toward something new, rather than the unchanging old reality. The officer said, "Oh." He probably had expected nothing more than a "Ha!" in response to his robbery joke, and he told me to go and have myself as nice a night as I possibly could. I answered that I would do that. Because with the truck empty of food, I was free and clear to go to where I really was headed this night. Which was to see Frankie.

I'd been to the farm many times over the years, but Fred and his Midgie, or at least one of them, had always been around, along with the couple of farmhands who do the milking and provide general help around the place. But this was a Saturday night during Fred and Midgie's hard-earned annual vacation, and they were miles and miles north of here, walking the boardwalk eating taffy and candy corn, listening to a band at the concert shell, reminiscing how they'd met at a big dance at the Casino and just look at the sorry state of it now. Frankie was home alone, running the place by himself for the first time and very tired after a trying week, as he'd disappointingly told me when I'd asked would we be getting together that Friday night as usual. Sure, I'd seen him each afternoon on deliveries, but I needed him for more than dairy products, especially in this confusing week. And once I arrived at his home, I knew that Frankie would realize the same was true for him. As invited to by the state policeman, I'd filled a small plate from the table at the police station. A brownie, another that was covered with frosting, a couple of sugar cookies, and some square blond cake slice that had a thick roof of coconut. Frankie would be happy to see me, and the food, I knew.

His farm wasn't that far away from ours, but located on the other side of the Quabbin gate. Actually, its fields abutted the far side of the cemetery of transplants that had become one of Lucy's favorite places to stretch her legs. She was a strong walker and I'd come to enjoy tramping behind, challenging myself to keep up with her pace, following her down row after row, listening to her narrate names. Oh, Cyprian! Oh, Asa! Oh, Stanwood! She'd stop to list dates of the comings and goings, and to give solemn readings of whatever bits of prayers or causes of death still were legible on the stones. Always, we'd end up resting on either side of a marker for poor Kittie Evans, cherished daughter of Zilpha and David, 1815–1832, once and forever "feventeen." Just like Lucy and I were right then.

"I wonder what happened," Lucy said one day.

I was on my elbows, carefully splitting a wide blade of grass to weave into a little ring. Thinking of making another one, for Lucy, if mine came out nicely. A ring identical to mine. In a few days, it would be so dried up that it would break if you mishandled it. But at least until that Friday it would be fresh and green and the very same as what I'd have on my finger. "When?" I asked her.

She knocked on the slate and said, "Then. What happened to her—what did it to her?"

I flashed back to my asking the same question, only of Victory, who was sitting on my bed in her honeycomb slacks, answering with the word *pharmaceuticals*. In the weeks after that, I'd waited for her to hide the bottle of Geritol she'd always kept on the kitchen windowsill to boost her iron-poor blood, along with the one containing tablets of Bayer for Pal's various aches, but both had remained in plain view up until and way past the day Lucy left, monuments to their great trust and confidence in the girl they'd taken in for the summer. I know people had health concoctions back when Kittie had lived, if not the earliest kinds of pills, so who knew—maybe this girl and Lucy had more in common than simply age.

"Poison?" It was the closest I could come without saying medication.

"Hmmmm." Lucy pondered, squinting up at the clouds. "Poison . . ." She rolled to face the stone and whispered dramatically "Tell us, Kittie—was it poison, Kittie?"

Kittie wasn't talking.

The cemetery—and the dairy—were in the direction you'd take if you were headed to the center of Belchertown, or to Amherst beyond, or to UMass farther on, where Frankie had received a full scholarship to study animal husbandry starting in September, a major that is not at all what it sounds like, I have to tell people who don't know any better. Come the fall, he and I would be at different ends of the country, farther away from each other than ever, but we'd meet back at the farm again next May. We'd

planned that forever, and forever was exactly what we were planning on: meet here for the next three summers, and the one after
that—just after graduation—have our wedding at the farm.

"Marry me marry me marry me."

Four years in advance, I knew every detail of that day to
come. A small and perfect ceremony at the farm, attended by
Victory, Pal, Fred, Midgie, Ma, Dad, our sisters, our brothers,
and the ponies. We got the idea from a magazine ad meant to
interest you in buying a diamond ring, in this case a small and
simple one aimed at people like us, who had absolutely no
money but a whole lot of sweet-smelling dreams. In the accompanying photographs, a young couple sat on a curb in the city,
dreaming of their wedding in the country, an event depicted
below that, the two of them standing in a meadow, a flower-
covered wagon as an altar, little-kid attendants in fancy shorts,
everybody wearing white, a goat there, even. From fifty-cents-a-
yard muslin and from the already-selected Butterick Sew-Easy
pattern 9502, size 10, I would make myself a dress that looked
as close to the one in the picture—a down-to-the-ground white
one with a lacy panel in the front and a fancy ruffle at the
neck—and I would have Frankie go out and rent an all-white
suit because I never did master the tailoring of men's clothing. I
would letter our invitations on parchment that I'd decorate
with a border of watercolored roses, then I'd take a candle and
burn the edges so they'd look eaten up by time. I'd roll each
and seal them all with red wax and mail them out in toilet
paper cardboards I would ask everybody to save for me
months in advance of that. Our guests would watch us being
led into the field by a pony train that Victory would arrange,
linking the six with clean, new rope she'd punctuate with pink
bows and all colors of flowers from the front garden. In the

middle of the field we'd stop at the cart and the priest that awaited us there to make everything legal and binding in the eyes of both man and God, and I'd lean my head on Frankie's big shoulder just like the bride was doing in the advertisement. There would never, ever be a nicer day.

And here's where I knew we'd live—right here, the place I was turning the truck toward right now. Fred had another boy, older and in banking, and a daughter who sat up in the front seat with a tiny black dog on her lap while her husband drove the three of them around in a tractor-trailer, crossing the country and turning around and doing it again. So if he truly wanted it, the Day 'n Night Dairy could be Frankie's one day. And there was plenty of room in the sprawling house to accommodate Fred and Midgie living there in all the hopefully many years until they passed away, and they wouldn't bother us one bit in the meantime. I would be nice and close to Victory and Pal, and, of course, the ponies. Many times I'd ridden Star down this long dirt driveway curving along between two high stone walls that marked the front fields. I was moving a little faster on this night—the road to the house went on forever and I was impatient. But, out of regard for the old truck, I took it easy. My reward was finally the sight of the enormous red house, its many windows edged with black shutters, its black front door all welcoming with a wreath of hydrangea Midgie had cut and hung to dry the summer before. Set on an angle away from the barn on the other side of the drive, big red letters on a bigger white sign spelled out

DAY 'N NIGHT DAIRY
FRED MATHEWS AND SON OWNERS/OPERATORS
REGISTERED HOLSTEINS

I parked next to the worn green Opel that Frankie had bought over the winter. It made me smile to see the little blue stuffed rabbit sitting up so alertly on his dashboard. The summer before, I'd won it at the Hardwick Fair, pitching Cheerios onto the moving turntable of a portable recordplayer and having them stay put, which is a lot more difficult than it sounds. I'd presented the toy to Frankie and he'd stood it up there himself in full view of the world. That's the kind of thing people do when they're in love, I thought to myself. A guy wouldn't be ashamed to put a toy rabbit on his dashboard because it was from his beloved girlfriend. His friends could say what they wanted to about that, but he wouldn't care. They had nobody, he had me. Let them laugh.

I picked up the desserts. The flimsy paper plate sagged and they all collided in the middle, chocolate and coconut sticking together, but what was wrong with that, really? I walked to the front door, which was always open and didn't that make you feel good, too, that you were free to just come on into this home and be made as welcome as if you actually belonged there, hello, Robyn, they'd call each time I entered and I'd take their invitation to sit at one of the rocking chairs next to the stove and to tell them everything that was new in my life since last time, even if that was just the day before.

But Fred and Midgie were away and apparently had locked up before they left. I found this out when I turned the big front door handle and gave a push. There was no buzzer, just a horseshoe-shaped knocker that a long time ago had been shining brass. I gave it three tries. Then another couple. Three more. I pounded a few times. Decided to try the more popular door, way in the back of the house, in the section they leased out to workers who had no other place to live. Nobody was staying there now, I knew, nobody since Willie left and got what most people would call a real job, with insurance and a paid vacation and a company picnic every July, and all he had to do was drive a van full of snack foods around to little stores on street corners all throughout Rhode Island and eastern Connecticut. His final week at the dairy overlapped with his first on the route, and for their goodness to him in the year and a half that he'd worked at the dairy, he brought Fred and Midgie two dozen double-packs of crackers pre-smeared with peanut butter, and another dozen accompanied by cheese wedges that amazingly needed no refrigeration. Willie's window had overlooked the garden I was passing right then. The garden with the trellis of the yellow roses that Frankie liked to bring me. Next to it, the windowshade was down and I caught the shadow of some sort of movement. Then heard a sound. I stopped to listen. To the noise. A small cry. A bigger voice. His saying, it's okay, okay. *Shhhhh*. Another, medium sized, hers, saying everything would be all right. But there was no convincing the baby, or me.

The back door was locked, too. I banged on it with a force I didn't know I had. Like how they say you call up amazing strength when you come across an overturned car with passengers trapped inside and with just one hand you right it. When I wasn't pounding, I was saying my name. That it was me! Robyn! I must correct myself—I wasn't saying, I was yelling. Yelling my name. As loud as I think I would yell if I were trying to save my life. Telling them that it was me out there making all that noise. Me, one of the many people who had been so worried. Who had felt so bad, and certainly some measure of guilt and fault. Who had bought the theories of inescapable sandpits and ancient well holes, of hungry mountain lion and bear, all those possibilities for Lucy and Amy offered by parents as their children circled the ring happily and safely. It was me doing the yelling. Me. Me who'd lost sleep, who'd been held close by Frankie and told to *sssshhh*. I was through with being quiet. I didn't care if there was a baby inside who might be scared by all this. I cared only that somebody in there knew that I was there.

I kicked and banged all my anger, at some point slowing, energy spent as I counted myself another innocent victim. Lucy had taken more than just one person away. My fists fell throbbing at my sides as, inside the house, a light flipped on, the talking ceased, the baby simmered down. Then, slowly, the door opened a crack, and Frankie's eye, lid at a convincingly pained droop, looked out at me standing there on a mashed heap of desserts, breathing fast like I'd sprinted over to the dairy rather than drove. I beamed a bunch of hatred into him as in the air around us I heard the supersonic tumble and crash of my trust and hopes and plans. Us. Gone. Just like that. A thousand awful things to say scrolled through my brain like song titles on a TV album commercial, the best ones done up in a different color so you'll certainly notice them. I opened my mouth at the arrival of one of the worst I was thinking, but, despite the opportunity, no words found their way out. I tried again. The eye waited. But I was unable to speak. None of it would have fit anyhow. You could play around with words for ten years and still not come up with the proper combination for how I felt at that moment. Awful. Dead. Betrayed. I moved. Extended my hand. Slowly, farther. Until it reached the doorknob and pulled it closed.

.        .        .

She had on the Illinios sweatshirt in the picture of her and him being led by the elbows away from the farmhouse, the photograph the city paper ran next to the front-page story titled "Baby-Snatch Teen Found at Dairy; Infant Unharmed." Beneath that was our name, written plenty of times, Panek this and Panek that, how she'd been invited here and stayed here and did her bad things while being here. But I didn't clip it out and save it because why would you want to hang on to such a thing? Anyhow, I didn't need to. A couple of juvenile delinquents in high school once doused the principal's car with acid, and for three years I stared out from homeroom at his light blue sedan looking like it was still dripping with a much lighter color. I imagined some kind of toxic thing like that had burned into my mind the images from that night, and that they would last another three years at least. Probably more like thirty. I didn't need to open an album to recall the row of cow tails that flipped when I turned on the barn light and zombied my way into Fred's office. The black rotary phone and the hour it took for the advertised zero hole to return to its place at the bottom of the dial and connect me to the operator, who did what I asked and hooked me up to the state police at the Quabbin Reservoir. The yellow bill marked "PAID IN FULL" that told how Fred was owner of five thousand custom-printed bottle caps was my focus as I heard a man say I'd reached the state police and that my call was being recorded and what was my emergency, please?

Think. Think. I had to think. Sure, it was an emergency that I knew what nobody else knew, but everyone there appeared to be okay—there were no bodies or carnage or house afire, no invaders, marauders, anything else that you would term an emergency. I was only calling to tell them one of the things that I now knew, which was what I told him now: "I found the baby."

I didn't say anything about the others. I figured they'd be caught—and if they weren't? I didn't care anymore. "At Day 'n Night Dairy," I added, answering the question of my location, and then I hung up, got myself to my feet, rolled the desk chair back into its slot, snapped off the lights, walked out of the barn, got into the red Ford, and drove out the long drive. Slowly over the ruts, in no rush.

I took the right and headed back toward the Quabbin, toward home, slowing and pulling to the side of the road, as is the law when you see the fast blue lights of a line of cruisers coming up over the hill and zooming past on their way to the scene of a low and true and far-reaching crime.

# · 10 ·

The neurologist said I have nothing in my head. That is good news."

The old lady was nearly yelling this, in the manner of some people who have next to no hearing and therefore no idea the volume they're projecting.

Her announcement banged off the cookie-sheet-metal sides of the old elevator that was taking me and her and her silent niece or daughter or whoever the other woman was down from the third to the first floor of Mary Lane. We moved according to the stamped and signed inspector-approved license, at one hundred feet per minute, descending jerkily to the newly reno-vated first-floor lobby where we would be free to go and able to exit under our own power—an option not available to those who, unlike this lady, but just like my uncle, did indeed have something in their heads. Something very wrong.

The night of the afternoon on which grownup Lucy had come back to the farm, I'd gone to the hospital to tell Pal. To ask him, I guess, really. What I wanted to know was this: Would it be okay if she helped sell the place? Would he mind? Was the idea crazy? Could she still be? And what about me?

Was there something wrong with me for even considering having her stay? There? At the farm? With me? After what she'd done?

I asked all those things, but, of course, Pal remained silent. He was staring up at the ceiling tiles, rapt like a movie was being shown up there. I waited for some dramatic look as he realized what I was saying—"She's back? Lucy? Lucy Dragon? Here?" But there were no words at all.

My uncle was the one on his back, but I felt I should have been in his place. Sprawled on a couch spilling myself to a psychiatrist, because only a trained and licensed professional could make sense of why I didn't just yell that I still hated her, scream that out at the same volume with which I once threw her name into the woods during the big search and my own into the dairy's back door. Why I let her even onto the porch, never mind in the house, allowed her to move into Victory's sacred bedroom. Why I even felt a twang of pride for the attention—actually touched that she'd come out of nowhere, after all this time, to help me. Me. And then, on the next step behind her as she went up the stairs, I'm thinking this is the person who ruined it all.

I waited for Pal to have some reaction to my news.

"Lucy Dragon," I prompted him. "You remember . . ."


I knew that if he could, he would. My uncle always truly had liked Lucy. Despite everything—including her going straight from the dairy to the police station to the youth home to the courthouse to juvenile hall to another asylum then to who knew where and then on with her life and never once contacting any of us to say she was sorry for all she'd put us through. No request to stop at the farm to apologize to Mr. Panek or

Miss Panek or to their niece, or to her parents or her grandmother or that nice young man with the big head, all the people she'd been informed were there on vigil in the police station
waiting room. She wanted to see none of us. Not a one. Just
ship her off to the next place she was going to be sent—that is
what she wanted. That was the word Officer Melley gave to us
there in the hall at the police station, where the six of us waited,
seated, silent, patting hands and backs, passing Kleenex and
pointy cups of warm water from the out-of-order cooler. Victory, Pal, me—none of us ever heard from Lucy. She didn't ask
the cops to swing her by the farm on the way to the police station. She didn't need anybody sitting next to her when she
heard she likely would face a plateful of charges straight off
*Kojak:* kidnapping, unlawful imprisonment, reckless endanger-
ment, and threatening the welfare of a minor child. The social
services people took Lucy from her cell to their van and then to
the first of the facilities she'd be kept in, and she never once
sent us a message of any kind.

Pal had a proverb he'd mutter sideways when people didn't
acknowledge your kindness: *"Wdzięczność poszła do nieba i pociągła
za nią drabinę"*—"Gratitude has gone to heaven and has taken the
ladder." The saying would have been perfect in the middle of
all this, but it was never once mentioned. Maybe my uncle
thought it, but didn't speak it. He just stuck to prayers of
thanksgiving, the kind that simply came rolling out of him
when I walked into the house that night I came back from the
dairy and he told me I looked like I'd seen a ghost. And I'd
answered no, I hadn't. What I'd seen was very much alive and
real. All three of them were.

At the police station that night, Frankie was the only one of
the two in custody who asked for a specific visitor in the little

room where they were holding him. But I refused to go. I went back to the farm. That August night I packed my trunk for Illinois. I never wanted to have anything to do with him, or Lucy, again.

But Pal's interest in the girl remained. Over the next couple of years, he would ask after her whenever we talked on the phone, like I knew any more about her than he did. Like I, rather than he and Victory, periodically received calls from her grandmother down in Virginia and could ask for an update at any time.

"Nope," I'd respond to the "Ever hear anything from that Lucy?" question he'd always slip into his half of our talks.

Fifty times over fifty calls, the same thing back and forth. But he wasn't doing anything but being interested.

So I really knew that having her back at the farm to help would be fine with him. Maybe I was asking if it was okay with me. Would he—would I—care if I brought into this personal work someone who really was not a family member? The biggest question: someone who was no less than Lucy Dragon?

I was back. She was back. I leaned my chin on the bed rail that would keep Pal from tumbling onto the floor if he ever did decide to move. I asked him, "Can you believe it?" My uncle gave no answer. So, for him, I shook my head.

The unspoken consent in my hand, four Debbie Wong cartons in a grease-branded bag on the seat next to me, I drove the red Ford back to the farm and found Lucy on the fence at the edge of the field, where we'd led the ponies to graze before I left to do what I'd described as just an errand. I'd urged her to stay behind, to take a rest after what had to have been a grueling drive, this being the weekend and all and Philadelphia being not exactly next door. I was surprised that Lucy had listened, and just as amazed that she was still pretty much exactly where I'd left her, sitting on the highest rail, Pan's head poking through the lower space to her left and she stroking an ear.

I carried the takeout over. I told her, "Feel free to stay as long as you like, I think Pal would appreciate your help."

"I know he would." Lucy was smiling. "Pan told me."

Okay, here we go. A too-familiar unease walked slowly up my spine. "Pan told you."

"Yeah, that Pal wouldn't mind." Lucy was happy saying this.

"Well, he doesn't. Doesn't mind. You're right."

"Pan said he knew that it wouldn't matter, my not being family."

I did take in a bit more air at that one, but, really, when you think about it, Lucy knew me. She also knew how this family worked and how it thought. Hers was an easy conclusion, not a tip from an animal.

"It's fine," I said happily.

"Pal always liked me, you know. And I liked him."

"I know."

"Then it's okay. I'm going to help you."

I could feel the bag of takeout almost ready to give way. I started moving toward the house, and kitchen table. Except for a hefty and unexpected serving of memories, I hadn't taken in a thing all day.

"Sure, I said." Then I added, because this is what I hoped: "It'll be nice."

And it began, a second and hopefully different summer with Lucy Dragon.

This one was all due to my own approval, so there would be nobody but me to blame if it mirrored the first in being anything close to unnerving. I did feel sort of ashamed when thoughts like that crossed my mind. Give it up—we were adults now. Time had passed, things had changed. Look at us from ten feet away: professional, courteous, accomplished, mature, smart. People grow. Get over things. Get better. Get on with life. I had. And Lucy had to have done all this, long ago, in order to get where she was now, a big-deal award-winning businesswoman with enough free time and extra money to just pick up on a whim and come out to stay here and help me for however long that took. Though I reminded her I only had the summer to pull this off, so if she was going to help me out, could she manage to help me out in that time, please?

"No problem!" she'd answered, all confident, like it was a given that you could unload an entire house and farm and huge parcel of land as easily as I was selling off the dozens of empty berry baskets, twelve for a dollar. "You'll see."

I felt more sure about having Jerzy's assistance. In the single week since I'd come back, he had already proved his worth seventy times. Jerzy had connections. From his work at the garage, and from his year-round life living in town every day, he knew everybody. Or, if he didn't know exactly all those people, he knew others who did. Or Jeannie knew them. And a lot of those people, now that Pal's things were available for sale, suddenly wanted or needed something that was his. A snowplow. An auger. Roofing slates. Size 12 Wellingtons. A pig.

Several of these customers looked familiar from my summers here long ago, but I couldn't for the life of me come up with their names. I registered them in my mind only by the items I watched them load into their vehicles. The man who took all the equipment for syruping. The loose brick guy, the table saw crew, the galvanized can folks, the deacon's bench lady, the laying hen people. The kid who wanted the biggest tire we had so he could make a tree swing like in olden times. The woman who bought a scythe for a Halloween prop even though she was warned it could be dangerous to carry around for a joke. The couple that nearly got teary when Jerzy showed them the antique grinder Victory had used to mix the stuffing for kielbasa and kishka, which would be their use for it, too. All these people knew what they wanted, and, with Jerzy's help, they went right over and located it, packing it away into cardboard box or trunk, or coaxing it onto a truck bed, into a wooden cage or rusting livestock trailer.

I let Jerzy determine the prices because he was smart and honest and he knew the current worth of old, used things as they were regarded in Massachusetts. My knowledge was of how much these items might unrealistically go for in a big city an entire coast away, where a goat would not be much in demand but where things like Victory's old wicker laundry basket, selling for ten bucks here on her old porch, would be given a pricetag ten times that in the snooty antique store at the end of my block. Jerzy didn't mind the extra responsibility, and when his customers were gone and out of sight, he'd come over with a handful of paper money or a check that had been made payable to me. Once a week or so, he gave me an up-to-date accounting of what he'd sold off, and on payday I'd add to his regular salary a percentage of the items sold. He always protested that. I never listened.

The newspaper story had sparked interest in everything that now had a very definite expiration date on it. Ahead were countless trips hauling more junk out onto the lawn, over to the big piece of plywood on which Jerzy had painted the words "TAG SALE." It amazed me what people would hand over money for, but then who was I to talk? I was the one putting it out there, pronouncing it worthy of at least a look, to join the rest of the necessities and curiosities being carted off with a slow but steady regularity. You might not notice right away, but head into the garden one morning to spray fresh water into the birdbath, and find yourself hosing down nothing but a necklace of alyssum and a bare circle of dirt where the concrete stem of the bath once had stood solid. Or spend a good half an hour searching through the cabinets beneath the sink for the largest of Victory's prized cast-iron fry pans, until you realize that not just that one but the nested set of all three of them have been gone for a good week now. It'll be tough but in time you might get used to not seeing the Evangelist goats out there standing with their front hooves on the top board of their fence—they went away last week with a woman in Wheelwright who hopes to make tourist soap from the milk of the four girls with men's names. That same person took the hammock, too, and is in the market for any farm implements covered with rust as for some reason she'd like to make a garden display of such things. She likes farm items in general, wanted to see everything Pal had. So next time you're opening up the feed bin, reach up, like you've done a million times for good luck, to touch the long-retired oxen yoke. Your hand will now be hitting nothing but the wood of the wall.

"People asked me did we have one," Jerzy would explain when I'd ask how did this or that manage to disappear from right under my nose. He'd produce the list he kept next to the socket wrench kit in a drawer that pulled easily from my uncle's workbench, and there the sold items would be noted in

Jerzy's underfed cursive: not only birdbath and yoke, but brass coatrack and wrought iron German shepherd, other surprises I was shocked to not have missed the very moment a customer removed them from the places they'd occupied since before I was born. I'd just scratch my head and nod and say, "Okay, fine," and then I would get back to whatever I'd been doing when I'd backed up to take a rest at the picnic table and sat down hard on the ground.

Some of the people who stopped by really weren't in the market for anything. They simply were nosy, felt it was not odd in the least to want to traipse through somebody's home, over their property, around their barn, for no other reason than to see what was there in the house where the crazy girl once lived. Like this was some kind of museum, or as much a Sunday-afternoon pastime as the pony ring once had been. Sure, I know that over the years I've been as curious as the next person about what exists just on the other side of the walls of my neighbors, or curious places I pass, but never would I consider marching through only because illness had afforded me the sad opportunity.

"That's because you're nice," Lucy said that first night as we ate our takeout on the front porch, she still with her old habit of keeping the helpings of different foods separated on her plate by a margin of a good inch. According to Lucy, a lot more people than you might imagine are not nice, and a good number of those types make a regular weekend outing of attending real estate open houses.

"You can spot their type when they're still stepping out of their cars," she told me. "Then they open their mouths, and what doesn't interest them really tips me off. They don't concern themselves with the condition of the roof, how close or far away are the neighbors, they don't ask the locations of schools or shops, about the swelling of the tax rate, whether there are any houses of worship for their particular faith. They say they just want to look around. And that's what they do."

They look in rooms, of course, and also down stairwells, in closets even, and sometimes Lucy actually catches them rooting around inside nightstand drawers and medicine cabinets.

I will not know what kind of people she meets here at the farm because she says she will not allow me to be in the house when any prospective buyers arrive.

"The homeowner should never be around during a tour," she informed me right off. "It just doesn't look right. You really shouldn't meet until the signing—which you actually don't even have to attend. You have enough to do outside, you can make yourself scarce when people are here, can't you?"

I said I could. I had the ring to tend, after all. "I can stay busy," I told Lucy, and I speared the few remaining Dr. Seuss-ish mushrooms left stuck to the side of a container.

She didn't answer. Just yawned silently, and stretched with agility. Darkness cascaded like rain. Stars brightened and made up the mythological shapes I never was able to locate. Frankie had known them all. Including the ancient stories behind each, and just how they related to the very place where you were standing on the planet right at that moment. I realized I hadn't thought about that skill of his in years, and I pushed it away fast.

As awkward as it might be, maybe we'd start approaching all that in the morning. A neat explanation for things done wrong. Hopefully a heartfelt apology. Maybe common ground. Right now, though, I'd no energy left to even think about where to start. I put the words out there: "Maybe we'll catch up with everything tomorrow."

Lucy nodded fast and said, "Tired," and stood up and put her hand on the screen door.

"I'm just next door," is what I said, though she already knew that. "Knock if you need anything."

"Thanks."

Now she was standing there playing with her chainy watch, the kind all my girlfriends are asking for from their husbands and showing off when we next bump into one another. Lucy had never been that into good jewelry. But I was going by how she was when I last knew her, a whole long time ago. In all those twenty-two years, I'm sure many things about her had changed. At least I was hoping they had. Because the both of us were here for the summer, and officially, if you go by the dates on the calendar, it was only the early part of June and the season hadn't really even started.

I let her sleep.

A courtesy I did not allow myself that first night.

With only a wall and a door and a little metal hook between us, I admit to being unsettled. Alone these past six nights, I hadn't been frightened in the least. But with her here, every normal little shift and pop of the house turned my heart into a window fan set on high. At some point after two-thirty, I heard a door open, and then footsteps moving away—to my relief— away and down the less-creaky side of the stairs as Lucy made her way down to the toilet. It felt like I'd been awake for the entire night. The bony hands of memories that once seemed buried just about as long as Kittie Evans reached up through the soil and found my neck. I was speechless as I watched Lucy, caught red-handed, being led from Fred and Midgie's house right into the plum BMW, which she then drove up the driveway of our farm. As if no time had passed between those two things. As if nothing had changed. A cheerfully bright morning arrived much too early and drilled a sunbeam through my eyelids. I launched myself outside, desperate for work I hoped would occupy my entire day.

Of course, I began with the ponies. The feeding and watering, combing, brushing, tacking, leading, attaching, spinning, filling the ring, latching the gate when the job was done. Each in their proper order and nobody giving any problems. I cleaned the stalls and I moved on, into the side shed. I nosed around, conscious I might not be alone. In this very place I once picked up a metal hand rake, with a fat black snake curled in the tines. That was long ago but it was also like right now, that liquid shape just inches from my hand. I cautiously flipped through the layers of grimy old storm windows standing up near the far wall. They'd be nice for making cold frames, maybe I'd make a sign pointing this out to handy people. Behind the final one was a heap of wood and metal—the molds Pal had built for making your name in cement.

Halfway through the 1960s, he'd ordered the plans through the mail and worked an entire winter to construct the alphabet. I remember Victory writing to me how making the forms that would make the letters was a lot more complicated than Pal had anticipated, but because he liked a challenge he was happy during all those otherwise dull months to be busy measuring and cutting and gluing and steaming and fastening. Each mold was made of wood, with eyes and hasps and strips of aluminum fastening the corners. Each weighed what had to be a ton, even though each was only the size of a typewriter. There were twenty-six molds, of course, plus an apostrophe that doubled as a comma, and a period, in case any need for punctuation arose. I remember watching him hatch the trial run—the simple five-letter PANEK that to this day is still set, solid and unchipped, level with the base of the grass around the mailbox down by the road.

Pal and I had poured the cement the night before, and then stood there watching like it was going to do something more than just solidify. He took my hand and put it to the side of the *K* mold so I could feel the unexpected miracle of a definite heat being given off by the cold, gray glop that filled the four legs of the letter. The next afternoon, we pulled the fasteners off and the sides fell away. "Tomorrow we will put them in the ground," Pal said. "After that, *Gdziekolwiek podróż cię zabiera, zawsze tutaj będziesz.*"— "Wherever you go, you will always be here." And when I looked down, and read my last name, I saw that he was truly right.

"Here I am," I said now, as I pulled the seldom-used letter *X* mold from the wheelbarrow and lowered it gently to the front lawn.

Frankie sent me probably twenty or thirty letters after that last summer. Probably closer to thirty, if I thought about it and counted them on my hands. He mailed them to Robyn at Sunset View Farm, c/o P. and V. Panek, because that was the only address of mine that he was sure of anymore. Thirty letters in three years, my name on the envelope and his return address— the farm—in the top corner, and the postage stamp adhered upside down, as he probably hoped I'd heard somewhere along the way how that was a secret yet universal sign of love.

He put next to nothing inside all the envelopes Victory forwarded. He'd mark the date and greet me—"Dear Robyn"—but he was reluctant to go on to the next thing, which normally would be, "I am fine. How are you?"

He wasn't fine. He knew the same had to be true for me. Or at least he could imagine. But all he ever wrote was, "I think of you."

I would try to imagine how he felt after having done what he did, but I never got too far. Some people's shoes you just can't jam your feet into, despite your best efforts.

"You can understand, can't you?" Ma started that, asking it on the back of the cover of a card that announced Hello For No Reason! She was always very nice about Frankie, as much his cheerleader as Pal was Lucy's.

"Frankie was confused," Ma wrote kindly. "That girl was crazy. He was just trying to help. He needs your forgiveness, no matter what contact you plan to have with him. So he can go on with things, his life, you know. He needs to come to terms with his part in everything, with her and that baby."

That baby part was not intentional, according to Fred and Midgie, whose holiday slammed to an end when Frankie made them the recipients of the one allotted phone call, which is really all they allow you in those circumstances.

"The girl just showed up there at the dairy," the two assured Victory and Pal when they drove over the morning after the arrest, hollow-eyed, to try to clear everything up, and to get me to at least listen to the apologies of their son, who had been released into their custody while he awaited the scary event of arraignment. "It was raining. She was soaked. The baby soon would have been drenched as well. She knew we weren't around. She knew Frankie was—is—a good boy. That she could go there and he would take her in. They had no previous plan. She just showed up."

Just missed her own baby. Just took the one from Fisherdick Road. Just knew that Frankie was my boyfriend. Mine. Just knew that he was alone. Just needed a place to hide. Just showed up.

"What could the boy do?" Midgie wanted to know.

She looked at me when she asked this. I saw Frankie lying to my face, then leaning in. "I don't know, Robyn," he'd told me a dozen times, and kissed me there in the barn, all over the best parts of my face, assuring me, "She'll be fine. I gotta get back." To play house with Lucy.

I had no answer for his mother, except: "Tell us?"

Well, he wanted to, Midgie said, but the girl, the girl, the girl, "the girl scared him. He didn't know what she was going to do—I mean if somebody is crazy enough to steal an entire person, who knows what else she's capable of?" No, Lucy didn't really come out and say she might harm somebody—or herself— but you don't want to take chances. At least Frankie didn't.

And because Frankie didn't know, he did what Lucy wanted: locked the doors, drew the shades, invited no one near, discouraged those who did approach, kept the day help far from the house, bought what Lucy'd requested from a store at least three towns away: diapers, bottles, formula, some little clothes, and a squeaky toy in the shape of a shoe, intended as a pet toy, but better than nothing. Paced the floor. Listened to the news. Did his long hours of work. And, as much as didn't seem too unusual, made excuses to keep away from me.

"He didn't want to do that," Midgie said apologetically. "He just was afraid."

In the thirty letters, Frankie said none of that. All he ever wrote was that he was okay and he hoped the same was true for me and that he was sorry, so sorry, so very sorry, and that he'd like me to write to him if I would like that, too, and right above his fast signature, he'd put, "I always think of you."

He couldn't know that I ever thought of him again. Because after that summer, I never contacted him once. I ran back to Illinois to mope for the remaining weeks of summer and to watch my mother arrange and rearrange all the items already so neatly packed into the new white steamer trunk. Then I flew off to Washington to settle in and study and keep so busy as to not allow myself time to think. Or to think about things other than Frankie, and Lucy, and the stolen baby, and my broken heart. But there always was sleep, and in dreams there Frankie would be, standing in front of me on the walk, in Fred's old uniform and steel-toed boots, metal basket in his right hand.

"I'm out of yogurt," Frankie'd say, and the world around him would disappear, just like that. He floated in blank space, a Colorform waiting to be stuck onto the scene of your choice. On the porch, a blank order form sticks out from the lid of the tin box. I watch my hand reaching for it, the fingers taking hold just where the printing reads "Day 'n Night Dairy—Fine Dairy Products of All Kinds" above the list of all the many offerings. And at the bottom, in Frankie's handwriting, there are the words "I think of you."

In this dream I go inside and the cold water pipe in the kitchen does its familiar little screaming thing as I turn the handle, then water of a temperature lower than that of the Arctic Circle shoots out into my hands. I tilt my face under the high faucet and keep it there until I can no longer stand freezing. I dry off with a worn linen tea towel that had been a calendar from 1971 and then I place the bottles in the Frigidaire. On their own shelf. Side by side, so they won't be lonely—a feeling that out in Washington, far, far away from Massachusetts and all it had been the scene of, I was getting to know well.

.     .     .

But real life can top a strange twenty-three-year-old dream any old day.

"Imagine," Victory would have asked had she been there to witness the scene and then relay it to you later on.

At the ring, I was waving good-bye to a teenage boy who'd been nice enough to bring his little sister for a ride. There was something wrong with her that you couldn't put your finger on. The walk, the speech, the angle of her gaze, everything just a hair enough off to get you noticing and wondering. Enough less-than-well kids had visited the ring in my time, and I always considered luckier the ones who had problems you could actually see, those being much easier to understand and accept than the ones invisible. You can put your hand on a cast or a bandage, you can monitor the mercury in the thermometer. In time, you can see the wrappings removed, the temperature slide down to the mark considered normal. There is relief, proof that everything is fine again and the way we think it should be.

Lucy had changed into sloppy clothes from the dressy get-up in which she'd dolled herself to greet two women from a realty company in town who were interested in working closely with her on the eventual big real estate sale and who were planning to split the resulting big commission. She'd informed them there would be no commission, that her work was being done as a gift to the family. They left shortly after hearing that.

"What got rid of them?" I asked when she came out to the ring.

For an answer that was no answer, Lucy pointed at the ponies and asked "Do you think they'd still hold us?"

I waited a few seconds, don't ask me why—maybe it was just the déjà-vu—then I opened the gate and advanced them until Pan was standing there in the opening. Lucy approached, lengthened the stirrup, and swung herself on. I tapped Pan and waited for Star. Hoisted myself into the little saddle. Reached over and closed the gate like I do at the beginning of each trip. Moved us forward.

"We gotta get a picture," Lucy said, and she hopped off to get her camera. Passing Star, she stopped suddenly and put a hand on mine and looked me straight in the eye. "I want to explain everything to you," she said, and right off I knew this would be it.

Even so, I'd always imagined that if I ever was going to get the story from Lucy, about Lucy—the Lucy who had lived here all those years ago—I was going to have to go looking for it. Not have it delivered to me. And never did I think I'd be hearing it right here, at the farm.

I pulled Star to a halt. And, because they were all connected, everybody else had to stop, too.

"You don't have to tell me anything." I almost looked around to see who'd said this, and then realized I'd been the one. Saying the opposite of what I wanted, just because I wanted to spare her. And at the same time, hoping she would cover every minute of everything I had spent so many wasted hours wondering about so many years ago.

"I don't have to tell you. I want to. I am here to help you, sure, but to at least explain myself. Now that I am myself, and not who I was."

Who she was, was confusing. I said, "Well, that's nice." Really, what would you say?

"It's not nice, you deserve it. You were good to me. You and your uncle, and Victory."

"Well, you're a nice person. You were a nice person then . . . you are . . ." I shut myself up. I didn't want to confuse her, or myself, being someone who for a big long span of time had thought of Lucy Dragon as wholly terrible. And, ask me on a bad morning, maybe I still could.

"I was nice, I guess," she said with a little shrug, "but I had some big problems. Ones I shouldn't have brought here. But it wasn't my choice to come here. I didn't have any choices back then. I got sent here. I got sent a lot of places back then."

Mr. Dragon was off at a shoe convention in Wilmington and Mrs. Dragon was just a couple blocks away from home unveiling a line of seaweed masks at a ladies' tea the afternoon Lucy went across the street to the home of the college boy who was to tutor her in calculus and instead gave her a good long private lesson in biology.

"I could have done better with the numbers, I let everything slide on purpose, to keep my grade down around a low C, just to display the need for more help," she said. "Which I got, a solid two months, every Tuesday just after I got home from school. I would go for my tutoring, then be back in time to help with the little kids and the supper. My parents would ask me if I was learning anything. I was telling the truth when I said I was, a whole lot."

They sent Lucy off to a Salvation Army home in the skinny left-hand part of Maryland that you never would know even existed unless you lived there or happened to look closely at a map of the state. The place was a dinosaur, gearing up to close after seventy-four years assisting pregnant teenagers whose parents had determined the babies would be surrendered for adoption. Modern times, the fresh legalization of abortion, and a society less critical of girls in this situation had deflated the once-steady need for the place. Lucy's parents fell into a more old-fashioned category that cared what the neighbors thought, even if one of their neighbor boys was half the reason for the crisis, and drove her up there in late summer, just before what would have been her senior year. She was enrolled in one of the last few groups of girls waiting out their trimesters at the drafty Victorian in the center of the middle of nowhere.

"My parents told everybody I was going away to a school for the gifted and the talented, that I'd won a sudden scholarship," Lucy said. "They told me they'd come back for me after the adoption. I asked them, 'What adoption?' I didn't have a say. Nobody asked me. It was their choice. Everything was their decision. I had no idea even where I was going. I ended up in a big shared bedroom with one girl from Georgia, another one from Colorado. It was the three of us and our three problems. Me and Bonnie and Jill, all of us wanting to have daughters even though we would never know a thing about them, including whether or not they would turn out to be girls."

And that's what did it. That's what threw her into the hole. According to Lucy, she was as regular as you or me all through the transplanting to Maryland and the boring months of sweeping halls and cooking meals and washing her increasingly bigger clothes, even all through the horrible stabs of pain that grabbed her the day before Thanksgiving while she watched *Happy Days* and played double solitaire with the new girl from Pennsylvania whose boyfriend would drive over on Saturdays and stand on the other side of the chain link fence and woefully make her one quick name—Rae—go on for five minutes. Lucy said she was normal, fine, okay through the hollow-sounding countdown into the rubbery anesthesia mask. Made it down to eighty-seven, which she imagined as the answer to an equation the college boy would assist her in working—one that put her under, so far that the requests for medical instruments and the cries and the whispered word "girl" seemed to float from under the door of another room a hundred miles down the hall.

Mr. and Mrs. Dragon came back to get her after that. Once everything was over and Lucy seemed recovered and packed her bag and sat on the cold front steps under the cement awning, feeling oddly thin yet fat at the same time, all full of something sad she couldn't put a name on, yet completely empty like she was made of nothing but air. Her parents drove up to the entrance and each gave her one small hug like she'd been away a couple days on a class trip and it was no big thing to see her again after five long months. Then her mother talked all about the new paint in the dining room and the hallway and the living room and the nook in which there is a brass coat tree for guests to use, wait'll you see the shade, mixed specially to match a peachy yellow she spotted on the inside of a seashell, you know the shells she uses as decorations on the table at her cosmetic parties because they look so, well, natural, and go with the product perfectly? You're going to love the color. Everybody says it's very calming. Everybody. Her father said almost nothing. Asked for coins once when they approached a toll that requested exact change. Asked Lucy did she want the radio just after they drove out the gate. He put it that way like he was going to pull it out of the dashboard and hand it to her. "Do you want the radio?" She answered no. "No, Dad." Then she thought about those last two words together, and she wanted to laugh.

"I stared at the new-paint living room walls while I took everything in the three different bottles with my mother's name and address on them, written for my mother to take 'when experiencing anxiety.' Each in their third of an unlimited amount of refills, and each dated the day after I'd been driven up to Maryland. What I was experiencing fit the bill, to say the least, so I helped myself. The peachy yellow paint was calming—my mother had been right. I got so relaxed I didn't care about a thing. I positioned myself on the new couch all covered with the Laura Ashley chintz. I could see right out to the street, the snow falling on my classmates as they walked to the bus stop. I could see past them to the home of the college boy now off at university and probably assisting somebody else with their education. The shade in his window was still hanging crooked, like I remembered it being all the afternoons I'd been on the other side of it, and it's strange and sad how you can be busy at what he and I had been doing in there and, sometimes, at the same time your mind can wander over to a shade and in the middle of everything that's going on and on and on and on, you're thinking how you would just love to get up and go make the window look nice and neat."

Where the Dragons put Lucy next was another home. Somewhere south this time, down past Richmond. This one for disturbed children. There, they didn't care if you'd already had a baby, if you were seventeen you still were considered a child. You had to go to bed when they wanted you to, wake up when they wanted you to, eat when they said, take this pill and only this one now, tell your troubles to that person at a certain hour, and repeat them to another person later in the day. You were encouraged to draw out your feelings, to fashion them from clay, to give them color with paint, braid them together with thick rug yarn. The art therapist hovered, frowning in her search for meaning—strokes that represented anger, dark colors that reflected sadness or loneliness, pencil marks that if stared at long enough started to resemble an infant. Lucy made bead bracelets for everybody there who would wear them, and she told the doctors that the combinations of colors held meaning for her, yes, that's right, they were helping her work out the great sorrow that had led her to try to do what she had tried to do that day on the couch looking out to the house across the street. In reality, she didn't know why she'd taken the pills. Except that she'd had a baby and then had no say in what happened to it. The bracelets were busy work that kept her mind off such things. Thinking, thinking of something else. Rather than where was the girl now? Who was raising her? What did she look like? What did she enjoy? Lucy didn't know any of this. So she made her bracelets. And after five months in the home for disturbed children, with spring here and the nice and bright holiday of Easter arriving the following week, she was determined competent to face the real world again.

Lucy had only been released a couple weeks. There barely was time for her to get used to her old bed again or to learn her way around the placement of the new living room furniture, the search for and selection of which had kept her mother occupied during Lucy's absence. Mr. and Mrs. Dragon sat her down on the fancy tufted couch, this one positioned with its back to the window, and informed her she'd be spending the summer away. No, no, this would be a private home. Back in Grandma's town, the one she came from. Where her father had lived as a boy. A farm, nice and quiet. Grandma says they have horses—many, many of them. And a girl your age there, even—maybe one who'll be helpful to you. "They said it like that—'maybe helpful to you.' You—strangers—were supposed to help. They—my family—didn't know the first thing about what to do with me except to keep sending me places."

And that's how Lucy ended up here that first time.

She was leaning against Pan now, and Pan, like a big dog, was leaning right back. I stood at the fence. Watched myself as I hung on even though I didn't need that for balance. Just because I felt like I needed an anchor. And Lucy went on to say, "I found her just by wandering around."

Back at home, she used to do that a lot. Way long before anything happened.

"I always found it hard to stay where I was supposed to, and maybe was nine or ten when I began sneaking out my window and I'd walk around the neighborhood. Looking at homes—when you think of it, kind of like what I do now, only for pay. I wondered what they were like inside, who was in there, what they were doing. Surely some of these places had to hold more interest and, I don't know—life?—than mine. I was at home in the dark, there, staring at houses. I never found it scary. It always was to me what the exact proper wall color was to my mother."

At the farm, there was as much darkness as there'd been at the home in Maryland and at the one down around Richmond. And no fences to confine anyone other than the animals. Lucy was with us only about a week when she began her night walks, finding her way through the fields and paths and getting onto Fisherdick Road all by her senses. Just like that. She'd had no plan, no guide—despite what the gossips had thought. She was on no search. She was just new to the neighborhood, new to freedom, feeling her way out of the woods and onto the tar of Fisherdick, and there was a neat row of houses, all worth some gazing. She roamed around the property of the Watsons. Of Mr. Clean. Of the Coburns and their garden. Then she came to the Suttons' new place.

The sight of the parents and their baby did it. That's what threw her into the hole again. Three of them there in a pyramid like some statue you'd buy on a whim to give a new mother. Even if it was ugly and tacky, she'd keep it. Because, yes, that's how it really is. The two of you really do stand there and stare at your kid, for minutes and hours and days at a time.

Lucy stared, too. Regularly. Five or so nights a week she was going out there, long before I ever caught her, and more often than I did. She liked the moving through fresh surroundings. How cold her skin got when she was first out of the house, then warmed up as she moved along the wall and into the field and beyond. Her favorite part was to get where she could see no lights, not from the street, not the one Victory kept on over the sink in case anybody had to get up in the night. Lucy would stand in the complete dark and pretend she truly was just like she felt—the only person on the planet. And then she'd resume. Traveling into the woods, over to the one street beyond, and to the backyard of the fourth house on the right, inside which lived a story with a happy ending.

"Amy—I didn't know her name then, but of course I learned it—Amy was younger than the baby I left in Maryland. But even so I'd look at this one and I'd miss . . . mine. I mean, well, she hadn't really been somebody I got to know, like you'd know somebody who could talk and all—I mean I never even saw her. They wouldn't allow that. But I knew her anyhow. I sat there in the tree missing the baby I had, who was given away, who somebody else now had. My baby. Watching the Suttons inside watching their child. Most of the nights, of course, they weren't in the room—they did have to sleep some-time—and that one night they were gone, and the window was open. The baby just beyond that."

First Lucy thought she'd just get up close. And she did that with no problem, sneaking over to the screen, and to Amy, who was awake and looking around and who did turn and spot Lucy and smile as she would have smiled at anybody because what did she know at that point?

It was like somebody else taking over. Somebody moving Lucy's hand to push up the screen. Reaching inside. First to play. Then next thing you know, she was walking away. Into the dark. In a fog. Holding Amy, who was loving it.

"The night was a little rainy, but off and on and kind of nice, too. We went to that fancy garden next door. To the bushes at the dead end of the road, the ones that smell like maple syrup. We moved toward the woods. I knew I had to put her back and I did turn and head that way, then I heard the man yelling the name. A woman, too. Only she was screaming it. I saw the front lights on, the backyard lights on now, my tree there all in the floodlights. I knew I was in trouble. Big. So I ran. I just held on to her and ran."

This is the part I'd always imagined. A million versions of what went through Lucy's head then. Why did she go where she went? So I asked, "Why the dairy? I mean, it wasn't right next door."

"I couldn't go back to you, to the farm. I didn't want to bring trouble to your uncle and aunt. I knew Frankie was alone there without any adults. I thought maybe he could help me figure out what to do, how to get her back without getting in trouble. I knew the path to the cemetery. The one from there to the dairy. I just showed up. And he took me in. He was a good person, you know. Somebody who would not tell because I asked him not to."

"He was a good person," she said, putting Frankie in the past tense like he was dead. Which, for all I knew, he could have been. Long ago, the charges lost him his UMass scholarship. Mortified his parents. Damaged their business, people around here being the kind who would not want their daily milk from cows from a farm that also raised a young criminal capable of such things as had been proven in a court of law. I knew he'd left town later that summer, but didn't go too far, the obligation of his suspended sentence being a visit with a probation officer every single week for a whole three years. Victory and Pal, who told me this, had to know more but I never asked them for it. "Frankie was good, I felt that I was not," Lucy was telling me. "I know better now. Though it's taken me a long while to figure that out."

It was that time of day and one of the ponies—I think it was Zoey—began the word. Chester followed. Then Star. All of them shook their saddles, shook off everything that was holding them there and back from what they wanted, which right now was supper. Their awareness and concern was limited to the very moment that was happening right then. Which is when they told Lucy what she and I could go on to decipher.

A neigh.

Then the silence in which her story floated.

Pal would be going off to a nursing home.

There was nothing more that could be done for him at the hospital. And there was no way I could care for him at home. I know all that because I asked.

It seemed logical to me that he could come back and live out his days in his own place, or for at least the rest of the summer. Before we moved to Illinois, my family lived on a street where nearly every house held another generation. Regular elderly persons and also the very infirm were kept around for years, until the last second, with their kids doing what they could. I remember collecting the week's paper money at the Sniegs', and finding *Babci* Snieg stretched out in a hospital bed placed where, just the week before, the fancy dining room table had stood. Beneath the dimmed chandelier, she looked dead already as the daughter lovingly brushed her mother's silver hair and didn't even turn as she called to me that my envelope was there next to the telephone, and to take it and buy myself something special with the change, would I please?

"*Babci* Snieg, yes, well, people don't do things like that now. They leave the care to professionals," Ma wrote me that summer on the back of a small card front that told me "You Are Invited!" The illustration was of an umbrella, which translates to shower, though it wasn't clear if this was one for a wedding or a baby. "Times have changed," she added, underlining that news, and the truth, in case I hadn't noticed that. And "Don't feel guilty—you're doing enough already," a nice comment I didn't feel was the case.

Up and down our street back then, my friends grew up in the same homes in which their parents had been born and raised, and in which the people who did that original raising still lived. The Falkowskis had both a grandmother and grandfather in a little apartment over their two-car garage. The Toruns had remodeled their TV den into a convenient first-floor bedroom for their *dziadek* once he started to lose his memory and wasn't safe in his own place, where knobs and handles for stove elements and hot water were just accidents waiting to happen. Things are different now—old people don't stay at home anymore if there is something wrong. Their children don't have the time to care for them. Or the space. Or the know-how if it's a very serious situation. Or, in some cases, they just don't care—why do you think they moved away from their parents in the first place? This is what I was told.

'Round-the-clock care, that's what was needed for Pal. Professional 'round-the-clock—nothing I would be able to handle. So I had to halt all my progress in the junk-selling world and the getting-to-know-adult-Lucy world and enter a new one—the dismal search for a place that most likely would be my uncle's very last stop.

I went to his hospital room to tell him what the doctors had told me. He'd said nothing in response, but then he hadn't said much of anything for the two months since collapsing in the kitchen and then giving me my assignment.

"The new place, it'll be an improvement, I promise. A nicer place, none of this hospital atmosphere. You'll feel like you're at a resort." I said all this even though I knew Pal had never been to a resort. And though I knew he was far from a kid I had to joke with as I handed down bad news. But sometimes words and things just come out of you. I went from him to home, to inform Lucy, who'd spent the afternoon at her laptop, putting out the word about the farm and scanning the web for possible buyers. All across the country, she said, there are people whose dream is to chuck it all and live in the country. She just had to go out and find them so they could find us. "They're out there somewhere," she said, and I confidently thanked her, as I was doing every day now.

Things were different since the pony ring. That's how I put it in my head—since the pony ring, where Lucy'd gone and done her explaining a few days earlier. We still wouldn't have been able to be each other's official biographers, but there was more conversation, and the mood, the air, the days in general, all were a lot more comfortable. If she'd asked me did I know who she was, I could have answered yes without feeling I was just trying to be nice. Sure, some of it hadn't been easy to hear, especially the name of Frankie Mathews spoken aloud more times in half an hour than I'd heard it in the last half of my life. Frankie Frankie Frankie. Kind of like getting hit each time, but a little less painful as the story had gone on.

I'd last seen him nineteen Februarys ago. In my last year of school, stuck with how to start writing a paper for psychology—the professor had printed the statement "This is a sentence" on the board and then asked for five hundred words on the double meaning—I was grateful for the interruption of a knock on my apartment door. And there he stood. Frankie. Probation served, bag in hand, no plans but to make things right with me. What-ever that might take.

"I'm, uh, I'm, you know, released. Done with it. Free." Those were the first things he said. I can tell you because I remember them exactly, for their awkwardness.

I had not a thing to reply. His being there was his being there, as clearly as the sentence on the board was stating its existence for us. This is Frankie. Right here. Mussed up from travel and looking tired and older even then. A sweater out-dated and too tight, jeans too short. All of him soaked in rain. I stood there, my hand on the doorknob, taking all this in. The messed look and the exhaustion and the age and the fashion that had faded. I hadn't seen him since that night at the farm, three years back. I worked my way to before, before the search, before Lucy disappeared, before Lucy arrived to begin with, back to when I was nine and startled to see him dashing from Fred's truck to the porch. It wasn't like you'd want to write it, no big fast dropping of all my anger and disappointment, but enough layers falling away there to get me to point him inside and turn the key and lock us both in.

We lasted two months. Not even, really. A little more than seven weeks. Each day of which I'd look at him and I'd look at us and all I'd see was all that was missing. Early on, the days were like how I thought we'd have it after the dreamed-of wed-ding ceremony at the farm, after the ponies with their ribbons, after the circle of relatives in the field, after him in the white suit and me in the handmade gown, after the head on his shoulder and the budget diamond on my finger. Our time was more than good the first few weeks or so, back again to the heart-revving sweaty waiting and waiting for just a wave from the opposite side of the street, a look aimed across the traffic right into you like a laser, and when the light changes and you do meet with not just a kiss on the mouth but celestial forces enfolding, lightning and gold and currents in a storm around you two, there, next to the mailbox and the trash can and the flyers for world peace now. Playing at being adults, the shared closet and the shared meals and the shared bed that was really the floor because a twin is a twin and even though we shot for being one every chance we had, the sad truth with lights off or on was that we still were two. Separate. And different. From each other, and from who we were three years before. I'd stand back and compare Frankie then to who he'd been, and he never measured up. Sure, things did settle, and walls cracked and parted. But behind them, each time, stood Lucy. Out there, somewhere, but right there, between us.

The kid at the ring long ago had been right about visible souls, and I should have listened. No, you don't disturb something once it's buried. You just don't. And Pal was right. He was in my ear, as much truth as consonants: *"Jak sobie kto pościele, tak się wyśpi"*—"As one makes his bed, so must he lie in it." Frankie was in my ear, in English, with the awkward things that are said when you realize it's just no good anymore. I thought of Lucy, and of Pal, and of Frankie, especially Frankie, as I watched him from my hall window, getting smaller and smaller as he made his way down the long flat wet street that led toward the bus station and off to whatever he would do with himself now, without me.

What I went on to do was search for him. For the Frankie I'd known. Before Lucy went over there and he let her in. I looked for him in every guy who looked at me. Blond ones, red-haired ones, white ones and black ones, the skinny and the obese, those who towered and those half my height. What I'd known in Frankie wasn't in him any longer. Maybe somebody else had it.

On ferries, in churches, outside men's rooms, above the faculty lounge. In the farmer's market, the fish market, the regular market, in bowling alleys, city hall, a dog shelter, a youth hostel. Piers, bus stops, liquor stores, coffee shops, a soup kitchen, numerous discos, and the set for the filming of a political ad. In the cocky grin of the water quality monitor who left me with Tina when she was just a shocking test result at the ironically named Planned Parenthood. Maybe I wasn't as smart, but there I was, the valedictorian in the next town. There I was, alone and with a child. There I was, Lucy Dragon.

I looked for Frankie time and again. I pressed on. I could have made a fine career of this if paid. For years and years and years. You can waste a good portion of your life looking for what you've lost. Always looking. Nearly right up to the day Mary Lane Hospital called to tell me about the emergency being experienced by Pawel Panek.

"I want to help you find a place, a nursing home, a rest home, whatever they're calling them now. For Pal." Lucy was serious, and her words had a tone, a sound, a level, that told me this was not so much a bit of information, as a fact. A done deal. No changing it. She was going to help.

"You're helping enough," I said. And I wasn't just being polite. She was working hard and I don't know where she was getting them all, but in the month since she'd arrived, Lucy had attracted what seemed to me an impressive number of people who wanted to view the farm. And in that time, even one couple who went so far as to put an offer in writing. It was way too low, but still, it was an offer. Maybe they'd think again, she said, and told me to leave it to her. While I was out putting kids onto ponies and bits of bric-a-brac into people's trunks, Lucy was doing the big work. Trying to find somebody to buy the entire place.

"But I have to help your uncle," she said.

"You are."

"No." Here, she looked down at the suppertime dish of green beans I'd passed her. They'd been picked from bushes planted by Pal back when he was healthy and capable, only weeks ago to us, but a whole entire lifetime for these beans. "I mean I want to help in a way that matters."

"Oh, selling the property, that's not enough." I made big eyes, a joke. It didn't go over.

"No, it's not. Pal was, he was very nice to me, when I was here before. And he didn't even know who I was. I want to do something for him, something that'll really matter."

She stopped there, but she could have gone on. She shrank before my eyes. Back to a seventeen-year-old version of herself, her dinner plate switched from the one that just seconds before held a chicken leg and a foil-wrapped baked potato and those beans to another overflowing with guilt and shame and other such bad stuff that you'd never want to have to put inside yourself.

"Whatever you want to do." I said that because I wished the look on her face would change.

As it turned out, I took care of everything. I would have included Lucy in the decision. But all that happened so fast, and that same day she had an appointment, a promising customer—a group of officials from a progressive area school that had the idea of using the farm as one big classroom for ecology and agriculture studies. It sounded so hopeful I wanted to stay home myself, but didn't want to miss my appointment at the Belden House.

Wesley Elmer had told me to start there. He'd been coming by the hospital quite often to sit at my uncle's side and rattle off all the news he'd collected at the dump and at Friendly's and at the Weir River Club. When he visited, he'd leave a slip of paper on the nightstand. He'd write: "Wesley Elmer was here." All in a line like that. So I would know that somebody, at some point, had been there with Pal. That somebody else cared. Because I wasn't going to hear this update from my uncle.

When a story was funny, Wesley Elmer would smack Pal in the arm for effect, in a way you would never think to strike a sick person. But he went and did it just like things were normal. Or he'd poke my uncle in the chest for effect if the person about whom he'd been speaking was particularly infuriating. "So I said, 'You (poke) fat (poke) little (poke) thieving (poke) bastard (poke).' And, you know, he brought my pig back that very afternoon." Wesley was friends with everybody, including the girl who was now running the rest home out in the Brookfields—or at least knew her when she was actually the age when "girl" would have been a proper term for her. She was the niece of an old friend of his, a guy named Cuckoo. What, I never heard of this guy?

"They used to have a pole-sitting contest every year down at St. Mary's. Every year Cuckoo Polanski would win. He could sit up there for days."

I shook my head. Wesley Elmer looked disgusted with me.

Cuckoo didn't register, but maybe if I'd seen his face, there would have been a connection in my head. I'd only been back a few days when I began to spot the first few familiar faces from all those summers past. On runs to the hardware store, the grocery and the discount shop, the bank and p.o. Filling my basket with Windex, Borax, Clorox, Bon Ami, Liquid Gold. Trash bags. Scrub brushes. Rubber gloves. Stickers and little stringed tags on which to write still more prices. An O-Cedar broom with the patented angled bristles that I hoped indeed would be true to the theme song and make my life easier.

I rarely knew the names of those whose eyes or noses or laughs clanged some old bell because names weren't a part of running the ring. Everybody who came there was just Pardner or Little Miss or Kiddo or Hey You. Bub, once in a while. Or Bo-Bo. At least that's what Pal has always called the riders, so those were the names I used.

I actually did remember Eileen's name. And her name was what I said when I saw her two people behind me in the fifteen-items-or-less aisle down at the Grand Z the week after Lucy arrived:

"Eileen!"

Twenty-two years previous, she had been a shy scarlet fever survivor that one of Victory's and Pal's friends used to bring over on the occasional Sunday drive, and then leave with me the rest of the day as a supposed favor because I was a child all by myself and so was she, so wouldn't it be nice for us to be friends. Like it was that simple, that just any kid would do the trick. It wasn't hard to remember the great chore it was to both run the busy Sunday ring and lift both ends of an entire half day's conversation.

"Yup," she'd answer when I asked her something that I was hoping would inspire a few remarks.

Or "Nope."

Or, more often than anything else, no words at all. Mostly, she'd stare at me, looking possessed.

That day in the store, grown-up Eileen wasn't buying food, as you'd expect somebody to be doing in a grocery. She was standing in line holding a lamp, midnight blue in shade and base, and so small it looked more capable of darkening a room than brightening it. But Eileen apparently didn't think so, because there she was, getting out her wallet to pay for it.

I looked from her hefty deck of credit cards to her hands, which bore an assortment of plain rings, all in gold and even worn by the thumbs. Otherwise, she looked like a lot of the people I was seeing around from the old days. People who had been kids when I was a kid. You couldn't help but be struck by how old they appeared. Faces drawn, skin hanging or bland, hair colored unflatteringly, jelly bodies encased in punishing jeans. They wore scowls, snarling down at carbon copies of themselves at age seven, frowning into their wallets, snapping at cashiers who bit back. We used to be the same age. Now, certainly they looked older than I did, and, certainly, I didn't look anywhere near the state of them. I couldn't. No way.

"Eileen!"

Finally looking up from her lamp, she said this: "Hi."

We ended up having enough of an exchange that I got invited over to her house. For that same evening. She told me she lived in a ranch past the Polish National Church, and on the back of the receipt for the lamp she wrote out directions so detailed that I without any problems and by the requested six P.M. found her neat little green-sided place with a pointless length of fence running down next to the road before stopping and angling into the ground. Next to the front walk, two painted cement deer stood startled but I didn't take it personally.

I was hoping the years had given Eileen some time to come up with a couple of topics of conversation. I brought something to kick things off, a small raffia wreath that had been hanging in Pal's kitchen. It had been in perfect condition, wasn't dusty or anything. I really should have brought something along as a hostess gift, and I figured why go and spend money? This was one less thing I wouldn't have to concern myself with pricing and putting out on the lawn to have somebody scoff at and push aside, or toss in the Dumpster when that day eventually arrived.

"Aw, you didn't need to go and spend money," Eileen informed me when I held out the thing that had to have materialized at the farm back when Victory was alive. Probably from the parish tag sale or something, not costing more than a dollar, which was a lot more than the value of a circle of hay tied at four points with a blue-and-white checkered ribbon.

"I didn't spend money," I assured her.

She didn't believe me. "You really didn't have to." But she took it from me anyhow and quickly yelled up the little set of front stairs: "Stubby—come'ere!"

We both stood facing the stairs, Eileen as silent as in the old days, and then came the muffled stampings of feet on the slate-hued wall-to-wall, *bam bam bam*. Stubby appeared, living up to his name, coming up to no higher than my earlobe. He was compact and strong-looking, hair like a kewpie doll's, kind of orangey-red and thin all around except for on top, where it stuck up in kind of an ice cream cone shape. He was shoeless, the rest of him still in a gray suit with loosened red tie. A little gold pin on his left lapel displayed crossed handguns.

"This is Robyn!" Eileen announced loudly enough to startle me. "Robyn from the old days at the farm. Panek Farm up near the Quabbin. The pony ring farm! Look what she gave us! Get a nail! Hang it up!"

Stubby crushed my hand in an earnest shake and asked me, "Chicken or beef?"

They were barbecuing on the deck just off the kitchen sliders. Stubby served us drinks in clear plastic glasses on the picnic table that had been built in a triangle shape. Eileen and I sat there and watched him do all the work. I realized it felt good to be waited on.

"Nice to see somebody from the old days, eh?" Stubby asked Eileen.

"Oh, what times we had!" she replied, with actual slaps to the knee. My knee. I smiled and nodded, though I was wondering if she was thinking of the right person.

"I used to love to go up to that farm! I used to beg my mother to take me. 'Please! Please!' I'd whine like that (she actually did here, for effect). I would have lived in that barn if your aunt and uncle had let me. I thought you were the luckiest kid I knew, getting to stay there like you did. Growing up, all we had for a yard was a driveway."

The things I was learning. Eileen had loved the farm! Had admired and envied me! It was part of a phenomenon I was witnessing since coming back, mostly since the newspaper story and the wave of folks coming for rides and the remembering. Many of the adults who approached me all had some version of a secret to impart, and usually the opposite sides of the memories I carried.

The burly bearded guy who bought the two-handled saw
had been the shy, skinny, shaggy-haired kid who delivered
papers to the farm for a couple of years in my early teens. "I
used to love your long hair," he told me quietly as he handed
me twenty bucks from a jam-packed money clip. "I was sad
when you cut it. Sad." Sad? I remembered him as extremely
shy, and his dashing in and out of his parents' station wagon
always with his face angled down. I couldn't recall him actually
looking at me, ever, once.

"You always gave me and my little cousins extra times
around," the vice-president told me when I went down to the
bank for Pal's bottom line. I squinted at her, scrambling. "I'm
Nancy!" she pouted, disappointed. "I wanted you to be my pen
pal out in Chicago. All winter long I used to stare at the map of
the United States and think how I could have had a pen pal living so far away." I remembered Nancy, whose father at the time
was the bank president and therefore a big huge deal in town. I
remembered telling her that I didn't care if it was her eleventh
birthday—she still couldn't shove all the other kids out of her
way to get to the front of the line. I remembered her kicking
me with her patent leather Mary Janes, very hard and twice,
and if you want to look very closely on my shin you can see
the scar to this day.

"The pony ring—what times!" Eileen was nodding, reeling
in memories that were a mystery to me.

I turned my focus to the peace of the lovely view behind
Eileen and Stubby's home. The yard that seemed to have no
real boundaries, just drifted from uninterrupted neatly cut grass
into high grass into a field and then off up a wooded hill. You
had to work to find some sign of a neighbor on either side of
the house. A portion of the hip roof of one of those pre-fab

Sears sheds could be spotted if you craned your neck to the right and stared into the hedges, something I knew to do because Eileen, obviously proud of their solitude, had pointed out this fact and then invited me to make the necessary gyrations. But if you didn't do that, all the world would seem to belong to Eileen and Stubby alone.

"This is gorgeous," I told them. Basting a pan of ribs set on the little redwood shelf that jutted from the gas grill, Stubby immediately shouted over: "Eileen should get all the credit," making it sound like she was responsible for geography.

"All I did was stop in an office," Eileen said, waving him away. "And find Peggy."

Unlike the six other employees in the realty office that used to be the Rite-Aid, all of whom pretended not to see anybody standing there at the counter, Peggy was the one who put aside her sandwich and Thermos and left her desk and came over when Eileen on a whim one day two Aprils ago had stopped in. She and Stubby were living in Monson at the time, in a collapsing lakefront cottage where they'd raised three kids, two of whom already had moved out. They'd talked occasionally about getting a smaller home, something farther away from the center of things, more removed from the harshness of real life that Stubby complained was a big downside of his job as a police dispatcher for the town. Eileen still couldn't pinpoint why, but that day she drove right up to the office and went on in. And later that afternoon, Stubby and Eileen were seated right where Eileen and I were, writing down an offer on a form on the triangle table.

"Just like that," Eileen said. "Peggy is fantastic! She led us right to the place we had in our minds, in our heads. And, she helped us unload our house just about as quickly. I tell you, when you're ready to have people look at the farm, you should call her. I'll get you the number."

She went to stand up and I touched her sleeve. "No need," I said.

"You're gonna do it yourself? Oh, don't. I hear it's very hard to sell a home, and plus you don't want to get taken. My friend sold her own home, and she did—she got taken. She did."

"Taken," yelled Stubby from over at the grill.

"I won't, I'm not going to do it myself," I said. "I have help."

Eileen looked relieved. "Fantastic! Anybody I know?"

I took a swallow of the iced-down Chablis and for the second time since she'd arrived I said her full name: "Lucy Dragon."

A whooshing noise and a "Whoa!"

Stubby jumped back from the grill, which was flaring a wide flame high over the flung-back cover.

"Turn it down! Down!" Eileen was screaming, Stubby yelling back how he was, he was.

"I am! I am!" And after a few seconds of his shuffling around with the control panel, down went the fire, like a big wave peaked and spent and being drawn back to the sea, exposing what it had thrown onto the beach, or, in this case, onto the grill rack: the three sorry, charred hunks of meat and bone that were to have been our supper.

So we had pork chops that were to have been the next night's meal. Parkerhouse rolls steamed inside a shell of tinfoil. Peas from a store-brand can and a big square of butter sliding around on top of them. And a nice macaroni salad that I would have guessed to have been homemade but that Eileen said she'd ordered from the deli counter down at the Grand Z. She also had stood in line and ordered a small container of cole slaw, the kind made with oil and vinegar rather than mayo because Eileen can't stand mayo, even to see it in front of her, even mixed in with something else, even if it's never going to touch her plate or fork. She just hates it. She went on about the mayo, trying to come up with the origin of her dislike. Texture? Color? Smell? She searched much longer than really was necessary, something Stubby pointed out to her, and she shut up after that. Which resulted in silence and Eileen's staring. Almost like back in the old days when she'd come to visit. Except for birds' noises, and the static from Stubby's scanner in a faraway room, it was all quiet there in the backyard, which would have been nice if you were alone to enjoy it, or if you were visiting people you were comfortable with, which was not the case here.

Eileen piped up. "That wreath. It's very nice." Then silence again.

After dessert, which was nothing more than a pan of brownies you can mix and serve in the same papery microwave pan, which was exactly what had been done, we left Stubby behind to scrape the grill down with a plastic gizmo that Eileen noted she had won at a card party at the home of Pauline Wojtowicz. "You remember her, don't you? She had the place at Beaver Lake with the pontoon boat. . . ."

"My summers here, I never got off the farm much," I reminded her. "Church, groceries, feed store, Mountain Park one Friday in July, that was about the extent of my seeing the rest of the world. Not that I had one complaint."

Eileen nodded and then segued into shaking her head: "You're really not going to . . ."

"Huh?"

"You're really not going to have her help you—are you?"

I didn't have to ask who was the her. I said, "Well, yeah, I am. She's a realtor now, you know. For her work. In Pennsylvania. She's in charge of her office. She's very accomplished. She's received awards."

"She's nuts."

I heard Pal in my head: *"Wiadomosci o czyn dobrych maja daleki podroz. Wiadomosci o złe czyny nawet dalszy"*—"Word of a good deed travels far. Word of a bad deed even farther." And, apparently, it can travel off into the future. Years ahead, still remembered with fascination. Like how my father used to slow the car down back in Illinois when we'd get near the former home of the guy who left his wife and baby to run off with the nun who taught him in ninth grade. The guy didn't live in the house anymore, nor did his former wife and baby. Still it transfixed us. We'd tell visitors, "Right there—that's the former home of the guy who left his wife and baby to run off with the nun who taught him in ninth grade." And they'd all go, "Ooooh."

Now I was living in one of those kinds of houses, a destination point for those still handing Lucy's story down through the generations. I saw plenty of them. Vehicles braking as they approached the cement letters spelling out "PANEK." I knew what the drivers were narrating: "Right there—that's the former home of a crazy girl who stole the baby . . ."

"She was crazy ages ago," I told Eileen, then I corrected myself: "Ever hear of mental illness? People get better."

I got in my car. Eileen leaned in the window.

"She's a criminal. A crook. A kidnapper—'Baby-Snatch Teen'—remember? She'd be a murderer, probably, if you gave her half a chance."

I turned the key. "I know who she is," I said, and I meant none of the adjectives Eileen was offering.

"Here." Eileen pushed a paper toward me and got her face a lot closer to mine than you would want somebody's to in normal conversation. She whispered, like there was anybody else around for miles: "Peggy's number. Call her before you get too involved with Lucy Dragon. Tell her you've found another realtor. Stay away from Lucy. If you have trouble, you call us. Stubby can help, him being with the police and all."

I didn't touch the paper, let it fall between the seat and door. "She was young," I said. "She had, she had problems then. Everybody does."

Eileen's eyes got big. Indignant, she claimed, "Not me!"

"Okay. Fine."

"I don't have problems!"

"Okay. Fine." I was backing out now, and Eileen was getting smaller by the minute.

"Not me!" she was shouting from next to the deer. "Not me! I don't have problems!"

The Belden House was a pretty mansion with a pillared entryway that got you thinking of the White House. At least the front of it did. Miss Polanski, who was waiting for me in the vestibule when I showed up for my appointment, explained how the place originally had been this one building. Stephenson Belden was the original owner, a Yankee antique whose porcupiney face was captured in a crackled oil painting hanging behind the reception desk. He'd become rich from figuring out some faster way to hitch horses to wagons back when things like that were important, and he was said to have been pretty stingy, except for when it came to the expenses of caring for his elderly mother, whom he loved more than anything. He'd willed his house and fortune to the town for the care of its aged residents, then and forever. A very nice thing to do, except for that, over time, so many more people were making it to very old age, and so many other old people from neighboring towns came knocking, that additional space was needed to properly shelter them all. In the 1960s, a long brick extension was added to the rear of the house, designed and constructed so perfectly as to be almost invisible from the street. If you were a stranger passing by, you'd think this was just another of the stately old homes that lined the street across from the common. This was what Miss Polanski pointed out to me, but I told her it wasn't necessary—I'd gone by the place a thousand times, and never once noticed the addition. But, honestly (though I didn't say it to her), until you have cause to go looking for a vacancy at this kind of place, or are headed into one yourself, you don't take much notice of the entire building, never mind the newer part it's hiding out back.

"Renovated five years ago to state of the art," Miss Polanski told me as we passed from the lobby of the original home down a corridor that led into the addition. Glass lined the top half of the hall. On the wall that made up the bottom, bright construction-paper collages that attempted to resemble trees were tacked in neat rows. Miss Polanski saw me noticing them, and said how this was just some of the enjoyment that Uncle Pal could have if he lived here.

"These were made in Art I," she said. "We have Art II, for advanced students, and Advanced Art for those who, well, are really, really, advanced." She ticked off on her fingers, but didn't have enough to help her count all the other classes: line dancing, interpretive dancing, chair dancing. Aerobics, yoga, tai chi, reiki, mindfulness meditation. Poetry, creative writing, and the always popular memoir. Gardening, nature identification, flower arranging. Film appreciation, book discussion. Chorus, musical instruments. Gourmet cooking. Computers and the internet . . .

Miss Polanski continued as we passed the doors for Recreation, Chapel, Men's, Women's, and Linens, and her narration reminded me of the catalogs I find in my mail every fall from local colleges trying to entice me out to growth-inducing non-credit classes I never have enough free Monday nights in a row to attend properly. I guess this was why they never used the term "rest home" any more—it sounded like there would be no time for that here. Miss Polanski noted that most of the offerings at the Belden House could be attended or accomplished from any position, so nobody here, whatever their limitations, would be left out of any of the activities. It was enough to almost make me look forward to old age. Flat on my back, nothing to do but finally learn how to properly construct tortellini.

"We have children from the local school paired with each resident. They write back and forth, it's so enriching. We have the town bookmobile here Tuesday afternoons. We have dog days—I thought of that title myself, do you like it?—well-behaved pets are brought in to visit those who'd like to pat a dog. We have a ballet troupe from Worcester that comes through every Christmas to perform part of a scene from *The Nutcracker* in each patient's room."

The dogs, Pal would enjoy that. Having some guy in tights leaping over his bed would be another thing. But according to the investigative TV programs and their well-hidden cameras documenting the horrors of elder abuse, there could be fates more dire than an overdose of contact and culture. It seemed the greatest torture my uncle would endure here might be having to sit through a reading of original poetry. I asked for the papers to sign.

You don't want to be too picky, and they really don't allow you to be, but I did have one request—that Pal be given a room with at least some version of a nice view.

"He's been outdoors most of every day of his life—until he—until this," I told Miss Polanski. "Is there a room where he'll maybe feel like he still is outside?"

We were in her office now. Like all the rooms and spaces at Belden House, it had the decor of a romance novel. Gardenias battled for space among the peonies and roses that exploded across the wallpaper. Above a small, pillow-strewn sofa probably meant to make guests feel that much more comfortable while they were in here making their difficult decisions, billowy pink curtains were tied back to reveal windows illuminated day and night by single electric candles nailed to the sills. The shiny wood floor was interrupted here and there with the kind of fine rugs Victory would have called Persian. A Tiffany knock-off lit the well-ordered oak desk that held the computer that held the data that Miss Polanski was now scrolling through with muted mouse clicks.

"Hmmm. I'm sure we can do something—let's see what would be best for Mr. Panek . . ." She frowned. Moved to a new bunch of lines. The computer made sounds like it was eating its way through a meal. Miss Polanski said, "Maybe . . ." Then she raised her eyebrows hopefully, only to crinkle her mouth in the final defeat.

I looked past the padded shoulder of her sky-blue linen suit to the mantle over the fireplace piled with a trio of fake birch

logs. On either side of the lavender-scented candles burning
steadily as an aromatherapeutic contribution to the atmosphere,
photographs told me a little bit about Miss Polanski. It
appeared she was actually a Mrs. Or at least once had been. An
elaborate carved frame displayed her as she had looked on her
wedding day at least a decade before, all secured into a sleeveless ivory satin gown, a forefinger inside the opera-length gloves
touching her chin as she gazed out a window into the flattering
natural light, the warm sunrise or sunset complimenting her as
the photographer certainly had to have predicted it would. My
eyes went from the picture to her left hand, which was busy
joining the right one in typing a series of commands. Quickly
and loudly. No ring, no more. What had happened between
that look out the window and this day that found her staring
into the monitor with the same now-gloveless finger at her
chin? What happens to people between there and here, you can
never really know. I guessed that for Miss Polanski, it was nothing good. Had it been a regular old divorce, I couldn't imagine
she would be still happy to be showing off her wedding picture.
I would have put my money on a tragedy. What had it been?
What had happened to him? How had she handled it? Had
Cuckoo Polanski proven to be of any help during the roughest
time?

"Here we go," Miss Polanski said, stopping the tapping. "I
think I know what to do."

Uncle Pal moved in the Tuesday of the next week. Room Number 116, at the end of the addition, the part that stuck out farthest into a hayfield that marked the end of the Belden House's
property.

We had to wait for a pending death, but it was worth it for

all concerned. Each of the two occupants of 116 had his own television set suspended from a holder bolted to the ceiling, and a clicker secured to the bed with a curly telephone cord, easily retrievable if it fell. Each had his own dazzling white lavatory, his own touch-tone telephone, his own set of oaky-looking shelves on which to display some personal items that might make him feel more comforted. But the view was what really mattered. It was like looking out the back door of the farmhouse: that field, then woods, no signs of man or the things he constructs. Eileen and Stubby's backyard all over again. Miss Polanski said the land had belonged to the Beldens, now was rented for haying, usually done by the farmer whose property abutted the far end of the acreage. Watching the hay grow, seeing it mown down, and, with luck, getting to see it being sown and sprouting anew the next season, all that could be easily observed by my uncle. With some shuffling, he landed the enviable window side of a double room also occupied by a gruff former restaurateur who didn't care about the view because he spent most of his day at the other end of the building, in a corner of the lounge, playing cards for serious money even though that technically was not allowed on the premises.

"Just like home," I said to Pal. And I added, pointing to the window, "Look!" even though his eyes were closed, as they were so often nearly two straight months now. They did open now and again, but you never had any schedule or warning. Next time they did, what a surprise he'd have.

"Thank you," I said to Miss Polanski, who'd guided the orderlies and me to the room, and then observed them gently placing Pal on the new bed. "Thank you."

"Not at all," she said. "It's my job. If he were my uncle, I'd want him to be happy."

On the shelf next to the window, I set the picture from Pal's dresser, the one of him and Victory and me in the mouth of the barn, Chester off to the side on a lead. Next to that I placed a small clear vase containing some flowers from the front garden—a bit of wild greenery and then just mostly daisies from an energetic clump of them that every summer blasts from between a couple of rocks next to the back door. I'd be there often enough to refill it, just as Victory had with the arrangements she'd always placed in my room. Next to that I put a black plastic comb, new, picked up from a bin of them next to the cash register at the CVS, then the blue plastic tub that held his teeth when he wasn't using them, the red vinyl pouch containing his reading glasses in case the great day of his actually needing them arrived, and the little statue of St. Francis that he'd always kept on his windowsill, pointed outside, so that the great and influential Francis, lover and protector of all members of the animal kingdom, could watch over the ones who lived on the farm beyond. The front of the statue was faded from all those years in sunlight, only the back showing the original true color of the Hershey-brown robe. Francis was the same guy who'd asked God to make him a channel of peace in the prayer on the trivet that used to hang above Victory's stove before I sold it out front for seventy-five cents. Here, in this new room, I pointed him toward my uncle. I figured it couldn't hurt.

Pal was at a point of pared-downness that Sister Beatitude would have envied, had she been vulnerable to such a deadly sin.

*"Bogaty jest ten który nic nie ma."* This Pal would have told me if he could: "Rich is he who owns nothing."

# · 12 ·

In between our obligations, Lucy and I eventually went and did a few of the things you might do if you were just here on a vacation, rather than tending to legalities and responsibilities and real life.

"You want to?" she'd ask, and I'd say, "Why not?" We left the red Ford behind, heading off in the plum BMW. "Wanna drive?" The car was lovely and smooth on the road and I enjoyed the difference from the truck. Windows down, we laughed and turned up the stereo. She had a changer that handled five discs, and fancy speakers that put you in the concert hall. She played jazz, which I've never understood, but, as I was seated next to Lucy, the notes were hinting that they could line up in a way I might start to comprehend.

One night we took a ride to Holyoke. But it turned out they'd closed Mountain Park ages before—both the amusements and the ski hill beyond that. You couldn't even drive up the access road. The carousel had been moved to a green in the downtown. Who knows what happened to the rest of the rides, whether or not the fun house had been leveled or was still standing and now truly scary. From the highway you could still see some of the undulations of the structure down which the roller coaster had charged, now a white wooden skeleton against the mountain.

We pulled through the gates of the cemetery of transplants. I parked us on Sunset and without a plan we both headed for the timeworn stone leaning at a sunken angle, the marker of Kittie Evans, cherished daughter of Zilpha and David, 1815–1832. Only feventeen, which we, now forty, truly spelled with an *f*, once had been as well. Our tickets were still good and our rides were continuing on way longer than the one that Kittie had paid for. Lucy put a finger on the years, both the ones that Kittie knew, and the ones that so far had been ours. And she said: "Imagine."

We walked back to the car as the late sun poured in golden bolts through the spaces between the white pines. There were trees and plants and some wildlife, certainly, but when it came to humans and you looked all around you, we were the only ones alive. And it was like twenty-two years ago as I got a wave of really feeling that way—alive—just for being next to Lucy, who on a good day could do that to you.

In silence we passed the entrance to the dairy sold twenty years back to some bigshot from Amherst College. Fred and Midgie had moved down to her sister's farm in New Jersey, not a place you'd right off think of as agricultural but you'd be surprised if you went down there and saw all that is grown. Fred and Midgie needed to get out of here and make a new start and that's what they did, pulling in a bundle from the college guy who restored the house to what it looked like when Fred's own parents had built it. He was known for being an astronomy expert, but he also was handy and he stripped away all the paneling and siding and Formica and shag, every bit of modern stuff that had been added over the years. The barn got turned into a heated riding arena for the fancy pleasure horses that grazed in the fields that passed in my peripheral vision. The boy who'd grown up there was on both our minds that second, two places at one time, using up every bit of space so there was not one extra thing you could be thinking about. But not a word about him was said.

We went to see Pal there in the nice bright room at the end of the hallway. He was flat on his back, face to the ceiling, sometimes looking, sometimes not, same way he'd been since May. And here it was nearly August. Next to him, on the nightstand, a little square of paper that read "Wesley Elmer was here" told us his friend had been by again. I sat and told my uncle how twenty-nine kids had come to the ring the Monday before, which had to be some kind of record for so early in the week. And in this modern age. They hadn't even arrived all together in a bus, which is how you might get that many at once. I recited the sequence in which they showed up because, well, what else did I have to say to him? I said, "Four, two, one, six from a camp, three, one on a bike, one, eight . . ." All the while, Lucy stood silent at the window, taking in the view of the pasture. The woods beyond to the farm property after that. When it was her turn in the chair next to the bed, she looked at Pal and, rather than ramble on, she quietly asked, "What do you miss most?" Then, like she expected one, or maybe could divine it, she waited for his answer.

Each summer I stayed at the farm, Victory baked up tradition.

Her mother—my grandmother—had taught her the recipe, way back when, in this very fireplace. Because that's how you cooked way back when in the old country. Over fire. Like a

Girl Scout. Even if you were making a cake. And that's what
the *dziad* was. A big long awkward roll of a thing baked over
the flames of a low and steady blaze, turned on a spit as if it
were a leg of animal being cooked in a historical exhibit.

It was a treat for the winter holidays, an event in itself that
resulted in a special desert that jazzed up one of the longer
nights of the year. But since I was never at the farm in winter,
Victory made an exception and baked one during the summer,
when you usually don't have the fireplace cranking and throwing off heat. Victory would wait for a cooler spell, or the pre-
diction of rain, then she'd make her decision.

I'd looked forward to making one the summer we had Lucy
there, mostly to the unveiling of that last, fascinating part, to
see her reaction, which from anybody is usually amazement
and sometimes enough to make people wish they had a camera
on them.

Pal would say it was a good thing we had our own chickens,
otherwise we'd go broke getting the fifty eggs the recipe called
for. As it was, we had to pay Fred for the two pounds of butter
that also was necessary, along with a mountain range of flour
and sugar. All this created a thick soup of a batter that Victory
mixed in a deep lobster pot and brought over to the fire. She'd
pour a ladle of it onto the hot spit, and when that was baked,
she'd pour over that another measure and that would bake as
well. It was my job to turn the handle, in between new portions
of batter. That went on and on as the cake grew, the color of a
pancake, uneven in shape and gnarled on the surface like the
cane of an old-country beggar, for which it was named. We'd
drink tea while the baking went on, brewed with a dark infusion of leaves like it's supposed to be. No bags here, tea was
purist style—first a scant pouring of the orangey water in which

the soaked leaves floated in their permanent pitcher on the kitchen counter. Then the rest of the glass—never a cup—filled with water hot as the pot could stand. Tea for everyone—and for the adults, the addition of something golden poured from a bottle kept far back on the shelf that you would hit your head on if you didn't duck when going down cellar.

We'd have people over these nights. Wesley Elmer. Alice in her car with Bernice, and Fred in his with Midgie. And they'd all have tea, too, or tea with the golden stuff, or just the stuff, alone, everything requiring frequent refills. When the last layer of batter was finished, my uncle would remove the spit from the fire and lean it against the bricks in a standing-up position. Then Victory would cut round slices that showed the mysterious rings of the cake, like those in a tree when you cut it down and see the history in there, how John Quincy Adams was president when this ring was made, and the Civil War happened when this one was formed, here's how big the tree was when the valley was flooded, and this was the size it got to the year that baby girl was stolen from Fisherdick Road.

On the exact date of our nation's bicentennial, July 4, 1976, about a month before she took Amy for seven days and left us for twenty-two years, we baked up a *dziad* for Lucy. I remember the porch door being open and a nice breeze traveling through the living room, bringing the lovely metal rain smell indoors to the dozen or so of us there in front of the fireplace, on the couch, the chairs, Lucy and me on cushions, Frankie seated next to me, his head against mine and flooded cinema-like in that tangerine light that illuminated my mind's recording of Lucy's leaning-in fascinated reaction to the rings, the way she half closed her eyes when she got her taste of them, like she wanted to block out everything else in the room and just concentrate on the sweetness. Pal began to sing. The slow one about the highland man who must leave his home, farewell my hills, flowered valleys, farewell my childhood of gladness. Even if you didn't understand the language, you would have fallen in love with this guy and it would have made perfect sense to go and empty your entire bank account to do what it would take to make it possible for him to stay where he belonged. None of us had any instruments with us, so it was my just my uncle's voice plain and unskilled but perfect because of that, the background being the snappings of the burning logs and the steady fall of the rain on the grass. He stopped his song in the middle of a line and said, "Listen," and we all did, to the sky pouring for an audience, and we were glad to have had this pointed out. Then my uncle started up again, the highland man walked off, and the singer hoped for his return. Everything ended with raised glasses and hey hey, Pal, once more please, applause, and his bowing briefly and several times.

The night Lucy and I returned from the amusement park and the cemetery and the road past the dairy I decided that, no matter the weather, I would bake a *dziad* while I told Lucy about my life. To try to give her, and maybe myself, the words that would describe how very much of it has been tied up to, reflected in, formed by what had happened that summer. To say how nobody since—not even Frankie himself—could measure up to who he was before Lucy carried Amy Sutton through the dark and to the dairy. Later the next morning, I decided to bake one anyway, to have something to keep us busy and occupied and thinking of things other than what had happened after the doorbell rang and Lucy got up from the kitchen table and I heard her sandals grind to a stop and then no hello or conversation, nothing, and so I went to find out who'd come by, and there I saw Lucy on this side of the screen looking out at the other side. At the milkman.

She and I had been working on breakfast. I'd gotten out Victory's cookbook, her only one, skinny with the red cover that she kept on the windowsill, where her Geritol and Pal's Bayer still sat waiting to jazz up somebody's blood or relieve their pain. The *Rumford Complete Cookbook,* according to the first page, back in 1950 was boasting more than six million copies in use. One of those copies had landed in Victory's kitchen, a whole book she got just because Mrs. Fenimore behind the counter at the drugstore had said that was where she'd found the recipe for the rave-drawing cereal macaroons she had served at the Protestant church bazaar. That was the only thing Victory ever made out of that cookbook, and page 171 was marked with a holy card depicting Our Lady of Guadeloupe and the barbecue-flame halo forever encircling her. My aunt consulted the cookbook every time she made them, which was about twice a month, and over the years you'd think she'd have come to learn the recipe by heart. But she opened it to where Our Lady was marking it without fail, and made the same thing, varying it only as the instructions suggested—that the two cups of flaked cereal could be Corn Flakes or Rice Krispies.

We ventured into new territory, cracking the spine and finding an entire chapter that told me how eggs should appear in some form in everyone's daily diet. I skipped down to the most essential—that eggs are one of the easiest foods to cook. Soft, hard, shirred, poached, fried, scrambled, deviled, creamed, curried, and something called planked. I got out half a dozen. Fresh. Victory had taught me about eggs long ago. Because Uncle Pal had gone to the time and trouble of adding the adjective "fresh" onto the hanging sign announcing that we had eggs for sale, Victory felt it was only right that we didn't tell a lie. Every morning, we went into the coop and collected the eggs, but of course not everything we gathered got sold instantly. So some that we stored in the extra refrigerator down cellar hadn't exactly been pulled from beneath a hen the very morning you were stopping to buy your dozen. Victory instructed me to place the eggs pointy side down into the cartons, and to put the newest cartons on the bottom shelves and move the older ones higher up. We sold the top-shelf eggs first, and moved the ones from below into the spaces the sales created. If any lingered longer than a couple of weeks, Victory would use these for our meals, testing them the way her mother had taught her, placing an egg in a bowl of cold water and seeing if it would sink or swim. The freshest sunk. Ones that had been around a while stood on their ends or bobbed low. We still used those. The oldest ones floated like they were awaiting rescue at sea. These were sent off to the compost, and I loved delivering those there, pitching them individually, even if I had a couple dozen to toss, merely for the reward of hearing their muddled cracks when they hit the decaying pile of refuse.

But these were fresh. Fresh eggs that just this morning had been left to us by Curly and Henrietta, Pandora, Queen Elizabeth and Red. Everybody else was gone by now, the twenty-eight others sold the day before to a man who knew Pal from his many trips to the feed store. The six that remained strutted around a suddenly cavernous coop, making their normal little worrying sounds, but now probably really meaning them, wondering who'd be the next to go. And I couldn't blame them—I was in charge of things and even I didn't know that.

I asked Lucy, "Remember Mr. Clucky?"

Many generations previous to the current chicken dynasty, the summer Lucy and I last were here, he'd been the best known rooster. Loved to ride in the truck. He'd pace around it until Pal was going somewhere, and would run after it if not invited along. My uncle made Mr. Clucky a car seat, a little cage on a box that would allow him to see out the window but still be contained safe, keeping his flapping wings out of Pal's concentration while driving.

"Mr. Clucky. Ha . . ." And that's when the front bell rang.

To say that Frankie surprised us is a great, diving understatement. The same goes for Lucy's surprising him back when she went to the door and saw his face. What it had to do to him to see her looking back, well, the wondering about this could have gone endlessly had a car not come up the drive and a swarm of Camp Fire Girls screamed toward the ring and Lucy shot a panicked look back at me and mumbled an "I'll go," then walked quickly, stiffly, to the back door. I moved to the place where she'd been standing and looked at Frankie through the wires like he was some kind of exhibit.

He was tan. But he was always tan. He looked more like Fred did back when I knew Fred, this just meaning that Frankie was older and wore some years visibly but in a lot less jarring way than many of those people I ran into at the hardware store. The bones of his face were more pronounced. His hair was still blond, and he looked like he'd gotten a recent haircut, everything all neat and straight at the edges, the back tail of his hair falling to the collar of a green T-shirt with no pockets that was tucked into tan pants that has loads of them. The strap of a good-sized duffel remained in his hand and it must have been tough to keep holding it like that, up and off the floor, all this time since ringing the bell and seeing Lucy there, and now me. I thought of the word *dumbstruck,* and then I went on to wonder did it have a *b* in it. I tried to imagine. How would the word look without the *b?* I was thinking, thinking, though I know it sounds so stupid, but I was thinking of anything other than Frankie standing there and saying nothing, there in front of me after all this time living in my head.

Then he spoke: "Robyn."

I stepped aside and slowly opened the screen. Put myself in front of him with nothing between us now. He let the bag go and the sound was like a body finding the floor. He brought his hands up, but to his own face like people sometimes do when a situation is overwhelming. Then he turned toward the ring and watched Lucy help a girl onto the saddle worn by Zoey. He turned toward me and what he saw then, well, I don't know.

He spoke: "Where did she come from?" The "she" weighed about a ton.

"Philadelphia."

No, no. "I mean—when, what's she doing here?"

I used to imagine. Often. Very, very often. For a lot longer than was healthy. Years and years past the one disappointment that colored everything for me. There must have been some shred of hope shoved to the back of the shelf, though, when you consider the time I put into my thoughts about him. I easily could fixate on what it'd be like the next time Frankie and I met. I pictured it would be at first greeting-card picturesque and then rocket into something that could be filmed for one of those channels they offer on hotel cable. I used it as a drug. Bored? Disappointed? Heartsick? Imagine how it would be if I ever did see him again. But nineteen years after last touching me, his hands were like a physician's. Careful, precise, like I was a pile of broken bones. He took my shoulders, moved me back, looked at me as if there might be visible signs of damage from my being here, alone, with Lucy Dragon.

"Are you okay?"

"Of course." And I pointed at him—"Are you okay?"

He almost laughed a little, and his eyebrows raised themselves. A scar ran along the end of the right one, something he hadn't had there as a kid, I can tell you, because when he was a kid I knew the square inches of him. A wound had been received and tended and healed and forgotten and I'd known nothing about it. Nothing. But that is what happens when you have no contact with somebody. You don't know. But, then, think—it was your choice. "I guess I'm fine. For somebody who didn't expect this—her—here."

What he did expect here was me. Up in Frankie's Vermont town, the paper had carried the story. The story about me. And the ring. The same wire story that Lucy had spotted in the *Philadelphia Inquirer,* the one that got her phoning associates to cover her absence, throwing together a bag full of clothing, heading to the bank, and then onto I-95 and north. For Frankie, the result first was more thought than action. He'd read the story a couple of times. He'd ripped out the page. Put it on his desk. Stacked mail on it, uncovered it eventually, lost it again, found it again, thought some more, piled more things on it, moved those eventually, and eight weeks after it had run, he'd made a decision. Knowing where I was and what I was doing, he decided he wanted to come down and see if there was anything he could do to help. To help. "I don't know (here he crossed his arms around himself), I'd like to do something for your family," he said. "All of you, always so nice to me . . ." He scrambled: "You know—I can help with the animals, the house,

I'm still good with all that. It's what I do. I work on a farm, a small dairy up past Putney. Organic. You know yogurt's most of the business. Mainly yogurt. Organic."

Frankie is an expert in yogurt. He wants to help. Here. This summer. He is standing twelve inches from me.

Asking about Lucy.

And I answer his question: "The Saturday after I got here. Late May."

His head shot forward. "The same week you got here?" He turned to the ring again. Lucy was talking with the troop leader, I guessed that from her beanie. "She's been here all this time?"

"Yeah."

"Doing what?"

"Helping, too. She's helping sell the house. That's what she does. Realtor." Like I needed proof, I reached over to where Lucy kept a little basket of business cards on the hall table. I took one out and held it up and pointed to her name. And to the slogan. "She finds homes for those who need them," I said, like an ad. "She's been giving lots of tours."

Frankie didn't look impressed.

"She's fine now." I was defending her, to him. Listening to myself, incredulous. He said, "She's . . . ," and he searched for the word that I went and suggested: "Okay?"

"Well, yeah—she's okay?"

"Sure seems it. She's like anybody. She has a town house and a Maltese and runs in fund-raisers."

"Just came here? No warning?"

"No warning. That story in the paper. It went all over the country, I guess. Like I said, she read it . . ."

He shook his head. "No warning."

I ventured, "Imagine."

And when it hit Frankie that he had arrived in the very same manner Lucy had, that was when he stepped forward and through the door, which, because sometimes you just have to go with what is swirling around you, I had pushed open for him.

Inside, I answered his questions. Telling the story Lucy had told me. Of what she said she'd done back then—a lot of which he knew—and what she'd been up to since then, and what she'd come here to do for us—me and Pal. About her not being crazy anymore, because, like she told me, you know that does happen—people do get better. It is illness, and illness can be cured. I told him about how well she is doing now, making her life finding homes for those who need them. Making her own in the meantime, way down in Pennsylvania, alone. No husband, no luck with anything like that. No kids, except if you're counting—but I didn't mention this—the one who's no longer a kid, who never was hers to begin with, who remains out there somewhere, unresponsive, or maybe simply ignorant, of Lucy's couple of extensive, expensive tries to locate her.

Frankie looked uncomfortable, even though I had fixed him up at the kitchen table with a cup of coffee in the chair he always favored, the tall-backed one nearest the porch door, at the end of the table where sits the person who at a fancy meal does the carving.

"She seems to be doing well," I told him. "I wasn't sure for a while. But I do believe her—you can put things behind you. She's not crazy."

"Ill," he corrected. "You want to say 'ill.' "

"Right—she's not ill anymore. Or crazy, either. You'll see." I stopped there. "You will see. There's no way of avoiding her in this small place."

Frankie kept quiet. And I think I knew what he was feeling—how there can be something stirring inside you that you didn't even know was there, and you look up from the pony ring and there's the big dark car rolling to your door. Or you hear a doorbell while you're making the eggs and you go to see who rang.

"Alcohol and cake. Great diet you people have."

Frankie was attempting a joke while holding out his glass. Lucy poured a bit of the tea infusion, I added hot water from the kettle on the hook above the steaming *dziad*. Lucy carefully put in the finishing touch, the old and golden stuff we found in its place at the back of the shelf on the way down the stairs.

We'd halved the recipe, considering there were only three of us, still making a nice enough dent in the surplus eggs down in the cellar refrigerator. I'd never seen Victory fool with the ingredients, so I wasn't sure what the outcome would be. But I was happy to see that, four layers into the effort, everything appeared normal so far, the way you'd like it to be.

"So, uh, Pennsylvania," said Frankie. "You like it." And "Tell me about your car." "Tell me about all the people who've been coming here and what do they think of the place?"

He was good, offering the broadest of topics for her to choose. Steered way clear of any of the serious stuff. It all could have been filmed for a documentary on superficial conversations. One-line questions, the same kinds of answers. How's the Sox and what kind of mileage does a car like that get and you see any movies recently? Nothing below the surface, hovering safely above, not one indication that would have you guessing these people had a history you could look up on the town library's microfilm.

I watched the two of them giving their answers, no music to
back them up, just the squeaking crank on the spit as I slowly
spun the *dziad,* the snap of the flames, and the unstoppable big
crickets noisy and outside where they belonged. Interest rates
and rainfall, mileage, a dilapidated house that a former Penguin
goalie fixed up and sold for four times the original price, everybody who comes here says no repairs would be needed anywhere in this place, just maybe renovation if you were the type
who wanted a more modern look and perhaps an upstairs bathroom. His stuff, well, yes, he likes his work, it's at a dairy, no
surprise. The main product is yogurt. Organic. Very good. He
is active in an over-thirty baseball league, second base. He lives
in a small river house he renovated, it used to be a bait shop.
He lives there alone.

Surprise.

Then hope?

I added the layers of batter during all this. Filled the glasses
with whatever was missing from them. Spun the handle some
more. In the tangerine light, Frankie and Lucy spoke enough
but said nothing.

The cake was ready. I propped it up against the hearth like Pal
always had. Sliced. There before us were all the rings. Their
own stories enclosed, wrapping around the next, entwined in
ways you could see only if you looked close, and even if you
made that effort, it was difficult to see the separation. One layer
connected to the next after being put near heat.

I served big plates. Added the maple syrup Pal had boiled
down just at the end of this past winter, when he was up and
well and good still. We ate and had seconds and thirds and
many more glasses to wash it down. From down the street, and

down the valley, you could hear the pops and whines of fire-crackers brought into the state under illegal conditions, their smugglers maybe daring to light them off in a trash barrel to give as sonic a boom as possible. Sometimes after one went off would come a light round of applause. People happy with the light or the noise or maybe just the fact they were all there. Sometimes that's all you need, after all. I wished I could remember the song about the mountain man. I couldn't. Give me the first word and I could have gone four stanzas. But there was no one there familiar with it—I know this because I asked. So at that time I just recited the idea. "Do you remember this, Lucy?" And she nodded, that yes she did, and I started how there was a man. He had to leave his mountain. That drove him to tears. But there was something about him being told not to feel bad. I think the person who sings the song tells him that—not to feel bad. Though I couldn't remember the exact consolation. But sometimes, just being told that is enough. That somebody would like you to stop how you're feeling, and get on with things.

The mountain man had been told this.

I wondered if he'd taken the advice.

# · 13 ·

The fall my family settled in Illinois, a fair filled the parking lot of the shopping center where every Wednesday we bought our groceries.

"Look!" Ma yelled out of nowhere that day, when we got near the noise. (Realize that she hardly ever yelled, for bad or good.) "Ponies!"

My heart shot into sixth gear. Other than a photo that Victory had sent me of the ring busy on the first Labor Day there I'd ever missed, I hadn't seen a real pony in nearly two months. I whirled around to spot what Ma had seen. A cloud of aqua cotton candy floated past. A tattooed hand held a disc of fried dough beneath a snowfall of confectioner's sugar. Standing near a skill game that dangerously invited you to shoot a BB gun at a paper bulls-eye, a tall clown turned toward an alleyway and hunched to light a used cigarette. I saw no ponies anywhere. Not a one.

"Where?"

Ma spun me around fast, by the shoulders. She crouched and pointed to help me find what she'd seen:

A carousel.

"Come on!"

Suddenly she had my hand and was walking a lot faster than I was, pulling me along, calling back to me: "Wow! Aren't they gorgeous? Beautiful! So lifelike! Do you see them all?"

I saw them. Horses, not ponies. And plastic. Or metal. Or whatever you make horses out of when you are not God. The herd of them was stalled, done with or not yet starting to circle. Frozen stiff, caught in all sorts of positions and expressions, most of them fierce or, at the least, unsettling. Necks arched. Legs curled in mid-gallop. Eyes wild, tongues out to the side, and teeth bared against unseen predators.

Cheery organ music played too loudly from somewhere hidden. A couple thousand pulsating bulbs covered most surfaces, all lit up and wasting who knows how much electrical energy even though it was only full-daylight lunchtime.

"Which one do you want?" Ma asked brightly. "Which pony?"

Before I knew what was happening, she was paying the man some amount of money from her little see-through plastic coin purse, and the next instant his dirty stranger's hands were gripping my sides and he was swinging me onto a pink horse that pawed the air way too frantically. Then he was at my side, picking up a leather belt attached to the big silver pole that ran down through the horse's neck and held the statue bolted to the floor.

"Ever been on a horse before, cutie?"

I just gave him a look. I could right away tell he was an idiot. As he buckled me in tight, he worked from the righthand side of the horse. You never, ever work from the right side of a horse. Even a fake one.

"You scared? Don't be scared now."

I turned my head away as he completed the safety precaution I myself had performed so many hundreds of times for so many hundreds of kids who were just about to ride a real pony that actually might hold the possibility of causing them harm. My face fried with embarrassment. The one good thing was the lack of riders—at least as far as I could see. My vision was blocked by the center of the carousel, a big fat column with paintings on it that rotated even before the ride started. They turned backward, making you feel like you were moving already. There was a picture of a man and a woman riding on a big black plowhorse that did not require saddle or bridle. Next was an Indian and his Appaloosa up on a cliff, surveying a placid river valley as it looked before anybody came along to wreck it and make it into some sprawling mess like my new hometown. The next panel was a bunch of old fashioned-looking little kids all in a line. Each of them riding out of a barn. Riding on ponies.

Trouble was, I knew real from fake. Then and now. It's an ability that's stayed with me all my life. So if I found myself even starting to think that Frankie's returning was due to anything other than guilt, I'd just shake my head at the silliness. Whatever we all had in common last time we were here on the farm, the denominator now was work. And that's what Lucy, then Frankie, had come back for. Their versions of penance, their confession prescription of a single Our Father and three Hail Marys and one Glory Be and a promise not to do it again. Not to be dumb or stupid or, if you can help it, crazy. They, and I, did the work that started as one early project and moved into the next and before you knew it, you hadn't eaten all day. On the kitchen table, Lucy dialed the phone and pounded her little computer, looking up only to give or answer a greeting, and she cleared everything away for the supper we ordered out. Debbie Wong or Theresa's or Debbie Wong again. We talked through the meals, but everything remained the polite bits said to the next person in line at the checkout or the p.o. or the funeral home. Then, at our own pace, Lucy and I would head upstairs and Frankie would go off to the porch and that would be that for the day.

Jerzy was elated that Frankie had come to stay for a while. They had absolutely no history—it's just that Frankie was what Jerzy needed without his even realizing it. Sure, I was strong enough, but two men could push and lug easier and swifter than Jerzy and I had been doing all these weeks. Big pieces of furniture appeared on the front lawn each morning, and, if they were still remaining, got carried in at dark rather than just covered by a tarp. Things were pulled from the gut of the barn that hadn't been in sunlight for fifty years. Pieces of tractors, metal shapes that had you guessing the use, wooden barrels, a grinding wheel, the tall wagon Pal used as a money-maker for a few autumns back when the chain of signs out front included the offer of hayrides and people still went and did such things as a romantic date. The more stuff Jerzy and Frankie dragged out, the more cars stopped, the more money was unfolded, the more things were carried and loaded and driven off.

"People like to browse, I guess," was Jerzy's conclusion.

"Not just to look at one or two or three things," Jeannie threw in one day during a visit. "Not that I'm being critical . . ."

But she was. I'd come to realize that she wanted the farm. For herself and Jerzy. He'd worked there so long, for so little, it just seemed right that he end up with it. But it wasn't mine to give, and that's what I'd have to do—give it—because Jerzy had very little money. I know this because he told me.

"I have very little money," he said plainly one day soon after I moved back and just before Lucy arrived. "No way I could get a loan, I don't know anybody rich. There's no way I could afford this place or I'd buy it in a minute."

"I figured that. I wish I could just give it to you, but I can't. It would be perfect. It's Pal's, not mine. And he wants me to sell."

"I have very little money," he repeated and went off to work again. To more moving, shifting, selling. All around us, things got very hollow. You'd walk in a room or around the yard and the sound would be different. Your voice would carry farther. Spaces expanded. Lots of things had disappeared. Others weren't going anywhere. Specifically, the ponies.

On a cool Thursday morning, Lucy came out and helped me groom. School of beauty all over again. She braided forelocks, fluffed manes, finished off coats with a dustrag like you do before a show. She said what I was trying not to think: "What about them?"

People wanted the ponies, sure. Oh, how cute! I'll take them all. What are you asking for them? But there was no price. Because I wasn't selling. I didn't know what I was going to do with them, but I wasn't going to sell. "Neigh," they would say to me out at the ring. Was that "Thank you" or "Do it and get it over with." I worked on the translation.

Into the second week that Frankie was back at the farm, an ease was settling in. One morning long before I came downstairs, some kind of talk was going on between the two of them. Lucy had been rising earlier than we were, and getting out of our way before we ever saw her, heading back up to her room or off into town. But the timing was off this morning, she later, he earlier, and there they were, hunched in from their seats across the table, serious eyes, voices turned way down low. I saw actual pictures above them, like how in paintings you see fires glowing from the heads of apostles and other holy types. These were more in detail, though, and fast, like flash cards. I didn't need to study to tell you the progression: Fisherdick Road. The woods. The dairy. The rabbit on the dashboard. The voices behind the shades. Frankie's eye in the doorway, the cow tails, the long trip the zero-hole took around the dial. What I firsthand knew about Frankie's life after that. What I'd been told by Lucy about the years since. My U-turn when I spotted them in the kitchen was recordbreaking.

I heard her "I shouldn't have . . ." and his "I didn't know . . ." and again her "I shouldn't have . . ." I left them there with themselves and their history and the filling up the gap between. Or whatever it was they were up to. They needed this—I was just glad something was happening after all the silence. I kind of wished they'd stay in there all day and say whatever needed to be spoken aloud. That last summer here was gone and everybody was fine now. Nobody dead, nobody lost, nobody taken, nobody crazy. In my housecoat I went out to the empty ring and leaned on the top rail and it felt like that afternoon all over again, keeping myself out there while Mr. and Mrs. Dragon and Lucy's grandmother got the big update at the kitchen table. I wondered who would appear suddenly, this time, asking for consolation. All I heard was an impatient pony voice from inside the barn. One soft neigh. And then another.

.     .     .

Lucy and Frankie weren't in there all day, just a good part of the morning. For so long that I finally crashed through and used the bathroom one time, keeping the shower running to allow them privacy and give them the knowledge that I was not eavesdropping. I went from there and to the barn and the ponies and the ring and four little blind kids who I allowed to climb all over the wheel and the animals to get the proper look they needed. Yelling and laughing and all of it better than getting on any of the ponies for five times around the world. None of the animals were going to complain about the touches, or be mean. None of them ever had been mean. Nor would they be. Standing at the gate, the woman who'd driven the blind kids over was enthusiastically shooting a whole roll of pictures. She said to me, "That your house?" and I said, "No." She said, "Oh." She said, "These your horses?" and I said, "No," and she said, "Oh." She said "That your man?" as I turned to latch the gate and there was Frankie standing in front of it like he'd instantly materialized from a spaceship. "No," I said. And she said, "Oh, too bad."

After that morning, Frankie offered them to me, the details of the talk. Lucy did, too, but I was in no need of what big and small stuff had been discussed at the table. Just was happy to know some words had been said to smooth things a bit. That the past would lift and not press on all our heads like it had been for so long without even our totally realizing. Take off a hat and it's then that you find how much it really was hurting you. That was what happened here. Relief of some sort. Easier days without it just being a show. As I saw it, what they'd come for had already happened—they'd done something to help.

I know fake from real. When something is put on and when it's truly meant. So when Lucy came out to the ring and stood there for a good ten minutes before saying, "I'm glad I came back," I knew she meant it.

I know fake from real. When something is put on and when it's truly meant. So when I went upstairs that night to find a little bouquet on my dresser, thick with tiny yellow roses, no card because what was there to say anymore, by me, or by him, I carefully removed one of the fullest rosebuds and put it in my top drawer.

And then, like that, like a wish you'd make, a guy from Boston wanted the farm.

He wanted the house. He wanted the barn. He wanted all the land. He wanted any and all junk that we hadn't yet gotten around to selling, either on the lawn or still inside the barn and home. With plans to enlarge the house and open a bed and breakfast decorated with our old stuff—which he referred to as quaint antiques—he saw potential in everything.

Just about.

"The ponies—feel free to take those home to your place," said the guy, who was named Harold. "I'm not an animal person and I'll have no use for them."

"I live in Seattle."

"Oh."

For the first time that summer, Lucy was finally letting me talk to a prospective buyer. Maybe because this one was so promising. She'd checked out his background and he'd not been making up his history of buying and renovating and opening to guests—one location of his down in Rhode Island becoming so exclusive that none other than Billy Joel was said to have spent a honeymoon night there two marriages back. "Ah, yes, the Piano Man." Harold smiled and reminisced briefly when Lucy mentioned she'd been reading about his other holdings. "The Piano Man, Billy Jo-el." The name came out of him like that. Jo-el.

"Be nice to him," Lucy told me, meaning Harold. "You can talk him up, just don't say anything that'll make him change his mind."

So when Harold came out from Boston the few times to measure, make notes, admire the views that one day might become his, I said nothing about the water that pools deeply in the corner of the cellar each spring and in other times of heavy rain. I kept quiet about the skunks that like to claim the space beneath the porch no matter how many barricades you create, and how, once they're there, you have to bug Wesley Elmer to come over with his Havaheart trap baited with Oreos. I went nowhere near the sad subject of how the old forest across the street was being surveyed a few weeks back, and that the engineer standing at the roadside with his fancy gizmo on a tripod had told me two dozen acres of it were being considered for a new patch of expensive homes—McMansions, as he called them, sounding disgusted even though somebody's dream of them was the exact thing paying his salary that day. I jumped sixteen years ahead, to imagine how the kids who would be raised in those homes might one day join the others already racing their cars down Route 9 late on summer nights, engines screaming unquaintly past the house in a reckless manner that could kill. But I didn't mention that to Harold, either.

What I did tell him was what I knew he would love. What all visitors here love. I told him about the flooded towns, and about the dead village, about the cemetery of transplants. I pointed at the opening in the woods where the paths started, and how you could walk for hours to a place that no longer existed. And that en route a lot of odd things might happen. Stories are good, especially when people believe them. And this guy did.

"There are books on that?"

I nodded.

"Well, I'm going to have to get them all."

I had them all. Pal had them all. First editions. Signed, too. I'd packed them away for myself weeks before. The cherished folder of clippings. Other than the ponies, who would be tougher to pack, these things really were all I wanted to take with me from this place. The words and pictures of what made the land the way it was, and what had filled it. Both the things you could see, like water, and the things beneath that you couldn't see but knew were there.

Frankie was with us for three weeks when he showed me the contents of the big bag he'd been holding there on the porch the day Lucy went to answer his ring.

He asked me out onto the porch one morning and pulled the duffel from beneath his cot. Unfastened it and pulled out three molds from Pal's alphabet set. The *R*, the *F*, and the ampersand. I'd never missed them, as I'd never had the time to arrange them in alphabetical order when I put them out on the lawn that first morning Lucy was here, and they'd been selling in bits, people finding a letter or spelling something that held a meaning. Which is what Frankie had been intending to do twenty-two summers ago. The July week that he took from here what would be necessary to set us in cement for all time: *R&F*.

"It's just that—I never got the chance to put in the mix—that was the same week everything happened." He leaned down to line them up neater on the wood of the gray painted floor. "But I was. I was planning on it, I was going to make them up. As a surprise."

"And do what with them?" I thought to ask this, but I let it go. Instead, I reached to pick up the *R* and lug it out to join the few letters that remained. Frankie answered what I hadn't asked. He said, "I was going to make them up and put them in the garden under the window. In the garden of what I always thought would be our house."

I had the *R* in my hands now. It was as heavy as the rest of the letters in the set. Even though it was empty. I thought of the Amherst College guy relandscaping. Reconfiguring the garden, tearing out the all-too-common perennials and replacing with the more unusual varieties, coming across the letters and their joiner, shrugging, digging them up with a big shovel and heaving them into the Dumpster he'd rented. Where they would have landed cracked and out of sequence.

"That's nice." I came out of my depressing imagining and corrected myself. "That was nice. Would have been. I'll bring this out front." And I pushed my way out the back screen door, leaving Frankie there on the porch, with the *F,* and the *&,* and himself.

Out at the ring, a lady was taking charge. There'd been no one there, so she was loading her three kids onto the saddles. Backward. The ponies didn't care and at the sound of the closed gate, Star moved forward and the kids got a good long chance to take in what they'd already seen. In case they'd missed something to begin with.

"John. Yeah, John." Frankie was talking about Gumby, who had really just been plain old John, the smart kid who'd wanted to become a civil engineer long before the rest of us knew what that was. "He became a civil engineer," Frankie was telling us. "Engineering important things. Bridges, you know. Lives alone. But has an enormous home and each of his two dogs—some kind of things with short legs, I know this because he sends me his picture with them each Christmas—each of them has its own bedroom. Him, then each of the dogs. Their own rooms."

"Imagine," I said. I meant both about the rooms, and that here was another one of us who'd never ended up with anybody. I made this point and Frankie said there'd been a divorce. Two, actually. The man was too nice. Got taken advantage of, got taken, period.

Lucy was stirring her tea and I noticed the spoon speed up. *Tink tink tink tink* against the side of her cup. "Where is this house?" I couldn't tell if it was for business reasons or another kind of curiosity.

"Ohio."

"Oh."

"What does he look like?" That was my question. And Frankie said, "Oh, like you'd think."

And Lucy went, "Oh," and stopped the spoon altogether.

We were in the kitchen. Three of us together. And at the same time alone. Lucy would like Gumby, only not the way he looks, big-headed and unglamorous. I would like Frankie, only the way he was before real life touched him. And Frankie, well he used the pay phone at Rollaway Lanes when we went into town, phoning somebody up in Vermont he once mentioned wanted him but he did not want her in the same way. And, more often, if you stopped and imagined, it seemed that what he'd want was me. Just the way I was in the here and now.

Cleaning stalls and changing the oil in the truck, washing the storms, hanging laundry, pinning his L.L. Bean to Lucy's J. Crew to my Kmart and back again. I'd catch him watching me as I painted the well house or cleaned out the henhouse. He'd tell me, "You remind me of your aunt." There wasn't a nicer thing he could have said.

More roses in the room, deliverer never seen. Regular, most every day now, as if Victory had heard her name and had come back and was up to her old summer routine of making me feel select. I stuck my head into Lucy's room one day to see if she was getting the same treatment. Her dresser, her nightstand, the little table by the window on which Victory always had displayed her potted mother-in-law's tongue, none of it held anything but stacks of paperwork, real estate sections, directories. No extra life. No frills. Lucy got no flowers from Frankie.

Nor did she get escorted. I alone received his offers to come along and help when I was headed off to the CVS, the p.o., the IGA, and the A&P. The town hall, the bank. Sometimes I allowed him along, sometimes I didn't. Sometimes he didn't even ask, just hopped into the front seat like it was his, Mr. Clucky all over again. I'd ask, "Don't you have anything to do?" and he'd say, "Loads. Let's go."

"Oh, he likes you but then that never stopped." This rolled out of Lucy a little sing-songy one day when Frankie and I returned from the hard errand of leaving in a cart at the door of the Goodwill seven Hefty trash bags containing all the clothing that Victory had not needed for a dozen years, and that Pal had no use for either. Lucy must have seen me get out of the red Ford wiping at my eyes after the silent trip back from town, as she must have seen Frankie put his arm around me and I

didn't go to move it away because coming from just about anybody right then, the gesture would have been welcome.

I looked at Lucy there at the kitchen table, updating her
website with the words "OFFER IMMINENT" angled across
the picture of the farm.

Harold made his offer the next day. Lucy filled out the yellow
carboned form as she took his call, and handed it to me when
she hung up. I saw the many figures and zeroes, and what they
translated to me was Stephenson Belden all over again. Enough
money for someone, in this case my uncle, to live out his days
in the utmost comfort. More than he could have hoped for.
More than any wild success with the toboggan run or the praying hands knot or the three-winged bantam ever would have
brought him. Way, way more.

"What do you think?" she asked.

"What do you think?"

"I think my work is done."

Frankie drove all the way to the health food store in Hadley
just to pick up a couple containers of the yogurt his dairy sold
at such places, hoping to one day get larger distribution
because not just nutrition-minded types but everybody in the
world could benefit from the cultures that went right from the
container to your intestines, where they did great things for
your well-being. Frankie thought we could serve it as part of
whatever dessert I was planning for the end of the dinner we
would be holding in Lucy's honor that night. A dinner, for
Lucy, who had done such great things for us in securing a fat-
walleted buyer, and Pal's future comfort. Who had done what
she'd come here for. To help.

## WE REALLY DO
## APPRECIATE YOU

Across the butterscotch box mix I wrote that with the red frosting you buy in a tube. I put it on too soon, when the cake had not yet cooled down, and the words melted in and spread out. You could still read the sentiment, but the lovely raised letters were no more. Even so, Lucy still got teary when I brought it from its hiding place up in my room, a big candle stuck in the *O* of the *DO,* and, because I had no free hands to do so, Frankie provided the applause as I entered the room with it lit and glowing.

"You did what you said you were going to do, and I really, really thank you." I held out my glass of golden stuff and toasted Lucy.

"This was for your uncle," she said, "who always cared." And at that mention the three of us lifted our drinks. It was a moment as nice as you could hope. The closing theme could almost be heard.

We toasted that again when Lucy said, "We did this together." And, again, after Frankie wanted his turn, and then changed his mind. We toasted that anyways, whatever it was going to be. Harold, and his money. Lucy's website, on which he found us. Wesley Elmer, and his faithfulness. Jerzy's, too. Frankie, though he saw no reason. The health of Pal. The memory of Victory.

The ponies.

Lucy said the words I'd been trying to push aside since she phoned Harold to tell him his offer had been accepted. I'd weeded the garden and made the roast and knocked around the empty rooms with a dust rag, all the while knowing they were out there, tacked and ready and waiting. As always. Where they were right then.

"Neigh," they said. "Neigh, neigh, neigh. Did you forget us out here?"

I went out in the darkness and opened the gate. I unsnapped Star and he trotted over to be first in line for the field. Then Pan, then Tony. Then Princess, then Zoey and Chester. At the fence, Lucy began to take off saddles and halters, I joined her, then opened the gate and all six stormed through, stretching twenty-four legs in a trot over to the pile of hay Frankie was spreading into a long line so there'd be no fighting. We all leaned against the fence and watched them eat. Tails waving, mouths very busy, their round chewings the main noise. Ponies' awareness and concern being limited to the very moment that was happening right then, they were wholly and perfectly happy.

# · 14 ·

That same night, I heard the sound from all those years ago, so identical it could have been a recording. The only crack in the dead quiet in which the farm was suspended each night.

There it was: the bedroom door opening, then closing. The feet on the stairs. The tidy snap of the front screen that all summer served as the front door.

I opened my eyes and it was at the same time new and familiar to see, where normally would be nothing but space between me and the appleblossom wallpaper: Frankie's face. Turned toward me, eyes closed in the heavy sleep that comes after such a day, and night. His lips were parted like he was just about to say something he was having a bit of trouble remembering and now had recovered it and just couldn't wait to tell. Even though I never had forgotten this was how he once looked in his sleep, I found myself eager to hear what he might say to me, Frankie suddenly here like an apparition and I, well, not seeming to mind it even if I couldn't remember whose idea it was. Wherever the credit went, it wasn't such a bad one. And to think I'd woken up this morning believing it would be just another day of getting rid of stuff and working the ring and the farm and dealing with people in need of directions on their vacation travels. And now, look, the farm sold. And twelve inches from my eyes—Frankie as he is now—you never do know what is around the next corner. Or outside your window. Where I heard the walking.

I concentrated. Opened my eyes wider like that would help my hearing. No, no mistake. There was somebody moving along, and away from the house. Somebody. There's somebody out there. Sit up. Watch it going from nearby startling reality to farther-away fuzzy dream shape that dissolves into a gone-from-here nothing. Squint to make sure. Rub your eyes. Stare into the black. Oh no.

I sneaked past the back porch even though I didn't have to— who was left at the house to hear me, to stop me, to ask where I was headed? It was habit, added to caution fueled by the reality that once again, I was taking this course, the familiar path that began with three and a half strides from my doorsill, right foot first, to the top of the stairs, thirteen steps walked on their edges for the fewest squeaks, sixty-three steps from the house to the empty and expiration-dated ring, and off into the field.

Lucy had started off at her usual time, the kickoff of the blackest part of the night. The rocks and ruts and woodchuck holes and mole furrows that didn't have me thinking twice twenty-two years ago suddenly were everywhere I stepped. I envisioned breaking an ankle or wrecking a knee, Lucy tripping over me on her way back from wherever she was headed, both of us landing in rehab, a double room—maybe in a room across from Pal's new one. But the same as ever was how I could sense the general path, and make out big shapes like trees—as well as the small shape, the moving one that traveled along the edge of the field, to the right-hand-side along the rock wall. Lucy had never learned to wear dark as a cover. Her T-shirt remained my guide as I followed far behind, watching her move toward the scary woods, then make the sharp cut to the right that left me scrambling for a prayer that this was just a walk to clear the head.

The path Lucy took still ran along the little wet rut that fed into a small swampy area where somebody—probably my uncle—had set three duck boxes on posts pounded into the muck. Bullfrogs sang before Lucy passed, then fell silent, then started up again. Bugs dove, annoyed, but I didn't dare to slap. As in the past, I waited until Lucy had disappeared into the woods before I crossed the field and somewhat caught up. I had to concentrate to follow her, sneaking along on my trail, my heart louder than my feet. Lucy didn't seem to hear any of this. She walked at the same good pace she used in the cemetery, no headstones to distract her as she was now calling on the best of her speed.

Everything led where it always had, to the dead end of Fish-erdick Road. I thought about Mary Ellen and Margaret and their parents, and I wondered what had happened to them in all this time. Outside their home, the red reflective letters stuck to a big cartoonish plastic mailbox read "RATELLE." Lucy passed that, and I watched her from behind the fat stand of birches that had increased in width over the years. She continued fast, past the Ratelles', taking a right onto the lawn just past the next house, the once-neat white ranch that did not appear to still have an owner who would care whether or not the drive-way was clean. On the lawn was our competition—a tag sale that looked permanent, heaps of stuff, dinner plates, a hair dryer on a pole, two TV cabinets with no glass, a pile of curtains still hooked to traverse rods, ten or so fishing poles poking from a green plastic basket, everything left out there with no covering. I traced Lucy's steps, crouching low as I passed the Ratelles' big front window. The inside was black, but you could make out a statue of a saint on a table. It was too dark to determine who it was. Some woman with a robe like they were always wearing back in the days when the most famous saints were alive and doing the noble things that eventually would get them martyred and years later inspire people to name churches and hospitals and babies after them. I awaited the noise from the Bertrands' dog. There was none. No dog no more, no barking any longer. Thankful for that lucky break, I veered in, as Lucy had, at the neat row of square-cut yews.

In front of me was the big barrel next to the garage. It no longer contained burning trash, now was more of a haphazard planter. A pointy bush of some kind grew from a dented crack in the rusted metal side. Past that, where the pizza-patterned vegetable garden once thrived, a round above-ground pool took up that space. A big dolphin standing on its tail, like Flipper used to in his show, bobbed eerily, big almond eyes appearing to look at you even once the face had turned. At the edge of the pool, a small yellow sign warned you not to dive, that the water was only five feet deep, that the owner was not liable for any injuries like the one drawn there, a stick figure hitting the bottom of the pool, his head snapped back at an angle you never want to see in real life. Above the sign, the dolphin rocked gently where the big explosion of corn plants once stood, and he winked to the left. I followed his direction with my own eyes, and there in the distance was Lucy. Way in the next yard over. Up in a tree.

It was small, like a pear or a plum, a type that would be easy to get up into without the use of a ladder or the flat of someone's back. There she was, in it. Five or six feet off the ground. Sitting and staring. At the house.

I knew the exact rock down by the wall that Uncle Pal once picked up and showed me three snake eggs. I never again went within fifty feet of it. To this day, I know what's under there, even if it's gone by now. I knew the Sutton house had to be still there on Fisherdick Road, but I hadn't wanted to go looking at it, or at who might be inside. Even if they were gone by now. All through the walk, I had a mantra going. Not so much the same words again and again, but the same thought—no, she's not doing this, no this isn't happening—all these sliding across my brain while we were headed on the same path, into the same neighborhood, into the same backyard, almost up to the same tree, and there she is doing the same thing she used to.

I hadn't been hiding here in years, since back when the neighbors were still angry about the construction of the new house obliterating the wild blueberry patch. I wondered if there even was anybody left here who'd remember that, who'd still miss the scrabbly bushes, their sour berries so small that it took you forever to fill a coffee can with them but, still, everybody fussing how they were so much tastier than the eyeball-sized ones you can pull off the cultivated bushes, three or four of those enough for a single muffin. The couple of fruit trees that had been spared by the construction job were still there, now big and gangly, untrimmed, the many suckers at their bases jutting skyward like spears. Nearby were a few smaller new trees, so freshly planted that they still bore the tags telling you what type they were, how deeply they needed to be planted, what kind of light they preferred, and approximately when, if you did all these things correctly, you could expect a blossom. I stopped in back of what, in better light, its tag could have informed me was something called a katsura, which, if you have the space, is one of the most beautiful trees that can be grown. In fall, the tag said, look for its heart-shaped leaves to turn bright colors—yellow, red, or orange—and don't forget to smell them then because the scent will be sweet. The katsura would grow to eight feet if you allowed it. But right now, this night, it was big enough only to shield me there as I crouched trying to see what Lucy was seeing. Which I was able to. Which was nothing.

Not only the geography of the lawns and the names on the mailboxes had changed over time. At this house, the little windows were gone, replaced by a big bay one that allowed the owners a broad and uninterrupted view of the yard. They just had to sit there and look out often. The tree Lucy sat in was now hung with bird feeders of all types. Tubes, trays, pots, one shaped like an acorn that you probably had to screw the cap off to get the seed inside. There was one for spearing fruit onto, and a wedge of orange and an apple was stuck there for the birds that preferred such things to eat. All of the feeders wore some type of collar or baffle meant to keep the squirrels away, probably unsuccessfully. Off to the side, a wide pedestal birdbath awaited, wired up year-round, I noticed, for a heater that would enable birds to drink warm water whatever the season.

What Lucy was staring into was no longer a nursery, or even a bedroom. It was now a fully equipped state-of-the-art home entertainment center. A small table lamp had been left burning as a nightlight, and its yellowish shade illuminated a dark leather couch and loveseat set at an angle to allow a good view out that big window. A huge series of shelves covered the entire back wall. A television the size of a billboard was the centerpiece. A stereo with several levels of buttons and readouts was bookended by speakers as big as refrigerators. Another player of some sort of discs sat to the side, on its own stand like it had been an afterthought. Fake-looking ferns crowned each, cascading gracefully. Framed posters depicted mountains done in a type of pastel paint that contained sparkles noticeable even in near-darkness. The place had the sterile look of a showroom, or a hotel suite, some place that gets vacuumed and dusted every morning, whether or not there is a need. There was nothing in there that would get you all transfixed. Except if you were an electronics salesman. Or if you were Lucy, hiding, staring, just like she used to.

Just like I used to, after watching nothing but her being seated up there so still and continuing to do so with no sign of stopping, I sneaked away. From several houses down, a dog did bark, a young-sounding one with a hint of howly beagle to its deserted voice. Back past the pool and the diver and the dolphin and the can and onto the street and past the junk and then the saint of the Ratelles', back past the birches, next to the swampy area, quieting the frogs again, sticking into the wet rut, along the edge of the field, keeping the rock wall to my left, back over the rocks and holes and back up the stairs. Back into my room. Back to where I used to be, but also back where I didn't want to be—back in the mindset that Lucy, indeed, was still crazy.

I did. I factored in the many ounces of the golden stuff that made even my walk back to the farm and back up the stairs a challenge, and an obstacle course of stepping around little hills of clothing Frankie and I had shed like rain coming off us once the door had been closed and hooked again. Sure I could be inventing all this. The three of us here still had my mind tilting at some sort of an offbeat angle, my senses as well. There was nothing out there, nobody. It was just the day getting to me. I heard Frankie shift to take over the whole small bed. I went back to claim what space I could, sliding myself under the sheet and putting my ear close to hear whatever it was that he was about to tell me.

My dream that night was of Amy Sutton. It was happening all over again. Fresh, with all the emotions new and just as awful as if you were awake and in the thick. There I was, there were the police lights and the dogs and the helicopter Veg-O-Maticking the air above me, the bawling mother and the father as frying mad as I've ever seen a person, waving his arms and shouting at Pal, and my uncle not who he was at the time but who he is now, stricken and out of it, but standing, and being yelled at by this man so distraught and Pal not really having anything to do with what happened. The silhouettes of people walking through the woods and forming a chain and calling AMY AMY AMY like a three-month-old baby was going to pipe up from some hiding place behind a big tree and call, "Here I am!" Impossible, sure, but in my dream, that's sort of what happened. I, only I, of all the searchers, first heard the tiniest voice. Initially a sound you can't make out and you concentrate to hear what this baby is saying, over and again, louder each time, until you realize that it's your very own name.

"Robyn," it whispered. "Robyn." Then louder "Robyn!" Enough to make your eyes fly open. And stare into the face of Lucy Dragon.

"Robyn—Harold's coming in thirty minutes. You have to get out of here. I'll neaten the bed. Get up!"

Lucy was not only dressed for the day that had begun without me, but was made up and jewelried and perfumed and letting out spearminty breaths, smiling, too, happy and excited, and, well, normal—the last thing being the surprising part if you'd been there in the backyard with me not eight hours before.

"Remember? I told you." She was pulling the covers down now, and that's when it hit me that Frankie'd been there, and now was gone. "So get moving!"

I crawled away from her at the head of my bed, harvested from the bedpost everything I'd had on for the walk, and dashed to the bathroom. The morning was as sunny and perfect as you'd want it on what would be your first real tour of the place that now truly was to be your home, not just a walk-through with decisions still to be made. The offer had been made, and accepted. The papers readied. Harold was on his way. Lucy was in her element. The night before had been a strange old story in my head. I'd been seeing things. She hadn't gone out there. I hadn't followed her. I know fake from real. And I'd made it up. I had.

The brother they called Peabrain became a senator four and a half years back. He drove to the Statehouse in Boston each and every day in a late model gunmetal gray Lincoln Continental that had been a great bargain but also a source of ire from constituents who felt he had gone fancy-boy on them since all the campaigning he'd done in his 1982 Chevette. Peabrain was a good and honest senator active in all sorts of causes far beyond the borders of his district. Arms dealings, ecologically sound trade, peace in foreign countries that had never known such a blessing. You might see him in the paper standing next to some of your most major world figures when they swung through. You'd look at the picture and think, "There's Boris Yeltsin. With Peabrain." Even long after you did remember what his name was.

His sister's name was another matter. But I knew that I knew it. I just had to think hard, which was what I was doing then, with great effort, thinking, thinking, rooting around the packed moving cartons waiting in my brain, bringing out to light old days in this place, any thoughts I'd stored from that time. Something, anything to think about. Other than the walk Lucy had taken.

I looked around for Frankie, but his silver Honda was gone. He'd hitched the ponies, so I had little to do but stand at the ring and watch Lucy converse with Harold and the woman who had a videocamera trained on the yard, walking along while she was shooting, which looked dangerous. From this safe distance, Lucy could have been anyone else doing her everyday work, living her regular life. Regular. Normal. Like anybody else. Except this wasn't anybody else who was coming out to the barn now, done with Harold, and the woman he'd brought along, unable to wait any longer to catch me up on what they'd said. Just as I couldn't wait any longer to say, "I followed you."

"Ha?" Lucy had been ready to tell me something good, I just knew it. Maybe some dirt on Harold. Maybe there'd been a fight inside, like some couples get into in the stress of looking at real estate. That was something Lucy'd warned me about, and since her arrival I'd seen a few bouts firsthand, even though I was always far enough away so as not to appear nosy. I didn't care about her news. I just didn't. I said, "I followed you."

Lucy stopped. She was a couple feet from me. Just a little farther away than you'd be in normal conversation. She stopped there. Ran a hand through her hair, which hadn't been in need of fixing in the first place.

"What?"

"There." I pointed. And she had to know what I meant as there is nothing but woods in that direction. Woods, and the end of one road.

"Fisherdick. To, to the house."

She looked blank. She had looked that way a lot when she first got here as a kid. She'd lost the expression along the way, but I guess could summon it when in need.

"I know . . ." I started that and she cut me off and stepped into the very wide space between us.

"You don't know anything."

What Lucy knew was everything—at least everything that Amy Sutton had filled out when enrolling on-line.

"She's there. On the Internet. She's got an on-line profile. Member name: Amy Sutton. Location: Massachusetts. Sex: Female. Marital Status: Divorced. Divorced—can you imagine—Amy, Amy, divorced? Already? Plus, I know more. Hobbies: Gardening, shopping, football (Go Pats!). Computer: Macintosh. Occupation: Healthcare worker. Personal quote: 'Walk this way'—Aerosmith. Aerosmith!"

I remembered getting our computer and signing on for the first time and Tina warning me against filling out such a form, one that would tell the whole world things about me. I thought she was being paranoid when she said, "You don't know who'll be reading that." And now I did. I knew—the likes of Lucy Dragon were out there. Reading about us all.

"Isn't that enough—what more do you want to know about her?"

Lucy raised her hands up like some people do while singing religious numbers. "I want to know if she forgives me." The words were slow and precise and like little bullets. I backed against the ring and out of their range. In the same meter, Lucy said, "I just want to apologize. I don't even know if she's in there. I just want somebody to know I'm sorry. Didn't you ever do anything that hung around your neck for your whole life?"

For me, it wasn't something I did. It was someone I knew. Lucy. There with me every day. Still here now. And, I have to admit, as trim as she looked, still very heavy for me to bear after all these years.

"Then go to the front door," I told her. "And in the daytime. Like a normal person would."

Ooops.

"I am normal," Lucy said and she was as defensive as you'd imagine. "What is it going to take for you to believe that?"

So then I started. "It's going to take you not sneaking off at night and going to sit in a tree. What am I supposed to think when you go and do that?"

"You can think how it's none of your business," she said angrily, and I remembered the warning not to get her mad. "You can think that maybe this time around I'm there for amends. I don't want to go to the door. I don't want to interrupt. I don't want to bring up a bad time. I did want to retrace some ugly steps, made by a kid with problems. I just wanted to shine a prayer on that house. Can you get that? I'm sorry for what I did. I'm different now." She looked it, then her face changed. Even more serious, and she put her words right

through me: "I don't just take things anymore. If I did, believe
me, I'd grab what you have in an instant and go."

Chilled, I closed my hands, almost instinctively, though I
had nothing in them to hold. I rented. Used public transit. Had
no claims on even my child, now an adult. The farm was never
mine, nor would it be. As for Frankie, whom I felt she meant,
you cannot steal what isn't possessed in the first place.

She went on, quickly, the speed was like the start of one
of the scarier rides they used to have at Mountain Park. The
Scrambler, the forward-then-reverse Bobsled. Starting with a
jolt and going too fast too soon. "Now, with the sale taken care
of, I'll be going, nothing more you'll have to worry about. I did
wonder about the Suttons' house—or whoever's it is now—
since I've been here, but I haven't gone over there one time,
other than last night. I wanted to take care of that before I left.
Time's getting short. I do have a life, you know—things, to get
back to. My days here are numbered."

What that made me think was, "Whose weren't?" I looked
at the ponies. If a mirror were nearby, I would have looked at
myself.

Lucy stepped to the fence, stood next to me. Pan was in
front of her. She leaned toward the pony and after a few seconds shook her head. Then, following some more silence she
nodded at Pan and said to me, "Fine. Okay. I don't expect you
to be able to imagine what it's like for me. To be me."

Ah, but I'd always tried, halfheartedly or totally. Even
before I saw her for the first time, back when she was still a
shocking word whispered from down beneath the clothesline,
ever since Victory sat on my bed in those honeycomb slacks
and asked me to put myself in Lucy's footwear. I've tried. And
there at the ring I did it again. I tried to imagine never knowing

anything about Tina except that she existed, and that she was out there being raised by somebody else through no decision of my own. What would that do to you? What would it do to me? What would I end up stealing and running off with? Where would I go? I put myself into Lucy's shoes for the millionth time. I stood where she stood now. I imagined.

I heard myself talking to Lucy as I'd talked to her mother. "Now, now," I said. "Now." I even put my hand on her hair. And whatever sound a defense makes when it falls inside you, I heard that right then. Loudly enough to know it was real. I said to her, "You're not going anywhere."

# · 15 ·

I phoned the MSPCA, which ran some farm out near the Cape that took in abused or unwanted horses. I called a stable over in Brimfield where each year a few lucky veteran thoroughbreds landed, rather than in a petfood can. I talked once again with Wesley Elmer, who liked only swine. I made like Jeannie and rang the newspaper.

The woman who'd done the original story was delighted to hear from me.

"That was my first time having a piece go out on the wire," she said, proudly. "You never know which papers pick it up—did you happen to ever hear from anybody out of town because of it?"

I told her, "Oh, a few," but I offered no names or dates or traumas in need of healing. I was on the phone with her while Frankie was setting the breakfast table and Lucy was opening the carton of eggs we now had to buy, the three of us some weird trinity of absolution and recovery, two of the three checked into our own private clinic of second chances, prognosis as yet unknown. "What I need, if you could," I asked the newspaper woman, "I was wondering if you'd want to do a story—the ponies are all that's left to go. And, honestly, there are some options, but nothing really feels right to me. Maybe, I don't know, maybe if you did a story, somebody would come up with the perfect place."

Perfect was what I wanted. And I didn't think it was too much to ask. Even though I was trying to think differently. Long after he'd been anything but, I'd wanted Frankie as perfect as he'd been the day I met him, back when my age had only one digit. But as Victory learned from her reading and her living, neat and clean and tidy unfortunately is not how life usually works out. And Pal would tell me, *"Jeszcze się taki nie urodził, co by wszystkim dogodził!"*—"A person who could satisfy everyone has yet to be born." As good as a proverb for its truth and hitting the target. I just had to remember it.

"An update. People love that. Day after tomorrow?" the reporter was asking. "I'll come by with a photographer in the morning. Have them at the ring and ready. We'll see what we can do to help."

That night, Frankie and I drove slowly up to Lake Wyola. Up 202, up the highway named for Daniel Shays, farmer and rebel and son of this land. Turn right at the Two Cows and keep on. Past the farms and the gates and up the hills over the valley, above the water that filled it. We'd asked Lucy along, and we'd been sincere. The signing was in two days. Why not give yourself a break in the meantime. "I'm fine," she'd answered, and the words floated there. She'd been out at the ring with Pan for a lot of the day. I knew that wherever the ponies ended up, this would be her final days with them. Pal was right that ponies last forever, but he was also wrong. Stand back and you could see. They were more like big old stuffed animals now than small young horses. Grayed, bony, looking sleepy even when they'd had nothing to do all day but rest, stiff with gaits like windup toys. "Arthritis," the vet had pronounced in what from me would have been a free diagnosis. "They're old, remember."

I remembered, both that and a lot of things. His whistling, and her laughing, and the ponies saying the only word they are able to, and I'm standing in the barnyard blinded by the sweetness in all this. And Lucy is next to me, her palm on Pan's neck. Reciting Pal: "Wherever you go, you will always be here."

And I say it back to her, the original way, the consonants and the vowels whirlpooling around the fact they deliver. That this had been a home for Lucy, too.

A couple of the ponies neigh. Her eyes don't move from the ring as she interprets.

"They want to tell you good-bye."

How long I'd been gone. That was the first reason Frankie gave for deciding to come out here. How long the newspaper story said I'd been away. He hadn't known I'd never returned after that summer. He knew nothing. If anything, he wanted this chance to make things okay. He was Lucy in the backyard tree. There, really, to finally let things rest.

My doing all this work, that was the second reason. "I just kept thinking of you here, alone, like the paper said you were. Alone. Too much to do here. I know this because I helped my parents clean out when they were leaving the farm. I knew it wouldn't be easy."

And then the reason you'd prefer to hear, the best saved for last. The kind they end movies with, breathed rather than spoken, not even words, really, but a heat that sends you walking backward into the appleblossom wallpaper and there

Frankie's sliding down saying all kinds of things into your heart and the one that manages to float into your consciousness is:

"Robyn, I was going crazy in my life without you."

Crazy.

And behind the door locked with the hook and eye, on my grandfather's small bed, the same one I had dreamed of sharing with my Frankie in my teen years, once the world beneath us returned and we rediscovered that we had voices for talking we spoke truth late late late into the night.

Somebody was ringing the doorbell. Knocking on the screen door. "Hellooo." Almost "Halooo," but not quite. The bedframe sold, I rolled off the mattress and onto the floor and got my bearings. Nine-thirty. This is how late you sleep when you're up most of the night and there are no roosters left to wake you. Instead, a reporter doing that job.

"Hellooo!"

"Just a minute . . ."

Pictures. And there I'd be, a mess. I poked Frankie with my foot. He was covered by the sheet, entirely, like a corpse. "The newspaper's here."

"I'll read it later."

The woman was in better health this visit. Pollen was a long-ago issue. Now she was concerned about bees. She was allergic and to prove it she opened her purse when I got out on the porch and brought out a scary-looking syringe all loaded up with a drug that would save her life if she got stung. All she'd need to do was poke it into her thigh. She motioned it down that way, then held the needle close to my face and thanked

God for modern medicine. I agreed. "The things they can do," she noted, and I said, "Right."

Then she said, "Well, where are they?"

"Who?"

And she pointed to the ring.

"The ponies."

"Oh, sorry, I'm, I've, I'm just up. It's my job to get them out there. We had a farmhand but now without us having much of a farm, he's only by once a week or so."

The photographer, this time a female as in-your-way as the first one had been stealth-like, said, "Yes. Jerzy. I know him," and she pronounced it like Pal used to. I stopped my walking when she said that, just to let soak in the sound it seemed I hadn't heard for fifty years.

We moved toward the barn door. "The ponies, they're in here, you remember." I said this to the reporter, who nodded and got out her notebook and clicked her pen all ready to start quoting what I was about to say, which turned out to be nothing. I was too busy looking into the stalls of Star. Pan. Tony. Princess. Zoey. Chester. And finding them empty.

I'd put the ponies there myself last night, before Frankie and I left for the lake. They never went into the pasture at the beginning of the day, just traveled right from breakfast to grooming to tacking to the ring. But I walked out to the field to check anyhow. Maybe Lucy had been up, let them out, not caring if routine got broken this late in the game. There was nothing but green out there. The big stretch that ran uninterrupted toward the woods leading to the dead village.

"Wait a minute." I said this to the reporter and the photographer and ran back to the house. Right through the big empty space at the side of the house where for, going on three months now, Lucy had parked her BMW.

The search wasn't of the proportions of what you see nowadays, no thousands of participants, nothing televised instantly, almost from the exact point at which you realize there is a problem happening right there in your own barnyard. That the girl who is staying with you, the one who you were wary of then won you over and seemed so nice, and you dropped your guard and fell into a good time, then she went and did what she did but that was years ago already and she came back for another chance and to help, and she honestly accomplished something for you, but now at the tail end of everything she got angry, and look. You were right in the first place. She was crazy all along, because look what she's gone and done now.

There was a two-person version of a small-town manhunt, or a combination woman-hunt and pony-hunt, wheels in motion shortly after I stared into Victory's old and empty room so long, right past the bed stripped of its linens as a courtesy, right into the small and totally vacant closet, its door open as if to underline the fact there was nothing inside. That Lucy's things were gone. That Lucy herself was, too. Along with six ponies.

"Now, how exactly would she accomplish this?"

Sergeant Melley had the same kind of notebook the reporter had been holding at the ready when I'd come back out of the house and made the excuse the ponies had been taken on a trail ride, I was sorry for the inconvenience but nobody had told me, they'd be gone, could she return later?

"I don't know how Lucy would do it, but she had to have taken them," I told him. "She was here last night, they were here last night, they're both gone."

"You're sure she was here last night."

I thought back. To the ring. The conversation with her. The one she'd had with Pan. The last thing she'd said. That Pan had said to her, to me.

"Well, she was here in the evening."

"Weddings take place in the evening. For crime, we say 'night.'" Sergeant Melley was annoyed. "What time of day was it when you last saw her?"

I shot him a look. "Day."

"Time?"

"I don't know." I looked at Frankie, leaning against the refrigerator. He shrugged and offered, "Five?"

"Cusp. Let's say night. She was here at night. You're sure the ponies were here."

"They were in front of me. She was to the side of me. We— he and I—we left for a ride. Up 202. We came back around ten or so."

"And you saw her then. You saw them."

"No." I'd seen none of them. Just the back of Frankie going up the stairs as he led me to my room. I didn't remember seeing her car, but then I hadn't been looking for it. Some things get so familiar that they could be gone for a year and you probably wouldn't miss them. My mother once changed the curtains in the den in Illinois and it took my father from Memorial Day to Halloween to even notice. I was thinking of the curtains. Thinking of my parents. Thinking of their den. They had a huge television set now, like the one at the Suttons' old place, they'd sent a picture of it at Christmas like Gumby sends pictures of his dogs. I was thinking of Gumby. Even if they had short legs, did his dogs have big heads in the way owners and their pets are said to resemble one another? I was thinking,

thinking, thinking, of anything but what was before me: a uniformed policeman summoned here for the same reason he'd
come twenty-two years ago:

Lucy.

Sergeant Melley took out his radio and called in a bulletin. Six
ponies were missing, he said out over the airwaves. Old ones.
Different colors. Probably all traveling together. His theory was
they'd gotten loose, so he expected they'd turn up grazing in a
neighboring field, imagine that sight. Imagine seeing them there
if you didn't expect it. They would be no problem so long as
they didn't take to the road, something I didn't want to think
about but also something I didn't think would be the case.
Lucy had them. Somehow, I was convinced.

There was no sign that she had ever been at the house. Her
file of paperwork was gone from the teacart, her blue barn
sweater was missing from its hook on the door to the porch, on
the bathroom shelf I'd cleared for her because having your own
space—even for something as frivolous as your toiletries—is an
important thing, there was no salon conditioner, no French
foundation, none of the foaming tea tree oil facial scrub I liked
to steal a glob of every time I felt particularly greasy at the end
of the day. Gone. All of it gone.

"I still think they're just wandering," the sergeant said.
"Come suppertime, you'll see them. As for Miss Dragon, well,
we don't know she did a thing wrong. She just went home probably. You have her number, you can try there tonight. She'll be
home by then, the ponies will be home by then. End of story."

But it wasn't. Because she wasn't, and they weren't, and
Frankie and I were out there way after night, or after five, or

whatever you want to call that time of day, the sun was going down and we were walking through the woods calling STAR PAN TONY PRINCESS ZOEY CHESTER until we started bumping into roots and stumps and a cloud of bugs descended.

"You know, there's bears out there in the woods," Wesley Elmer told me when he phoned after hearing the APB on his scanner. "But there are! Black bears. Old ponies like that, there'd be no chance of getting away."

I thanked him for his optimism and hung up and went out to the barn. The size of something that's not there is bigger than the actual thing. The absence of the six animals crowded the place. Hulked over me. I checked each stall with each saddle neatly placed on the stand outside. I looked right through to the half door that opened to the field. The field with its gate open to the woods and everything beyond. All ready to accept the lost when they decided to come back from wherever they were. Long ago, Pal'd had a sky-blue parakeet that escaped one day, flew right out the front door no one was supposed to open because the bird was loose for exercise. But Wesley Elmer let himself in, and let the bird out. We placed its small cage on a table in the garden, the door of it open to an over-flowing food dish, new cuttlebone, fresh water. Like the thing was going to fly past its old confines and think, wow, I gotta go back in there—forget the big open world! We never saw the bird again.

I felt better about our prospects for the ponies. If they really were wandering, they knew where they'd been treated so well for so long. They'd return. "Right?" I asked Frankie this when he came out to the ring, where I'd stopped on my way back to the house. The spokes of the wheel looked like a game you'd play. Spin it and get whatever answer points your way. "They'll be back," Frankie said, and he closed the gate and brought me into the house.

Lucy's answering machine did her picking up each time we phoned the number on the card, both the cell and the regular ones, all bouncing to the tape at her office. I had Frankie do the speaking—he could control himself better than I could. He could sound like there was nothing at all wrong. He could say without any giving away in his voice that we were disappointed we didn't get a chance to say good-bye, and would she call us to let us know she'd returned home safely. He could say a pleasant good-bye at the end.

We sat at opposite ends of the kitchen table and listened for the hooves that never came clopping across the driveway and into the barn. For the neigh that did not announce the time away over and done. I felt like I did when I used to wait for Tina to come up the stairs after a party. The same sick feeling when more and more time went by without a sound. I started staring over at the telephone on the wall, like one of the six would think to call and ask could we come and get them because their ride had left without them. But not one of them ever did.

Slumped on the table. That is how I spent my last night ever at Panek Farm. That morning at ten, in a little office down by the Odd Fellows Hall, Howard's attorney would meet with Pal's and the papers would be signed. The place would be Howard's then. Left for him just the way he wanted it. With all the junk right where it was. And, through no effort of our own, without the ponies.

We dialed Sergeant Melley that morning, but he was on the road somewhere, reported Stubby from his post at the dispatch desk. No, he said, nobody around had anything animal-related to report, except for a cow drinking out of the lake in front of an A-frame on Shoreline Drive. No, we weren't missing a cow. Six ponies, remember? The ponies from the Happy Trails Pony Ring? Pal Panek's ponies?

Pal Panek.

Pal.

"How'm I gonna tell him?"

Frankie didn't answer. Just drove. I knew what he was thinking—would it matter what I said? If I said anything at all?

"I have to tell him. But, I really think he'd know anyway."

Frankie didn't answer, this time because he agreed.

He'd not been to Belden House before this morning. So he couldn't have been amazed that, for a beautiful morning, the front of the place was deserted. Usually you had to pick your way around wheelchairs, walkers, people being led by the arm as they got their fix of clean fresh air. The sidewalk was clear. There was nobody on the porch. Blocking the door. We went on in. At the reception desk, only the portrait of Stephenson Belden was there to greet us. He looked down on a hall eerily vacant. "Usually it's wall-to-wall with people and I'm not kidding," I told Frankie in a whisper. "They even have them in beds out here, lined up like they're cars waiting to get onto the turnpike. Only nobody's going anywhere."

We left the old section and continued through the hall into the newer part of the building. On either side of us, collages attempting to resemble four-legged animals were displayed in neat rows. We passed the doors for Recreation, open, nobody in the usual semicircle, working at chairobics. Chapel, door open, not a soul. Men's and Women's, I didn't look, and the door to Linens was closed. At the pink nurses' station, computer chairs stood empty and a phone beeped with no one running to answer it.

"Here," I said, and we turned the corner to the hall down which Pal's room could be found. Along with the entire population of the Belden House.

They were standing in the hallway. Residents jammed into doorways of the rooms on the right. All the chairs, walkers, beds, staff members we'd missed on the way in, here they were. Nobody was talking. If there were words they were the kind said when a baby is shown. Ooohs and aaahs and look and cute, all drawn out and awestruck. I knew they got cable at Belden House. There had to be something very good on in the middle of the day or—and you'd hate to think this—one of those kinds of international tragedies that has you glued to the screen and turning the volume to the highest if you have to run into the other room for a second. We passed one room, and the next, but there were so many little gray heads in our way that we couldn't see the attraction. Three more rooms later, there was Pal's. I was feeling maybe as sad as I had the first time I saw him back in May. The one thing he cared about, I'd gone and lost. Or allowed to be taken. No matter the method, the ponies were gone. Gone.

We squeezed past the lady in the doorway whom I recognized from her post reselling store-bought Baby Ruths at a rolling table with a sign announcing "The Canteen." I always bought something from her, she never said anything to me. But today it was, "Well, hello, good morning, you just come on in!" She swept her hand toward 116, where the cardplayer was seated on his bed in a gray leisure suit, shuffling with his back to us, his usual partner, in plaid jacket and tie, leaning against the closet, looking away as well. Just past him, there was Pal's bed, and Pal, head positioned toward the light of the window. Face in the direction everyone else was looking. Through. And out. To the green expanse where, just a few feet from the glass, Star stood, looking in.

"There's another one, another one," the canteen lady said excitedly as Zoey came into view, walked a few feet and then put mouth to grass. Halfway across the pasture, Princess preened, scratching her face with a rear hoof.

"I think there's about eight or nine of 'em," the lady said. "At least eight or nine."

"Ten," said the gambler. "There's ten, I know, because I've been counting since I saw them when I got up this morning. And that was five, thank you. See? One more." Chester went over and knocked his head into Star and they took off at enough speed to get a cheer sounding from down the hall.

Like a model, Tony strolled into our sight, then out, en route to new grass somewhere in front of the neighboring room.

Frankie was up at the glass now, making sure even though there was no need to check. No way the animals could have been anyone but who they were. Which was Pal's ponies. Here, with Pal.

I looked at the gambler, who was making notes—1 blond, 1 patterned, 1 white—probably to settle a bet. "Do you know how they got here?"

He shrugged. "Yesterday no horses. Today horses. I been here six years. Never saw so much as a sparrow out there. Talk about going out of your mind. Now this. Horses everywhere, probably ten or eleven or twelve. Running around, doing horse stuff. Horses! Just like that. Overnight. You think it's the drugs at first, but if it is, we all must be on the same thing."

"They're ponies, excuse me," said the canteen lady. "Ponies. Small horses—ponies. And they arrived last night in a big white truck that drove up to that gate way over there (here she pointed), followed by a fancy car like my granddaughter drives but I've yet to get a ride in. And a woman got out and shook hands with the farmer and got back in her car and left. You think I can't see—I can see perfect. So there. Remember this: they're ponies."

"What's the difference?" the gambler snapped back, and his friend against the closet began to tell him. Using as much detail as if he'd studied all night for this, he told the gambler surprising things, that yes, ponies are actually horses, only they're short ones, that many types of ponies have in common the admirable attributes of being strong, compact, hardy, and blessed with good endurance, that if you looked at a map of our great world you could trace the various breeds' beginnings. That each type of pony was equipped with the proper types of coats, thick ones covering those from the frigid regions, lighter ones on those from warmer areas, powerful legs carrying the ponies who spent their days climbing up and down rocky slopes. Wherever they had originally come from, the man said, all are easy to train and can be useful in many ways. Packing. Farmwork. Light harness. And for riding. "Ponies like these," the friend said, "you could ride them for years. Because ponies live forever."

I went over to the visiting side of Pal's bed and took a seat in the chair and spotted the first piece of paper: "Wesley Elmer was here." And, placed behind that, a second.

"Lucy Dragon was here."

She'd been here. She'd been at the other end of the field, out where Star and Chester had landed after their run. She'd

been at the farmer's. Making some deal about the ponies for
whom, true to the line on her business card, she'd found a
home.

"Lucy," I said to Frankie over by the corner, even though I
didn't have to.

I looked at Pal's eyes. Open and staring out. You'd have to
be coming to see him as often as I did in order to tell this. But
he was happy. I know fake from real. And today, Pal was genuinely happy.

Over on the shelf, his little statue of Francis watched my
uncle, watched the people watching the ponies. I picked up the
saint and set him on the windowsill so this great and influential lover and protector of all members of the animal kingdom
could have the view he'd been missing. Could beam his channel of peace out into a world grateful for the smallest measure
of it. Could send it out past the field and the farm and the
town beyond, down the Connecticut River Valley to skim the
sea and make a right where Pennsylvania begins. First stop,
the first city. Home of a girlfriend real not fake, perfect in her
being less than that. As good and as bad as the next person,
crazy as the next person. Who came here once and did something people still remember. Who returned to do something I
won't forget.

Out the window now, Pan stood. Beautiful white Pan of the
roadside tag sale. I wanted to think that in the depths of his
timeless floating, Pal was riding Pan like she'd been in her
prime, as he'd been in his, out of the ring and past the busy
coop and the windows-open house and the boomerang garden,
onto the avenue of green and to the end of the great field, into
the wild scrub that begins the deep woods that lead to the dead

village beyond. I watched them until they disappeared. Both never happier, or healthier.

Out the window now she spoke a neigh audible through the glass. I moved over next to Frankie, and the canteen lady and the gambler yelled for us to get out of the way, who do you think you are, those are our ponies!

"Horses."

"Ponies."

Take the sound and translate it to what you want. Next to Frankie that morning, in the one word from Pan, I heard the opposite of the last thing she had said to me through Lucy—I heard a hello. And Frankie, he heard something different.

"Imagine" is what he made it out to be. "Imagine."

But that wasn't necessary.

Look out the window. Look around. There is no need to imagine, when everything you want already is real.

THE  MOST  BEAUTIFUL

PLACE  IN  THE  WORLD

This 1988 edition is published by Arch Cape Press, a division of dithilium Press, Ltd., distributed
by Crown Publishers, Inc., 225 Park Avenue South, New York, New York 10003, by arrangement
with Friendly Press.

Printed and Bound in Japan

**Library of Congress Cataloging-in-Publication Data**

The Most beautiful place in the world.

   Reprint. Originally published: New York, N.Y. :
Friendly Press, c1986.
   1. Photography, Artistic.   I. Maisel, Jay,
1931-
[TR654M667   1988]       779'.092'2      88-3399
ISBN 0-517-66564-6
h g f e d c b a

# THE MOST BEAUTIFUL

# PLACE IN THE WORLD

IMPRESSIONS OF TEN MASTER PHOTOGRAPHERS

EDITED BY JAY MAISEL

ARCH CAPE PRESS
NEW YORK

This has been a collaborative work. It's been a pleasure to be able to work with photographers of this caliber and to have a part in presenting some of their favorite photos of their favorite places.

I'd be remiss if I didn't thank the other photographers who I couldn't include, not because of any lack on their part, but simply because we couldn't fit in all the fine work that we saw. Special thanks to Stu Waldman and Marty Goldstein who conceived this book and who were provocative and encouraging.

Joe Suplina, in his design, resisted the temptation of cleverness. His layout respects and enhances the differences in each photographer's attitude.

My most heartfelt thanks to Emily Vickers of my staff who let me ramble on about who and what I needed and then went out and contacted, cajoled, coordinated, interviewed and finalized everything. She put up with delayed mail, delayed decisions (my own ambivalence) and completed the enormous number of details necessary for this book. She was essential if not indispensable to this project.

My final thanks to you, the reader, who allowed us to bring this quality of seeing to an eager audience.

Jay Maisel

EASTERN SIERRA

VENICE

RAS MOHAMMED

PALOUSE

MOROCCO

MAINE WOODS

NEW GUINEA

SAHARA

QUELIN

NEW YORK CITY

# CONTENTS

Location photography is character study. Each place, like each person, is unique, with a style and personality of its own. It is character, not famous sights or gorgeous sunsets, that makes a place truly beautiful. For me, the photographer has only one job: to reveal that character and communicate it to the viewer; to have him not only see a place but feel it and "know" it. Otherwise, it's just a pretty picture.

*The Most Beautiful Place in the World* had to be more than picturesque. I wanted beautiful defined in the widest, most subjective sense possible. It had to come from both the place and the photographer's own experience of it. I wanted a book that would not only please the eye but stir the senses; that would not only show the face of a place but look into its heart; that would reveal both the endless wonders of the world and the equally endless ways of experiencing it. For in the end, "the most beautiful place in the world" is always inside each of our heads.

Jay Maisel

# EASTERN

# GALEN

# SIERRA

# ROWELL

I love mountains. I guess everyone does. The first time you see a mountain peak, words like wonder, awe, majesty are no longer clichés. If anything, they don't express enough.

In terms of elevation, the Eastern Sierra are relatively ordinary. Their tallest peaks are dwarfed by those of other continents. Yet the mountains possess a unique magic, a grandeur all their own. It's the grandeur of primeval landscape, of strange light and color, of wildlife. It's the grandeur of the earth itself.

John Muir called this area "a gentle wilderness." One can see why. Wildness coexists with the green and familiar. Nestled in the midst of harsh desert peaks, there suddenly appears an ancient, lovely forest of bristlecone pines. Southeast of here, sand dunes lead to Death Valley. Yet nearby, the springtime landscape comes alive with fields of wildflowers. Drive north and you're at Mono Lake. A "solemn, silent, sailless sea," Mark Twain called it. Towers of white tufa rise above the waters and, by twilight, the landscape has an otherworldly look.

The high point of the range is Mount Whitney. It is the highest peak in the original forty-eight states, and has a spectacular sheer vertical drop, thousands of feet into a deep glacial cirque with permanent snowfields. Viewed from the east at dawn, Mount Whitney's face is a deep crimson reflected against the snow.

The entire Eastern Sierra escarpment is nothing less than a vast biological and geological edge, a place where the Great Basin ends with startling suddenness. The contours of the land lie exposed as if on some natural topographical map. A hiker can trek cross-country for days on end, without trails, finding personal landscapes, discovering new vistas, constantly being surprised and exhilarated at each new turn.

I guess those words—surprise, discovery, exhilaration—sum up, for me, the Eastern Sierra experience. As a Californian, it is a place I return to again and again. No matter how often I climb its mountains, explore its hidden lakes and valleys, I am filled with the same sense of excitement as when I first gazed upon its landscape.

CALIFORNIA          NEVADA

E A S T E R N     S I E R R A

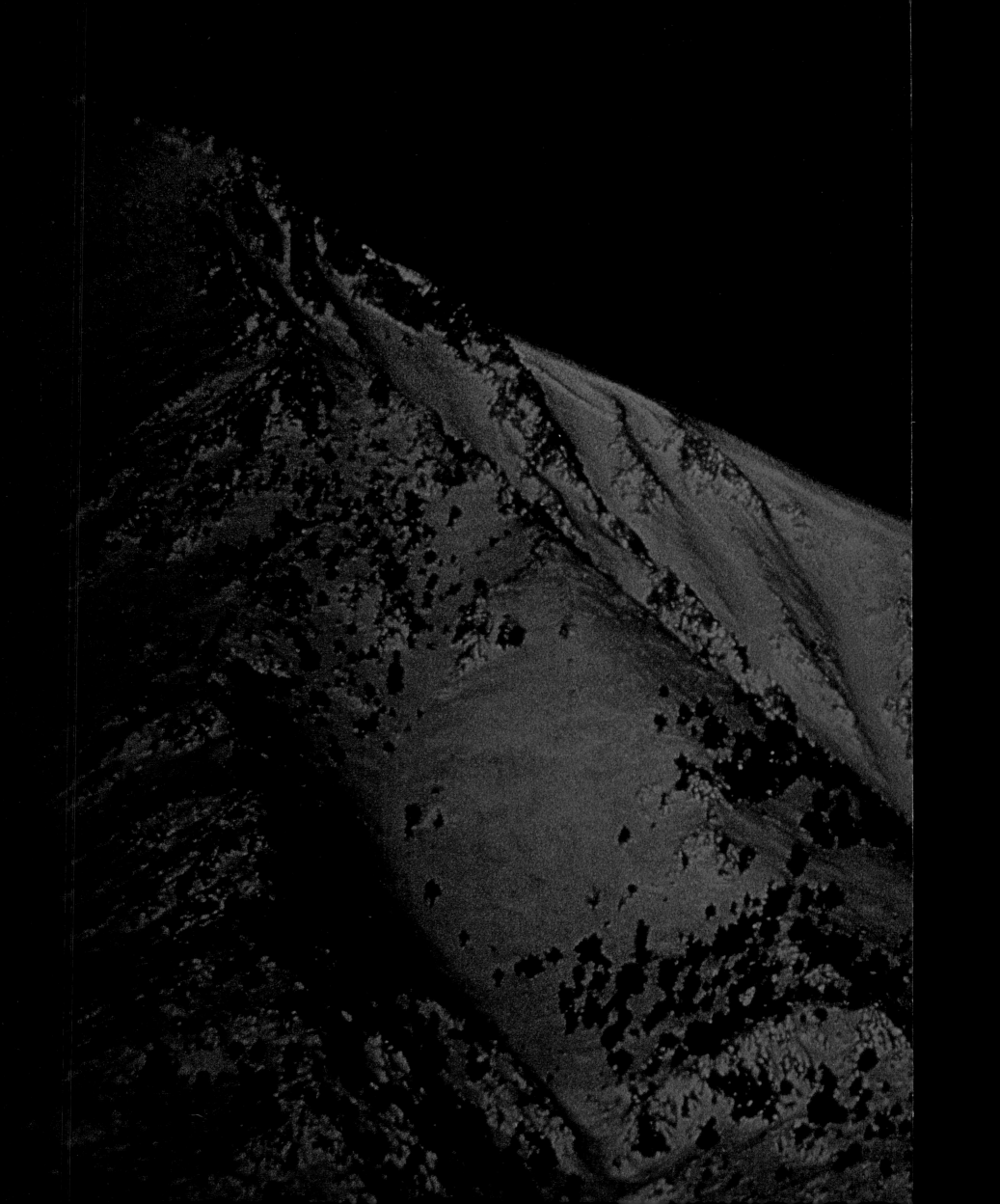

*Summer flowers
in a sagebrush meadow
near Grant Lake.*

*A climber ascends*
*Pratt's Crack,*
*Sierra Nevada range.*

*A climber stands atop a rock*
*pinnacle near Mt. Whitney, the highest*
*peak in the original forty-eight states.*

*A winter
moonrise over the
Sherwin Plateau.*

*Aspens in the fall,*
*Lundy Canyon near*
*Mono Lake.*

*Next page:*
*Alpenglow on the east*
*face of Mt. Whitney.*

*Late summer*
*snow beneath*
*Mt. Williamson.*

*A winter sunrise*
*on a Bristlecone Pine*
*in the White Mountains.*

*A storm over
the Palisades
range.*

*Next page:
Sunrise at Tioga Pass,
Yosemite National Park.*

*A single cloud catches the last light over a split boulder.*

VEN

ERNST

ICE

HAAS

Some places are unique, originals isolated in their own history and appearance. I love these kinds of places and, for this reason, I love Venice. It is incomparable. There must be legions who would join me in my opinion. Anyone who has ever visited Venice feels he has been enriched by a very special experience. For me it is the most romantic and poetic city in the world.

Venice is a grand old dame; slightly decadent, witty, wise, satirical, quite realistic, but tolerant in everything which has to do with the pleasures of the senses. Live and let live is what she preaches. If she gives you the illusion that you have a very intimate relationship with her, you soon find out you are not alone. Venice is as fickle as a cat; a courtesan, she gives herself to anyone who can afford her.

Which city in the world satisfies all your senses? In Venice you have the sensation of being in a living museum. Walking along the canals and narrow streets you experience living theater unsurpassed. There are hundreds of small bridges to walk over. But you can also glide under the same bridges for a totally different perspective, while you listen to the gondolier sing his songs. Venice is art as total environment.

Venice is a challenge and a confrontation. Whatever you see has been seen, whatever you hear has been heard. It's a real test of daring for anyone who wants to find his very own Venice. Everywhere you stand or walk, another painter, poet, writer, or composer has stood before you.

You can study her schools of painting, music, and architecture, her many mixed styles from Byzantine-Gothic to Renaissance. But the style which is purely Venetian is a combination of lightness, mildness, elegance, and tolerance. There are cozy, narrow streets to stroll, museums for inspiration, gondolas for closeness, romantic hotels for intimacy, and of course churches for confession. Incomparable.

Light, water, and stone are the three basic elements of Venice, and every season creates a new display by shifting and mixing the immaterial and the fluid with the material and solid. Whatever you see along a canal will be reflected in the water, and it is reflection which is the greatest transformer in this city. Every view has as its mirror image a never-ending variation of swimming color abstractions. No halfway sensitive human being can be untouched by this magic. It will bring out the artist, the hidden poet, the dreamer, the walker in you.

So many negatives are changed into positives. The crumbling walls, patinas, and bleached colors create a symphony whose title could be The Beauty of Decay. Likewise, it was not the sun that inspired the great painters; no, Venice in the fog, Venice in the rain, created the masterpieces.

Venice invites you to walk, sit, drink, think, taste, but most of all, to see. See for seeing's sake; absorb, discover, be open to surprises, and then, accept. This eternal Lady will force you to love her.

You will gladly succumb.

*The city of Venice is illuminated on a wintry*
*New Year's night as seen from San Giorgio.*

*Right page: Every morning the city of Venice feeds*
*the pigeons who make the piazza alive.*

*Huge Italian flag hanging down on the Piazza San Marco.*
*The Piazza San Marco is called the Salon of Europe.*

*A mosaic seen from a different perspective changes the colors.*

43

*Hundreds of gondolas decorated in the fashion of ancient
times compose the Historical Regatta in September.*

*Right page: Inlaid stones adding splendor to the Piazza San Marco as
viewed from the Bell Tower during the flood season.*

*Next page: Reflection of the Bell Tower in the flooded Piazza San Marco.*

The city for lovers.

Left page: Walkways crisscross the piazzas during the flooding season.

Preceding page: The balcony of the horses at Basilica San Marco.

*A typical canal scene with gondolas and a painter
on one of the many canals of Venice.*

*Gondola returning home in the sunset near Piazza San Marco.*

*Right page: A gondolier's hat awaits its owner.*

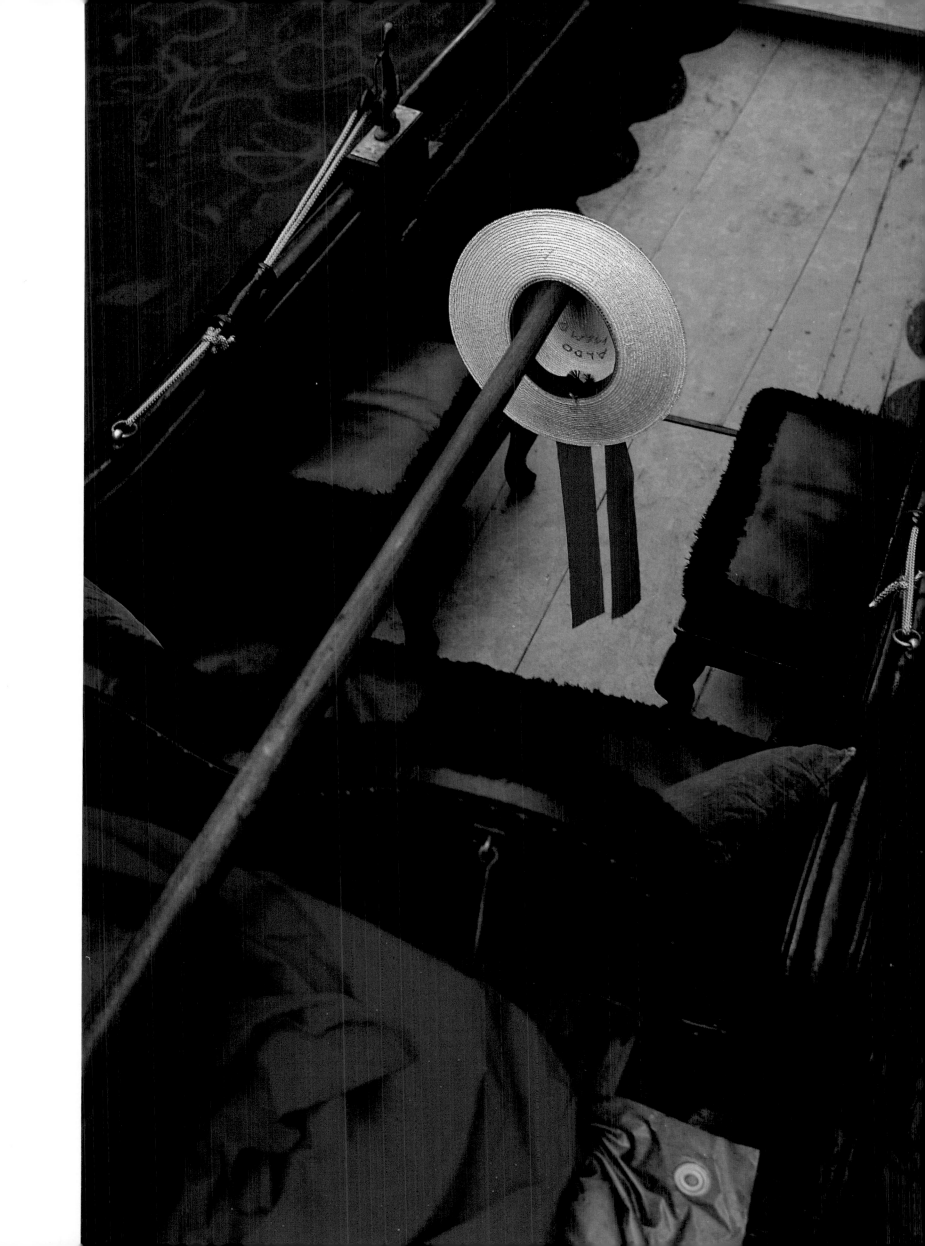

*Lovers on a foggy November night.*

RAS MO

DAVID D

HAMMED

OUBILET

Anne and I sit, backs to the reef wall, at Ras Mohammed. We are motionless, our exhaled bubbles creeping up the sides of the wall, seeping to the surface sixty feet above. We look into the deep water. It is a blue darker and richer than lapis lazuli. Below our fins, the reef wall of Ras Mohammed drops into blackness. Above, the late morning sun pushes shafts of light into the sea. Orange anthias fish swarm out from the reef. A passing silver jackfish dives into this endless school. The whole reef flinches from the attack. Then the anthias fish swarm out again, darting, feeding, picking up bits of plankton from the sea. It looks like orange clouds against a deep blue sky.

In the open sea, fifteen short-nosed gray reef sharks circle. They do not see us. They circle. Then suddenly the group dissolves and sharks—males chasing females—make fighter-plane passes at each other. A male suddenly bites a female on her flank. It is the mating dance, the courtship of short-nosed gray reef sharks. It is a secret of the sea. It is December in Ras Mohammed.

Ras Mohammed is a jewel that sticks out from the tip of the Sinai peninsula. Like a *V* the two northern arms of the Red Sea embrace the Sinai. On the east is the Gulf of Aqaba; on the west, the Gulf of Suez. All the waters from both gulfs pass by the tiny peninsula of Ras Mohammed. The Gulf of Aqaba is deep, in places six thousand feet deep.

At the very end are two sunken coral islands—the North and South Islands.

At low tide they barely break the surface. They are perfect reefs, full of life, covered with soft coral, then veiled with schools of brightly colored fish. The confluence of waters, and the rich marine life of the reefs create in Ras Mohammed a complete underwater universe.

Anne and I have watched great schools of snapper, batfish, barracuda, jack-fish and unicorn fish pass as if in review. We have seen hammerhead sharks, manta rays and turtles sleeping on ledges. In midsummer we have been surrounded by a vast school of blue parrot fish who have come together to mate. It is a frenzied time. This temporary school, literally explodes in all directions. At one end of the Ras Mohammed reef, there is a city of anemones filled with yellow clown fish. At the other end of the reef, there is a perfect shipwreck—the *Yolanda*, 220 feet long, sunk in 1979. The sea is now in the inevitable process of converting the *Yolanda* into part of the reef. A school of glassy sweepers has taken up residence in the bow section. In this perpetual steel twilight cave, lion fish with pectoral fins extended, looking much like harmless drifting flowers, hunt the glassy sweepers.

At the end of the harsh, hot Sinai desert lies this peaceful blue curtain of water. Underneath the deceptive cover is a phantasmagorical world; one filled with violence and beauty, fantastic shapes and pure colors, ever-shifting light and shadow.

Ras Mohammed is a memory that seems like a dream.

EGYPT     JORDAN

SAUDI
ARABIA

RAS   MOHAMMED

RED SEA

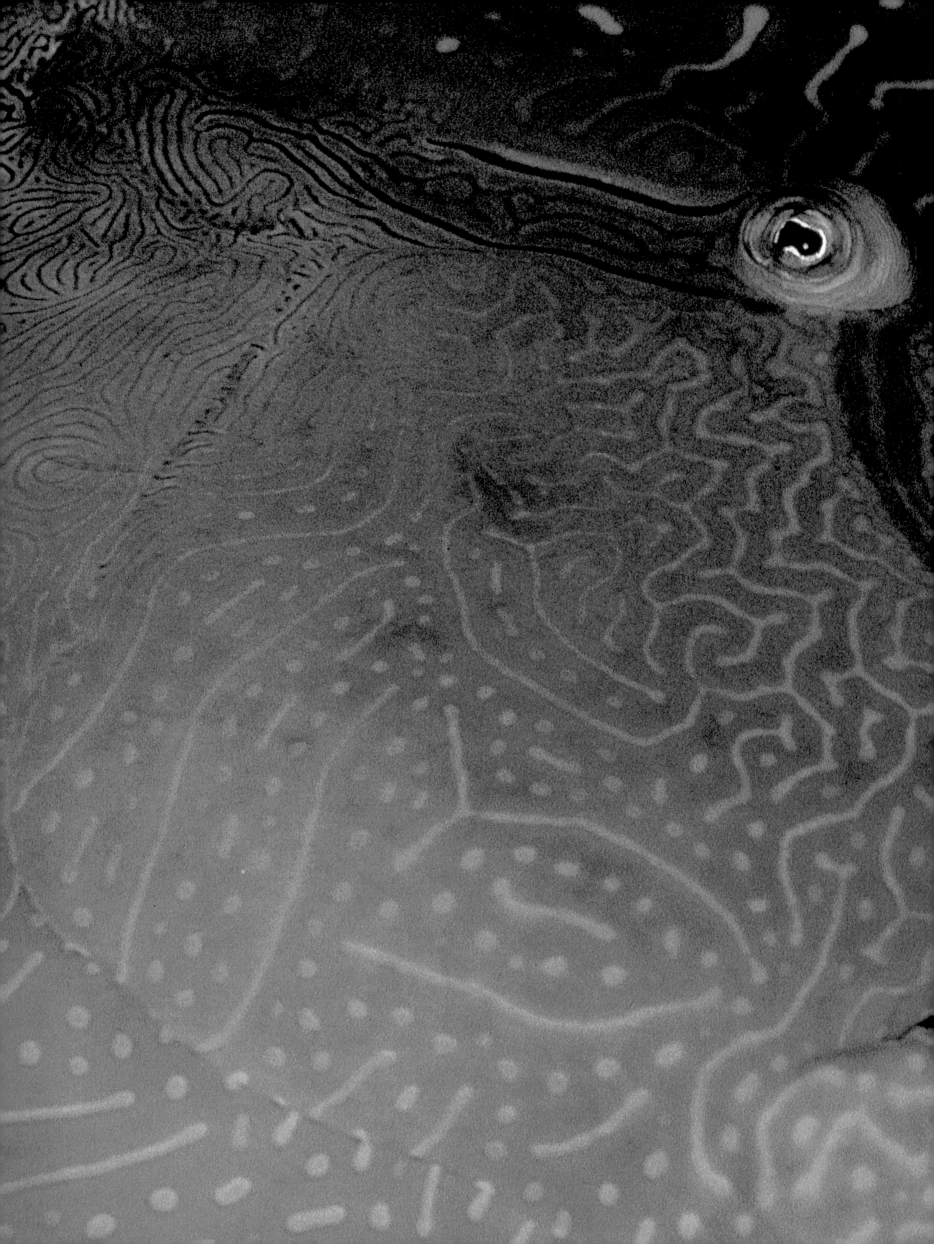

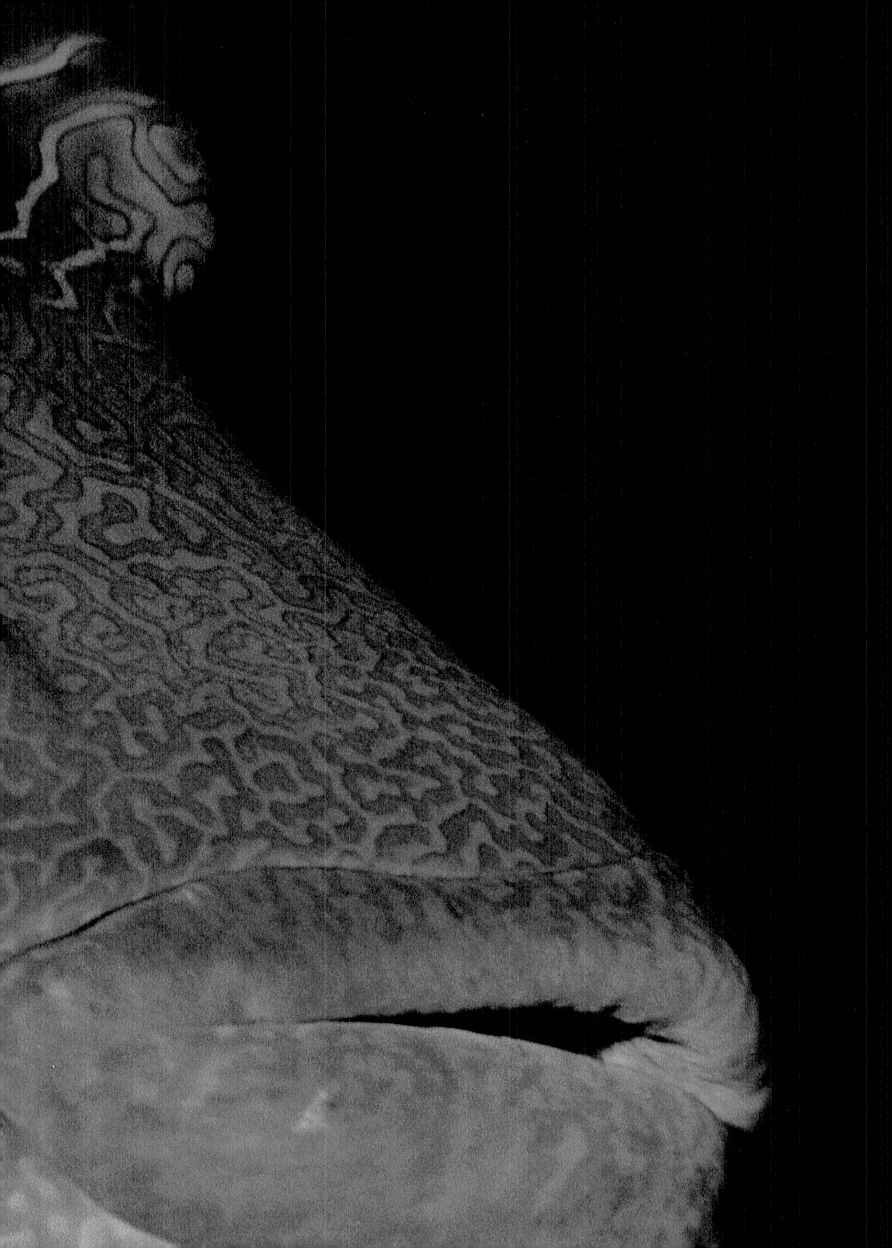

*A Fridmanii fish.*
*This tiny, two-inch-long*
*plankton eater is found only*
*in the northern Red Sea.*

*Reflection of a reef. The sky in*
*this picture is the perfect reflection*
*of the reef on a flat calm day.*

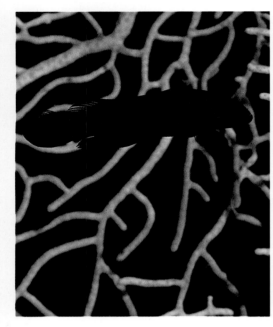

Nickii, a rare sand-dwelling fish,
swims in midwater. This male
has yellow pectoral fins and is
dominant among the fish school.

Diver
and large
gorgonian
coral.

*Divers swim
above a wall of
glassy sweepers.*

*A very red deepwater
gorgonian coral.*

*Next page:
Glassy
sweepers.*

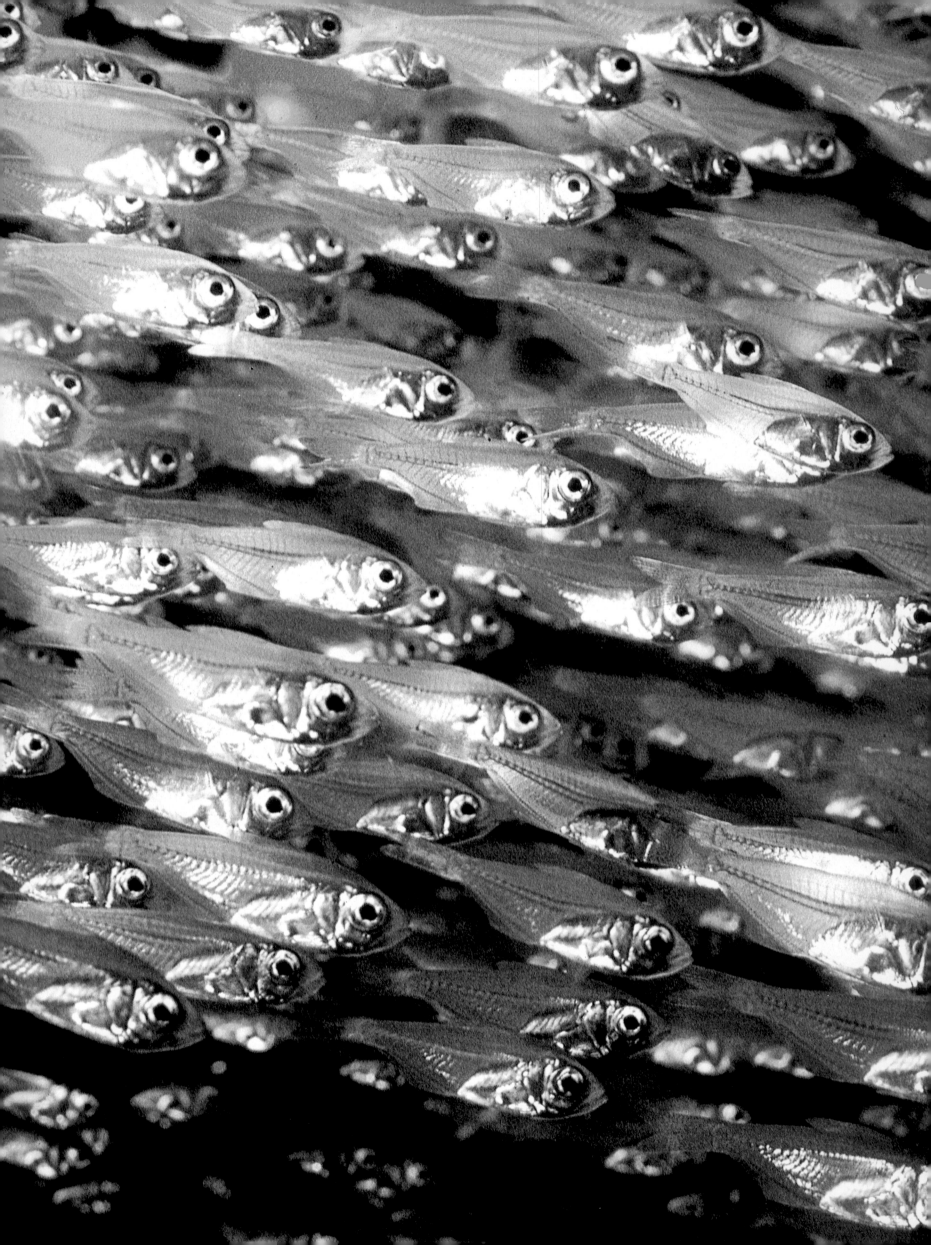

*Anemone and clownfish.*
*The poisonous tentacles of the anemone*
*protect the clownfish. The red*
*is the outside skin of the anemone.*

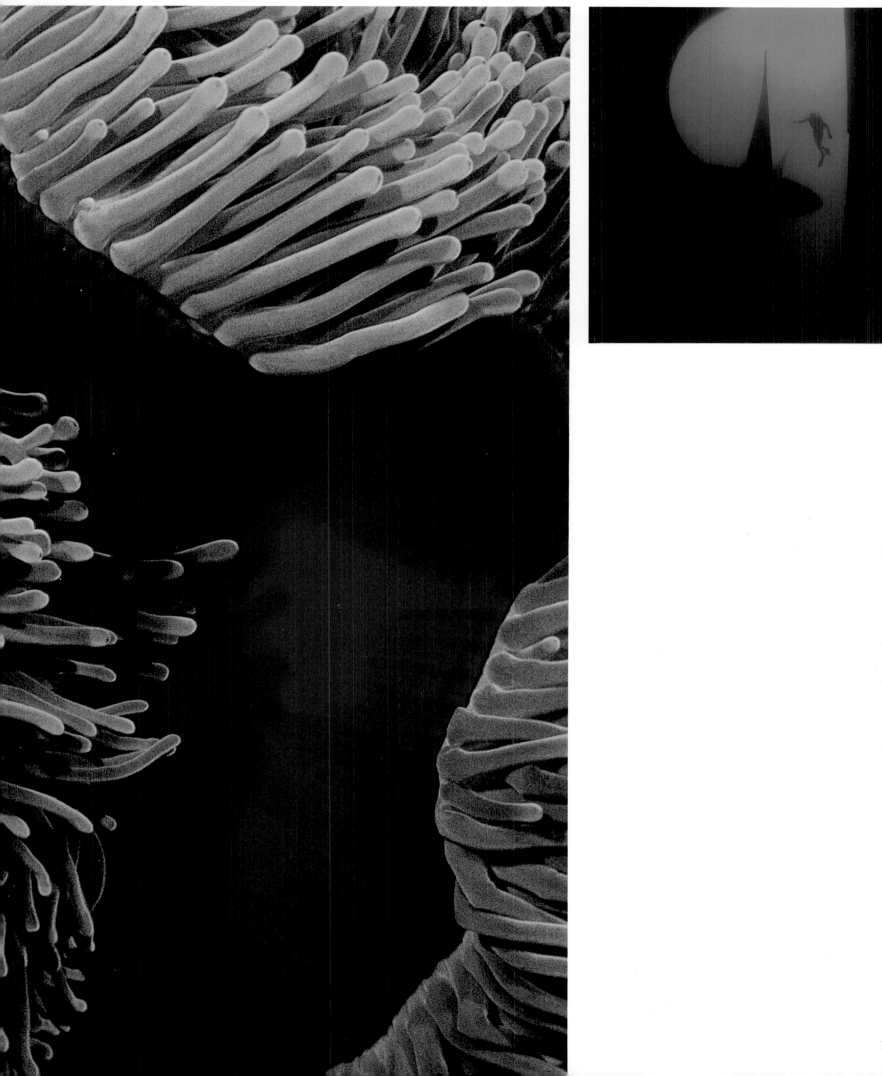

A supertanker over
one thousand feet long.
A diver inspects its
massive single propellor.

Next page:
The undersea
desert.

*Two yellow-disk
butterfly fish hide
under a coral ledge.*

A deepwater gorgonian
coral surrounded by
anthias fish.

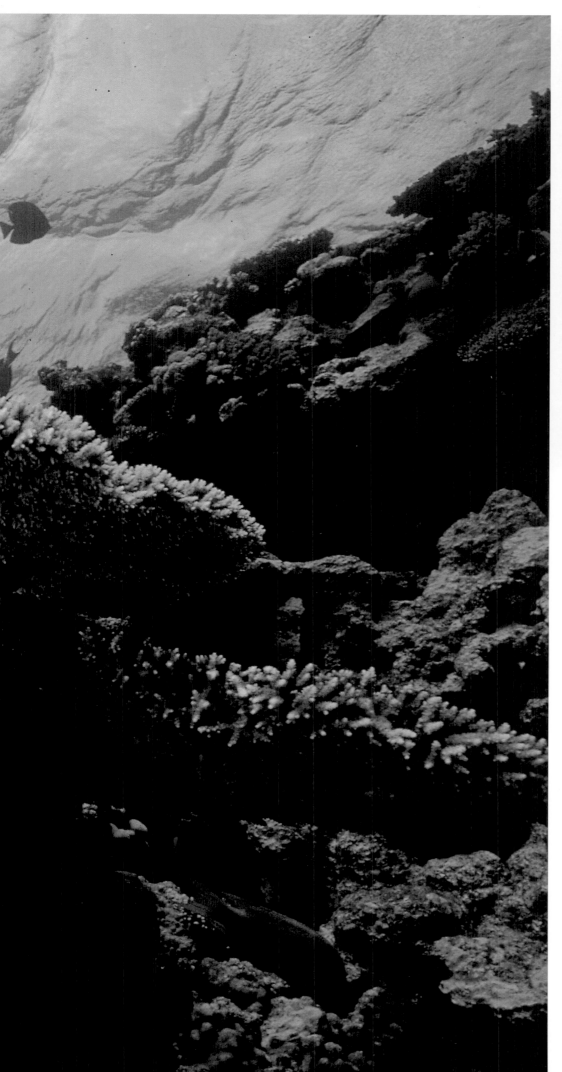

*A dolphin leaps at sunset in the Straits of Tiran.*

The peninsula of Ras Mohammed thrusts out from the very end of the Sinai Peninsula.
It straddles the Great African Rift which geologically divides Europe from Asia.
The water at the tip of Ras Mohammed is almost five thousand feet deep.

PAL

GEORG

USE

GERSTER

As seen from the air, cities are intriguing and intricate. Mountains are bold and spectacular. But farmlands are works of art.

Thousands of hours flying above the world's rural areas has convinced me that the farmer, sculpting the earth with his plough and harrow, painting the land with the variegated colors of his crops, is an unintentional artist. By simply doing his job, he provides the viewer with a spectacular open air museum.

Palouse is the Louvre of farmlands. Four thousand square miles of rolling hills, straddling the border between southeastern Washington and Idaho, it has the perfect combination of topography, weather, crops and farming methods to produce a stunning collection of what I call land-art.

A comforting reality about farmlands is that the best conservation methods also produce the best visual results; ploughing and planting on contour, strip cropping, crop rotation, channelling run-off with terraces, all transform farmlands into graphic, abstract natural works of art. Palouse, because it is beleaguered by torrential rains and sudden thaws, must practice the most careful and up-to-date methods of conservation. The Palouse farmers' husbanding and stewardship of the land both saves the soil and produces these spectacular scenes.

Once the reverse actually occurred—the land-art helped conservation. A soil conservation agent named David Hein had one of my Palouse photographs hanging on the wall of his office. One day a stubborn local farmer came to his office. For years, he had resisted newfangled conservation methods on his 2,000-acre Palouse farm. The loss of topsoil was running up to 156 tons per year. Suddenly, amazingly, the moment he saw my photograph, he did a 180-degree turn.

"If you can make my farm look as fantastic as that," he told David, "go ahead."

Subsequently soil losses on the remodeled farm dropped to innocuous levels. Later, David and I took a flight over "my farm;" resplendent now in its newly acquired zebra beauty of contoured stripes of fallow and wheat. David told me, "You saved the country millions of tons of the best agricultural soil."

It was a wonderful feeling. At times I have mixed emotions about chasing beauty from above while below farmers are in the grip of a prolonged drought and severe economic conditions. Being aloft does not mean being aloof. I'm thrilled that my visions of this beautiful land can inspire those who are responsible for it.

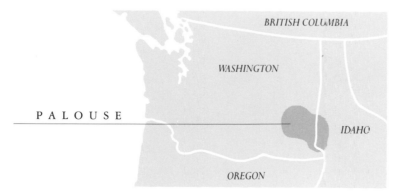

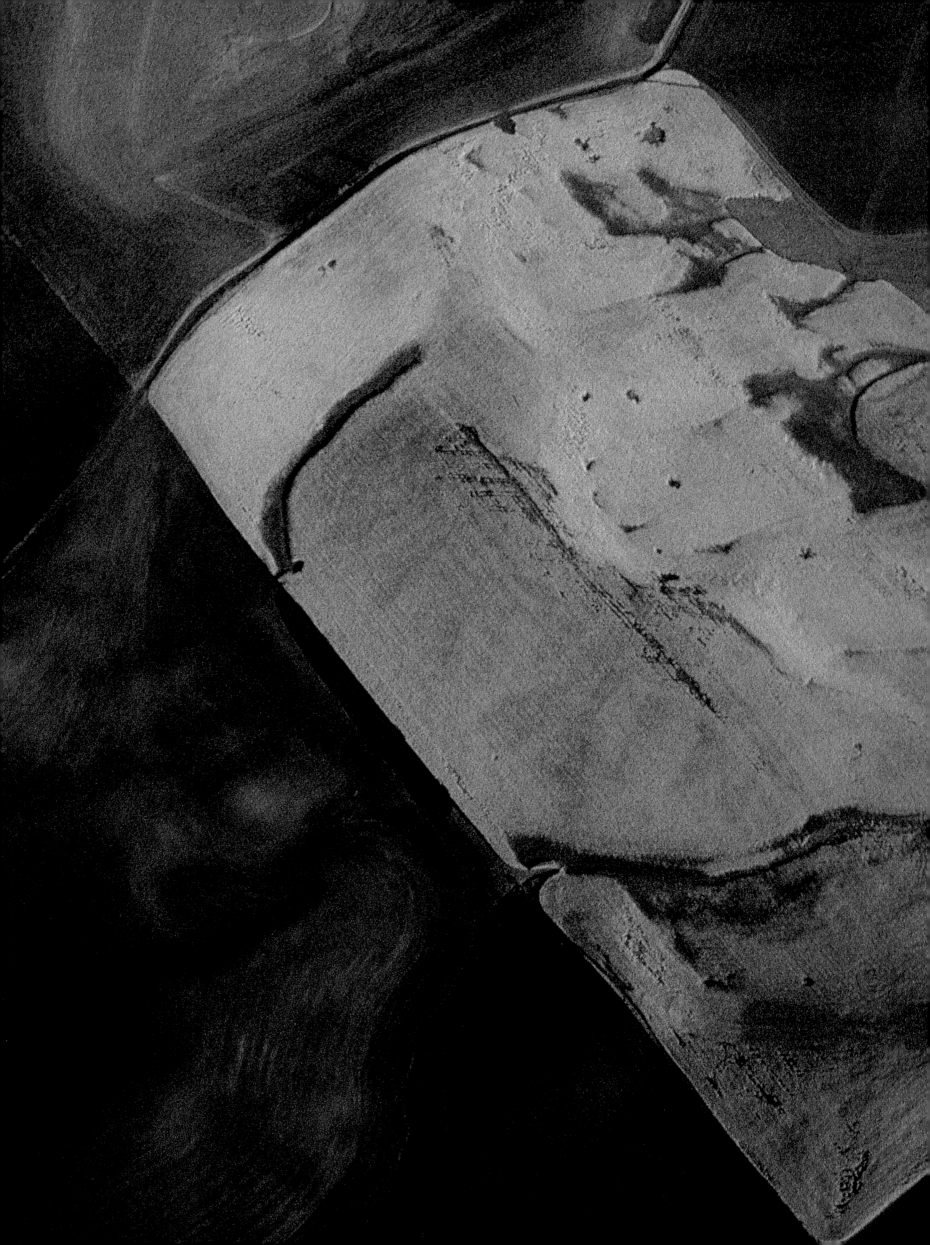

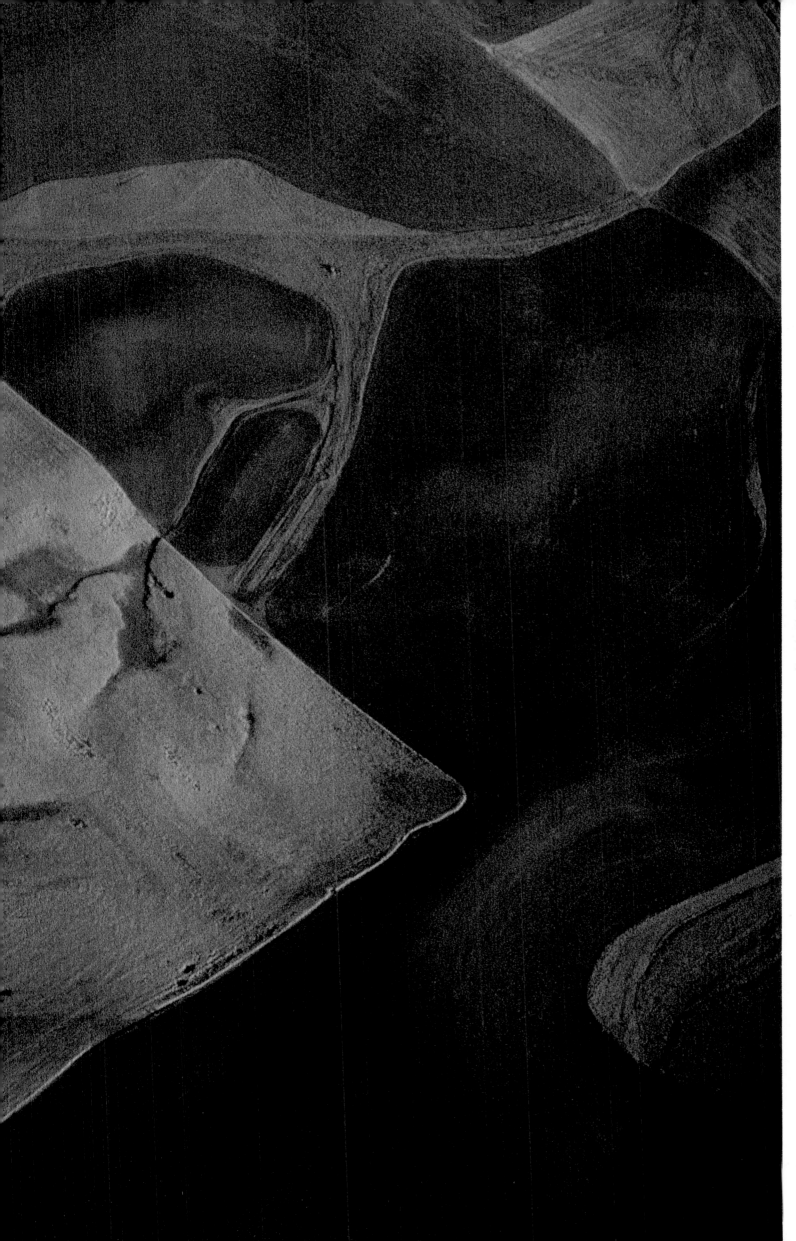

*Whitman County,*
*Washington.*
*The yellow is rape*
*near harvest-time.*

*Idaho.*
*Preparing the*
*soil for winter*
*sowing.*

*Near Pomeroy,*
*Washington.*
*Crop rotation:*
*fallow land and*
*wheat just harvested.*
*The rotation reads:*
*wheat-peas-fallow.*

*Whitman County,*
*Washington.*

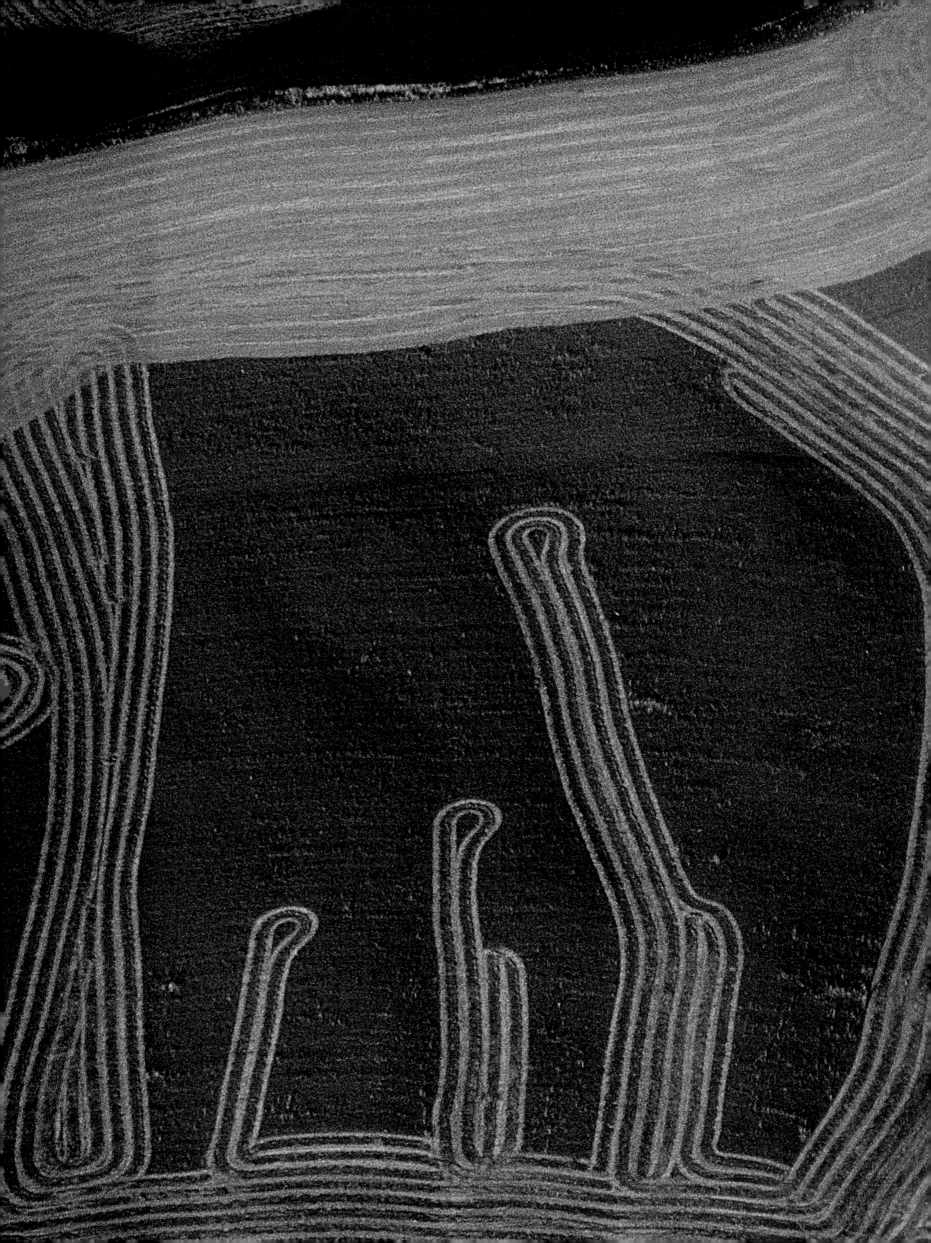

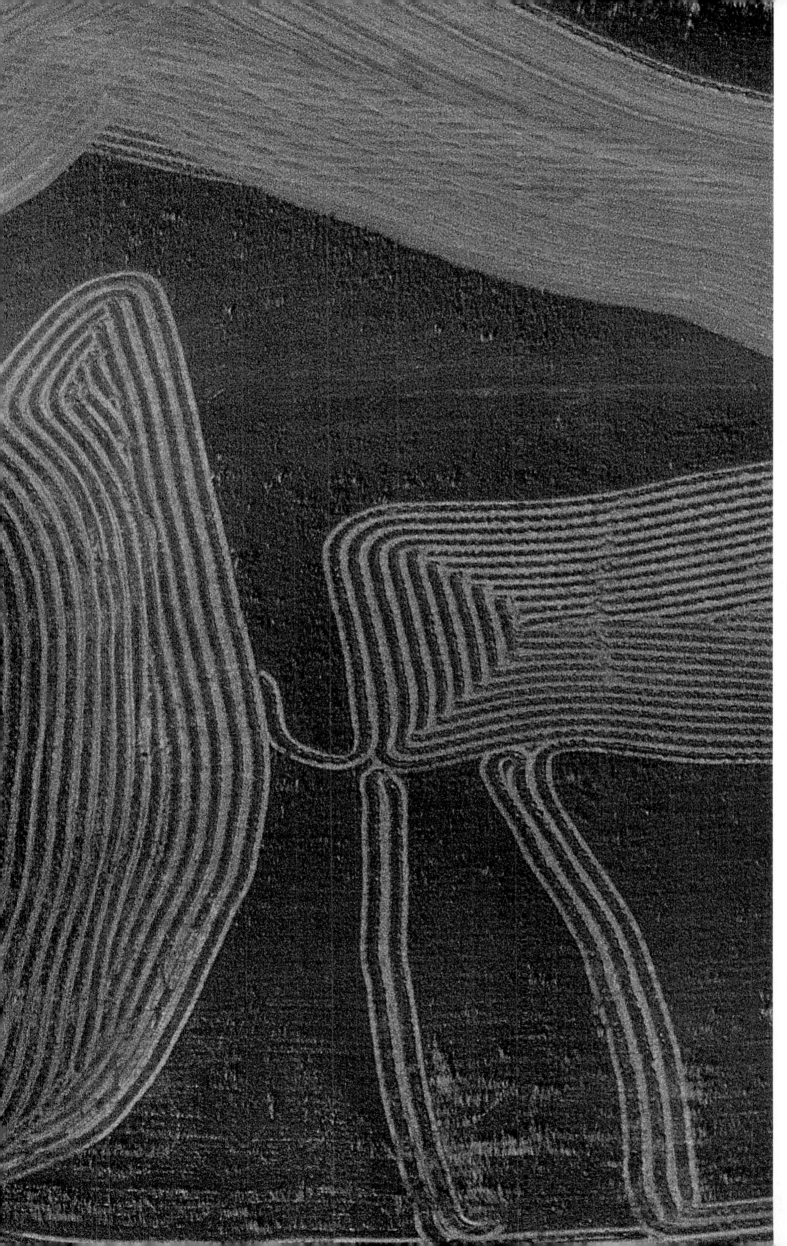

*Lentil field in
the Palouse Hills,
Washington.
The lentil is
ready to be
harvested.
A harvesting
combine already
has started work on
the upper part
of the slope.*

95

*Sewage treatment plan of the pulpmill near Lewiston, Idaho.*

Burning the straw
of harvested wheat,
Whitman County,
Washington.

*Washington.*
*A spring picture.*

*Harvesting dry peas,*
*Whitman County,*
*Washington.*

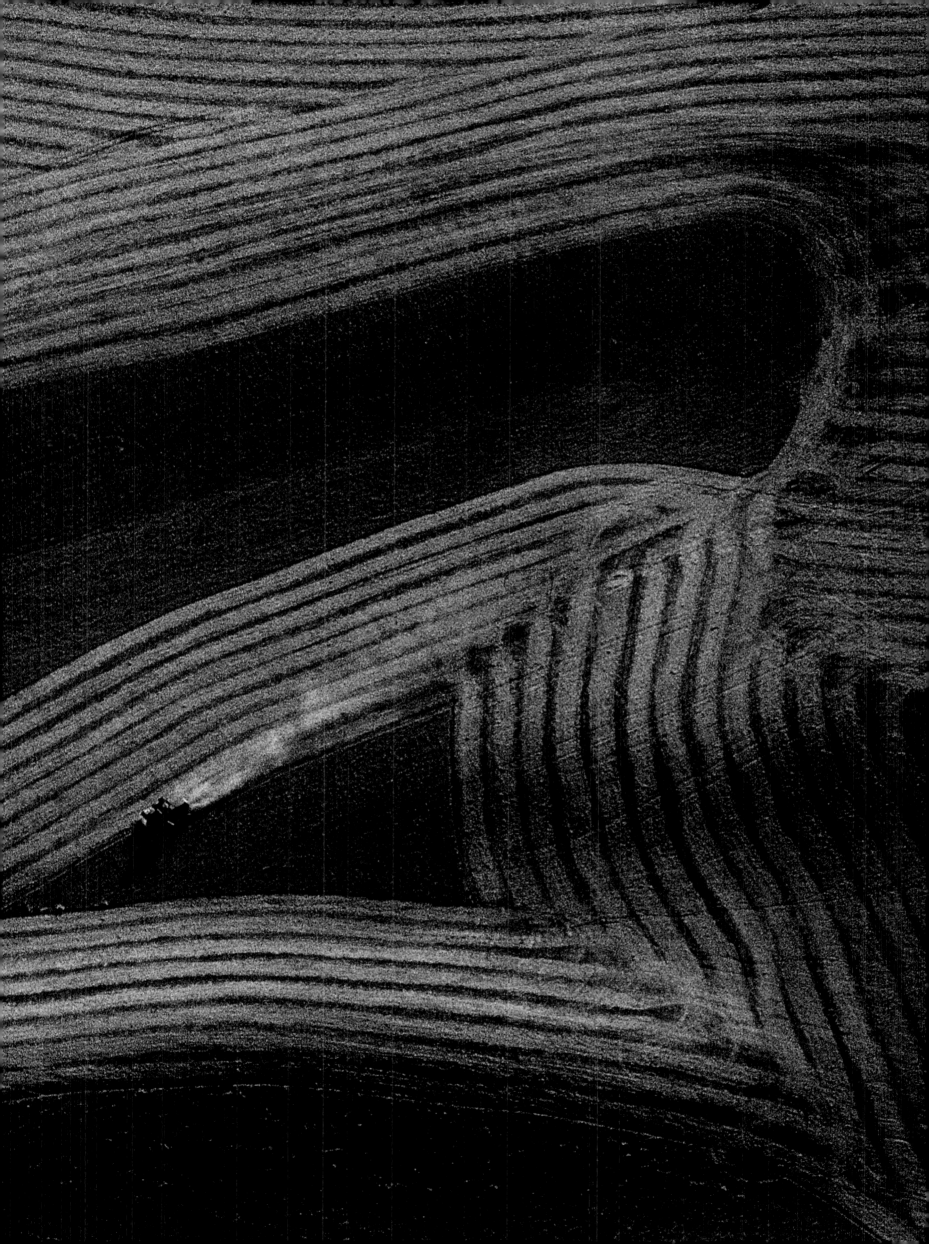

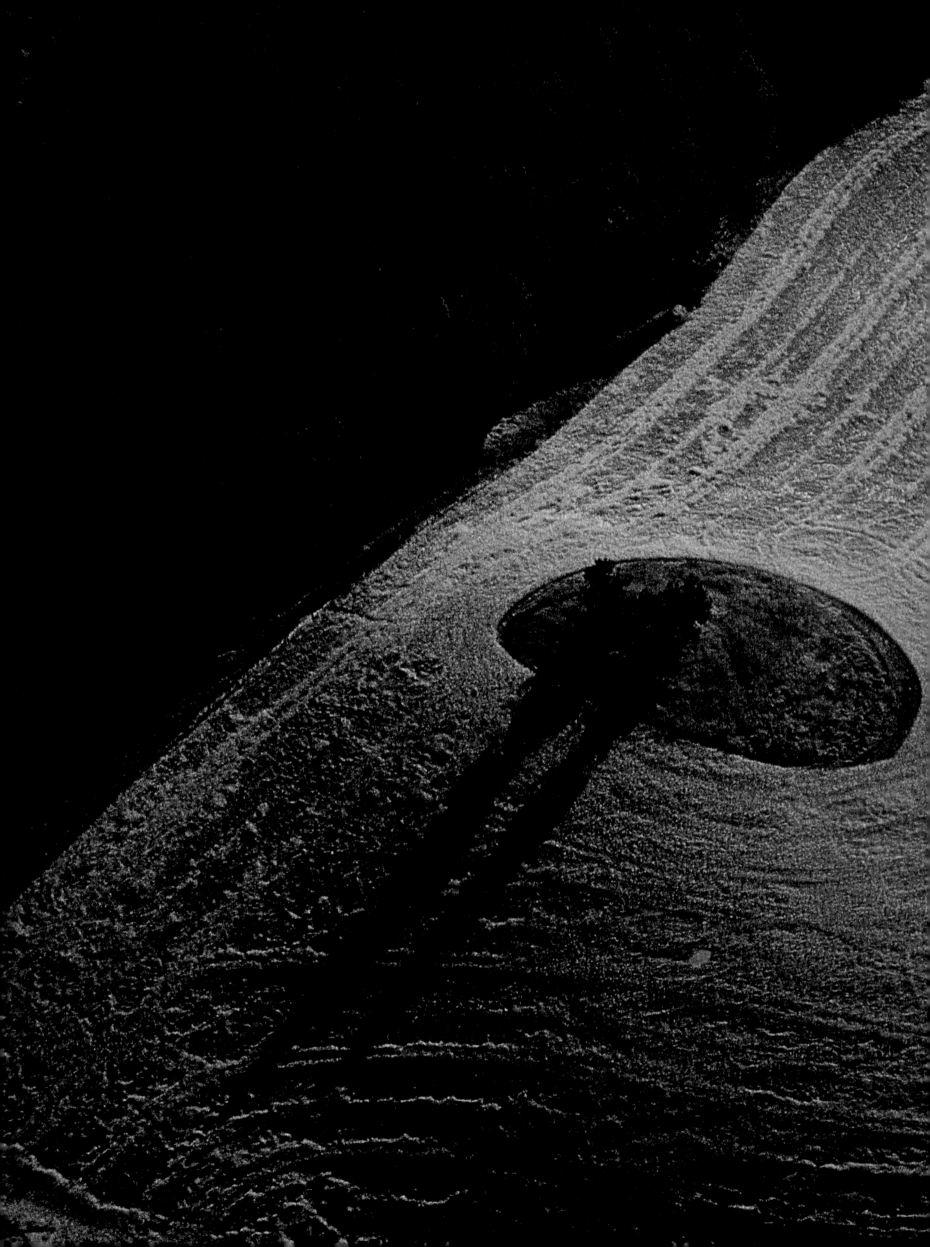

expression on his face: the light, the shapes, the colors were all exactly the same. I almost screamed, "My picture!" It wasn't. It was Morocco laughing at me.

Morocco constantly teases and frustrates. The faces beg to be photographed. But the people who own those faces refuse. To them a camera image is a theft of themselves. I persist. I'm sure many give in because they think me mad. Sometimes I play a game with the women, a flirtation. They hide and, in their hiding, they show themselves. Sometimes, it is an absolute refusal and I make the refusal the photograph. I am shameless. How can I tell them that what for them is a violation is for me an act of love?

In the end, Morocco can be admired, adored, hinted at, but never possessed. It is forever elusive: shifting shadows, floating robed figures against a landscape that is at once endless and timeless.

Morocco isn't so much a place as an obsession. I fell in love with it twenty years ago, and it still holds me in its grasp.

Morocco defies definition. It is forever contradicting itself. In the towns one sees the new nation: growing, evolving, finding a place in a new world. In the countryside and the small villages, it is another place. Nothing happens here that hasn't happened before. Today and yesterday have the same meaning. This became dazzlingly clear to me in a tiny village, near a tiny crossroads. There, years ago, I took a photograph that I especially liked. It was of a man with a fez on his head, walking in a particular direction. I believed that I had captured a specific time and a specific place. Years later, I happened to be standing in the same village on the same spot at the same time of day. Suddenly, I saw the same man with the same fez, walking in the same direction with the same

OCCO
RUYAERT

MOR

HARRY G

*Unharvested wheat field surrounded by grass. White areas are ash, from the latest eruption of Mount St. Helens.*

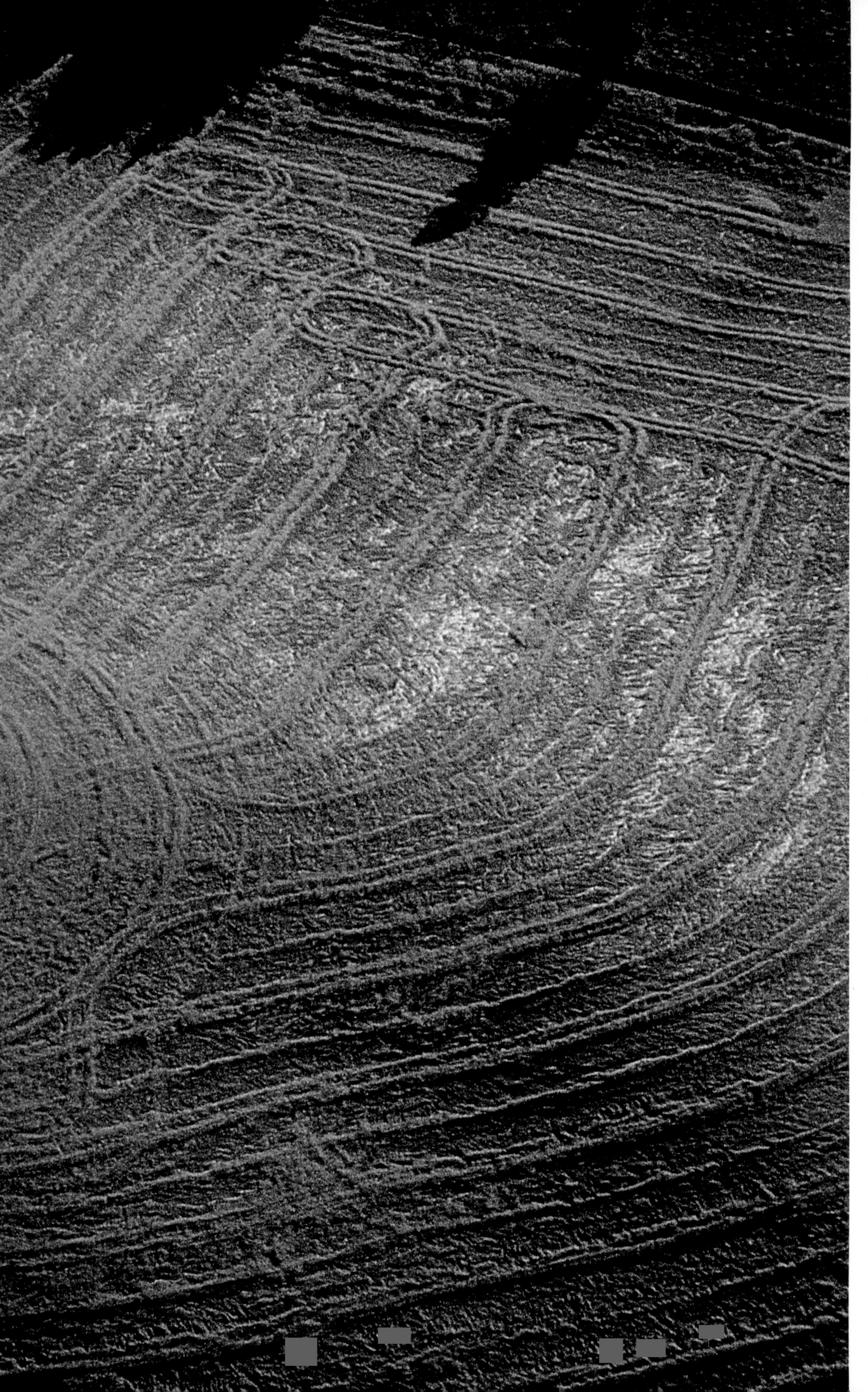

*Idaho, near Lewiston. After the wheat harvest.*

*Essaouera: Shadows of palm trees in city walls.*

*Marrakech: Jemma El Fna Square.*

*Essaouera: The old woman on the right was walking so slowly that it took her fifteen minutes to advance a couple of yards.*

*Essaouera: Man with red fez sitting in the sun.*

*Atlas Mountains: Berber girl.*

*Ouarzazate: This was once a small desert village; it is now an administrative town.*

*Chechaouen: Mountain village in the north.*

*Tinerhir: Women coming for weekly celebration and praying on the tomb of a Marabou, an Islamic saint.*

*Erfoud: Woman with a baby on her back. She was trying to avoid being photographed. When she turned her back on me, the baby appeared.*

*Marrakech: Young girls during the festival of Marrakech.*

*Tafraoute: Women in a market selling eggs.*

*Imilchil: In the Atlas mountains every year in October, there is a big meeting where men come to find a bride. The festival is called "the engagement festival."*

# MAINE

# FARRELL

WOODS

GREHAN

There's no one thing that makes the Maine woods a special place; no famous site or landmark, no largest this or greatest that. There's simply this wonderful forest situated a few hundred miles from anywhere, overflowing with life.

But there are things that will always stay in my memory. Cadillac Mountain, the first place in the United States where you see dawn. There is nothing quite like being at its peak, waiting for the sun to rise out of the chilly Maine mist and realizing you're about to be the first person in this country to see the beginning of another day.

And the moose, which is an extraordinary animal. Apart from its tremendous size, it has a presence which is at once comical and very noble. The first time you come upon a moose in one of those immense clearings, it seems as strange as seeing a rhino or hippo. But after you've been to the woods again and again, the moose becomes almost like an old friend.

And spring. Or rather the week right before spring, which epitomizes what the great photographer Cartier-Bresson called "the decisive moment." All the tree branches are at that final stage of budding when you feel them about to explode with new leaves. The flowers are already in full bloom, so the woods' floor looks like an enormous palette. It's a fleeting moment, one where you can actually feel the constant renewal of life in the woods.

Autumn in Maine is truly the autumn of our dreams. The woods, endlessly vast, saturated with color: autumn in its purest form.

But as I said before, it's not one thing that draws me back to Maine every year; it's everything. I once did a piece on Thoreau for *National Geographic*. As part of my research, I read his journal, which covered every day of his life for forty years. Recently I found something that summarizes my feelings about these woods.

*September 14, 1852: Be not preoccupied with looking. Go not to the object, let it come to you. When I have found myself looking down and confining myself to the flowers, I have thought it might be well to get into the habit of observing the clouds as a corrective. But no, that study would be just as bad. What I need is not to look at all but a true sauntering of the eye.*

I find that delightful. It captures the essence of the Maine woods: a place where the eye can saunter and always be fulfilled.

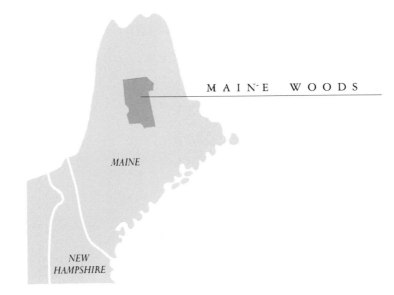

MAINE WOODS

MAINE

NEW
HAMPSHIRE

*Woods reflected on pond.*

*Yellow Lady's Slipper, Acadia National Park.*

*Right page: Spring seeds on pond.*

*Spring woods.*

*Wildflowers.*

*Next page: Allagash waterway wilderness.*

*View north from Cadillac Mountain.*

*Next page: Brook falls.*

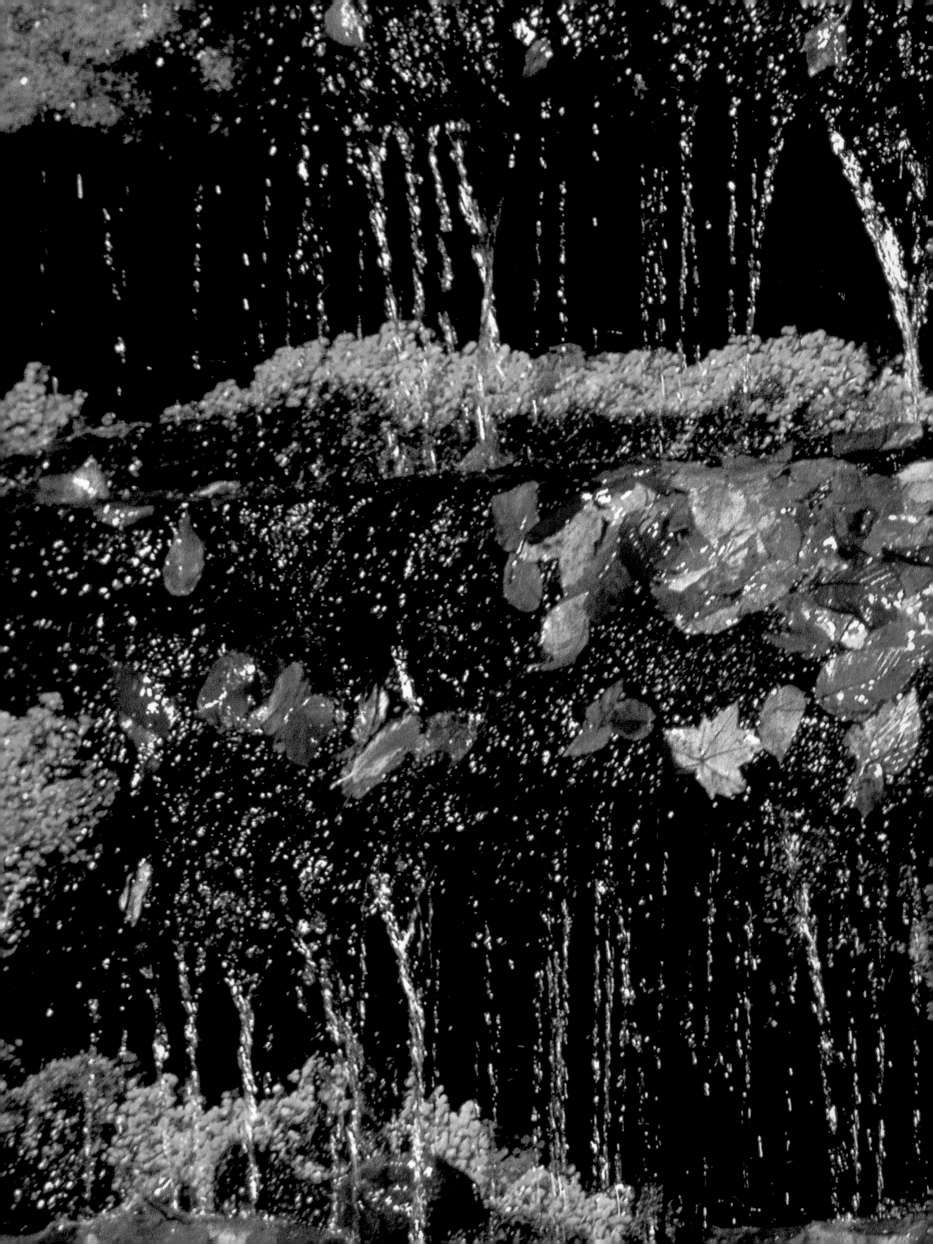

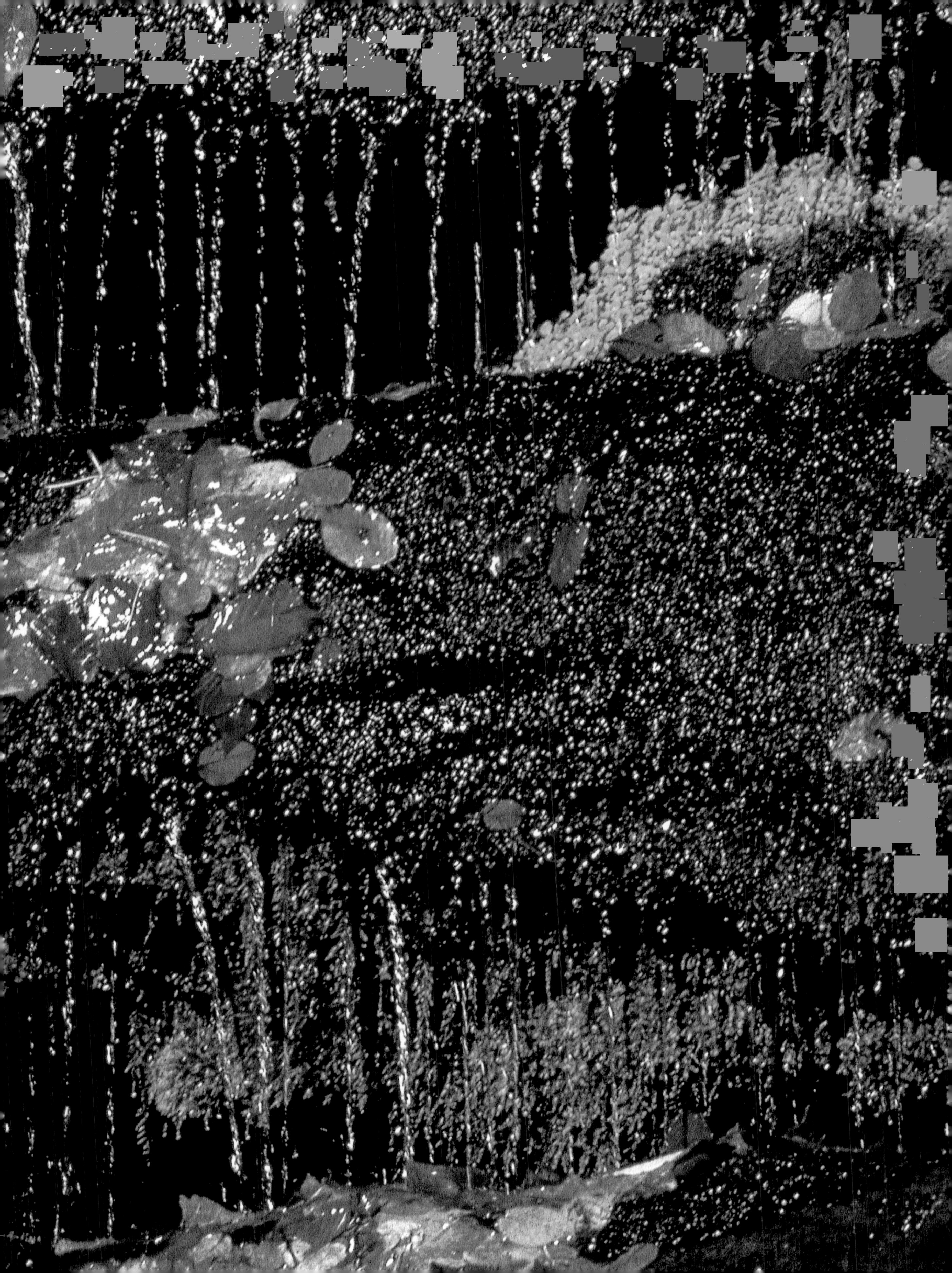

*Autum foliage, Baxter State Park.*

*Right page: Merrybells.*

NEW G

BURT

UINEA

GLINN

Choosing the most beautiful place in the world was, for me, quite difficult. If I had been forced to choose on physical beauty alone, I couldn't have made a choice. How could you choose between the sun rising over Mount Fuji and your first sight of the Grand Canal in Venice; between the ambers and ochres of autumn in Rome, and the glistening dew on a green rice field in Bali.

I was able to settle on New Guinea because, for me, its beauty is not just turf-deep. It is the people and the life that make it shine.

New Guinea is a fascinating, unique culture on the edge of disappearance. Unlike the people at the Kyoto festival in Japan, these people are not costumed. They are wearing the very fabric of their lives. Of all the marvelous places I have visited, I could probably go back to most of them and recapture some of their magic. New Guinea, the way I saw it, will never be there again.

These pictures were taken essentially in two distinct areas in New Guinea. In the highlands, the temperature is moderate, everything is green, life is easy and the natives spend all of their creative efforts decorating and adorning themselves. All of the decorations have religious overtones, but they are totally self-centered. Mudmen build their masks and daub themselves to represent the spirits of the dead to frighten their opponents; these efforts are not god-directed, but self-directed. In the lowlands, on the other hand, the temperature is hot and humid, the land is difficult, almost impossible to cultivate. Life is anything but paradisal, so the efforts of the people are directed to appeasing and appealing to the gods for protection and for making life easier. Here, instead of decorating themselves, people have built soaring spirit houses and carved magical figures, all in the service of the gods.

To be able to photograph these incredible people just before the arrival of cloth caps imprinted with the word Yamaha (caps which are taking the place of the feathered headdress) was an exhalting experience. In that way, at that time, this place meant beauty: a haunting, unmatchable beauty.

NEW GUINEA

AUSTRALIA

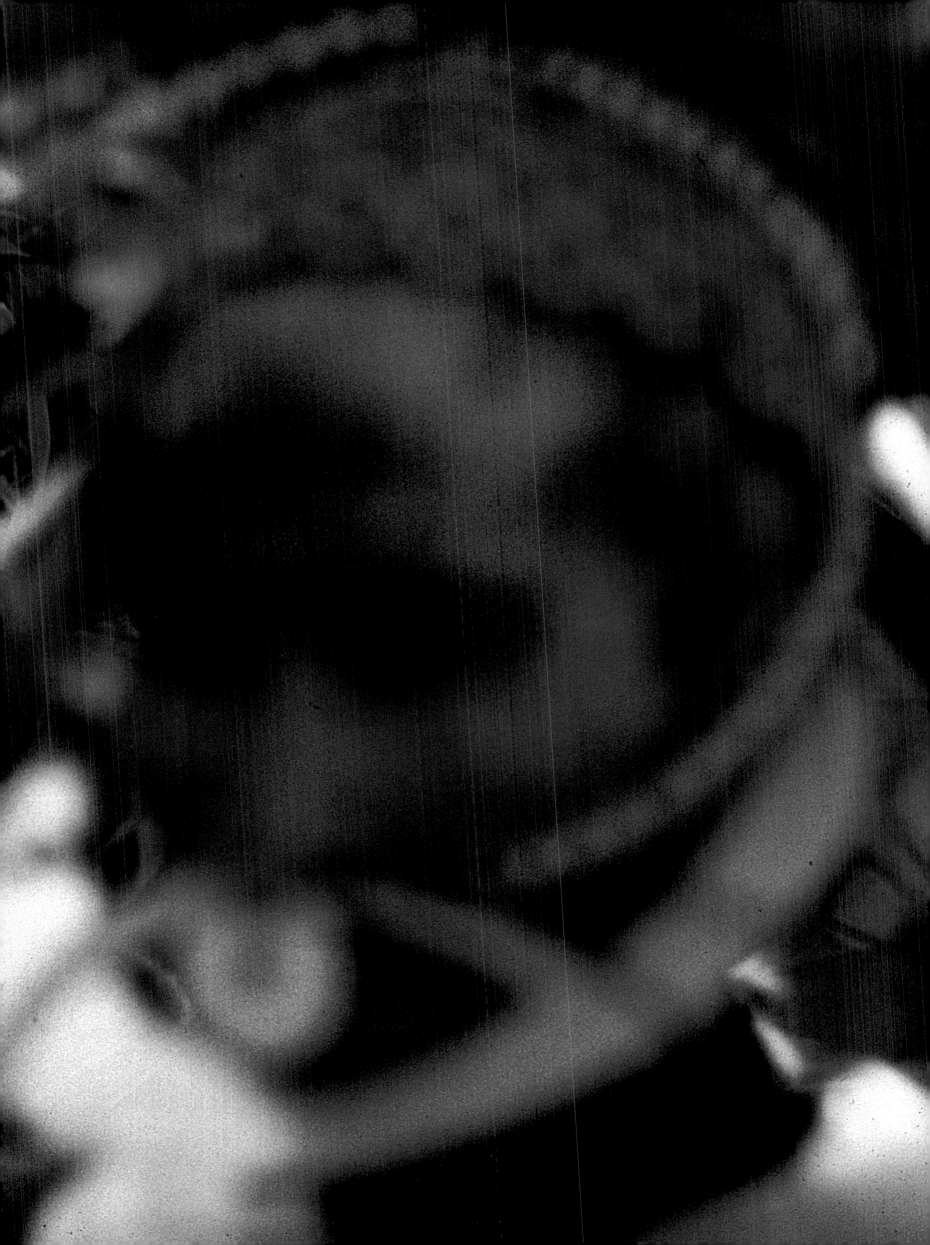

*Three men inside a spirit house near Maprik blowing homemade*
*flutes into hollowed-out, carved idol resonators.*

*Left page: Gathering of highland tribesmen at the annual Goroka fair.*

*Man leaning against the pillar of a Tamberan, the center of Sepik men's ceremonial life. The post is carved into an ancestor figure. The crocodile face represents the Wagan, a water spirit.*

*Right page: Men putting up lintel on spirit house underneath the painted bark facade. The lintel is carved and painted inside the unadorned spirit house in a period of days. Men who carve and paint stay inside the house without food and drink, totally naked from the beginning until the project is completed.*

*Next page: These are highland warriors, spear-carrying natives of Mount Hagen. They are wearing fiber aprons, gold-lipped shells and brass plates in their noses and on their foreheads' and plumage of Greater Bird of Paradise feathers.*

*Rear view of a spirit house in the area of Maprik.*

*Right page: A highland dignitary.*

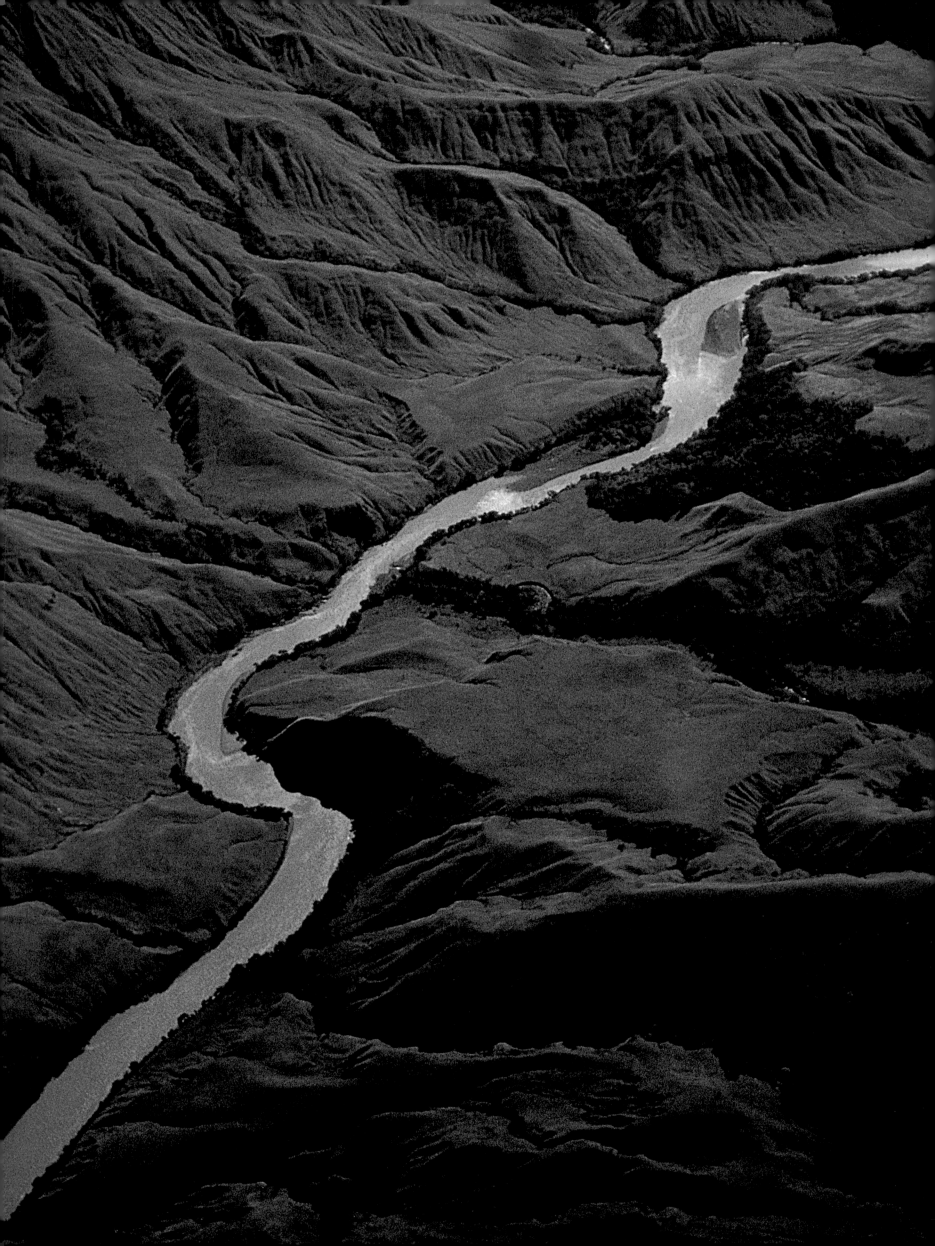

Gathering of spectators at Mount Hagen sing-sing. This is a very rare and
unpredictable occurence coming every six or seven years. At a sing-sing, the host tribe
displays its wealth of feathers and shells and kills an enormous quantity of pigs.

Left page: The river flows through the foothills down to the sea.

Next page: Mountain people in their daily garb walking across the ridge
in an area near Mount Hagen.

*Left page and below: Front and back view of woman. She is painting herself for the Mount Hagen sing-sing. Her headdress consists of eagle plumage and Greater Bird of Paradise feathers. The shell necklace is a sign of great wealth but the plastic arm bracelets are the beginning of the end—the encroachment of the 20th century.*

*Next page: Mudmen from a village near Goroka in the highlands. They are made up to represent spirits and ghosts and perform a kind of danse macabre before ceremonies. This one preceded a village pig killing.*

SAH

KAZUYOSH

ARA

I NOMACHI

From time to time I hear the desert calling me.

The voice haunts me deep in the night, when I sit exhausted, lost in a maze of thoughts, and putting away my pen, take an absent look at the twinkling lights of distant buildings. Once captivated by the desert, you find yourself aching for it when you are returned to the routines of urban life. You become aware of the vacuum within yourself. It sounds like wind blowing over the horizon, or sand running down a slope. It is the desert syndrome, incurable unless you stand on that blank horizon.

My first contact with the Sahara came thirteen years ago. I was without any particular purpose, but an obscure urge drove me south across the Algerian Sahara. When I cleared the Atlas range, the horizon suddenly unfolded before me. To be honest, the sight of the infinite blue of the overhanging sky frightened me. The straight line of the asphalt highway looked as if it fell into an abyss. It was just a week's trip, but I was simply overwhelmed by the sheer expanse of the Sahara.

The more I knew of the desert, the deeper was my attachment to the life of the Taureg, one of the nomadic tribes of the area, known by the veils they wear. Until the French came and settled there, they had long controlled the camel routes. They had lived a life as free as the wind. Closed to the outside world, they kept tradition and lifestyle intact as they wandered.

The Taureg men I met had piercing eyes. Their faces struck me as a creation that had been polished with sand and wind and the horizon's edge. Each of them wore a meter-long sword as he rode a camel across the desert—the figure of a lone fighter who was born out of sand only to return to sand.

The days of those Taureg now seem to be numbered. The serious drought during the past few years has left their precious wells, many of them as deep as a hundred meters, dried up, one after another, turning them into graveyards for the animals they herd. The once-proud Taureg will soon be gone, leaving nothing but the infinitely dry and blackish-blue skies.

I have been a witness to various dramas. A friend of mine, desert-possessed, took a lone trip across the Sahara on camelback. He died embraced by the desert. For another man I knew, traveling to the Sahara had become life itself. He would come home totally spent from the desert journey. Then he would work hard just to make enough money for another trip to the Sahara. He just could not help placing himself on that desert horizon. He would bring home stories about the sweat and dust he saw in the Sahara. When he resumed his life in the city, he would try to write more, only to realize that, once he left the Sahara, he had nothing worth writing about. Heaving a sigh, he would only listen to the voice of the desert rising from the blank page.

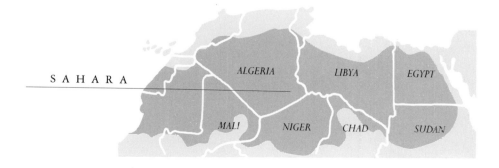

SAHARA

ALGERIA　LIBYA　EGYPT

MALI　NIGER　CHAD　SUDAN

*Cattle gather for water, near Tahoa, Niger.*

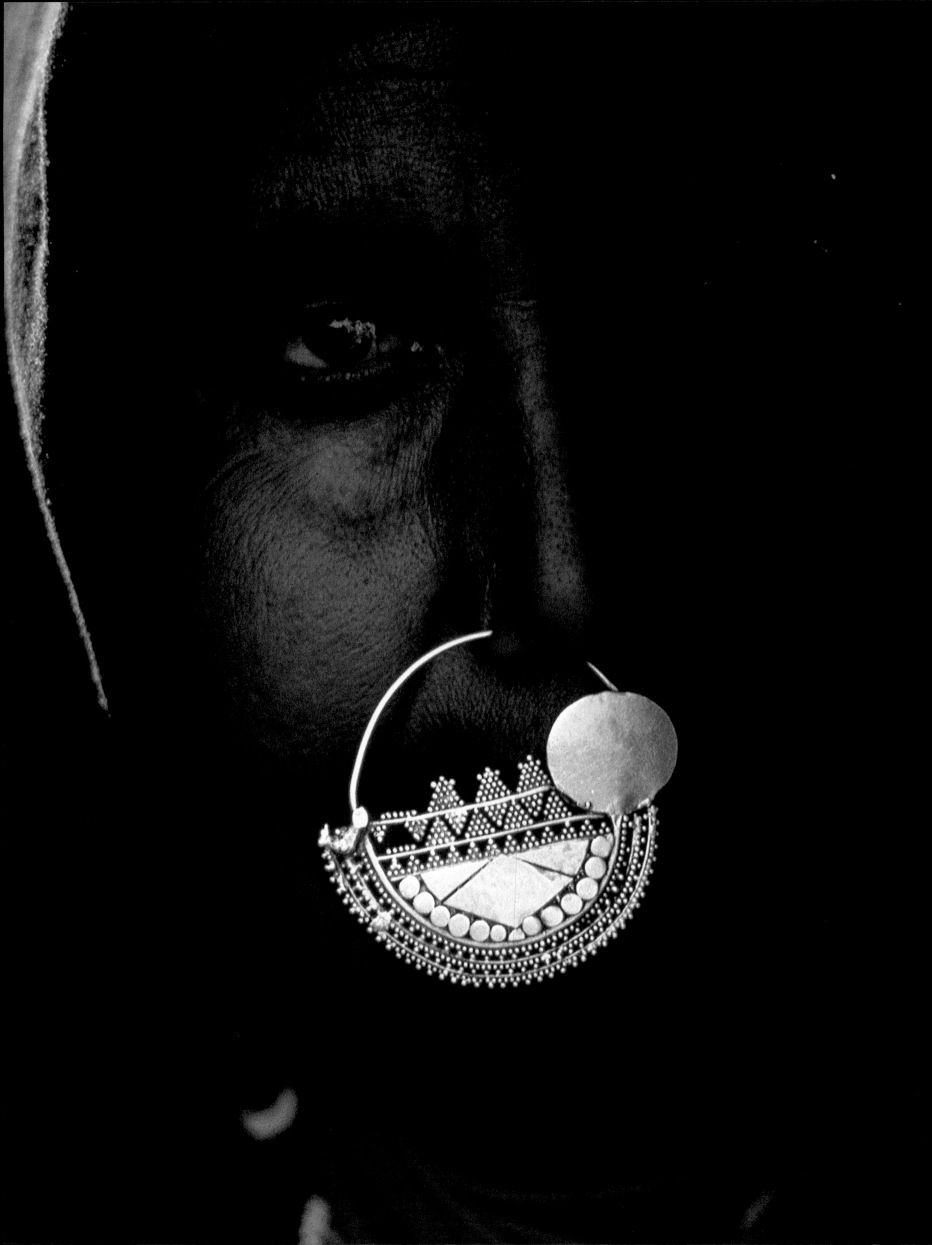

*Left page: Woman with golden nose ring, Oasis Bahriyah, Western Desert.*

*Sandrocks, eroded by sand, Southern Algeria near In-Guezzam.*

*Taureg girl, Northern Niger.*

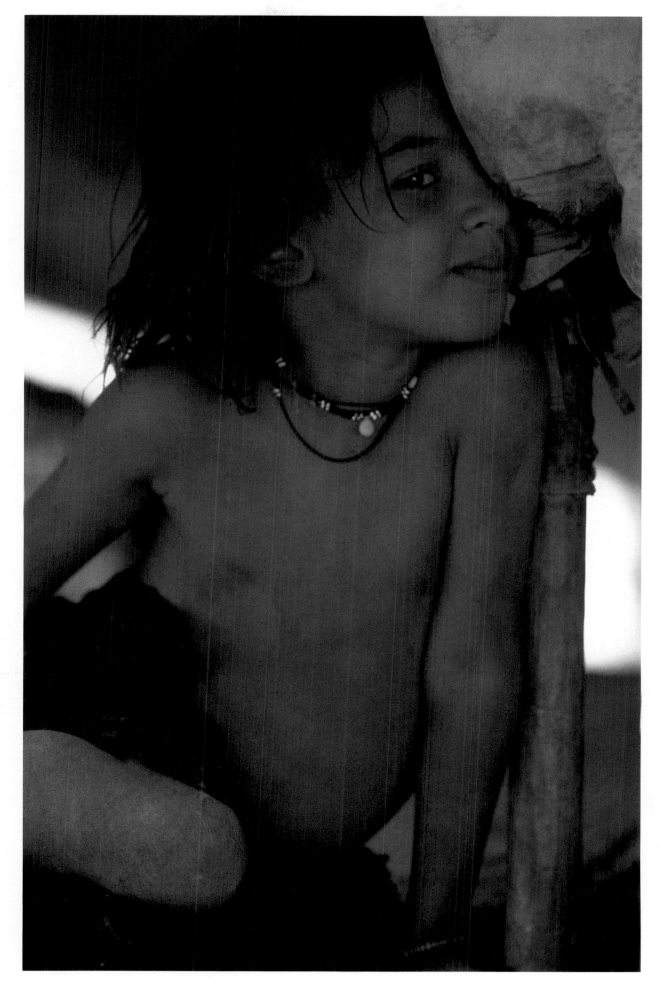

*Left page, top: Oasis under sandstorm, Kerzaz, Algeria.*
*Left page, bottom: Grand Erg Occidental, Algeria.*

*Next page: Young Taureg, Tamanrasset, Algeria.*

*Leader of a camel caravan rests in the shadow of a camel.*

*Sandrocks, Tassili-N-Ajjer, Algeria.*

*Left page: Cattle drinking water, Northern Niger.*

*Next page: Caravan consisting of 264 camels.*

Women visit a grave, Ghardaia, Algeria.

*A boy walks through shadowed sand dune, Kerzaz, Algeria.*

QUE

HIROJI

LIN

KUBOTA

I think I dreamed of Quelin before I saw it. It's possible. Quelin is a landscape that looks more like fantasy than reality. More likely, my dream came from something literal. Before I left for China, I was shown those famous paintings of the mysterious mountains of Quelin. Even though these works were hundreds of years old, and as far as I know, the artists couldn't fly, the mountains were painted from above. They captured my imagination and I knew then that I had to shoot Quelin from the air.

This was in 1979. China's door was opening very slowly, very cautiously. Chartering an airplane for photography was unheard of, especially for a foreigner. I persisted. I pushed. I cajoled. Finally, after receiving authorization from the Joint Chiefs, the Ministry of Foreign Affairs and the Central Committee, I became the first person to depict Quelin from the air.

Or maybe not. For when I went aloft, I was amazed by more than the spectacular landscape; those artists hundreds of years ago had gotten it exactly right! They seem to have painted Quelin's mountains from the seat of an airplane. Perhaps they *could* fly. Or perhaps Quelin does appear in our dreams.

Anyway once I had my plane I kept shooting. I went aloft again and again. They weren't the most ideal conditions, even for an experienced aerial photographer, (which I wasn't): a vintage biplane, an open door, shooting while held by parachute restraints, a large format camera, slow shutter speeds, always waiting for the plane's vibration to abate. But an opportunity like this comes along once in a lifetime. I didn't complain.

But it isn't just that opportunity and the mountains that make Quelin the most beautiful place for me; it's the people and their life. They give it a completeness. They make the fantasy of Quelin real. Mountain areas are often spectacular, but barren. Yet Quelin is lived-in, almost homey. Generation after generation has worked this land, through dynasties and revolutions, surrounded and inspired by these other-worldly mountains.

During the Cultural Revolution Madame Mao actually banned the scenery of Quelin. Nobody could visit it; it wasn't political enough. Perhaps she was right. Quelin doesn't inspire revolutions. What it says to us all is, "This too shall pass."

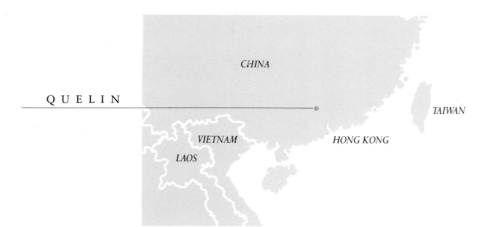

*Gaotian: just before sunset.*

*Gaotian: rice paddies prepared for transplanting.*

*Village of Zhongman. Stone pathway between rice paddies serves as a divider and footpath for villagers.*

*People ploughing with water buffalo, Gaotian. The farm implements are very primitive. The methods of farming have probably not changed much in hundreds of years.*

*This is Gaotian again. This gives you an idea of what one of those peaks looks like from below.*

*Next page: Early morning in a small area just south of Yangshuo. This is one of the most beautiful areas of all Quelin.*

*Early morning on the Li-Jiang River. There is no bridge at this point, so people ford the river on bamboo rafts.*

*Fisherman on the Li-Jiang River. The river bottom is very rocky, making net fishing impractical, so the cormorants do the fishing.*
*The fishermen tie the necks of the birds so that they are able to grasp the fish in their beaks, but unable to swallow them.*

*Strange Peaks Village. The green vegetation in the foreground is lotus flower.*

*Gaotian sunrise. The color is very unusual for this area due to the high humidity. I only saw this color once in all the time I was in Quelin.*

*North of Yangshuo.*

RK CITY

AISEL

After a visit to New York a tourist hails a taxi and asks the cabbie, "Can you take me to the airport or should I just go to hell?"

New York is a tough city—too hot in summer, too cold in winter, crowded, noisy, expensive, and dangerous. I've never wanted to live anywhere else.

Its beauty lies in its vitality and diversity. The pace and the energy is staggering to me and *I'm* a native. I treasure a walk in my neighborhood; the view from my home is spectacular. I live in a city which has not only a downtown, but a midtown and an uptown—all different and all full of visual delights.

I've taken my camera worldwide, but New York is my first love. Photographing New York is like trying to take a bite out of an elephant. It's the one place that can truly be called bigger than life. Into its physically tiny boundaries are packed spectacle and change unmatched anywhere.

Buildings disappear, new ones sprout; neighborhoods change quality, cabbies change nationality; senior citizens get older, cops get younger, and the rents always soar. The New Yorker, battle-scarred by strikes and blackouts, survives in the heartland of the cynic, the skeptic and the paranoid. New Yorkers think they're sophisticated, but they still retain the awestruck wonder of children.

New York is dream and nightmare, beautiful and ugly, with thousands of wonderful special events and a totally decaying infrastructure. The light and the skyline can break your heart. The visual power is special, like no place on earth.

To a true New Yorker, no matter where you are in the world, if you're not in New York, you're "out of town."

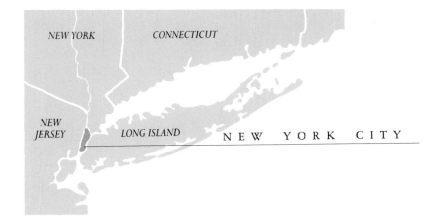

*Telephoto
of 57th Street
looking west,
summer's day.*

*Golden City
from Weehawken,
New Jersey.*

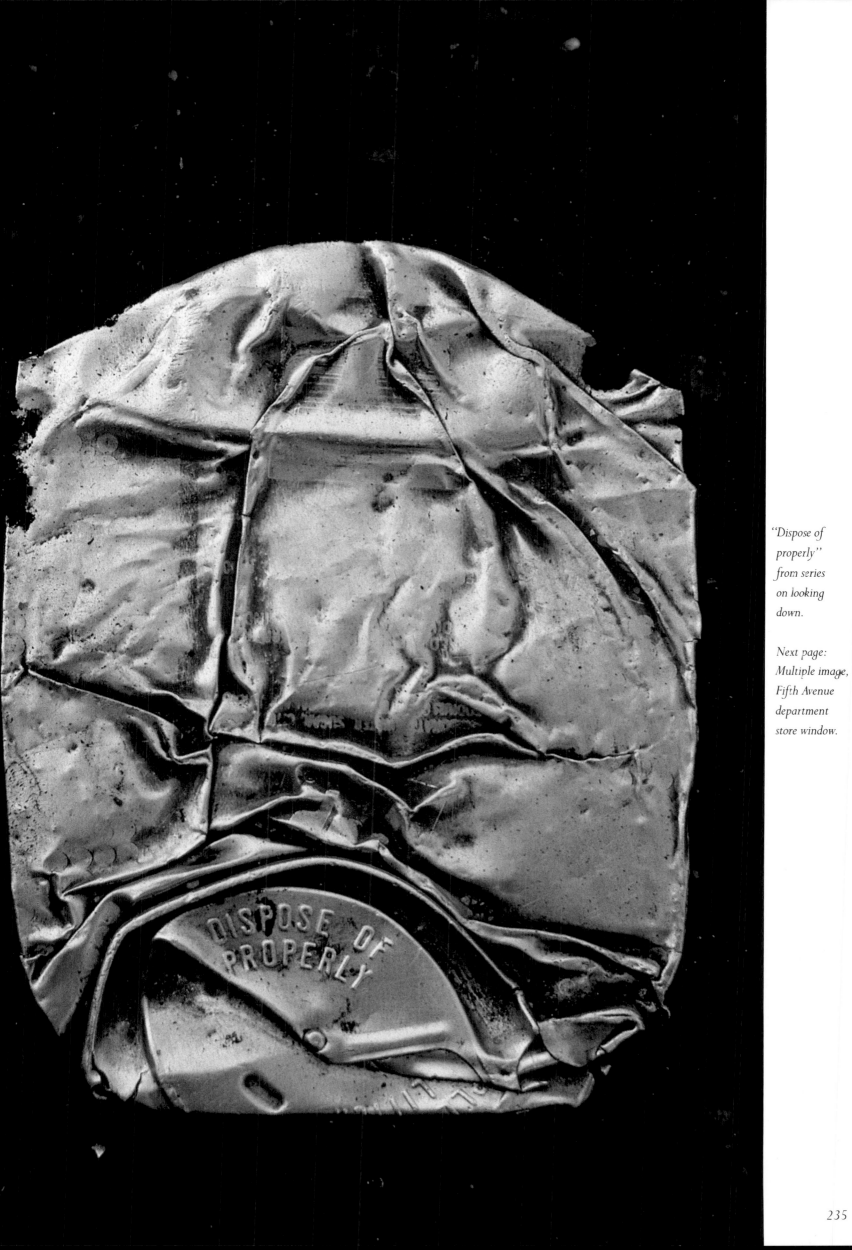

*"Dispose of properly"* from series on looking down.

*Next page: Multiple image, Fifth Avenue department store window.*

235

Crushed
taxicab.

Keith Haring
wall mural at the
corner of Houston
and Bowery,
since destroyed
and replaced with
something far less
beautiful.

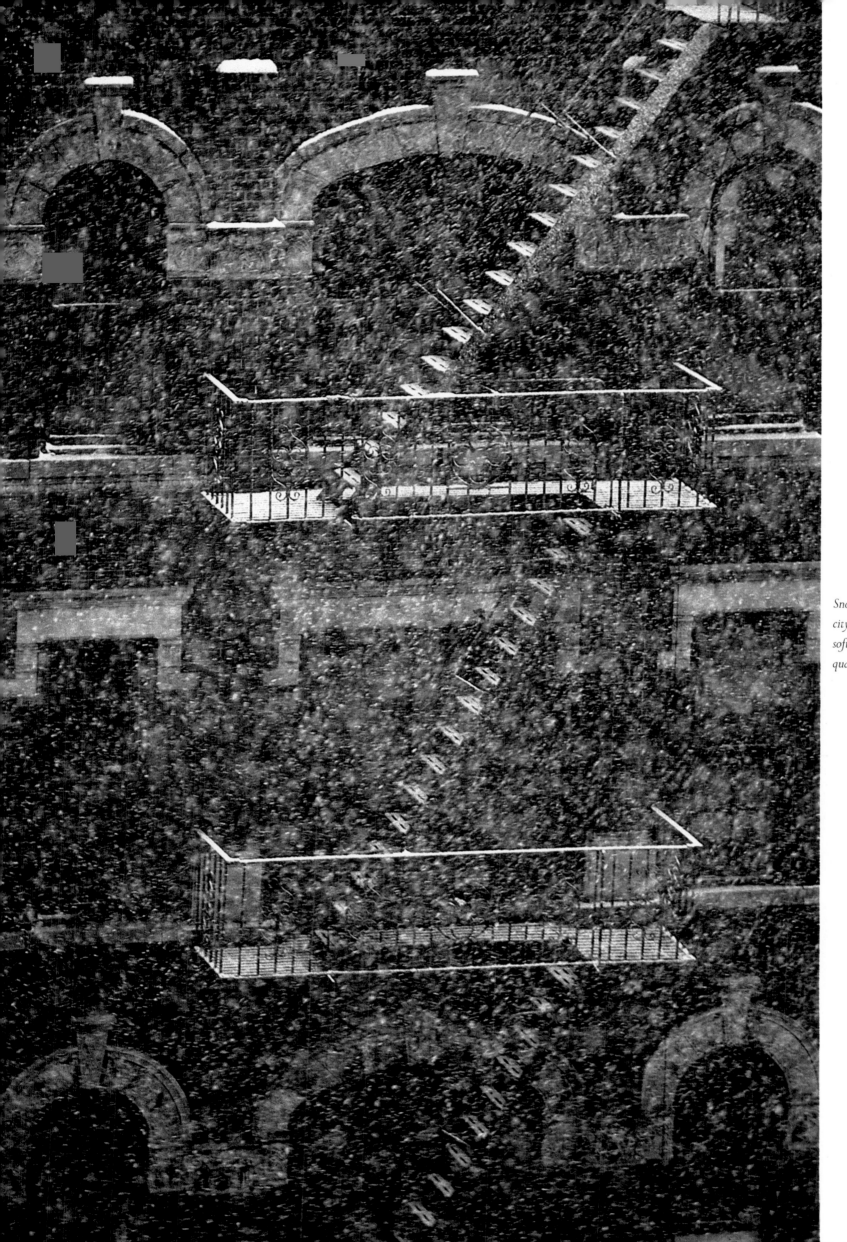

*Snow in the city adds a softening quality.*

*Woman with
birthday present,
Chinatown.*

*Man with
headband,
Washington Square.*

An abandoned dock
near Canal Street
(now destroyed)
that a group of
avant-garde artists
took over for their art.

The Statue of Liberty.
All photographers
are preoccupied with
how close they
can get.

"Don't Walk"
sign on a corner
near the World
Trade Center.

A view from
42nd Street and
Third Avenue.

Preceding page:
Sunday in
Central Park.
New Yorkers
understand that
the bike's in
the tree so it
won't get stolen.

*Helicopter view of Yankee Stadium at dusk.*

*I've been
shooting the city
from the sixth
floor of my studio,
for over
seventeen years.
This one was a
magic moment.*

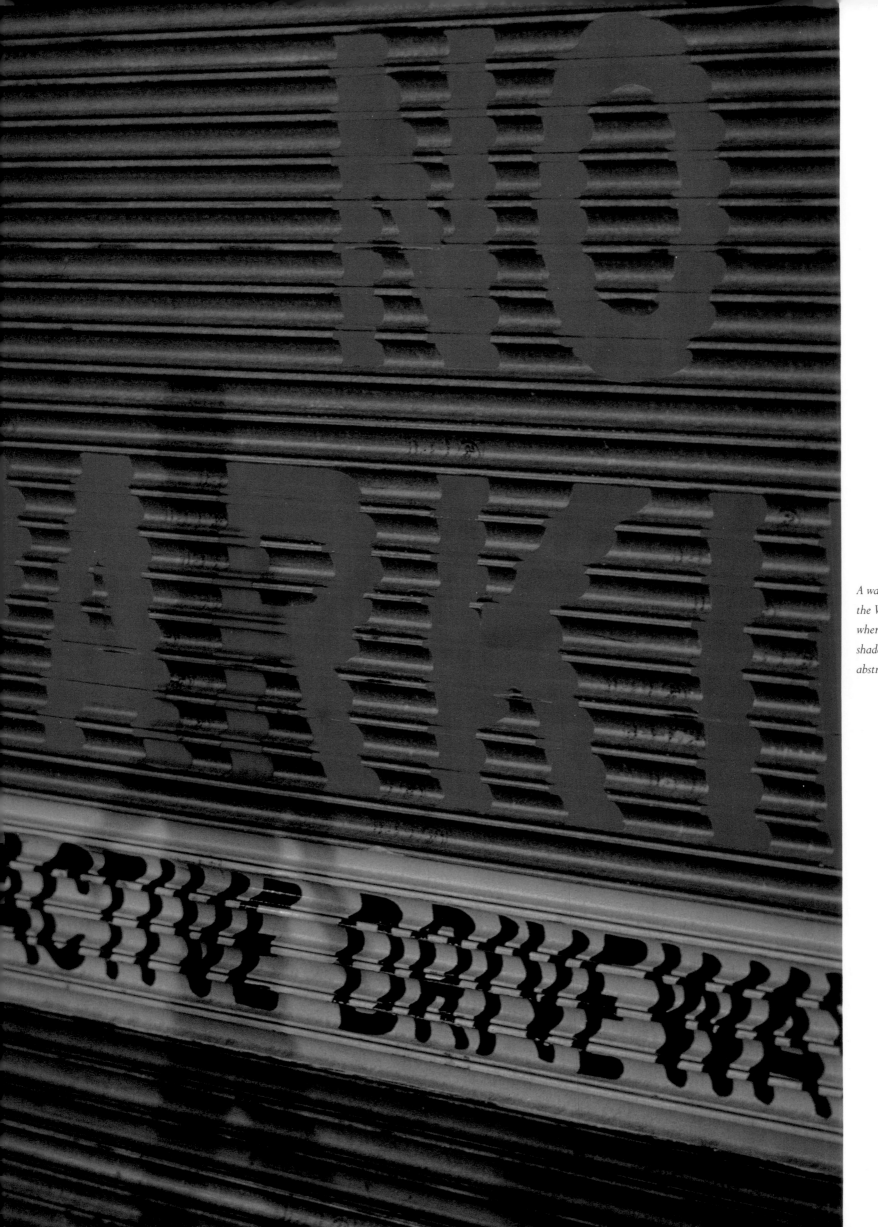

*A wall in the West Village where color and shadow become abstraction.*

*David Doubilet was born in 1946. He begin snorkeling at the age of eight in the cold green waters off the north coast of New Jersey. By the age of thirteen he was taking black and white underwater photos with his first camera—a pre-war Leica.*

*After attending a pilot course in underwater photography at the Brooks Institute in Santa Barbara, he began to pursue his career. Since then he has traveled to all the waters of the world, most often for the National Geographic society, but also for Time, the New York Times Magazine, Skin Diver, Stern, and Mondo Sommerso.*

*He is one of the most honored photographers in his field, winning awards from organizations all over the world, and his work has appeared in countless exhibits and books featuring the underwater world.*

*David Doubilet lives in New York with his wife Anne (also a diver/photographer) and their eighteen-month old daughter.*

*Georg Gerster was born in Winterthur, Switzerland in 1928. After receiving a Ph.D. in Literature and Philology, he began free-lancing as a writer-photographer in 1956.*

*Since then he has traveled extensively for magazines such as National Geographic, Geo, Time-Life, The Sunday Times Magazine, Match, Zoom, Graphis, Epoch, and Omni. He has contributed to nineteen books; the latest is entitled* **Below from Above** *(Abbeville Press), published in 1986.*

*He has had one-man exhibits in Basel, Paris, New York, and Tokyo.*

*Burt Glinn first became known for his spectacular color coverage of the South Seas, Japan, Russia, Mexico and California, each a complete issue for Holiday magazine. He has since worked on major assignments for magazines such as Life, Geo, Esquire, Travel and Leisure, and has appeared in foreign magazines all over the world. With author Laurens van der Post, he has produced two books*—A Portrait of All the Russias *and* A Portrait of Japan.

*Glinn has won awards from Harvard College, the University of Missouri, the Overseas Press Club, and two gold medals from the Art Directors Club of New York. He has served three terms as president of Magnum and is currently Chairman of the Board of that organization.*

*He is married to Elena Prohoska and has a son, Samuel Pierson, who was born in 1982.*

*Farrell Grehan studied at Pratt Institute and the Art Students League. In 1953, he bought his first camera, and a few years later became a working photographer.*

*Grehan was one of the select contract photographers for Life magazine and produced many memorable photo-essays, especially on art, modern dance and ballet. Aside from Life, he has been published in Sports Illustrated, Fortune, The Saturday Evening Post and National Geographic.*

*Farrell Grehan lives in Piermont, New York, on the west bank of the Hudson.*

*Harry Gruyaert was born in Belgium in 1941 and moved to Paris twenty years later. He first became a fashion and advertising photographer, working for magazines such as Elle.*

*In 1965, he visited Morocco and began to take up reportage.*

*Aside from his many trips to Morocco, he has photographed all over the world including India, Europe and the United States. His work has appeared in such magazines as Geo, Zoom, and Photo. He has had exhibitions in Paris, Stockholm, Tokyo, the International Center of Photography in New York, and the Walker Art Center in Minneapolis.*

*In 1976, he was awarded the prestigious Prix Kodak for his work on Morocco.*

*Ernst Haas was born in Vienna, Austria in 1921. He attended medical school, but his strong artistic bent led him to the camera. In 1947 he held his first exhibit in Vienna. In 1949 Haas joined the cooperative photo agency Magnum, and launched his memorable "Returning Prisoners of War" story.*

*Since coming to the United States in 1951, Haas has had one-man exhibits of his work at the Museum of Modern Art, Asia House, the IBM Gallery, Rizzoli Gallery, and the International Center of Photography. Haas also wrote, directed and narrated a series of four half-hour programs entitled "The Art of Seeing," which were aired on WNET-TV in 1962.*

*Photo-essays of his have appeared in leading magazines and photo journals, including Life, Look, Stern, and Geo. Haas is the author of* The Creation, In America, In Germany, *and* Himalayan Pilgrimages *and has contributed to the Time-Life Book Series, including* Venice *for the Great Cities Series.*

*Hiroji Kubota was born in Tokyo in 1939. He began his career as a photographer in 1965 and spent the next three years covering the United States. In 1968 he began to travel all over the world and, in 1971, he became associated with the Magnum agency. In 1975, he covered Pnom Penh and the final battle of Saigon. Since 1979, his career has been spent photographing China.*

*Kubota's work has appeared in Geo, The New York Times, Newsweek, Look, Life, National Geographic and other major international publications. In 1985, a major exhibition of his China photographs took place at the International Center of Photography in New York, and in Japan and China. His book,* China *(W.W. Norton) was published in 1985.*

*Jay Maisel was born in 1931 in Brooklyn, New York where he studied graphic design with Leon Friend at Abraham Lincoln High School. For one year he studied painting with Joseph Hirsch. After graduating from Cooper Union he worked at Yale with Josef Albers on color and with Buckminister Fuller on geodesic domes.*

*In 1954 he switched from painting to free-lance photography. Since then he has done editorial, corporate, advertising and personal photography. His work has been exhibited widely and his fine art prints are in private, corporate, and museum collections. Books include* Jerusalem, San Francisco, Baja California, *and* America, America.

*Of many awards, he is proudest of the St. Gauden's Medal from Cooper Union, and the Outstanding Achievement in Photography Award from the American Society of Magazine Photographers*

*In 1986 he is scheduled for a one-man show in China and New York which will coincide with the publication of a book on his photographs of America.*

*Kazuyoshi Nomachi was born in the Kochi prefecture of Japan in 1946. He took up photography in 1969 and began freelancing in 1971. He has made several trips to North Africa, Sinai and Central Asia, which resulted in the books* Sahara *and* Sinai, *published in five languages.*

*Between 1980 and 1982, Nomachi photographed the entire Nile river, from its headwaters to the Mediterranean, which, in 1983, resulted in a book, exhibition, and featured articles in Life, Stern, Figaro, Oggi, and others. A second book on the Sahara was also published in 1983. In 1984, he was awarded the prestigious Ken Domon prize for his book and exhibition on the Nile. In 1985, his book on the famine in Ethiopia was published.*

*Galen Rowell was born in Berkeley, California in 1940. He began serious mountaineering while in his teens. Since then he has participated in expeditions to Everest and K-2, made the only one-day ascent of Denali and Kilimanjaro, and accomplished the highest complete ascent and descent of a mountain on skis.*

*As a full-time photojournalist, he has made ten journeys to Alaska, eleven to the mountains of Asia, and many other trips to ranges in Africa, Canada, New Zealand and Norway.*

*He has worked for magazines like National Geographic and has published six books, including* Alaska: Images of a Country *(text by John McPhee) and* Mountains of the Middle Kingdom.

*Rowell's work has been exhibited in the International Center of Photography, the Los Angeles County Museum, the Denver Museum and in a major exhibition, now on national tour, entitled "Mountain Light."*